I0836090

SEAL OF ROME

SEAL OF ROME

EDEN MADDOX

SEAL OF ROME
Seal of Rome, Book 1

CITY OWL PRESS
www.cityowlpress.com

Cover Design by MiblArt. All stock photos licensed appropriately.

Edited by Danielle DeVor.

For information on subsidiary rights, please contact the publisher at info@cityowlpress.com.

Paperback Edition ISBN: 978-1-64898-561-4

Digital Edition ISBN: 978-1-64898-560-7

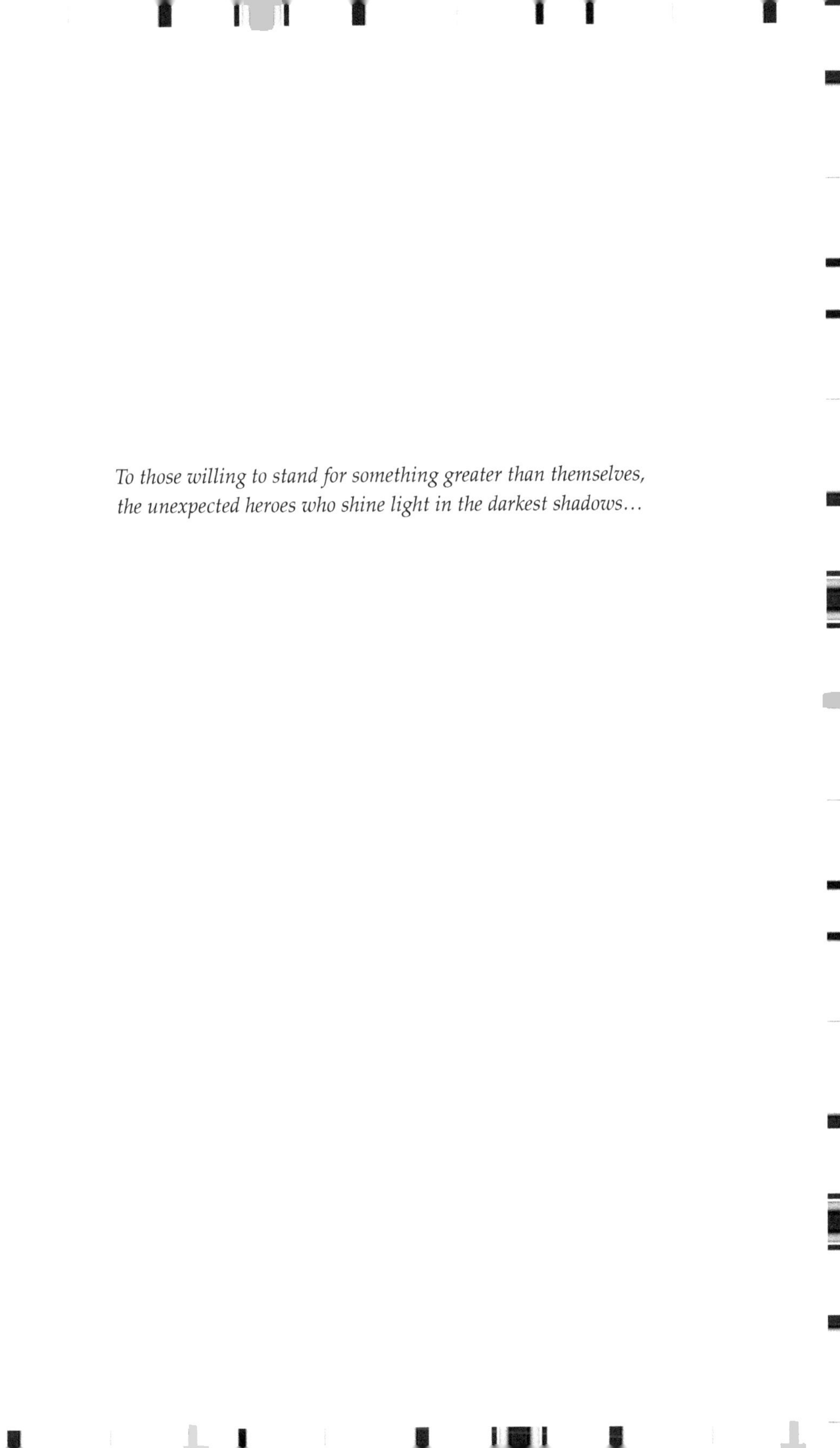

To those willing to stand for something greater than themselves,
the unexpected heroes who shine light in the darkest shadows…

A Note from the Author

Dear Reader,

Thank you for taking a chance on this wild journey through my eclectic imagination. This gripping genre mash-up molds page-turning action, romance, intrigue, and suspense into an epic story that transcends the typical clash of heroes and villains.

While set in Ancient Rome, *Seal of Rome* is a reimagining of history that borders on fantasy. It is violent and brutal. It is unapologetic in its portrayal of the human capacity for cruelty, but also our ability to do good. It will make some readers uncomfortable, so please proceed with caution.

Please also be aware that the "history" presented in this fictional story is a creative interpretation of facts and extensive research, stitched together to form a modern narrative relevant to our present human experience. All characters and events are made up, and the "facts" presented are done so with modern values applied to the interpretation of history. "Caesar" is a general term used to address the Emperor and not indicative of the *actual* Caesar. There's a reason the Emperor himself is never named.

Because *Seal of Rome* isn't about what happened. It's about what *could* happen when we humans roam our broken worlds with our selfish and selfless spirits. It's about the people who build barriers and those who tear them down. It's a testament to the horrors of what we do to one another, and the beautiful way we heal and love beyond reason.

But most of all, this story is a reminder that even in the darkest of shadows, there can be flickers of light, heroes who emerge against the odds to give us hope. Although, you can't site the "events" you're about to read, you *can* cling to our shared duty to take care of one another and fight for a better world no matter the cost.

SEAL OF ROME
GLOSSARY OF TERMS

Atrium–The central receiving hall of a Roman house with a cut-out in the ceiling open to the sky.

Capulus of a gladius–The hilt or handle of a *gladius,* often carved from bone or wood and designed for a firm, balanced grip.

Cuirass–A piece of armor covering the torso, made of metal, leather, or composite materials to protect the chest and back.

Editor of Games–The sponsor or organizer of gladiatorial games, often a politician or wealthy citizen seeking public favor through lavish spectacles.

Exedra–A semi-circular or rectangular sitting room, typically attached to a *peristyle,* used for conversation, relaxation, or displaying art.

Fibulae–Decorative brooches or pins used to fasten garments, functioning like safety pins and often ornate.

Flagrum–A Roman whip with multiple leather straps, sometimes weighted with sharp metal or bone used for severe punishment.

Gladius–A short, double-edged Roman sword used in close combat.

"Imperator," "Princeps," "Caesar"–Generic terms of respect to address and reference the Emperor.

Insulae–Multi-story apartment buildings housing the urban population, ranging from poor tenements to modest middle-class dwellings.

Lanista–The manager and trainer of gladiators, responsible for their purchase, upkeep, and sale to game organizers.

Litter–A curtained, couch-like vehicle carried by slaves, used by the wealthy for private transport through city streets.

Ludus–A gladiator training school where slaves and volunteers were housed and trained for gladiatorial combat.

Munera–Public gladiatorial games initially given as funeral offerings but later evolving into popular entertainment sponsored by elite citizens.

Murmillo–A heavily armored gladiator with a large rectangular shield and crested helmet, typically fighting against a *retiarius* or *thraex*.

Paenula–A heavy, hooded cloak worn for travel or bad weather, made of wool or leather.

Palla–A draped outer shawl worn by Roman women over the *stol*a or tunic, similar to a cloak.

Palus–The wooden post used by soldiers and gladiators for weapon training, simulating engagement with an opponent.

Peristyle–A columned courtyard garden at the back of a Roman villa, serving as a private retreat and social space.

Praetorium–The commander's residence and headquarters within a Roman fort or military camp, often elaborately furnished.

pilus PRIOR–The highest ranking centurion in a Roman cohort, commanding the first century for the second through tenth cohort.

Primus gladiatorial fight–The featured bout of a gladiatorial game, often showcasing the most skilled or famous fighters.

Primus pilus–The highest-ranking centurion in a Roman legion, commanding the first cohort and serving as senior advisor to the legatus.

Retiarius–A lightly armored gladiator who fought with a trident and net.

Secutor–A type of gladiator who wore a smooth domed helmet with small eye holes, designed to combat the *retiarius* without being snared by his net.

Spatha–A longer sword than the *gladius;* used by cavalry and later by infantry as Roman warfare evolved.

Stola–The long, sleeveless dress worn by married Roman women as a symbol of respectability and status.

Tablinum–The master's office or reception room in a Roman villa, situated between the atrium and the peristyle.

Triclinium–The formal Roman dining room featuring three couches arranged around a low table for reclining banquets.

Trident–A three-pronged spear used by *retiarii* gladiators and symbolically associated with Neptune, God of the Sea.

Vestibulum–The entrance hall or foyer of a Roman villa, connecting the gate or street to the atrium.

Codex Fidelium: Lex Silentii

Excerpt from the Lex Silentii ("Law of Silence"), the sealed charter forming *Septem Fideles,* included in the Codex Fidelium:

And let it be that in service to the principles hereby forming the foundation of this decree, a clandestine cohort of dedicated soldiers shall be established consisting of seven faithful warriors ("Septem Fideles").

Neither the threat of harm nor death shall tempt these agents into betrayal of their oath in word or deed. They shall be as ghosts, seen but unknown, forsaking all natural pursuits in service to their emperor and sacred duty.

It is hereby decreed that these seven warriors shall be chosen for their extraordinary valor, intellect, skill, discernment, and integrity. They shall swear with their lives to form an unbreakable coalition founded on the following sacred articles:

I. FIDES (Loyalty)

The Faithful shall swear allegiance to Rome and Septem Fideles above all personal ambitions.

II. SILENTIUM (Silence)

The Faithful shall operate in the shadows, performing their duties with discretion and covert means, never to disclose the existence of Septem Fideles.

III. OBEDIENTIA (Obedience)

The Faithful shall hold all orders governed by The Seal to be sacred and true, acting with authority and without hesitation.

IV. SACRIFICIUM (Sacrifice)

The Faithful shall be called upon to suffer the body, mind, and spirit to grave harm in service and preservation of the Greater Good.

V. IUDICIUM (Judgment)

The Faithful shall serve as judge and administer of justice for all matters governed by The Seal, operating swiftly and decisively within the constructs of their exemplary displays of integrity and discernment.

VI. PIETAS (Moral Duty)

The Faithful shall be the voice of the oppressed, fighting for those who cannot fight for themselves, upholding the principles of The Seal above all earthly decrees.

VII. CUSTODIA (Guardianship)

The Faithful shall bear the agony of Malevolence and the yoke of Chaos in order to preserve Peace and Security for the masses.

Let it be that The Faithful Seven devote their lives to the articles herewith ordained in this sacred document, even unto death. Upon acceptance, The Faithful Seven shall demonstrate their devotion and permanent adherence to these articles with a corporal seal, seared into flesh, forever binding them in service to this decree.

May The Faithful Seven be revered with veiled acclaim as Ghost Warriors, Servants of Rome.

Little Flower
Fountain District
Hades Hand
The Veiled Iris
Insula of Argus
Carbo's Tavern
Crassus Pass
Brick District
Tiber River
Seal of Rome
Eden Maddox
Villa

AMETHYST HILL
URSUS VILLA
ARENA
ROMA
SEAL OF ROME

Ghost warriors
Servants of Rome

Jason
The Slave

JASON

They are afraid. They are afraid. They are afraid.

The stink of urine and feces burns my nostrils as my pre-fight mantra claws through my head.

For six hours I've waited, chained with the other gladiators in the underbelly of the arena. I squint toward the bright sunlight streaking through the gate leading to the arena sand. Maybe it's been seven hours.

They are afraid.

With a steadying breath, I close my eyes and visualize the coming fight.

My victory.

My death.

Thunder from the audience above echoes below the stands, making communication impossible. Not that we would speak anyway. Too many have fallen, stripping the words from the four of us who remain.

We watch through the bars of our cell as slaves drag the mutilated bodies of other fallen warriors through the stifling passageway to clear the field for the primus fight.

I whisper a quick prayer for my dead comrades, souls who shared this cell just moments before. Today's games are death matches, rare but significant.

In a few minutes, I will be another casualty if my master has his way. Why he stripped my champion status and slated me for execution, I still don't understand.

"You four. Let's go," a guard shouts, drawing us from our meditation.

As the chains are removed, I brace myself for war.

The rusted iron gate of the cell swings open, and my fellow gladiator Ino steps through while tossing a weak smile in my direction. Basinus follows with a hard slap on the back. Musa grunts and looks ready to gut me right here in the shadows. He's always hated me and is likely the only one relishing the coming violence of today's publicity stunt.

Our morbid parade moves down the dreary corridor before stopping at the gate leading to the sand. I watch in silence as slaves hand the other gladiators their weapons and make last-minute adjustments to their armor. Wearing nothing but a leather subligaculum—essentially a loincloth—I resemble the prisoners executed hours before more than the champion gladiator I am.

My fingers curl into fists, my nails digging into my palms.

I've fought many primus matches, but never like this. By stripping me of my armor and weapons, they've turned what should be a breathtaking display of skill and strength into yet another of the disgraceful executions that open the games.

I tear my gaze from my brothers-turned-enemies to study the movement of legion troops through the gate. The proud men demonstrate their military prowess in tight formations that would impress the gods as much as the emperor they're honoring with these drills. It's a stunning display, a worthy prelude to a primus fight, which makes the coming slaughter even more incomprehensible.

Finished with their demonstration, the soldiers clear the sand, and the primus match is announced. A guard waves us toward the entrance, and I nearly stumble when my bare foot comes down in a pool of vomit. Disgusted, I scrape my sole on the sand to rid myself of someone else's terror, but the stench is now attached to me. Musa's amused chuckle further steels my resolve.

They expect me to die today, but I've been fighting death since the day I was born.

The crowd cheers when my opponents emerge, but they erupt when I step into view. The deafening roar rumbles through my veins as thousands of spectators belt their approval for their champion. The gods themselves must hear the cries, looking down as they always do to feast on the carnage supposedly in their honor.

I scan the towering stands stretching high in all directions. The endless tapestry of undulating color ripples in a nauseating mix of blurred activity. It's beautiful in a macabre way. The barriers of class, sex, race, and creed have been brought down by one thing: the chant of a name.

My name.

Musa is growing more livid by the second.

My blood pounds as I force myself toward the center of the arena. I try to absorb the booming encouragement from the stands, but the glare of the sun off my rivals' armor nearly blinds me.

Ino's smooth, domed helmet of a secutor obscures his face, while his large rectangular shield forms an intimidating barrier that could do almost as much damage as the sharpened gladius in his right hand.

Basinus, fighting as a murmillo, appears even more menacing with his elaborate, decorative helmet. It's easy to ignore the gladius in his hand when staring into the eerie molded scowl of his bronze face shield.

Musa, a retiarius, parades beside them with a venomous sneer that concerns me more than his net and deadly three-pronged trident.

In the mounting tension, they stare me down with predatory intent, spinning their weapons with the grace of a fifth limb. I barely recognize the men who have shared every second of my existence for months. Fear begins its insidious spread like it always does when brothers transform into monsters.

"They are afraid. They are afraid," I whisper to myself, taking courage from my personal mantra.

It began when I was eighteen. My first match in the arena—an encounter with a demon of spikes and steel.

I won that one, barely, but more importantly, I witnessed fear as strong as my own. An opponent may look intimidating, but it's an illusion. They aren't invincible. They face the same death I do.

They are afraid.

A cold sweat breaks out over my body.

The sun reaches down, charring us with its merciless flames. Perspiration tickles my skin as it drips down my arms and bare chest, taunting me while we wait for the signal. I feel exposed without the typical armor of a murmillo, and I'm practically naked without my gladius. By denying me a weapon, my master, Opius Plinius, has done more than sentence me to death. He's humiliated me by lowering my status on the sand from champion to common criminal.

I mumble another curse for the cruel lanista. All I've ever done was bring the ludus owner wealth and glory. This morning's infuriating confrontation replays through my head like it has since the moment he relayed my death sentence.

"I've brought you the gladiator, Jason, as instructed," the guard announces as he leads me into the peristyle.

"Excellent! You may wait outside," Opius Plinius says, waving him away.

My gaze follows Balbus from the room, mostly to postpone the moment I have to face my master. Distant shouts and clanging metal echo from the training grounds into the garden courtyard at the center of the villa. A serene breeze drifts over us carrying pockets of lingering morning coolness and the scent of fragrant flowers. The harsh contrast of the gentle trickle of a marble fountain to the violence outside has me gritting my teeth.

Exquisite beauty blended with casual atrocity is the pinnacle of the Roman way.

Plinius takes a step toward me, forcing my attention to his pinched features several inches below me. He scans my short beige tunic before resting his gaze on the raised brand seared into my upper arm. The letters "OP" forever mark me as his property.

While he studies me, I can't help but notice how his brash ensemble for today's spectacle shamelessly screams his status as a social-climbing freedman. His expensive wool tunic is dyed a deep crimson, just a few careful shades off from the imperial purple. An embellished gold brooch fastens the richly woven cloak draped over his shoulder, making it clear he expects to be seen and admired.

No one will be fooled, though. He's dressed like an equestrian, well above his station, but no amount of wealth will remove the stain of a man who's amassed a fortune by exploiting others and prostituting his fortune to the whims of the elite. It's said former slaves make the harshest owners, and Opius Plinius presents an excellent case in the way he runs his ludus.

I despise him for his cruel ambitions and pretentious claim to a status he doesn't deserve, but as with everything else in my existence, I have to be content with the promise of justice in the afterlife.

"Jason, my boy, how is your shoulder?"

I fix my gaze on the tiled floor to keep the grimace from my face.

"Better, my lord."

My arm isn't dangling uselessly at my side, so it's not entirely a lie.

"I heard Musa delivered quite a blow at yesterday's training."

"Yes. It's hard to defend against a cowardly attack from behind."

I feel my master's probing gaze, but I don't dare to meet it. An insect scampers over the elaborate mural of Mars beneath our feet.

"True, it was an unfortunate incident. I heard Musa received ten lashes for the unsporting maneuver."

"Yes. And I received five for failing to block it."

His grating laugh echoes off the stucco walls and columns. "Well, then, I suppose you won't let yourself be surprised from behind again."

"That's certain, my lord."

A chill runs through me at the way he continues to study me. My gaze creeps to his penetrating stare before darting back to the floor.

"I trust you are still able to fight despite your injuries?"

"Of course, my lord. I'm always ready."

"Good. That's excellent," he mutters to himself.

When he pauses again, fear curdles in my stomach. Something isn't right. The master of the ludus doesn't waste time on pre-match pleasantries with the gladiators.

Sunlight from the exposed center of the ceiling reflects off the garish gold signet ring on his finger. A similar jewel-encrusted version hangs from a gold chain around his neck.

"You have honored this house with many victories," he continues in a strained voice. "You are our champion. As you know, you will be fighting the primus today."

"Yes, my lord. I won't let you down."

Plinius clears his throat. "No, you never do. In fact, that's why I've summoned you. I wanted to give you the good news in person."

A gust of hot air rushes in from the rectangular opening as an ominous sign. Nothing about my master's strange hesitation signals good news.

"It seems the Emperor has heard of your dominance in the arena and directly requested you fight the primus."

I inhale deeply to calm the rising panic spreading through me. Considering today's elaborate munera are celebrating the Emperor's one-year accession to the throne, it was *good news when he made the announcement to all of us yesterday. Plinius called me here for another reason.*

I tighten my fists behind my back when he releases a heavy sigh.

"Jason, you're a prodigy, one of the best we've ever had within these walls. I'm sure you can understand the importance of this fight."

"Of course, my lord. As I've said, I will not disappoint you."

"No, of course you won't. That's not my concern." He clears his throat and scratches at his round, balding head. "My fear is that we have no opponents who can prove a fair match for you. It is they who will disappoint."

My stomach churns as my pulse pounds. "My lord?"

"We not only have an opportunity to impress the Emperor with a fight of the ages, but we have an obligation. That's why I have no choice but to even the odds. The reason you have not been informed of your opponent is because I've been honored to furnish gladiators for the entire primus pairing."

"I'm to fight my own brother?" I ask in surprise.

His lips curl in an uncomfortable twist. "The Emperor demands to see the best Rome has to offer, and since you dispatched Getha's best man last month, you no longer have an equal in the great ludi of the region. The closest come from our own house—Musa, Ino, and Basinus, none of whom would last a minute in the arena with you."

Sweat breaks out at his temples. He fidgets with the gold brooch at his shoulder. "They have just been informed of their honor as well."

They?

"I'm to face them together?" My steady tone belies the throbbing in my veins.

Plinius nods. "I know it's customary for the retiarius to face the murmillo or secutor, but for this match, they will be allies." His gaze drops to the brand on my arm. His brand. "You will also be unarmed."

I stare at him. All air ejects from my lungs.

"Unarmed? Is this a joke?" I snap before I can stop myself.

Plinius flinches and takes a step back. "It's the only way to even the odds."

His wide eyes silently plead with me to understand the rationale behind my death sentence.

I barely hear him once the simmering fire within me flashes to life.

"This isn't a match, it's an execution!"

"Careful, boy," he hisses. "You might be my champion, but that only makes you my favorite dog."

Rage burns through me as I dig my nails into my palms. "What have I done to deserve this? Have I ever disobeyed you? Have I ever done anything but make you fat with wealth and celebrity?"

I wince from the hard backhand. My cheek stings as Plinius shakes with anger.

"Watch it. You are worth your weight in gold only as my tamed animal. For your sake, I hope you learn where you fit in this world."

He hesitates before his ire melts into a sly smile. "Then again, after today it may be an irrelevant lesson. Guards!"

Outwardly, I show nothing as Balbus and his men rush into the room and grab my arms.

Inside, the fire explodes into a roaring blaze.

If rage will be my only weapon, I'll wield it with abandon.

Hours later, I study my opponents on the sand, searching for any advantage, any weakness, that will give me a chance at survival. I know they're doing the same, but they don't have the instinct or natural ability I have.

No, but they have weapons and numbers. I'd trade advantages in a heartbeat.

I draw in another deep breath to calm the growing panic.

Focus.

The lowest threat is Ino. Although I can't read my friend's expression through the slotted face shield, he apologized for the coming travesty after the announcement was made. I've spent many hours mentoring him and even helped fasten the red leather arm guard to his right forearm. He shifts his weight from foot to foot, absently gripping the base of his gladius. The large rectangular shield in his other hand looks threatening, but the cumbersome size and weight will slow him down. More than that, my friend is clearly conflicted about the entire affair and will pose a more latent threat.

Basinus is a bigger problem. Although he shared his lunch ration with me in recognition of the imminent massacre, he now holds his gladius and shield in a focused, tight grip. As a fellow murmillo, he has the most to gain from my demise. He may not have a personal vendetta like Musa, but with me out of the way, his status can only rise. The glistening bronze and dramatic red plume of his helmet add to the air of smug pride beyond his typical on-sand persona. He'll launch an immediate attack.

The greatest threat, though, is Musa. With our bitter rivalry culminating in a violent altercation during yesterday's training, the veteran retiarius is practically frothing at the mouth for a chance to stab me in the skull. His net and trident will be my toughest challenge, even though I'd typically be least concerned about a retiarius.

Eager cheers quickly morph into violent boos as the crowd evaluates the scene developing on the sand. I'm not surprised, given the picture of their favorite champion practically naked and unarmed against three opponents.

It's a criminal's death. A humiliating execution. Curses rain down upon Opius Plinius for the unfair slaughter, even if they secretly salivate over the bloody showdown about to come.

Who doesn't love the story of an invincible champion turned prey?

I have no doubt that epic storyline is part of the reason I'm in this position. I'm a celebrity, a fact that Plinius is happy to exploit for all it's worth. The wealthy flock to the ludus for a chance at an illicit encounter, lining up to experience the rush of running their fingers over my body in an exhilarating gamble that could result in a deadly bite as much as forbidden pleasure. I'm a household name, hunted by the elite and idolized by the masses.

And I hate it.

The fame, the wealth, the suitors—it's all meaningless when I'm still a slave. As Plinius says, "a dog." To them I'm an animal they fear as much as they admire, which only makes me a more desirable commodity.

Many of my brothers embrace the life, lulled into a false sense of freedom by the charade doled out by those in power. But I never had a stomach for lies. Instead, I pour all my energy into the only thing I truly own: my mind.

I have one passion—survival—and dedicate every skill, thought, emotion, and heartache to that singular purpose. My deep-seated rage, tempered by intelligence and icy resolve, has turned me into an impossible opponent.

It's a rare combination—one that does, in fact, make me worth my weight in gold. I'm sure the decision to sacrifice me at today's games was made begrudgingly. Such a price would only be paid in service to the Emperor.

They say I'm a blessing from the gods, but that's not my story. I'm not a product of heaven but of a hades that began the day I was born.

By the time I was sold to Opius Plinius at age sixteen, a lifetime at the hands of monsters worse than death had seared me into an iron statue of power and wrath, perfect for the arena.

By age twenty-three, I've lived the life of men twice that. I've killed seventeen, wounded countless others, and been beaten, raped, whipped, and scarred into a statue that can now stand weaponless against three opponents without a flinch except to wipe the occasional drop of sweat from my eyes.

I am indeed fearless, and the most dangerous kind—I'm not afraid to die.

I'm also not afraid to kill.

MUSA AND BASINUS LUNGE FIRST, AS EXPECTED. INO HOLDS BACK, SKEPTICAL OF THE mismatch, but in all honesty, I would have preferred a direct attack instead of the latent distraction my friend now serves.

I spin to the left, dodging Musa's net, but end up colliding with Basinus' shield instead.

Dazed, I hit the sand and instinctively roll away, barely escaping a hole in my lung when Basinus follows up with a thrust of his short sword.

Sand sprays into my eyes, but there's no time to shake off the sting. I jump up from the ground and leap back, narrowly missing Musa's three-pronged spear.

Frenzied shouts erupt from the stands just before a sharp pain spreads up my leg. I turn to see that Ino has finally entered the fight, his gladius now wet with my blood.

Hit in the calf, I limp several paces away to regroup, eyeing my opponents with a stony gaze that dares them to strike again. I may have courage, but I need a weapon if I have any chance at survival.

Sadly, my best bet is Ino's sword. The gladius is my strongest weapon, and Ino's compassion makes him my weakest opponent.

"Ladies and gentlemen, your grand champion!" Musa mocks, swinging his net again.

This time, I'm prepared for the attack and dive forward instead of backward. The surprise maneuver allows my aim to best Musa's, and I snatch the net from the air, yanking hard to pull him off his feet.

A cheer erupts from the spectators as Musa becomes a new obstacle for Ino, who stumbles and loses his grip on his sword. Prepared for that very outcome, I kick Ino in the chin to keep him down and dislodge his protective helmet. With a leap and a forward roll, I end up behind the line of opponents, now armed with a gladius.

The crowd is roaring.

Musa curses while Ino stays down, still disoriented. Basinus shrieks and charges from my right, but his advantage is now lost. I parlay his weak thrust into a devastating front kick to the shield that sends him to his back. I've just raised my foot to crush his nose through his helmet when I catch movement to my right. Spinning around, I manage to block Musa's trident before Basinus grabs my ankle and yanks me to the sand. Ino lands a solid payback blow to my face.

I cough through choked lungs, clawing at the ground to get away, but they're quickly on me, dragging me back to their circle. Blood streaks the floor of the arena, giving testimony to my weakened state. Violent boos from the crowd descend upon us.

Three-on-one is impossible odds, and despite my gallant efforts, I've lost. After everything I've fought and survived throughout my life, I'll meet my end like a petty criminal. I can almost sense the crowd's anticipation for the inevitable death of a god who's proven to be only a man.

Except, I'm not ready to die.

Musa drives his trident to deliver the death-stroke, and I deflect the sharp prongs with my bare hands.

The stadium ignites.

A lethal blade rips into my palm, but I ignore the pain and use all my strength to shove Musa back.

After freeing my bloody hand, I recover my gladius and roll into Basinus' shins, knocking him to the ground again. Without hesitation, I shove my short sword beneath his flared neck guard, while issuing a brief goodbye to my friend. It all seems to happen in a single sweep, and I quickly return my attention to the two shocked opponents who remain.

"How many lives do you have?" Musa grunts, drawing himself back into a fighting stance.

Ino's brown eyes fill with fear instead of frustration. "I will surrender to you if it comes to it, Jason. I swear it."

I almost laugh at the absurd promise, an easy oath now that favor has shifted.

Still, I'll show mercy if the Emperor calls for it. The match is far from over anyway, as evidenced by my tenuous grip on the gladius due to my damaged flesh and the slick ooze of my own blood. I'm amazed I can hold it at all, given the state of my hand. I rip off one of the strips of cloth around my arm to wipe the handle and wrap my hand as best I can. Then, I toss the sword to my left hand, which sustained much less damage.

"What about you, Musa? Will you surrender as well?" I taunt. "That way, you can wait until I sleep to drive a knife into my back."

"Are you calling me a coward?"

"I have five lashes from yesterday's training proving exactly that. There's a reason it takes three of you to even the odds!"

Enraged, Musa explodes forward, just as I hoped. He lunges with the trident, and I twist so it only grazes my side as I come down hard on his other wrist.

My gladius jerks from its collision with flesh and bone, while Musa shrieks in agony. His severed hand dangles from a small ribbon of skin, still clutching the net in a useless display of former power. But I don't revel in the victory. My own hands are barely functional after their clash with the grisly trident.

Instead, I pivot toward Ino, the only remaining threat. We both know he'll have to put on a better show if he has any chance of the Emperor sparing his life.

Ino has confiscated Basinus' gladius, recovered his own shield, and now charges forward with a fury that looks impressive, but could be easily thwarted by a skilled fighter. When he hits the sand, I return to Musa and stare down into his murderous eyes.

"Mercy or death?" I ask him, even though he'd never give me the same courtesy.

"Do you actually think I'd bend a knee to one of Lepidus' sluts?"

Musa barely finishes the insult.

The stadium explodes at the second execution, and I place my foot on his lifeless body to remove the gladius from his neck.

"What about you? It's time to choose," I say, facing my friend.

Ino shoots a quick glance at the Emperor's box. "I won't be granted mercy. Not yet," he says in an anxious tone.

I follow his gaze for a brief scan of the elite patrons. He's right. He'll have to do a lot more to impress the crowd.

"Charge me," I hiss.

"What?"

"Do it. Strike me in the right arm with your dagger."

"But…"

"Do it!"

Ino hesitates before pulling the dagger from his belt and lunging to my right. I wince as the blade slices into my skin and lodges in the dense muscle of my upper arm. I fall to my knees in a dramatic display, while Ino pretends to wipe blood from his gladius to give me time to dislodge the dagger from my bicep.

I gasp at the pain as I yank it from my body. Blood gushes from the new wound and coats my arm in a deep red sleeve. It's not a deathblow, but it will weaken me considerably and force a more even fight.

Part of me regrets showing mercy as I stagger to my feet.

"You don't have to do this," Ino mumbles, resuming his stance. "Plinius won't be happy at our manipulation of the outcome. He doesn't believe in mercy and hates being crossed."

"I'm going to stumble again and drop the dagger," I say, ignoring him. Now's not the time for sentimentality. "Wait for my signal, and we'll give them a fair match."

Ino obeys, and soon the arena is filled with the clanging of steel on steel. Plinius may have promised three deaths in today's primus, but I sense the growing excitement of the crowd. They're hungry for an underdog victory against the most sporting of the three challengers.

"They're beginning to favor you," I whisper as our blades come together and I shove him back. "They respect you for hanging back in the beginning and giving me a chance."

"Enough to spare my life? I'm no match for you. My fate will hang in the balance of their opinion when you beat me."

I survey the riotous stands. "I don't know their minds yet. They already have two deaths to satisfy them. That may be enough."

I send Ino back with another blow and wait as he regains his footing.

"Knock me down again and give me time to recover my weapon. That will win you more favor," I say.

Ino frowns. "This isn't right. You and I both know you could gut me with your eyes closed."

I grunt as our swords meet again. "And you and I both know I don't want to. Quit moaning and hit me. We can gossip later."

Ino smirks. "Fair enough. Brace yourself."

I do, but the air still rushes from my lungs when Ino collides with my chest. I fight the instinct to hang onto my weapon and allow the sword to drop a few paces away. Ino plays his part and, with a subtle bow, steps back as I push myself to my knees. My injuries are starting to take their toll. I will have to end this battle soon or I'll be the third body in the ground after all.

The stadium buzzes with anticipation when I push to my feet and stagger toward the gladius. Ino waits, charging again once I regain my stance.

This time, I don't hold back and easily overcome the other man with an elegance that comes as naturally to me as breathing and sleeping.

When Ino falls with my sword at his throat, there's a collective gasp from the crowd. All heads turn toward the Emperor.

I raise my eyes as well, daring to confront the richly dressed occupants of the prestigious private box above us. I feel the lust and awe oozing from the aristocratic spectators. I'd probably recognize several as discreet visitors to the ludus at some time or another, but my focus rests solely on one man: the ruler of the Roman Empire.

His eyes are fixed solely on me.

When our gazes lock, I nearly drop my sword at the surprise connection. There's something unique in his expression. Something I've never seen before. Not desire. Not envy. Not even awe.

Respect, maybe. Admiration.

For a split second, I've earned the attention of the most powerful man in the world.

"Spare him," the Emperor announces, acknowledging the chants of the crowd.

I clench my jaw in relief.

Stepping back, I reach down to Ino, who grasps my wrist. The stadium roars as I tug the other man to his feet. We salute the Emperor and then turn to accept a shower of praise from the witnesses who came to watch us die.

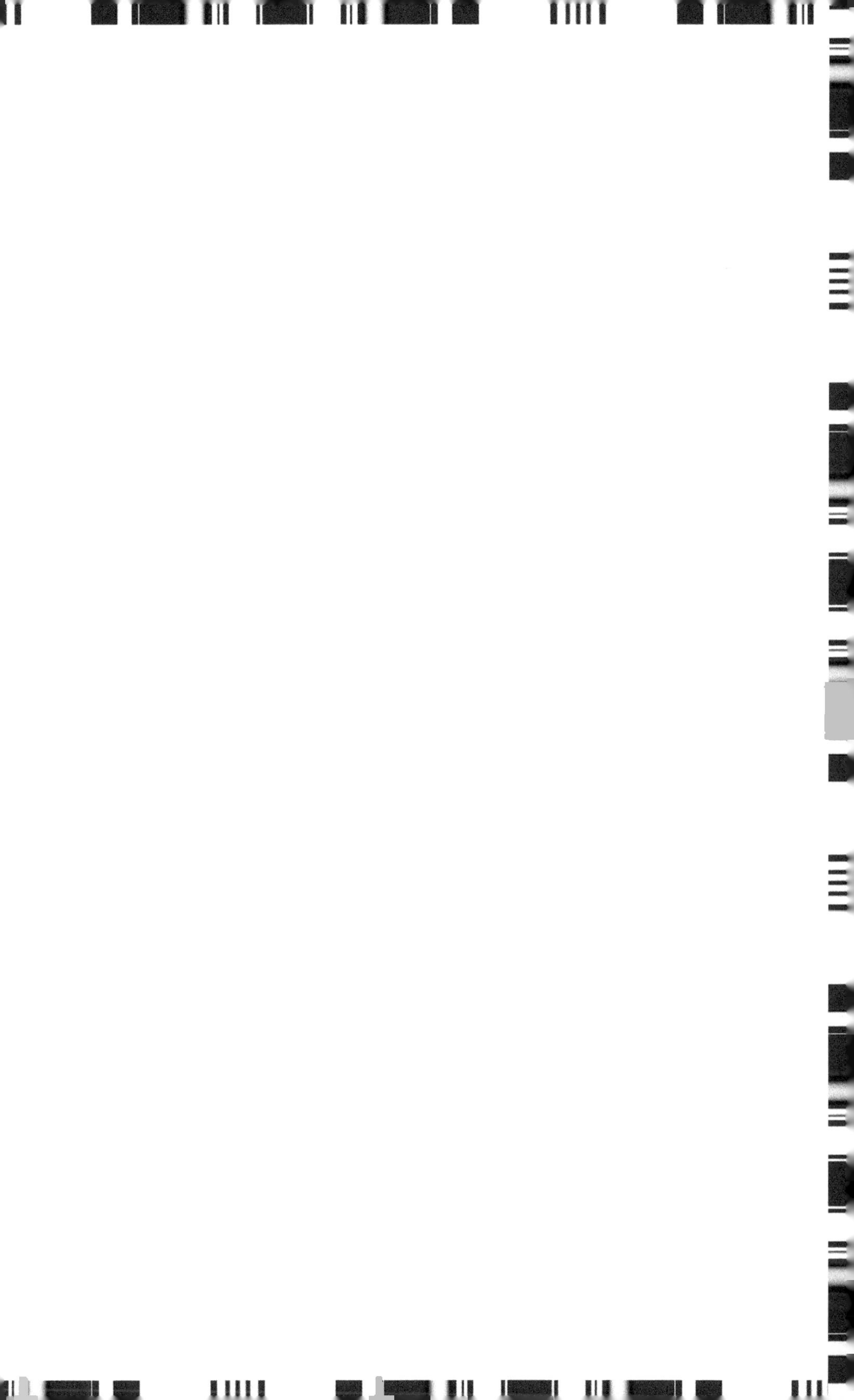

Tacitus and Argus

The Soldiers

TACITUS

"Argus, my friend! Slept with the horses again last night?" My taunt drifts toward the bear of a man lumbering up to the end of our row.

His unintelligible grunt as he squeezes past the cramped spectators supports my observation almost as much as his wrinkled tunic and bloodshot eyes.

"You would know. Your mistress was among them," Argus quips.

His late grin reveals a missing bottom tooth, while his calloused hand runs through short, copper-toned hair. Sunlight reflects silver strands littered throughout a close-cropped beard, highlighting the twelve-year age gap between us.

"At least I have a mistress," I return.

His grin widens, splitting the thick scar grazing the right side of his face. "Just one? A handsome Adonis like you? Here."

He slams a small wineskin against my chest, and I capture it with a targeted eye roll.

"You haven't missed much," I say, settling back on the stone bench. I return my attention to the dull soldier drills taking place on the arena floor. "I expected more, given the Emperor's attendance today, but so far, it's just the usual executions and pathetic sparring. Even the re-enactment was boring. General Nepos' victory at Jupiter's Pass. Remember that? We were at that battle and I barely recall it. Opius Plinius belongs in the country if this is the best he's got."

"So, what you're saying is, I should return to your mistress and finish what we started?" He lifts a scarred brow, and I return a dry look.

"General Severus sent us here for a reason."

"What reason? To punish us for losing last week's pay to that conniving Gaul?"

"Probably," I snort. "If I recall, you lost more than our pay, which is why he's pissed. Please tell me you brought food as well. I'm starving."

He narrows his green eyes on me. "Have you still not learned to cook? That prissy equestrian upbringing did you no favors, kid."

"Elite generals don't need to cook," I mumble, snatching the stale bread he holds out.

"No, but disgraced centurions do."

I wince, grateful when a reverent hush falls over the crowd. The Emperor must have signaled the start of the primus because a trumpet blast echoes through the arena. The simmering buzz of the tightly packed stands shifts into tense excitement.

"Finally! Got here just in time," Argus says with a smirk.

He inches closer as the bodies around us jostle for a better view. My response is cut off by the booming voice of a herald standing in the center of the arena floor.

"Esteemed citizens of Rome! In honor of His Imperial Majesty, the most glorious Princeps, it is my privilege to announce the premier exhibition of today's magnificent spectacle! From the house of Opius Plinius, you will bear witness to thrilling combat featuring the bravest, most victorious gladiators Rome has to offer!

"People of Rome, I present to you the murmillo Basinus, the secutor Ino, and the retiarius Musa. All three will join forces to face your invincible champion… *Jason the Fearless Murmillo!"*

An explosive roar engulfs the arena. The stone benches seem to shake at the thunderous cheering and stomping of the crowd. I fear for the slaves and women crammed into the flimsy wooden tiers at the top of the stands.

But the deafening commotion quickly shifts into confused silence.

My pulse picks up as I strain forward, trying to peer past a large man screaming obscenities. Soon the collective shock transforms into a chorus of boos.

"Frax…" Argus exhales the curse in disbelief. His additional two inches gives him a better vantage point.

"What am I missing? I can't see past this ogre." I lean to my left but still can't see much through the swaying bodies and flailing arms of the irate spectators.

"It's Jason," Argus explains.

"The gladiator they just announced? Impossible," I joke.

"Hilarious. I meant, he's supposed to be a champion murmillo, but look at him. *Caenum*…look at his opponent."

I finally find an opening for a clear view of the sand.

"That looks like Musa, the retiarius," I observe. "I've seen him fight before. Quick delivery, but weak mind. Easily riled. Once he—" I stop. Dread seeps through me when I spot the rest of the lineup.

The boos become outright curses, and I shove the merchant in front of me to the right for a better view. He twists back a furious glare but shrinks at Argus' warning look. My friend's thickly muscled build, tall stature, and menacing war-earned scars mean he rarely has to use the gladius he so skillfully wields. The threatening presence that struck fear in enemy soldiers is more than enough for the urban civilians back home.

I'm less intimidating physically, but it wouldn't take long for an opponent to regret picking a fight with me, either. Coming from a prestigious military family, I've been training to lead Rome's great legions from the day I learned to walk. Up until six months ago, it seemed that my destiny to become the youngest senior officer—not just in the Sixth, but the entire empire—was all but secured.

Now, I'm a disgraced nobody embedded in a sea of commoners watching other men fight.

My fist clenches around the stale bread when I see the champion gladiator they call Jason. The scars on my back feel as if they're burning through my tunic like they do whenever I'm confronted with gross injustice.

"*By Pluto's chains*…he's not only unarmored, he's unarmed," I murmur.

"You *sputax* sons of harpies!" Argus shouts.

"A man deserves a chance!" I add to no one in particular. "It's practically an execution."

"A shameful slaughter, that's what," Argus spits out. "Soldier or slave, a warrior deserves respect if he's earned it."

Despite the intense heat, a sudden chill moves through me. "Is this why Severus sent us?" I ask, leaning close so only Argus can hear. "Did he know about this?"

"Probably," he grunts. "What a joke. Let's go. I'm not watching this."

I cast a surprised glance at my friend. "You're leaving? Do you really think he sent us to watch the execution of some gladiator?"

"How should I know?"

"Because he gave *you* the instructions. What exactly did he say?"

Argus glares at me but drops back to his seat. "Not much, if you must know. He said to be here, so…" He gestures over his body in impatient testimony. "I have no idea why he insisted we roll around among the vermin and piss of the stands while he pals around with the Emperor over in his private box. Look at him, whispering sweet nothings in the man's ear while we bake our faces off in the sun."

I shake my head, accustomed to my friend's unfiltered mouth. I'd say it will get him in trouble one day, but it already has. Many times. The irony that *I'm* the one who ultimately got us flogged and dishonorably discharged from the Sixth isn't lost on me.

"He's a retired general who won three wars and delivered an entire continent to the Empire," I return. "He's outlived every politician in Rome, including two emperors. You don't think he deserves a little shade and a few figs?"

"Shut up, they're starting!" Argus snaps, waving me quiet.

"Says the man who was about to walk out," I grumble.

"I stayed, didn't I? Oof. That had to hurt. Knocked straight to the floor by a shield. That's the worst."

"Not as bad as that." I wince as Jason takes a sword to the calf.

Argus jumps to his feet. "This is a joke!" he cries.

Shouts of profanity rain down around us. Shaking fists and obscene gestures obstruct our view as growing hostility spreads over the crowd. The authorities are about to have a riot on their hands if something isn't done. What were they thinking with this charade?

I peer in the direction of the Emperor's box for a glimpse of Severus, but I can no longer see through the angry spectators.

"The man is a legend in the arena," Argus hisses, glaring at the action below. "He doesn't deserve to go out like this. He's earned much better."

I nod, forcing away haunting images of my own brush with brutal injustice.

A sudden cheer erupts from the benches, and I duck into an opening to see Jason snatch the retiarius' net from the air and turn it into a weapon of his own.

"By the gods, he's got the sword!" Argus yells, pointing at the sand. "Take that, you *bestiae filii!*"

"Still wish you'd left?" I toss with a smirk.

His eyes narrow in mock disdain, but he's too excited to take the bait.

"Get him! Get…yea!" Argus jumps up and down, spraying wine all over us.

I laugh as the red liquid stains my light blue tunic. Maybe this will be a real match after all.

Then…disaster hits.

An eerie pall settles over the crowd when Jason crashes to the ground and absorbs a barrage of blows. A deep crimson stain traces his defeat over the sand as the opponents drag him around, putting his shame on display.

Jeering swells around us, but Argus and I maintain a respectful silence. Jason's fate is too close to what ours could be one day. Memories of a horrific night six months ago gnaw at the recesses of my mind. The night *my* blood painted the sodden ground.

He's not our brother, but he's a warrior and that's enough. A warrior deserves a courageous death.

"He didn't have a prayer," I mutter.

"This is wrong," Argus growls. "Better to face the lions than this humiliation. Better to..."

We launch to our feet when the defeated gladiator blocks the trident and shoves it away.

"Did you see that?!" Argus cries, grasping the stranger beside him. "Did you?!"

"He grabbed it! Just like that!" the man shouts back with animated gestures.

Chaos spreads over the packed benches as fans jump and cheer. There's bumping, shoving, and shouting, but no one seems to care. In this moment, we are all one body. One witness staring into the face of the impossible.

"The kid is a god. Look at how the retiarius rages!" I laugh.

The angry fighter will be dead soon. I may not know much about these gladiators, but I know war better than my own existence. Musa is rattled, which makes him weak. A skilled warrior like Jason should have no problem taking advantage of the situation.

"He got him!" Argus shrieks. "He took out the murmillo! *Thunder of Jupiter!* One down!"

The stands swirl in a frenzy. Strangers cheer and embrace as though they've known each other their whole lives.

The impossible becomes even more probable when Musa loses his net-hand to Jason's sword, just as I predicted. Controlled anger is a deadly weapon. Wild fury is a death sentence.

"I don't believe it," Argus muses, staring in awe. "He's going to do it. He's going to win this thing."

"Incredible," I mumble under my breath.

"He's just toying with the last one now," Argus laughs. "Probably enjoying the glory of the crowd and his final moments of victory."

I squint at the sparring gladiators and shake my head. "No, I don't think so. Look closely. See how Jason drops his strong side so the secutor can take the advantage? Now, look around us."

Argus furrows his brow and then follows my gaze to the spectators who have morphed into a raucous circus. His eyes widen in understanding.

Despite the heat, the smells, the sweat, and cramped conditions, the audience is salivating over the action below. I've never seen such fervor, such hunger for a fight. Such admiration for a pair of opponents.

"The champion isn't playing the secutor. He's playing *us,*" Argus whispers.

I grin. "My guess? He wants that poor kid to live."

Argus shakes his head in disbelief. "Brilliant."

"Extremely."

"It should have been impossible."

"Should have been."

We exchange a knowing look.

This is why Severus sent us.

Mallia

The Patrician

MALLIA

"Oh, wonderful. Now we get to watch a boring military parade," the Emperor's niece huffs.

Aurelia twirls a ringlet of blonde hair around her finger as she glares at the hundreds of legionaries marching in perfect formation on the sand below. While sweat-soaked slaves remove the bodies of the victims from the previous events, a full cohort from Rome's elite Legio IV shows off their military splendor in honor of the Emperor—and their former legatus who now serves as the Emperor's top advisor.

Not that either of them is paying attention. The Emperor and his confidant have been in deep conversation at the entrance to our private box since the end of the last fight.

Their hushed voices have me beyond curious, but I'll likely never know what could be important enough to make them miss their own parade.

Aurelia hasn't even noticed her imperial uncle's strange behavior. It's not surprising since she rarely notices anything but herself.

It's said her ancestry dates back to the goddess Juno, which is ridiculous, of course, but formidable enough of a possibility to grant her immunity in elite circles. At the very least, there are no volunteers willing to challenge the gods on the matter. Her companions bear her vanity out of respect for her title and fear of her (possible) divinity.

And I would know. I see it almost daily.

As the only child of the esteemed Senator Lucius Mallius Justus, I often find myself in the company of Rome's elite, including today's invitation to join the Emperor and his entourage in their private box at the games. Supposedly, there's a surprise match for the primus of the lengthy festivities, but the terrible heat is making the thought of waiting for such an eternity almost too much to bear. It's certainly too much for my entitled companion.

"*To the lions with Hades,* this ridiculous inferno," Aurelia hisses at whatever deity is listening. Hopefully, not Hades. "Really, I'll never understand why we must suffer through all the pre-match fanfare. We all know why we're here. Let's skip to that."

My nod of agreement is only because I'd rather not be here at all. Skipping any part of "the day's festivities" seems better than sitting through it.

"I'm surprised the arena is so packed, given the heat," I say, fidgeting with the soft linen of my pale gold palla.

Aurelia's painted lips twist into a grimace. "Of course it's packed. Jason is fighting the primus today."

"Jason? He's a gladiator?" I ask the silly question only to punish her scolding tone. I hate when she treats me like a child.

It seems to have worked when she retaliates with a smug caress of her expensive pearl earrings I'd been admiring earlier.

Somehow, I contain my eye roll as I force my attention back to the military demonstration. The soldiers are now running shield drills, which I find much more enjoyable than all the gruesome blood and death we've witnessed today.

I will never understand this lust for violence, just as I will never understand the obsession with gladiators. They are men—brutal men—who spar other brutal men. If the violent man also happens to be handsome, gods help us, these people lose their minds. I've never seen this Jason fight, but that's probably because I haven't been to the games since the last time Aurelia dragged me here. I seem to be the only one in the Empire not fawning over him.

"Really, Mallia, I must speak to your father about raising you in a cave. You! Come here!" she shouts at my maid. "What's your name again, girl?"

"Danae, my lady," she says softly, head lowered.

She's careful not to look at me or we'd burst out laughing. We often joke about Aurelia's theatrical snobbery and petty adherence to social etiquette.

Case in point: pretending she doesn't know the name of the slave she sees almost every day when I visit.

"Danae, you seem like a bright girl. Have you heard of the gladiator Jason?"

Danae glances at me for direction, and I give her a quick nod—along with a subtle smirk. She covers her own amusement well.

"Yes, my lady. I have heard of him. They call him *Jason the Fearless Murmillo.*"

Aurelia claps her jeweled hands in triumph. "See there, Mallia? Even your slave knows more than you."

I sigh and squint into the sunlight to feign some interest in the action on the sand. "Okay, so he's a murmillo."

"A murmillo? He's more than a murmillo."

"Let me guess, he's also your lover," I say in a bored tone. "Should we start on the wedding arrangements?"

Aurelia scoffs, accustomed to my sarcasm. "You joke, but soon you will understand. Perhaps even you, my pretty little skeptic, will be impressed."

Unlikely.

She casts a quick look at the Emperor and leans close. "Besides, it's not just the women who sing his praises. It's my uncle who brought us here, not I."

Surprised, I glance at the powerful man, suddenly more interested in the gossip.

"The Emperor is a fan? Really?"

"A fan? Silly girl, emperors aren't fans of anything except their armies. But yes, he's taken quite an interest in this particular slave for some reason."

I squint toward the iron gate where the gladiators will enter as if the mysterious man will suddenly appear. Maybe I am a tad curious.

"Because of his accomplishments in the arena?" I ask.

Aurelia huffs and resumes her absent tug on the lone curl left free of the intricate braids covering her head. "How would I know such a thing? You, there!" she snaps at a servant. "Closer with that fan!"

The man scurries forward and angles the large bronze fan in her direction. As much as I hate the way she treats her slaves, I don't hate the additional air breaking up the brutal heat.

She signals a cupbearer who rushes over to refill her chilled wine.

When the slave offers some to me, I shake my head with a gentle smile. In this heat, it's the mint water I crave. Danae catches my longing glance at the other pitcher and signals the cupbearer holding that one.

I mouth a *thank you,* and she returns a knowing smile. I have no idea what I'd do without her.

"He's an enigma," Aurelia continues, drawing me back to the conversation. I don't even remember what we were talking about. "Different than the others. Everyone says so. He's a champion that spurns all the pleasures that come with such a status."

Ah, right. The gladiator.

"Interesting," I hedge, taking a refreshing sip of my drink. "That's rare."

"Naturally. He's a rare specimen. I've only been in his presence twice, but his very essence smolders with a fire you can feel in every recess of your body." Aurelia fans herself for emphasis.

"I see. He sounds—"

She waves me silent. "I'm telling you, Mallia, when he looks at you with those blazing eyes, you can't help but fall under his spell. And his body—so warm and hard. All muscle and scars everywhere. It's enough to make you burn from the memory alone."

My fingers tighten around the cup as I squirm on my cushioned seat. I cast an uncomfortable scan around us, grateful no one seems to be paying attention to us.

The truth is, I have heard of Jason. Of course I have. I just refuse to be part of the hype and fawn over a slave like a fool. I'd rather die than have others react to me the way I'm now cringing at Aurelia's obsession.

This conversation certainly isn't making the scorching sun any more bearable.

By the time the main event is announced, I've given up on the prospect of surviving this tedious day. But a quick look at the Emperor piques my interest again. He's *still* at the back of the box, engaged in an intense exchange with the retired Legatus Severus. Based on their grave expressions, whatever they're discussing is infinitely more interesting than anything Aurelia has said since… ever.

"There he is!" she cries. "Look at him. Magnificent," she breathes, forcing me back to my current torture. Aurelia practically drools as she leans forward for a better view. It's not personal, but I already hate this man for making my life miserable with his magnificence.

Our vantage point is good, and maybe my resentment eases slightly when I survey the gladiator in question. There are four on the sand, but it's not hard to identify Aurelia's crush. Only one draws my immediate attention.

But it's not his stunning form or the carved features of his handsome face that attract me. It's his somber stance.

I'd been expecting a cocky smile, a flirtatious glint, any of the self-important gloating typical of the elite gladiators as they parade for the masses. The others march around like they expect to be worshiped, but this one stands solemn and ominous, projecting a dangerous calm like a stalking predator. His bearing exhibits a stony resolve, and even more incredible, he doesn't seem to notice us. He certainly isn't basking in the infatuated admiration of the crowd like the others.

The young warrior is focused, angry…and unarmed.

"Wait! Where's his armor and his weapon?" Aurelia cries, pointing a jeweled finger toward the sand. "He has no weapon! They mean to kill him! Uncle!"

The Emperor halts his conversation with Severus to glance at Aurelia. I see his subtle nod to the general before returning to his seat. He adjusts his robes as a contingent of slaves rush over to offer snacks and beverages. He takes a cup of water but refuses the bowl of figs.

"Yes, Aurelia?" he asks in a resigned tone.

"They mean to kill him!" she cries. "Opius Plinius is a monster!"

The Emperor's lips twist slightly as he settles back in his chair.

"A monster? You don't like your gladiator's odds, I presume."

My friend's icy blue eyes narrow in resentment. "Of course not! Three-on-one with no armor or weapon? It's absurd! You should have Opius Plinius executed for this travesty!"

He barks a short laugh. "Execute a man for a match billing? That would be a first."

Aurelia squints a cold stare at him. "I know you agree. You've always been impressed with that gladiator. I know that's why we're here."

"I have been. And I'm looking forward to seeing what he does with this challenge."

"Challenge? It's a massacre!"

His face takes on the same quiet amusement it does every time his niece makes her internal drama public.

"Relax, my dear," he says in a soothing tone. "Jason is a very valuable asset of Opius Plinius. I do not believe he'd present this pairing if it were as unbalanced as you seem to think. I'm surprised you have so little faith in your man. I've heard rumors you wagered a small fortune on his last fight."

A scowl spreads over her delicate features as she crosses her arms and stares back at the sand. I suppose only an emperor has the power to silence her.

Oh, to be an emperor.

"Fine, but if he dies, you will have a terrible time consoling me," she pouts.

"He's a gladiator, my dear," the Emperor says with a smirk. "He faces death like you face breakfast every morning."

"Well, it's a waste, that's all."

"What is? His life or his Adonis physique?"

I can't stop a snort at the Emperor's taunt. Aurelia is seething.

"Fine. Joke all you want, Uncle, but I don't know why you're pretending you don't care. I heard you talking about him plenty of times over the last few weeks."

"Silence!" he hisses, drawing several surprised glances.

Aurelia has struck a nerve, which is something I rarely see. The Emperor isn't known to be easily riled. He's a severe man, proud but not arrogant. It's funny how I respect him greatly, but I can barely stand his niece, who adores me.

I glance at the action on the sand, curious about this mysterious gladiator who can stir up the most prestigious box in the arena. Maybe there *is* something special about him.

As the match wears on, I don't like how my attention stays riveted on the man. I especially don't like my body's reaction to the way he flexes and moves with fluid grace that almost makes me forget we're witnessing violence.

It kills me to admit that maybe Aurelia is right for once. The gladiator is... fine. Yes. He's magnificent.

Maybe it's the unfair circumstances that tug at my naturally compassionate heart, but with each passing second, it becomes harder to watch him take blow after blow. Aurelia is beside herself when the three opponents converge on the young warrior and drag him over the sand.

"You have to stop this!" she pleads to her uncle, who doesn't seem to hear her.

Once again, the Emperor's reaction surprises me. He's looking for something, studying the activity below with an intensity beyond what's required for an afternoon of entertainment. His fists are clenched around the armrest of his chair, his jaw set. A troop of nude dancers could perform right beside him, and he wouldn't glance their way.

Still, what shocks me the most isn't the Emperor's interest, or Aurelia's crush, or any of the improbable action happening in the fight below.

What haunts me for days to come is the moment a common slave grabs the prongs of a bloody trident and causes the most powerful man in the world to exchange a discreet nod with his general.

Severus
The Advisor

SEVERUS

I wait as the Emperor leaves his companions to meet me at the top of the box.

"It's done?" he whispers, leaning close.

I nod. "Opius Plinius was not happy about the arrangement, but I paid him well as you requested. I also swore him to silence."

"If he loses Jason today, he will be fully compensated. That's more than he can say for other matches."

I study the sand, watching the first cohort from my former legion parade the grounds with all the discipline and precision I'd expect from my men. I used to miss military life. Now, I've learned the real wars are fought in the imperial palace.

"I suspect the lanista will lose his champion today, but not to death," I say, rubbing my stubbled chin. Even after five years of retirement, it's strange to feel the scratch of facial hair on my fingers.

The Emperor searches my eyes with a severe expression. "You have incredible faith in this boy, don't you?"

"He's one of the best I've ever seen, Imperator."

"You don't think he's too young? Argus and Tacitus are seasoned soldiers. This boy isn't even twenty-five."

I swallow a laugh at the logical but unnecessary concern. "You tell me how much age matters after you see him fight today. Besides, Tacitus is only seasoned by experience, not by time. He is young, a prodigy in his own right."

"Fair point. Still, what about this gladiator's popularity? Everyone knows him. There are statues and impressions of him all over the city."

I nod, recalling the vendor stand of carved figurines we passed on our way into the arena. A ridiculous trend, but gladiator worship doesn't even graze the list of sins polluting this gods forsaken city.

"Yes, and his fame will work to our advantage, at least as much as our detriment. You must trust me." My firm voice relaxes the worry lines in his face. My friend is only a year older, but the stress of an empire has aged him more than decades of war have aged me.

The Emperor is a man of integrity, a man cursed by a great love for his citizens who will never know the agony he carries for their well-being. After a long string of self-serving tyrants, I'd almost given up on the hope that Rome would ever have the honor of a leader such as this.

Now that he's here, I will do everything in my power to keep him on the throne—including challenging the very dominion of Evil's stronghold over this empire.

"Besides, when you see Jason fight, you'll understand why all other obstacles fall away," I add in a softer tone.

"I'm looking forward to it. If he passes this impossible test, I'm not sure what else he'd have to prove other than his loyalty."

I allow my gaze to lift to the Emperor's astute brown eyes, something I never do lightly. "He will pass. He's the one, Caesar. I knew it the moment I saw him, the moment I watched him wield a sword."

The Emperor's lips settle in a thin line. "I hope so, my friend. I'm trusting you with my life."

My heart beats faster as the gravity of this moment settles around us.

"I know, and I'd lay down my own for yours. We all would, but he's the one. I'm sure of it. May the gods strike me down if I'm wrong."

His lips twitch with suppressed humor. "You're never wrong."

"Perhaps one day, but not this time."

After a short pause, the Emperor releases a heavy breath. "Then so be it. I have no choice but to trust you."

I return a firm nod. "You will not regret it, my lord. Securing Jason is all that remains to re-commission *Septem Fideles*."

Chapter I

JASON

"You cowardly *bestia filius!* What in Hades was that?" Opius Plinius growls, storming toward my cell.

Every inch of my body burns in protest as I force myself up while the guards open the lock, but I refuse to confront my master's rage from a weakened position.

"I thought you'd be happy that I won, or was the plan for me to die?" I spit out.

I know it's a mistake even as the words leave my mouth, but I have no patience for the man after what I just survived at his whim. The irony of his calling *me* a cowardly son of a beast is too much.

Plinius flings an irate hand toward a guard, who smashes his vine stick into my side. The blow to the existing injuries sends me stumbling into the stone wall.

"You insolent dog! I saw what you did! Giving Ino a heavy advantage to turn favor toward him. You manipulated the crowd. You usurped the role of editor!"

Bracing a hand on the coarse stone, I glare at him through clenched teeth. "We gave them a show. That's what you wanted, wasn't it? You should be on your knees *thanking* me for turning a joke into a spectacle worthy of an emperor."

A blow to the face, followed by a strike to the ribs, leaves me on the floor, coughing in agony. The low-ranking guards close in, surrounding me in eager anticipation. I feel their violent thirst. Former gladiators who hate that their glory has faded have been waiting for this opportunity for a long time. It's no accident

Plinius called on them for this confrontation instead of Balbus and the usual contingent who respect us.

Plinius leans toward me, eyes bulging and nostrils flaring. "What I *want* is for you to learn your place! For you to understand that you are my animal." His rancid breath leaks from thin, cracked lips to coat my face. "As such, you do not think. You do not make decisions. You do not play games with my life! Do you think the Emperor is an idiot? He's an accomplished military man in his own right. You think he didn't notice your vanity?"

"*My vanity?*" I retort with a cold glare. "What vanity? It was survival! Admit to what really angers you. You sent me out to get slaughtered, and now you're livid I came back alive. You can't stand the fact that a slave beat you at your own game!"

"Vah!" Plinius bellows a harsh cry and snatches the vine stick from the guard. He rushes at me, and all I can do is hold up my arms in a weak defense. Wild, imprecise strikes land hard and fast, grinding me into the floor.

He draws back abruptly, and I clutch my side, choking for air. My body is on fire as recent stitches hang open and scrape the skin they're supposed to be mending. Blood from the reopened wounds stains the surrounding walls in a bitter premonition of my coming fate.

Plinius retreats a step and surveys me with lethal precision.

"Clean him up again," he barks. "I want him as healthy as possible for next week."

"Next week, my lord?" a guard asks.

"Next week, the others will learn that no one plays me for a fool. Not even a champion. Fortuna be cursed."

ARGUS

I stare toward the small window cut into the wall of my one-room flat. Sunlight leaks through the cracks in the shutter, mixing with tendrils of smoke from a neighbor's dinner preparation. Animated arguments clash with shrieks of playing children from the surrounding insulae in the apartment block, but the noise does nothing to mask the news echoing through my head.

The concerned soldier waits nervously in the open doorway, but I have no words for him. None of his report makes any sense.

"You're sure the woman you saw was Iulia?" I ask, turning back to my former brother-in-arms.

"I'd swear on my mother's grave if she were dead," Erasinus says with a solemn expression. "I saw your wife in Ephesus, my friend. Our legion is passing through Rome, so I came as soon as I could."

"*Frax…*" I mutter, scratching at my short beard.

Ephesus. That can't be right.

"I wish I had better news."

With a grunt, I brace a fist on the rough, plaster-coated wall beside the door. "I'm not sure there is such a thing when it comes to that woman."

Erasinus offers a crooked smile. "If it makes you feel any better, she doesn't appear to be with another man."

It doesn't.

"What about my boys? Any sign of them?"

Erasinus lowers his gaze and fidgets with the military belt cinched around his off-duty tunic. My own belt from my service with Legio IV Custodia Sacra hangs above my bed beside a relief of a griffin, the insignia of the Fourth. My years serving under Legatus Severus in the Fourth were some of the best of my life.

The opposite was true of my subsequent ignoble stint with the Sixth. That cursed scorpion can burn in hades.

"I'm sorry, no," Erasinus says in an even tone. "They weren't with her. I followed her for as long as I could, but my centurion kept us on a tight leash."

Of course he did. As would any centurion worth his rank.

I sigh and tap the wall with my knuckles. "Well, thanks for the update. At least I have closure."

"Happy to help." He twists a weak smile but continues to hesitate at the threshold. "So, how are you doing after…well, you know…"

I wince and grit my teeth against the sick feeling in my stomach. It's a fair question. I haven't seen Erasinus since that fateful night. But talking about it hasn't gotten any easier.

I have no interest in reliving the moment I lost my career and Tacitus lost everything.

"Great," I huff sarcastically. "Nothing more noble for a career soldier than guarding storehouses."

My friend grimaces and studies the griffin on my wall. "Do you ever miss it?"

"The life or the Sixth?"

"The life," he says with a laugh. "I know very well how you feel about the Sixth. Understandably so."

Yes, I miss the life. Every cursed day.

"Nah. It's good to be back in Rome," I lie.

Erasinus returns a knowing look but doesn't call me on the fib. "And… Tacitus? How's he doing after everything?"

A shudder moves through me at the mention of my closest friend. My brother in every respect except blood. There aren't enough hours in the day to answer a question as complex and ugly as that one.

"Pretty good."

I straighten to attention and salute before he can make any more impossible inquiries.

"Well, thanks again, soldier. Good luck to you."

"Same to you, Argus. Good health and long life."

He pivots on the small landing to descend the stairs back to the building entrance. I close my door and lean against it.

Ephesus. *Pluto's chains…*

I need to find Tacitus.

ARGUS

It's often said I'm the brawn and Tacitus is the brains of our duo, but I prefer to think of myself as the enforcer for his brilliant and strategic mind. He may be more than a decade younger, but we've fought and suffered enough to be equals.

Now, as disgraced soldiers, we're equal outcasts.

"You're telling me Iulia is in Ephesus," he repeats for the tenth time since I found him in our favorite tavern. Nestled on the ground floor of a nearby apartment block beside the public baths, this place is owned by another veteran of the Fourth and doesn't water down the wine as much as the other establishments in Crassus Pass. Carbo is always generous with pours to fellow soldiers and lets us use the small back room attached to the crowded main area.

The alcove may be as loud, smoky, and cramped as the rest of the tavern, but at least we have some privacy free of prying eyes.

"It's not going to make it less true the more times you make me say it," I mutter, taking a large gulp of wine. Tacitus hasn't even touched his. Clearly, he's not having the greatest day either.

He releases a long breath and shoves a hand through his medium-length dark waves. With his straight nose, long lashes, and perfectly proportioned aristocratic features, he looks like he belongs at a senator's banquet instead of a battlefield.

However, his artistic beauty is a cruel illusion. A marble bust chiseled with the violence of a sculptor's mallet has faced less pain than this man. Definitely less injustice.

Behind those haunted brown eyes is a cunning military mind, fierce bravery, and deadly skill. Underestimate the former first-cohort centurion, and you will have a gladius in your throat before you can finish your insult. Besides Legatus Severus, Tacitus is more of a soldier than any man I've served with in my twenty years in the military.

"How in hades did she get all the way to Ephesus?" he asks, squinting through the dim lamp light.

I shrug and scratch at a dent in the wooden table. "How should I know, but Erasinus swears he saw her when his legion marched through."

"*Juno's breath*…what are you going to do?"

I lean back against the soot-stained wall. "What can I do? Even if I went after her, what's the point? I don't know if my boys are there, and I sure as hades don't want her without them. Even if I find them, they're almost grown now, and I have nothing left to offer since my discharge. There's no inheritance to start their lives as men. They'd disown me, too."

Tacitus shakes his head and stares into his untouched spiced wine. "Unbelievable. I'm sorry, my friend. Truly."

"I'll drink to that." I drain my cup and slam it back on the table. Hopefully, the server heard the sound and brings the pitcher.

"Atia's birthday is coming up," Tacitus says quietly. "She's turning sixteen."

"*Caenum*…"

I straighten from the wall and rest my forearms on the table.

Searching his troubled expression, I breathe a silent curse for the gods over the way they've tortured him.

A muscle moves in his cheek as he stares at some invisible target with a hard expression.

"Will your father marry her off?" I ask after a long pause.

Tacitus shrugs, still not looking at me. "I don't know. I haven't heard any rumors of it in the few circles that haven't shunned me."

We sit in silence for another long stretch, each absorbed in the pain of lost memories.

"Do you ever regret it?" I ask in a reflective tone.

His gaze shoots to me. "My decision?"

I shrug, settling back into the stone bench carved into the wall. "Yeah. I mean, I know why you did it. But look at us now. I wouldn't blame you if you wish you'd chosen differently, given everything it cost you. Everything you've lost."

Tacitus flinches and closes his eyes. After a long exhale, he opens them and fixes a resolute stare on me. "It's been a nightmare, but how can I regret it, Argus? What kind of person would that make me?"

A fraction of the person he is. It would make him just like the spineless braccas *responsible for what happened that night.*

Instead, he'll always be an unsung hero living the shameful life of a criminal.

Anger at the injustice burns fresh, and I have to force it back down. The past is the past.

Releasing a heavy breath, I toss a wry smile his way and lift my empty cup. "Well, my boy, it appears it's official. Neither of us has a family now."

Tacitus barks a harsh laugh. "I'll drink to that," he echoes.

And empties his cup.

JASON

A curse filters through my lips as the guards shove me against the tall wooden post in the center of the training grounds. An eerie silence spreads over the line of gladiators watching the familiar scene. At some point, it's been each of them. Right now, they're grateful it's not.

The morning sun reflecting off the freshly combed sand shows no remnants of the last punishment doled out on this spot. The post itself is less innocent with its chips, gashes, and dried blood. I can only wonder how much of it is mine.

Much less than it's about to be.

I cast a dark look at Plinius as the guards anchor my arms above my head with thick, iron chains. The hot metal cuts into my wrists, stretching my body until the stitches applied to last week's wounds strain in protest.

"This filthy dog has betrayed us!" Plinius shouts as he parades before the gladiators and guards. "Embarrassed our house in front of the entire city, the Emperor himself!"

He stops beside me with a cold scowl.

"A gladiator fights. A gladiator kills. He does not show mercy. He does not mock the system set in place by the gods."

His murderous gaze digs into mine. "This is my message, Jason. They will remember this as well as you will."

I glare back, fists tight with suppressed rage. "This has nothing to do with honor," I hiss through clenched teeth. "This is about your own humiliated pride."

Plinius goes deathly still. Without warning, he rips at the laceration on my leg.

An anguished gasp expels from my lungs as hot blood runs down my calf.

I will be dying today. I've known since the moment the guards came for me this morning that it would be my last. How the gods must be laughing that I'm about to die for the sin of cheating death. My only hope now is to provoke the cruel man into granting me a quick one.

"You can't stand the fact that the gods have mocked you," I growl with a taunting smile. "You sold your soul for their favor, and now they scorn you for your hubris."

Predictably, Plinius roars in anger and grabs the rod from Balbus. He smashes it against my back so hard, my ribs crack from the impact with the post. It only takes two more blows for my knees to give out.

My head hangs low as I fight for air. I want to say more. The gods know my brain is packed with insults I've endured my entire life, but nothing will surface. There's no breath left for provocation, no strength to fight, and a new terror seeps in: that I won't be able to convince Plinius to kill me before he has the chance to deliver his "message."

My fate is sealed when he relaxes his fury into chilling resolve. He returns the rod to the guard and wipes the blood from his hands. With a dramatic sigh, he addresses his audience again.

"This traitor seems to think he is a god among men. Better than all of you, and even more than his masters. I believe it's only fair that each of you has a chance to defend yourself against his challenge. Line up! Ino, since this maggot clearly felt your life was worth more than his, you will go first. Choose your weapon."

Nausea sweeps through me as his cruel sentence becomes clear, but I bite back any response. Let him play his sadistic games. I only lose by allowing him to enjoy it.

Plinius steps back with an icy sneer. "You fared well in the arena, despite your lack of arms. Let's see how you do with no hands."

SEVERUS

"General Severus! What a surprise! We're honored by your presence," Opius Plinius gushes as he glides into the atrium. His cloud of attendants follows close behind, and as usual, he's dressed like he's come from the Imperial Palace, not the breakfast table.

Social climbers—especially freedmen—are exhausting. I hate that I have to indulge this one.

"Thank you for your time, Plinius," I say with a tight smile. "I know you're a busy man, so my visit will be brief."

"Of course! I'm at your disposal. What can I do for you?"

I study the short man's nervous tug at the brooch on his shoulder. His gaze darts from an ornate fountain to the tiled mosaic on the wall and back to me. It's a strange reaction for someone who's just pleased the Emperor with his offerings, especially one as vain as Plinius. I expected him to assume I've come to extol him and sing his praises.

"Based on our previous conversation, I think you know why I'm here," I say.

Plinius scratches at his temple, still not looking at me. "Do I?"

The idiot can't possibly have forgotten our discussion the day before the Emperor's games. I grunt in frustration.

"The champion, Jason. I wish to speak with him," I remind him in an impatient tone.

Sweat gathers on the man's forehead, and I brace against a sudden rush of unease. Something is wrong. Come to think of it, this ludus is eerily void of activity for this time of day.

Plinius clears his throat. "I'm afraid that's not possible."

"Why not?"

As the Emperor's closest confidant, I'm not accustomed to being denied.

"Well... he, uh..." Plinius glances into the shadows behind him. I follow his gaze but can't see past the decorative columns leading into the rest of the villa.

Another shiver runs through me when he shifts on his sandaled feet. I cast a discreet warning glance at Marcellus, my loyal soldier-turned-bodyguard. Based on my companion's grave nod, he's sensing something is off as well and signals the other five men forming my cohors singularium to prepare for conflict.

"Jason was severely injured, my lord. He's still recovering," Plinius explains in a weak voice.

My gaze sears into him. "I'm not asking to watch him fight. I just wish to have a conversation. He was standing on the sand the last time I saw him, over a week ago. Certainly, he can rest on a mat while we talk."

Plinius cringes and examines his dusty feet. "Yes, certainly. I understand. Still, the infirmary is a nasty business. Blood, vomit, I could never subject a man as worthy as yourself to such conditions."

"I've fought wars my entire life. You think I'm intimidated by a little blood? Where is he? I don't have time for all this discussion."

"My lord—"

I step toward him, slinging the train of my black military cloak behind me with a rough hand. "Take me to Jason, or I swear the Emperor will confiscate this entire ludus so I have free rein to do as I please. Your choice," I spit out.

By the gods, I might kill him myself.

"Yes, my lord! Of course," he whimpers. "This way."

I shake my head in disgust as he finally obeys the simple request and leads us from the atrium.

My discomfort returns when the man guides us through the lavish villa toward the training grounds, instead of the bowels of the gladiator quarters as expected. I alert my men to stay vigilant at the break from protocol.

"Your infirmary is outdoors?" I ask in a sarcastic tone.

I swear, if he's still wasting my time…

Plinius stops just before the gate leading outside, wringing his hands. "No, it's…I suddenly remembered Jason is no longer in the infirmary."

"Really," I clip out. "Well, it's fortunate that you remembered this before we found ourselves unnecessarily stuck in that place of blood and vomit."

"Yes, it's just…"

Fed up with his sniveling, I charge past him into the sunlight.

When I spot the reason for his hesitation, my entire body goes cold.

Horror sucks the words from my lungs.

No…

"*Thunder of Jupiter…*have you lost your mind?" I roar, turning on him.

Plinius shrinks and ducks behind his guards. "He was insolent! He violated a gladiator's sacred duty to put forth his best efforts in any fight! He mocked us! Insulted the Emperor!"

"You vicious animal!" I growl, storming toward the post where Jason's body hangs in a bloody mass of mangled flesh. "*To the lions with you!* You will burn for this!"

No one would call me a sensitive man by any means, but right now, raw emotion cuts off my breath. My rage overflows with each step I take toward what's left of the young gladiator.

"*Bestia filius*, Plinius! May the gods curse you with eternal vengeance. You have no idea what you've done!"

As I approach Jason's broken body, the scene around me fades. My men, my duty, all the many witnesses looking on in stunned silence mean nothing in the wake of the horror in front of me. This is beyond evil. This is…Gods, I don't have words. When the young man stirs, I forget about the vile lanista responsible for the carnage. My only thought is on saving this boy's life.

"He's still alive! Jason, can you hear me, son?" I rush around the post and lift his chin, searching his bruised and bloody face.

His eyes flutter open but only return a blank stare.

"He's alive!" I call to my cohors, waving them over. "Get him down. You, there, bring my litter!"

"What are you doing?" Plinius cries, rushing toward me.

"Taking him where he belongs," I bark.

"You can't do that! He belongs here!"

I fire a glare that sends him back a step. With a bitter curse, I toss a bag of coins at his feet and watch as they spill onto the sand like the spray of blood it's seen so many times.

"I think you will agree that's a fair price," I hiss. "Especially now."

"He's not for sale!"

It takes all my strength not to murder him right then. "If you'd like to challenge the Emperor on the matter, you are welcome to follow us back to the palace and present your case, but we'll be taking this slave with us. Marcellus, load him onto my litter and give me your horse. I'll ride back. Out of my way," I growl, shoving past the disgusting man.

Chapter II

MALLIA

I watch my distorted features ripple in the marble fountain of the palace peristyle. Stray tendrils of dark hair flutter over my face in the reflection until a cloud of floating rose petals obscures the vision.

Typically, the private imperial courtyard near Aurelia's suite is one of my favorite locations for our visits. Today, though, the royal niece has a crisis, which means the rest of us do too.

"I just don't understand how my brooch could be lost," she whines from a marble bench beside her favorite myrtle tree. "Can you imagine? Stealing from the Emperor's only relation! Who would dare?"

A gentle breeze carries the scent of roses and the song of chirping birds throughout the garden as I run my fingers through the soft floating petals.

"Are you certain it was stolen, my lady? You didn't just misplace it?" I force enthusiasm into my bored tone.

"Silly girl! It's been in my family for generations. It belonged to Juno herself!"

I swallow a snarky response and focus on the cool water tickling my skin. "It's very unfortunate, my lady. Well, you have half the Guard searching, so I'm sure they'll find it."

Aurelia whimpers, and I glance over in time to see her wipe a fake tear from her charcoal-lined eyes. Who that display was for, I have no idea.

"Yes. You're right, of course," she sighs. "Sometimes, I think—"

Urgent footsteps clap down a neighboring corridor, followed by shouts of muffled commands.

"Gods have mercy, what's that commotion?" Aurelia hisses, straightening on the bench. "Fausta!"

"Yes, my lady," her maid answers, rushing to her side.

"Go find out what's going on. The noise is making my head spin!"

The servant nods and scurries off toward the disturbance.

"I swear I will not live to age forty," Aurelia mumbles, massaging her temples. "This stress is more than I can bear. I can't imagine how you get by, my dear."

I bite back a snort and return a polite shrug. As the daughter of a wealthy, highly respected senator, I suppose I manage the hardship of a pampered existence quite well.

"We can be grateful for these pockets of serenity," I say.

Aurelia adjusts her blonde ringlets around her shoulders and settles back on the marble bench. "Yes, well, you must distract me from my torment. I've heard rumors of your engagement. What of that?"

I wince and grip the edge of the fountain. I'd much rather discuss a possibly stolen brooch.

"Mallia?"

With a deep breath, I resume the absent swirl of the petals. "My father has come to an agreement with the family of Primus Placidius Pius," I say in a casual tone.

"Pius! But he is only of equestrian status. A merchant!"

"Yes, but a very wealthy one."

"Hmpf. Still." She motions to a slave, who rushes over with a bowl of grapes.

"Primus is the eldest and due to take over his father's fortune," I say, plucking a cluster of fruit from the bowl offered to me. "He's a highly sought-after bachelor."

"Despite his three noses?" Aurelia quips, shoving a grape in her mouth.

I fight a smirk. "Being attractive wasn't on my father's list of qualifications."

"But it should be on yours. You don't seem as opposed to the idea as I would have thought. He must be twenty years your senior."

I swallow my reaction with a half-chewed grape.

Of course, I'm opposed to the match. I'm not a hopeless romantic, but what girl doesn't dream of love and passion? I fantasize about burning with the fire I've heard so much about as much as the next dreamer.

But none of that matters in the world of elite politics. I was raised on duty and formalities. Principles and expectations.

Besides, the Emperor's outspoken niece is the last person I'd consult with any objections. I'm young but not stupid.

"He is experienced, it's true," I say. "But he spends most of his time traveling, which would leave me free to pursue my own interests."

Aurelia's mischievous grin makes me think she heard something very different than what I intended. "You devilish girl. You will take many lovers, then. Now I understand your plan."

A hot gust of air rushes over me. "I was referring to reading and studying," I mutter.

"Please," Aurelia scoffs. "You are much too young and beautiful to give up on the hope of passion. Really, Mallia, you must…Fausta! Thank the gods. What is the news?"

The servant bows and approaches. "I have learned that General Severus has returned to the palace with a severely injured man."

Aurelia's slim fingers fly to her lips. "Really! Why would he bring the man here?"

Fausta continues staring at the tiled walkway. "I don't know, my lady, but Severus is with the Emperor now. The commotion was from the man being carried to Telemon's lab."

"They took him to our private physician? Who is this stranger that he would receive such an honor? A visiting king? A victorious legate? Speak up!"

Fausta bites her lip and tugs at the sash around her beige tunic. "I'm not certain, my lady. I'm confused by the events as well."

"You must have heard something," Aurelia snaps. "What are the rumors then? The slaves always talk."

"The rumors are that the injured man is a slave," Fausta says hesitantly. She casts a fleeting glance at her mistress, and I feel my own maid's tension behind me. "The talk is that he's a gladiator from the House of Opius Plinius, called Jason."

SEVERUS

"What do you mean you brought him here?" the Emperor hisses after dismissing the attendants from his private study.

His brown eyes dig into mine as I brace for battle. "I know it's not what we discussed, but I had no choice."

"No? Because I can assure you, the correct *choice* was not to steal a gladiator from his master and bring him to my house!"

The Emperor rarely questions my judgment, but this is no ordinary indiscretion. The stakes are catastrophic, but I don't regret my decision. Knowing Jason is a few rooms away in the care of a gifted physician instead of dying like a discarded criminal chained to a post makes any consequence worth the confrontation.

"We've invested weeks, months, into *Septem Fideles*," I say in an even tone. "I could not let an idiot like Opius Plinius throw it all away on a misguided whim."

The Emperor slows his pacing and scrubs a hand over his face. Brows knit, he studies the stack of scrolls on his desk.

"You've picked a difficult fight, Severus," he says, deep in thought. "Plinius may be an idiot, but he has friends who are not. You put everything at risk over a slave."

"Not just a slave, my lord. You saw what he did in the arena."

He swings a dubious look at me. "Indeed, the battle was impressive, but his victory may be less so if it has left him near death and in need of sanctuary."

I shake my head and approach my old friend with rare fervor.

"That's what I'm trying to tell you, Caesar. Jason's injuries were not from the fight. You saw him walk off the sand, just as I did. It was Plinius's own hand that nearly killed him this morning in retribution. When I arrived, the boy was strung up like a condemned man and barely alive from a brutal punishment."

The Emperor stiffens, his gaze narrowing on mine. "Punishment for what? Should we be concerned your boy can't be controlled?"

Embers of resentment burn hot at the memory of the gladiator's torn body.

"I doubt that, my lord," I growl. "Based on Plinius's own testimony, I'd venture to say the gladiator's mercy for his rival that so impressed you did not impress his master."

The Emperor raises his eyebrows. "You're saying Plinius beat his own man for allowing another to survive the fight? That slave paid him a huge service by earning the crowd's favor with a noble battle, thus preserving a valuable gladiator."

I nod and adjust the ornamental chest plate fastened over my tunic. "Exactly. But the man is too stupid to recognize justice and common sense. It's not surprising when he himself appears to be a sadistic fool."

The Emperor sighs and shakes his head in slow arcs. His expression softens as he leans against the edge of the desk. "It was bad, then?"

A sharp twinge cuts through my chest. "Horrific. It's amazing the boy is still alive."

"*Caenum*..." the Emperor mutters, rubbing at his eye. "Then I will speak with him and see if we can salvage something from this mess."

My fingers clench around the hilt of my gladius. "I'm afraid that won't be possible, my lord. He wasn't conscious when we returned from the ludus."

The Emperor winces, anger burning in his eyes. "No doubt a blessing from the gods to show him the same mercy in return. Take me to him."

"Of course, Imperator."

Slaves waiting outside the study straighten to attention when we emerge, but the Emperor waves them off. Their curious gazes follow us down the long colonnade lining the peristyle connecting the private imperial chambers.

Sunlight from the open roof above the family's personal courtyard filters through the marble columns lining the corridor as the Emperor and I make our way toward the physician's clinic. With each step, I sense the growing tension among the staff. It's not often the head of an empire shows obvious concern for a slave, but there's a reason I serve this man with limitless devotion.

By the time we reach Telemon's lab, my heart is pounding as old anger mixes with new fears. I don't know what to expect, except that we've started a war that cannot be undone.

Telemon and his assistant glance up in surprise when the Emperor's determined expression propels him through the open threshold into the medical study. The respected Greek physician looks about to speak, but quiets and moves aside at our approach. I follow the Emperor past the writing desk, racks of scrolls, and well-stocked apothecary, straight for the marble worktable.

The compassion on the Emperor's face when he sees the injured gladiator lying face down is exactly why I would give my life for this man.

Telemon has already begun cleaning Jason's wounds, which only makes them look more severe in their definition. His back is shredded with stripes and lacerations from various weapons. His deep battle wounds nearly invisible among purple and black patches littered over his body. He's barely recognizable as a man, let alone the stunning gladiator adored by the masses less than a week ago.

"*Thunder of Jupiter*," the Emperor whispers, scanning the carnage. "Plinius did this?"

Teeth clenched, I return a tight nod. "He said it was a gladiator's duty to put forth his best effort in a fight. He called Jason's mercy for the secutor 'insolence'."

We exchange a long look, and the Emperor's eyes flare with anger. "He's a monster, then. As you've said. There's no other explanation. You did the right thing, Severus."

"Thank you, Caesar."

The Emperor studies the victim for a long moment. A muscle moves in his clean-shaven cheek before he releases a heavy sigh.

"It will be quite a mess for us, but I agree with you," he says in a low voice. "You had no choice."

He straightens his robes and addresses the physician. "Tell me when the boy wakes. I'll speak with him then."

Telemon lowers his head in a deep bow. "Of course, Imperator."

The Emperor nods with a grave expression, and his gaze flickers back to the injured gladiator on the table. "Be sure to save this man's life. He is important to me…he is important to all of us."

MALLIA

"Jason is here?" Aurelia cries, jumping to her feet. "*Juno's breath,* what do I do? Counsel me, Mallia, for I am about to faint from the stress of it!"

I fight the urge to shrug as I shift on the bench to face her frantic pacing. The truth is, I have no idea what one does when an injured gladiator shows up in one's home. I can honestly say in my short life, it's never happened.

"I don't know, my lady. I suppose if he's here, it must be for a good reason."

"I should go to him, shouldn't I? Check his status?" She starts toward the corridor that was alive with activity moments before and then stops. "No, of course I can't. It would make a scene." She spins back to me. "You must go."

I flinch and stare at her. "Me, my lady? Why not send Fausta?"

"Fausta? No. Oh, Mallia, please!" She rushes toward me and drops to the other end of my bench. "Fausta is dutiful, but not nearly intelligent enough to navigate this delicate situation. You must discover what you can without raising suspicions."

"Suspicions of what?" I ask, now concerned. What exactly is she proposing I do?

"Suspicions of my interest, of course. It would cause such a stir for the Emperor's niece to inquire of an injured slave."

"But not a senator's daughter who's a guest in the palace?"

Aurelia furrows her brow and chews on a nail. "You make a good point. Oh, this day! How will I survive it?"

She sinks back against the edge of the fountain and closes her eyes.

"I can send Danae. I trust her with my life," I say, mostly to end this ridiculous non-crisis.

Aurelia opens her eyes and glances over at my maid. "No, that's not good enough. It needs to be you."

"But my lady—"

Aurelia's soft hands grasp mine with a firm tug. "Please, Mallia. I will trust no one else."

Her blue eyes plead in a way that don't allow for refusal. I know from experience there's no point resisting her schemes once they've solidified in her mind.

I manage a tight smile and signal Danae as I push to my feet. My light blue palla catches on a rose bush, and Danae helps free the draped linen. Who would have guessed that when I chose this outfit, it would be for a spy mission, not lounging in the imperial gardens like every other day?

As Danae and I weave along the tiled pathways toward the column-lined corridor, images of the stunning gladiator creep back into my head. His stern, fearless expression. The way his body flexed and moved with such fluid grace. Maybe part of me is actually curious about this development. I have so many questions, so many inconsistencies to explore, and with each step down the marble walk, I try to ignore the excitement climbing in my chest.

A gladiator at the Emperor's palace is certainly intriguing. At the very least, it will be more interesting than listening to Aurelia speculate about it.

"Telemon's lab is this way, my lady," Danae says, leading us to the rooms lining the far side of the peristyle. My maid has spent as much time at the palace as I have and is more intimately familiar with its hallways and crevices. She must know exactly where to find this mysterious gladiator. If the man is injured, no doubt the physician will want to care for him with direct access to his equipment and herbs.

Danae shoots back a reassuring smile, and some of the tension in my shoulders eases.

I wasn't exaggerating when I said I trust Danae with my life. She's more than my maid. She's my friend, and like a sister. She was four years old when she was assigned to care for me as an infant and has been a protective presence in my life ever since.

Danae turns the corner and waves toward an open doorway I've passed on previous visits but never entered. She peeks inside, and a relieved smile spreads over her lips. She must have guessed correctly.

My heart pounds as we move into the room. Glancing around, I freeze beside a large desk.

The physician stands over a body on a table at the other side of the room, but it's the great retired legate Severus beside him that has me stalled mid-step. The men block much of the view of the patient lying on the marble worktable.

"Yes, what is it?" General Severus asks, turning toward us with a somber expression.

Telemon looks over as well, and I draw in a breath.

"Forgive me, my lord," I force out in a steady tone. "There is talk of a gladiator on our grounds, and I was sent to investigate."

His brow lifts as he scans me and then Danae. "I see," he says in a droll tone. "I can guess who *sent you*. What's the lady's concern?"

"She—I mean, *they*—are concerned for their safety." The lie stings as it rolls off my tongue, but I'm not sure how else to navigate this situation. I wasn't expecting witnesses to Aurelia's nosy request, and certainly not an encounter with one of the most powerful figures in Rome.

General Severus nods gravely, and I relax at the spark of humor in his eyes.

"I'm sure that is her primary concern," he says with a smirk. "You may tell *your friend* that the rumors are true, but she need not worry. The gladiator is severely injured and will be well-guarded. He poses no threat to her safety."

"Thank you, my lord. I'm sure she—*they*—will find much comfort in that assurance."

"Yes, I'm sure," he echoes dryly.

I feel Danae's amusement beside me. She's probably enjoying the general's sarcasm as much as I am.

"Well, then I won't bother you with any more questions," I say, turning toward the door.

"Wait. Stay for a moment."

Surprised, I hesitate for a step and then turn back.

"Would you mind giving us some privacy?" Severus directs at the physician.

"Of course, my lord," Telemon replies with a reverent air. "We've done all we can at this point, anyway."

Severus nods, and I bite my lip as the physician brushes past me with a brief scan.

Now alone, anxiety swirls in my stomach beneath the general's scrutiny.

"You're Mallia Justa, are you not?" he asks.

"I am, my lord."

"Is it Lady Aurelia who sent you?"

I take a deep breath and manage a stiff nod. Severus remains silent, turning something over in his mind, and I use the opportunity to study him as well. While we've never interacted directly, we've crossed paths plenty of times in the palace.

The man is slightly older than my father, probably in his late-forties, and holds a hardened edge that comes from a life of war. Silver strands sprinkle his short dark hair, matching the coloring of a close-cropped beard. His esteemed military status reflects further in the modified legion attire he wears. A black cloak with red lining cascades from his shoulder, contrasting a perfectly polished bronze chest plate. His crimson, knee-length tunic is slightly longer than the typical soldier tunic and lined with subtle gold trim. Although retired officers typically don't bear arms within the confines of the city, Severus' studded military belt fastens a worn but impressive gladius to his right side.

Beyond the striking officer bearing, however, there's depth in his gray gaze, a certain warmth unexpected in a man as weathered as a legendary general typically is. His gentle humor about the situation comes as a charming surprise, and I relax slightly.

"Maybe the Lady Aurelia has done us a favor after all," he says, adjusting to face me. "I've never had the pleasure of speaking with you directly. By all accounts, you're an impressive young woman."

Heat spreads up my neck and into my cheeks. "Thank you, my lord. My father is a respected senator, and my bloodline can be traced back to—"

"I'm not talking about your family. I'm talking about *you.*"

His kind smile removes the harshness of the rebuke. Intrigued, a tiny grin sneaks onto my lips as well. He doesn't seem intent on elaborating, however, and motions for me to join him by the injured gladiator.

All warmth drains from my chest when I see the patient clearly for the first time. My stomach rolls with each scan of the young man's broken body. How in Jupiter's name is this person even alive?

"His master did this to him," Severus says in a bitter tone.

My eyes widen as I survey the living corpse before me. "For what crime, my lord?"

"For the crime of being more noble than he."

Shocked, I glance at Severus, but he's still studying the slave with a pensive expression. "It's a cruel world we live in, my lady. No one understands that better than this young man. He's suffered more than anyone will ever know, more than anyone should."

My heart constricts for both of them as I take in every detail of the scene. It's clear the general cares deeply for this slave, and I wonder why. Nothing about his demeanor indicates lust or hero worship.

"Will he live, my lord?"

Severus sighs. "I don't know. I'll do everything in my power to make it so."

I believe him, and something about the confidence in his tone soothes the ache in my chest.

"We were at his last fight," I say, breaking the tense silence.

"Yes, I remember seeing you and your maid in the box. It was an impressive showing for him."

"It's strange that Opius Plinius would abuse such a valuable slave. He must be worth a fortune after that victory."

The general darts a surprised glance at me.

"Indeed. It's a confusing turn, to say the least. Unfortunately, many men are guided by ego, not by wisdom."

"It looks like the lanista was driven by something more vile than ego," I mumble and then wince at my slip. "Forgive me. It's not my place to make such a judgment."

Severus flashes a mischievous smile. "No, I suppose not. But as an accomplished legatus and confidant of the Emperor, I *do* have the privilege. Opius Plinius is a sadistic *bracca*."

I bite back a snort, but our amusement fades when we return our focus to Jason.

"I can't imagine his pain," I muse quietly.

Severus' jaw tightens, but he doesn't respond.

"What's your name, child?" he directs at my maid.

"Danae, my lord." She seems as flustered as I am by the man's deference.

"Danae." He turns with great ceremony to face her. "I believe I can trust you as much as your mistress. When the two of you are alone, I'd like you to discuss what you've seen and carefully consider everything I've said. But you must do me one favor." His attention crosses to me again. "Don't tell the Emperor's niece about our encounter."

"Aurelia?" I ask in surprise. "Why not?"

His fingers wrap around the top of his bronze chest plate in a casual grip. "If my instincts are correct, you already know the answer to that."

His smug confidence has me shaking my head with a smile of my own.

"Don't misunderstand me," he continues. "I'm not asking you to lie to dear Aurelia, simply be brief with the details. You know her sensitivity. The truth isn't a story for such a person. I can't share any more at this time, but one day you will understand."

I glance at the young gladiator again, and my heart cracks open. My privileged brain can't even begin to comprehend the violence necessary to leave someone in this state, and maybe I'm already starting to understand what Severus is saying. Aurelia cares about Jason's fate to the extent that it interrupts hers. She'd have no sympathy for his suffering—no interest other than gossip—and the thought of turning this brutal injustice into an afternoon diversion makes me sick.

"No one deserves this," I say softly, tracing the torn flesh with my eyes.

"No. Least of all him."

A shudder runs through me as we watch the young warrior fight for each breath.

"I'll do as you say, my lord." My promise comes out hoarse, and I clear my throat. "I will also pray for his recovery."

He breathes a heavy sigh, and I glance over in time to see him blink back a film of moisture. I'd be surprised by his strange reaction if this entire encounter hadn't been a complete mystery.

"Thank you, Mallia. I am in your debt," he says in a solemn tone. "If you see Telemon on your way back to Aurelia, tell him I wish to speak with him."

Chapter III

TACITUS

"Where's Severus? I thought he was supposed to meet us here," Argus grunts, dropping to the bench beside me.

I shrug and finish off my second cup of wine. The server comes over to refill it and delivers a fresh cup for Argus. The alcove at the back of Carbo's tavern was occupied when I arrived, so we're forced to cram into the packed main room. Grating laughter and violent debate echo off the low ceilings and dirty plaster-coated walls.

"He's probably detained at the palace," I say, staring at the empty stool across from us.

"Ha! Eating fattened goose liver and quail eggs, I bet," Argus grumbles, swiping his cup from the table. "Meanwhile, we're stuffing our faces with stale bread and rancid lentil stew."

I shake my head and trace a crack in the clay cup. "Will you ever stop whining? *Caenum*, Argus, you're worse than a child."

"Eat ashes," he retorts as he signals the tavern slave for more drink. "I'm going to attribute your insult to too much wine."

"And I'm going to tell Severus you complain about his diet every time he's absent."

"Vah, it's a legitimate complaint!"

"I'm sure when you're a military hero and friend of the Emperor, he'll be happy to share his quail eggs with you. Until then…" I shove the plate of stale bread toward my friend.

"Until then, I've got you for company," Argus mutters.

"You could do worse." I point a thumb toward the table hosting our drunk rivals against the far wall. A lewd scene of Bacchus and his naked revelers covers the chipping plaster behind them in a fitting tribute.

"Ursus's men?" Argus growls. "What in hades are they doing here?"

"They must also have a taste for stale bread and rancid lentils," I quip.

Argus lands a violent stare in their direction. "Well, they'd better have a taste for steel because they're about to get a dagger down their throats."

I snort a laugh and tear off a chunk of bread. "You wouldn't dare. Not here. With just the two of us? There are at least six of them. Probably more outside being served on the street-side of the bar."

"We've faced greater odds in battle."

"Without risk of the gallows!"

"It would be worth it," Argus mumbles through a long swallow of his wine.

"Well, your execution will have to wait. There's Severus."

We wait in silence as Severus winds through the drunken patrons in our direction. With the hood of a gray wool cloak drawn over a simple beige tunic, his disguise makes him look more like one of Argus' plebeian neighbors than the second most powerful man in Rome.

"Tacitus, Argus. Sorry, I'm late," Severus says as he takes the stool across from us.

"It's no problem, Legatus. We understand how busy you are," Argus coos.

I shoot a quick side-eye at the sudden reversal. "Is everything okay, sir?" I direct back at Severus. "Your message seemed urgent."

The general quiets and scans the tavern. His eyes settle on the far table. "I didn't realize Ursus's people would be here."

"We didn't either. They usually don't come this far north."

"I wonder what he's up to," Severus growls.

I lean in. "I heard he has a man in the Senate."

With a dramatic gasp, Argus flutters a hand to his chest in mock horror. "Are you suggesting one of our glorious senators might be corrupt?"

I cast yet another irritated glance at him. "You know what I mean. A senator on Ursus's payroll is more dangerous than the typical aristocratic pig looking for kickbacks and bribes. Ursus does nothing if it's not for blood."

"Tacitus is right," Severus confirms, and I enjoy Argus's pout more than I should. "But that's not why I'm here. Not yet. There's been a setback to our plans."

"For *Septem Fideles*?" Argus asks.

"Quiet!" Severus hisses. "Not so loud. Especially not with them so close." He fires another glance at the raucous table by the mural. "Yes, with *Septem Fideles*."

My stomach sinks. "We're no longer being commissioned?"

Severus tucks the hood further around his face. "No, it's not that. The problem is the final member of your team is currently at death's door."

Argus and I flinch in surprise and lean across the table.

"That would mean you and the Emperor decided who our comrade will be," Argus whispers. "Let me guess. Marcellus."

"Marcellus? *My* Marcellus?" Severus replies with a chuckle.

"He's a great soldier," I say.

Severus nods and waves off an approaching server. "Yes, but we're not interested in great soldiers. We want the elite. The best of the best. We need value beyond someone who simply excels at following orders. We need warriors who can think, make instant decisions—difficult decisions—at great cost to themselves. Someone who is willing to die for what they believe but skilled enough not to."

"Is that all?" Argus says with a smirk.

"I found you and Tacitus, didn't I?"

"Well, yes, but…"

"And you don't think I had similar attributes in my prime?"

"You still do, Legatus," Argus gushes. "There's no one more qualified to protect the Emperor than you. I've been honored to fight by your side all these years."

Gods, he's insufferable.

Severus tilts his head and lifts a dark brow. "Then you know I hate when you salute my tail, Argus. I'm no longer your legatus."

Argus narrows his eyes and sinks back against the wall. I snicker at the barb and then go still at a sudden thought. I snap a look at Severus.

"The gladiator," I breathe out, barely above a whisper.

Severus meets my gaze, all humor draining from his face.

"That's why you had us attend the games last week," I continue, thinking out loud. "He is the third. He is to be our brother-in-arms."

Argus scoffs and punches my shoulder. "A slave? Really, Tacitus? Come on."

I glare at him. "Don't be a hypocrite. You were as impressed as I was. Besides, since when did we care about things like status and class? When a man sheds his blood beside you, he is your brother. End of story."

"Not all soldiers believe that," Severus points out.

"Not all soldiers are elite," I return, earning a smile from him.

"True enough."

"You're both serious!" Argus cries and then shrinks at Severus's warning look. "Well, sorry. This is a lot to absorb in a whisper," he hisses.

"I'd like you to meet him," Severus says in a firm tone.

"So you expect him to recover?" I ask, my heart rate picking up.

"Pray he does. The imperial physician is tending to him now. I just left a meeting with Telemon and the Emperor."

Pray? Good luck with that. The gods have had no interest in me for a long time.

"I'm sorry to bring it up," I say, "but how do you know we can trust him? If he's a slave, he has more reason to hate the Empire than protect it."

"We haven't confirmed his loyalties yet," Severus concedes. "Still, I have no concerns in that regard. Jason is a fierce warrior, but also intelligent and discerning. He's not vindictive, which is a big reason for his dominance in the arena."

I study Severus, surprised by his confidence. "You've been watching him," I conclude.

He returns a grave nod. "For a long time. He's the one. I'm sure of it."

"Then that's good enough for me," Argus says, draining his cup and slamming it on the table.

"Of course it is," I quip.

"It'll be good enough for you too. You'll see," Severus assures me.

Maybe. I've been betrayed too many times to place much value in words. But Severus is no ordinary man. His opinion *does* carry weight, and deep down, I want to believe him. The gods know I need to believe in something again.

"When do we meet him?" I ask. "I thought you said he was dying."

Severus taps his knuckles on the pine table. "And there, gentlemen, is our challenge."

JASON

Voices. Light.

Searing pain.

I fight to open my eyes, but even that small effort proves to be too much. I give up with a groan.

"He's waking up!"

More activity.

Footsteps.

A cold sensation on my face. Soft and wet like a cloth.

"Jason, can you hear me?" A female voice. Foreign. I don't recognize it.

Ashes, everything hurts. Why didn't Plinius just kill me? Does he hate me so much he let me live to endure this agony?

"Please, Telemon. Can't you give him something for his pain? He can't even speak," the woman says.

"I already did. If the gods choose to wake him now, there's nothing else I can do."

"Water," I croak.

"Water!" the woman echoes, followed by commotion nearby. "Here."

I try to sit up and realize I'm on my stomach. I doubt I could have moved anyway.

"Here, let us help."

New voices. A man, older than me but not ancient, confident and tested.

Hands grip my arms and pull.

The agony is excruciating, and I'd be sick if there was anything in my stomach. Somehow, I'm able to control the pain as hands continue to yank and twist my aching body in directions I'm sure it can no longer go.

"Be careful, Argus! Gods have mercy, you're going to shatter the one bone in his body not already broken."

"*Rot with worms.* I'm a soldier, not a wet nurse!"

"Thank the gods. No infant should be subjected to your care."

"What? You think because you assisted Crastus for one minuscule campaign, you're now a qualified medicus?"

"At least I know not to manhandle a guy who's been through hades and back! It doesn't take training for that, just half a brain."

"*Shrieking harpies*! You both are giving me a headache," a third, distinguished voice mutters. "I can't imagine what your bickering is doing to this poor boy. Jason, son, can you hear me?"

Something about the mix of command and concern in the man's tone encourages me to try harder. I force my eyes open and focus on the new sights in an effort to take my mind off the other senses. After some time and stern concentration, I manage to squint at my blurred surroundings.

Several faces hover around me, none of which I recognize.

One is younger, most likely my age. The second is probably in his late thirties. The last man must be in his forties.

I try to respond to the distinguished man. My mind wants to speak. The words are blasting through my head. They just won't come out.

"He's trying to say something," a woman says.

I can tell the new hands on my arm are hers. Her skin is rough like the others, yet gentle. Hands that know hardship but belong to a person with compassion and tenderness. I've never been touched by hands like that before. For some reason, I need her to know that.

"Thank you," I rasp out.

When the woman comes into focus, I can tell from her simple but elegant braids, the fine linen of her olive tunic, and an additional beige palla draped over her shoulder that she serves a powerful family. Her sweet smile matches her touch.

"Welcome back," she says as she brushes my cheek.

I glance around the room, certain I must be dead. I don't recognize a single object.

"I'm not at the ludus," I mumble.

A stern man decorated in modified military attire comes into view. "No, son. Plinius will not hurt you again. You are at the Emperor's palace."

"The Emperor?" I exclaim, then wince from the effort. "I don't understand. What about Opius Plinius?"

"He's an animal," the distinguished officer spits out. "When I saw what he'd done to you, I brought you here before he could kill you."

"It would have been merciful to let him," I mumble before I can stop it.

The others exchange a look, but no one insults me with an argument.

"You must be hungry," the man in charge continues. "You've been unconscious for two days."

Two days?

I stare at my fingers, now poking through thick bandages around my hands. Clean and free of sand and blood for the first time in a long time. The clean skin makes the bloody circles around my wrists stand out even more.

"He had you beaten and flogged," the man says as he lowers himself to a stool beside my linen pallet. "I will guess it wasn't the first time."

"It wasn't the first time that week," I grunt, still confused by this entire turn of events. "I'm sorry, but why am I here again?"

The man smiles through silver and black stubble. "I suppose now that you're awake we should introduce ourselves. I'm Legatus Severus. These are my men, Argus and Tacitus, both former soldiers. That person at the desk is Telemon, the Emperor's physician. He saved your life."

I nod to them before resting my gaze on the woman.

Severus's gray eyes soften with affection. "And this is Danae, the maid of Mallia Justa, daughter of Senator Lucius Mallius Justus."

Danae returns a gentle smile that feels so out of place in my violent world. None of this feels right. I've spent plenty of time in infirmaries over my life, but never one as clean and well-equipped as this. And certainly not with a crowd of concerned strangers monitoring my recovery.

While I'm grateful for the introductions, and even impressed by the presence of the esteemed Legatus Severus, I still have no idea what I'm doing here. What *any* of them are doing here.

"My lord, I thank you for removing me from Opius Plinius and addressing my wounds, but I still don't understand. Won't he return to claim me?"

The worried look they exchange makes me uneasy.

"It's not likely, son," Severus says with a tight smile. "You belong to the Emperor now."

Shocked, I can only stare in silence. Dozens of questions spill into my head, but I don't dare ask them. Slaves don't have the luxury of answers.

To be fair, the others seem just as surprised at Severus's announcement.

"Well, there's a twist for you," the older soldier says, letting out a breath. His thick scars and close-cropped hair would fit well at the ludus. "I suppose nothing should surprise me anymore."

"Of course he'd purchase the rights to him. It makes perfect sense," the other soldier replies. "How else could this be possible?"

Severus releases an exasperated sigh. "The harpies bicker less than these two," he mutters. I try to smile, but my lips won't move. "Well, I think we've burdened you enough for one visit. We'll let you rest."

The powerful man rises and signals to his companions. "I'll be back to check on his progress tomorrow," he tells the physician on his way to the exit.

I watch all four leave without a word, still not sure if I should be concerned or relieved.

MALLIA

"How was he today?" I ask Danae as soon as we're alone in my quarters, back at my villa. "I know what you told Aurelia at the palace, but I want the truth."

It's been excruciating waiting so long for a real update, but we've been taking Severus's warning seriously. Based on Aurelia's excited reaction to what little Danae *did* reveal, I understand the general's position. Aurelia seemed to have no interest in the gladiator's well-being, just the gossip related to it.

Danae sighs and begins helping me remove the pins from my hair. "It's true he's awake, but he's far from recovered. He's in terrible pain. All we can do now is wait and pray."

I frown at the memory of what I'd seen the other day. "The whole thing makes me sick. I hate injustice, Danae. It's infuriating."

"I know, my lady. And I love you for it."

I return her smile with a weak twist of the lips. "I know it was the lanista's right. I know it happens all the time. I just..." I stop, not sure how to finish that sentence. I haven't even finished the thought in my head. What exactly is it that's bothering me?

Sure, memories of my encounter with General Severus and Jason the day of his arrival have left my compassionate heart pounding in anger. But what I'm feeling now is more than that. I can't erase that initial image of the beautiful gladiator from my head—standing in the sun, squinting at his opponents, seemingly powerless, but without a trace of arrogance or fear. I've never seen anything like it. Not from a gladiator. Not from any man. He was a statue.

A breathtaking, living work of art.

The truth is, I was silently cheering for him by the end of the fight—not because of the many reasons those around me shook with lust for bodies and blood, but because I had too many questions. I wanted to understand this person, this enigma who had captured the heart of the masses, yet seemed to have no interest in it.

What kind of person shuns celebrity and adoration? What would it be like to be near him, to hear his voice? What secrets rage behind that hard, focused stare?

It's ridiculous, of course, these haunting thoughts from a single look. A fantasy more than anything else. Still, whatever the answers, they don't stop the questions—and I've been sending Danae to "assist" the physician during each visit to Aurelia's home.

When Danae had returned to announce that Jason was awake, it was all I could do to hold my tongue until we arrived home and I could get the full story.

"Was General Severus with him again?" I ask.

Danae nods. "Yes, and he brought two of his men with him. I believe their names were Argus and Tacitus. One was seasoned. The other was considerably younger but of some status. From his bearing and intonation, I would guess he was of the equestrian class."

"And they gave no indication of their interest in Jason?"

I bite my lip, suddenly shy about my questions. Maybe it's the strange, forbidden heat flooding through me as I think about the gladiator at the center of it all.

Danae shakes her head. "None. The legatus obviously cares about him, yet Jason didn't seem to know them. It's all very strange. Apparently, he belongs to the Emperor now."

"The Emperor?" I straighten in the low-backed chair and angle my head toward Danae. "What would the Emperor want with a gladiator? Did you have any interaction with the man when he woke?"

Danae's hand stills on the comb in my hair. Tilting her head, she chews on her lip in thought. "Yes. He thanked me."

"He *thanked* you?"

"He could barely speak, but his first words after asking for water were to thank me."

Another surge of warmth spreads through me. My fingers close around the handle of the polished bronze mirror.

"You think highly of him," I say, studying her closely. Every motion, every flicker of movement in her expression matters. She's an excellent judge of character.

Danae blushes and resumes freeing my hair from the coils and braids. "I don't know him, my lady."

"Still, you witnessed what I did in the arena. It's not in my head. There's something about him. General Severus sees it, too."

"It appears so. He is significant somehow."

"I want to see him again."

Danae flinches in surprise, her gaze darting to mine. "My lady?"

"I'm serious. There's a reason General Severus has involved us in this situation. Tell Severus I'm ready for the truth, and I want to speak with this gladiator now that he's awake. General Severus will take care of the arrangements."

Danae's eyes scour my face in alarm. "My lady, I—"

"Relax," I rush out through a chuckle. "I have no interest in visiting a gladiator for the same reasons Aurelia pines for their loins. If General Severus thinks I should be connected to this turn of events, I want to know why."

After a short stand-off, I lift a brow and she sighs. She knows she'll lose once I commit to an idea. And *this* idea is lodged in my head.

The gladiator's first words were to thank her. How can a warrior so lethal and mistreated be governed by humility and gratitude?

It doesn't make sense. Then again, nothing has made sense since the moment the young champion stepped onto the sand and turned a blistering afternoon of violence into a breathtaking display of sacrifice, skill, and grace.

"I'll speak to General Severus tomorrow, my lady. Just please be careful. Good intentions can be just as dangerous as bad ones."

Chapter IV

TACITUS

The shadow of an olive tree provides some cover as I survey the imposing ten-foot gate of the immaculate urban villa. An outer wall flanks both sides of the thick oak panels, obscuring the meticulously curated garden behind it. Passing strangers admire the polished bronze bands and lion-head knocker, but the familiar sight only has my stomach in knots.

My childhood home stands exactly as I remember, except for the fact that I'm no longer welcome inside.

I tug the hood of my light wool cloak tighter around my face and shift forward for a better view. Visiting my family's villa in the Amethyst Hill neighborhood of Rome was a mistake for many reasons, but once my legs started moving, they didn't stop.

Today is Atia's sixteenth birthday. My sister is a woman now, maybe even engaged, and all I can do is imagine the smile on her face as she enters the next stage of her life.

I squint through the slow-moving traffic for a full view of the gate, as if by some miracle my little sister will appear in the vestibulum behind it. But every time the path clears, I'm rewarded with only a pair of snakes etched into the dark green paint. My family doesn't even know I'm back in Rome. Most soldiers who've been issued a missio ignominiosa are banned from returning to the city after their discharge.

"Tacitus?"

I spin around and shrink from an old woman trying to peer past the hood.

"Murria," I say with a gasp.

"Oh, my boy!" My former nursemaid's frail arms wrap around me like mine did to her when I was a child. "How we miss you! Does your father know you're here?"

"No! And he can't. Please don't tell him," I plead, stepping out of her embrace.

Her watery eyes fill with compassion as she raises a gnarled hand to my cheek. "Of course, my dear. You should know that most of your family didn't agree with his decision to disown you."

I set my jaw and look away. "That fact means little when it's his will alone that determines my fate."

Her expression hardens with determination. "No, my boy, *you* control your fate. He made a decision that affected your path, but it's you who will decide how it impacts your journey." A sad smile softens her features. "You're a good boy. You always were. A special boy, and you will do great things. I know your sister believes that."

I flinch from a stab of grief. "How is Atia?"

Murria hesitates, as if selecting her words carefully. "She's well. She misses you…as do your mother and the servants."

I wince and force a nod. My gaze flickers back to the gate and the hidden memories beyond.

"You know I'd come home if I could," I say with a hard stare at nothing.

"I know." Murria takes my clenched fist and smooths it between her calloused fingers. "And *you* know I love you as if you were my own."

Tension eases behind my ribs as I force my gaze back to her. "I know," I echo with a weak smile. She returns it and then releases my hand.

"After the confrontation with your father, we had no idea what became of you." Her gaze moves over my face, down my light blue tunic, to the gladius strapped to my waist, and back up. "I'm just glad to see you're alive and well."

"I'm alive anyway," I mumble in a bitter tone.

My former nurse rubs my arm in comfort like she's done so many times. "Yes, and for now that is enough."

I shift my focus to the procession of a wealthy senator being carried in an ostentatious litter. His private security and parade of attendants swarm the enclosed vehicle carried by slaves. In this cursed city, one can only guess if the man's small army is a justified precaution or a laughable pretension.

I glance back at the bolted gate of my father's house. "Tell Atia happy birthday and that I love her?" I hate how my throat closes around the words, but I've always lost my edge when it comes to my little sister.

"Of course." Murria squeezes my wrist until I look at her again. "You take care of yourself. We keep praying that one day all will be forgiven."

I force a tight smile and gently pull away. She will have to pray until the end of time, then.

Without another word, I turn and disappear down the street.

ARGUS

Again? *Caenum!*

I slam the door to my flat in frustration. Once again, my insula has been invaded. The utensils on the small shelf near the cooking brazier have been rearranged. The stool that usually sits beside the table is now under the partially shuttered window.

With fresh alarm, I stalk toward the worn wooden trunk at the foot of my bed, but the few valuables I have are still nestled safely inside.

After pushing to my feet, I check the window and look down to see a stack of crates ascending from the street. I thought the gods had smiled on me the day this slightly larger corner flat on the first floor became available, but maybe they were smirking instead.

I pull the shutter closed as tightly as the damaged latch will allow and cross to the kitchen area of my one-room flat. Grumbling to myself, I inventory the provisions packed into jars, baskets, and sacks. Like before, several chunks of bread are missing from the fresh loaf I bought this morning. An apple and a handful of walnuts are also missing from their respective containers.

Another curse escapes me for the brazen thief. Same as last time. Nothing stolen except a few small bits of food. I shake my head and return the stool to the table.

MALLIA

"I understand I've piqued your interest," Severus says in a light tone as we carve a leisurely path through the imperial gardens.

He invited me for a walk almost as soon as I arrived at the palace for my daily visit with Aurelia. The invitation suited my friend, since she also seemed to be in the midst of her daily headache.

Danae follows behind with a vigilant stare as the legatus and I meander along the tiled walkways. I know my maid set this up—and that she wishes she hadn't.

"You have," I say. "Usurping my maid to assist with schemes that would do nothing *but* pique my interest has worked, apparently."

Severus rumbles a brief laugh. "I've been accused of many things, but subtlety was never one of them."

I return his easy smile, enjoying the way the sunlight reflects in his gray eyes. While he's handsome in a rugged, unassuming way, there's also a mystique I can't quite define. Beneath the air of authority and intelligent humor, his eyes hold the sense of a burning secret that's always intrigued me.

"Well, your plot has accomplished its goal, my lord. Here I am. So, what is it you want with a senator's daughter?"

Severus glances at my face before motioning toward an inviting pergola to our right. Wrapped in ivy and fragrant jasmine, the marble columns and intricate lattice work provide refreshing relief from the morning sun.

I take a seat on the marble bench, surprised when he remains standing several paces away.

"I don't want anything from you at this time, other than to spark a friendship and open the lines of communication," he says with a distant look.

I scan his refined, rigid profile for more clues into his unexpected response. "But why? I'm nobody. A powerless girl under the command of my father."

A slight smirk lifts his lips as he twists back to me. "A nobody, huh?"

"You know what I mean." I fiddle with the silk of the pale rose shawl draped from my shoulder. "I have connections because of my father, of course, but I don't have money or status of my own."

Arms crossed, he leans against the marble column to watch a peacock strut past us. "I do know what you mean, and I also know you're wrong if that's how you value your worth."

He straightens abruptly to face me. "Tell me something. What are your thoughts on the gladiator?"

My pulse picks up at the odd question. I shift on the bench. "The gladiator? You mean the injured one brought to the palace?"

Severus huffs a short laugh. "Come now. We're alone. There's no need for pageantry. You know which gladiator I mean. Or did your maid act alone when she approached me about this meeting?"

I pray I'm not blushing, but my cheeks feel hot. Hopefully, he'll think it's the sun. I fight the urge to press a hand to my burning skin to find out. "You seemed to appreciate Danae's help when I've sent her. I only wished to understand more about the situation."

A knowing smile plays on his lips as he scans me. "Ah. So, this is a favor to *me.* You have no personal interest in the boy's status? You've never given him a single thought since that first encounter in the infirmary?"

"He was unconscious during my visit," I defend, allowing a hint of noble resentment to surface.

It only seems to amuse him more. "True. But you still have opinions. You must, if you're interested in seeing him again."

"I..."

"Or did I misunderstand that part of your maid's request as well?"

A huge part of me is hoping Danae can't hear any of this from her location further down the path. This meeting is proving to be a mistake, just as she warned.

"Come. You saw the fight," Severus persists. "You heard what his master did to him afterward. That's enough to form an evaluation. What are your thoughts? What is it you saw that day in the arena?"

I clench my jaw and stare at my sandaled foot dragging over the tile walkway.

He's right, of course. I have thoughts. Lots of them. Certainly more than I should. But I never considered expressing them, and can't imagine what they have to do with this moment or the esteemed man standing beside me.

Still, it's a simple enough question, and maybe it would be good to let the storm in my head find some release before it crushes me.

"If you must know, I saw a man stand fearless against impossible odds," I say in a conversational tone. "I saw him act without hesitation when necessary, but show restraint for the same reason. I saw him suffer to gain an advantage." I stop and meet his patient gaze. "I saw him show mercy when he had every reason for vengeance."

Severus returns a grave nod. "As did I, my lady. As did I."

With a deep sigh, he pushes away from the column and joins me on the shaded bench.

"And what of the punishment he received after the fight?" he asks in a pensive tone.

Confused, I shift to face him. "What do you mean? I never saw any such thing."

"No, but you saw the effects in Telemon's lab. You saw the state he was in and can guess what happened after his victory."

I lower my gaze, a dull ache forming in my chest. "You're referring to the abuse that almost killed him," I say quietly. When he nods, I draw in humid air.

"Well, if what you've said is true, then it seems a great man was tortured for no reason."

Severus shakes his head with a stern look. "Actually, no. There, you are wrong. Jason was at death's door for a very specific reason. He was punished for vanity. Ignorance. Fear."

I stiffen and narrow my gaze at him. "How? I saw none of that in him that day in the arena."

Severus's eyes soften with a sad smile. "Not in him. In us. The elite."

The ache sinks into my stomach. Sweet floral aromas suddenly burn my nostrils and twist through my lungs.

Severus adjusts his black cloak behind him and settles onto the bench. "Our society is very generous to the wealthy," he continues, staring at the mosaic floor with a wistful expression. "It gives us an existence even the gods would envy. We fear those who threaten the order or remind us that we may not deserve our status. We were placed on a pedestal by nothing other than our bloodlines, and persecute those below for the same reason. It's an illusion built precariously on chance, and we punish those who don't conform or fit our ideals. We especially hate those who threaten to expose the brittle premise that protects our status."

Pluto's chains, did he really say that out loud?

Heart pounding, I scan the area for witnesses. His words border on treason, especially for someone so close to our supreme Princeps.

My breeding screams at me to protest and close my ears with disdain, but maybe that's his point. If I'm truly honest, those questions have haunted me for as long as I can remember. Just because it's treason doesn't mean it's false.

"You're saying Jason is a better man than his masters, which makes them feel threatened," I reason quietly.

Severus flashes a quick smile in my direction. "You're getting it now."

I let out my breath, feeling sick. "That part, yes, but I don't understand what any of this has to do with me. Why confess these things to me? We've barely spoken before this moment. Again, I'm no one. Just a girl."

The amused secret he carries returns to his gray eyes as he studies me. "You're still insisting on that, are you? Let me ask you something else. Your friend Aurelia was with you that day at the games, seated right beside you with the same vantage point. What do you think she saw?"

I watch the breeze ruffle a patch of hyacinths to the left of the path leading to the pergola. Buzzing insects and chattering birds fill the long silence with their relaxed song.

It's a good question. Layered. Maybe I'm starting to understand after all.

"She saw sex," I say in a distant tone. "Blood. Entertainment."

Severus remains quiet, letting my words sink in.

After a long pause, he straightens in his seat and waves around us.

"You see it, Mallia. You see like I do. Like the Emperor. Like my men, Tacitus and Argus. Like your lovely maid, Danae. You may be young, but you see what most don't, and that, my new friend, is what I want from you. I want your vision, your compassion, your intuition, and perspective."

"And this Jason?"

Severus frowns, his gaze hardening on something in the distance. "Jason sees clearer than any of us."

SEVERUS

"Severus, my friend. I've been anxious for your arrival. What news?" the Emperor asks as he waves me into his private study.

I set my jaw and close the door behind me. "The rumors appear to be true, Imperator. Vibius Acilius Ursus is marrying his son to the daughter of Senator Marcus Aratus Varro."

The Emperor goes still behind his desk. His hand tightens around the scroll he's holding.

I considered softening the blow when I received the confirmation, but I knew he'd prefer the direct approach. The Princeps and I don't play games with each other, which is partly why we're both still alive.

"I was hoping for a better report," he says in a grave tone.

I nod, scratching at the stubble on my chin. "I was hoping to give you one. Varro has a significant following in the Senate. Almost as large as Senator Justus."

The Emperor drops the scroll and leans back in his chair. "Justus is a strong ally for us. His daughter Mallia is a good friend of my Aurelia, is she not?"

"Yes. And hopefully a good friend of yours soon."

He straightens, brows furrowed. "You've spoken to her."

A slight smile pokes through my gloom at the memory of our garden interview this morning.

"Mallia may be young and small in stature, but she'll be as strong of an ally as her father. More importantly, she may be *Septem Fideles*' best hope to protect you and save your Empire."

Chapter V

Jason

I strain to my elbows at the appearance of a beautiful young woman in the doorway. Telemon has left on another call, leaving me alone for a rare moment. I can't help but wonder at the convenient timing of this particular visit.

With her fine jewelry, the elaborate styling of her silky brunette hair, and the expensive fabric of her pale gold tunic, the visitor perfectly models the rich elegance of Rome's elite. She's exactly who I would expect to find in any room of the imperial palace.

Except this one.

"Don't try to get up," she says in the crisp accent of the senatorial class.

Tension ripples through my sore muscles when she crosses toward me and settles onto the stool beside my cot. She shouldn't even be here, let alone lowering herself to my level.

"I'm Jason. A slave, my lady," I explain, thinking she might be confused about my identity.

A hint of wry humor breaks into her smile. "I know. We all know, believe me. General Severus sent me to check on you. My name is Mallia."

This is Mallia?

I balance higher on my arms, straining to support my weight. I don't know what I was expecting regarding the senator's daughter Danae and Severus have been discussing, but this woman isn't it. Maybe I thought she'd be…older?

I study the rack of surgical instruments on the wall, unnerved by the way her light brown eyes trace my broken body. It's been over a week since I arrived at the Emperor's palace. I can't imagine how awful I must have looked that first day, if this is what I am now. I've never been much for embarrassment, but a prick of nerves writhes under my skin at her intense stare.

"They should have warned you," I say, flickering a glance in her direction.

Her intense concentration slides over my wounds. "Warned me?"

"About my appearance."

Pretty, charcoal-lined eyes find mine, and I swallow an uneasy surge at the sudden connection. Her frown is a fascinating blend of compassion, anger, and curiosity.

"They did, but I'm not sure how you prepare someone for this." There's a trace of disgust in her voice, but it doesn't seem directed at me.

My fingertips dig into the blanket at my side. "My master made his fortune training men to tear each other apart. If any place is equipped to destroy a man's body and soul, it's a ludus, my lady."

Did she wince? I still don't understand why she's here.

"You can call me Mallia," she says quietly.

I bite back a laugh. "No, I can't. But thank you."

She twists a weak return smile, and the slight flush on her cheeks stirs something long dead inside me.

I force my gaze to the shelves of supplies again. I've never felt anything like the odd quiver in my stomach. The gods know I never feel *anything* except anger, fear, and pain. It's been that way for as long as I can remember.

Maybe it's the herbs Telemon has been feeding me.

"I suppose you're right," she mumbles, still scanning me with confusing familiarity like the others do. As if we're old friends, even though I don't recall ever meeting any of them.

I don't understand this sudden interest in me. I'm not even valuable as a gladiator anymore. What if I never fight again? I'm nothing without a sword. No future, no purpose. If that happens, then Opius Plinius' sentence was far worse than death. Better I had died valiantly in the arena where I belong.

"Well, even if you refuse to use it, my name is Mallia," she continues in a conversational tone. "My father is Senator Lucius Mallius Justus."

"I've heard of him. He must be a regular guest of the Emperor, considering how often I see your maid. And now you," I add with a smile.

She tugs at the light pink palla draped over her gold tunic. "Actually, no. It's the other way around. I'm a close companion of the Emperor's niece, Aurelia."

Dread sinks through me. Dark memories creep in, and I shake off the inappropriate reaction. It shouldn't matter if she's close to someone I can't respect. I have no right to any feelings on the subject.

"She's mentioned you've met in the past," Mallia continues, scanning my face. "She speaks of your encounters often."

I sense she's testing me, but I don't know why or what she's searching for. Did Aurelia send her? She must know I'm in no condition to be of use to her.

Jaw clenched, I ignore the churning in my stomach.

"Yes, I'm acquainted with the Emperor's niece," I reply as evenly as possible.

Mallia's probing gaze runs over me, but she won't gain any insight. You can't survive the life I have without the ability to become stone.

"She's quite taken with your eyes, apparently," she quips in a sardonic tone.

My gaze snaps to hers, and her late grin draws a rare one from me.

Maybe she's not much of an admirer of the Emperor's niece after all.

"My eyes," I say dryly. "Yes, they all visit for my eyes."

She blinks away with a shy smile, and I don't like how my pulse picks up. Sure, she's beautiful, but it's the glimpses of a complex mind behind the breathtaking exterior that's turning this encounter into a dangerous game—the qualities that made me doubt she'd enjoy the company of a shallow, spoiled woman like Aurelia.

"Anyway, such affairs are none of my business," she says, waving her hand.

But the way her curious gaze creeps back to me says otherwise. I can only imagine what ugliness she sees in the filtered sunlight. I'm not sure which is worse, being openly objectified with lust or pity.

"Well, sadly, I'm out of commission at the moment," I say, testing her as well.

Her shock transitions to more embarrassment, providing another intriguing contradiction. In my experience, patricians feel no shame, especially in the presence of slaves. We're not people, and they can do no wrong. It's up to everyone else to submit to their idea of decency.

"I only came to introduce myself. I'll leave any undressing for the physician," she returns sharply.

Is she upset?

"A noblewoman with morals. How rare," I say, trying to ease the strain.

Her dark brow arches in challenge. "Not so rare. I'm sure you've just been asked to serve a disproportionate share of the opposite."

"You're referring to your friend Aurelia?"

She straightens on the stool, eyes wide. "No, of course not. I would never insult her. I meant…"

Her shoulders relax at my smile.

"I'm only joking, my lady. I'm sorry for making you uncomfortable. The truth is, I know all about you. I'm a captive audience on this cot. Thanks to you, I have a wonderful nurse whose only flaw is to talk incessantly about her goddess of a mistress. Even General Severus has mentioned you. He has a lot of respect for you and your father."

Her expression clouds over, and my stomach sinks. Fear creeps into my bloodstream. I must have taken my familiarity too far, something I rarely do. It just…felt different with her. *Real.*

I blink hard, all humor fading. "I'm sorry, my lady. I didn't mean to offend you. I overstepped. I—"

She shakes her head like she's in pain. "Stop apologizing."

I can't breathe as her entire demeanor hardens. Eyes clenched shut, she appears to be fighting a violent internal battle.

My head rages with one as well. The room spins with silent accusations of how badly I messed up this encounter. All I wanted was to put her at ease. She looked so uncomfortable and…*frax*.

She has the power to make what Plinius did seem gentle.

"I'm truly sorry, my lady," I rush out.

Despite the searing pain, I fight to push up from the cot. I don't even know what I'm hoping to accomplish. It's not like I can kneel at her feet or do anything other than—

She gently shoves me back down.

"I said stop." Her tone is softer now. There's a tremor in her voice that hints at stifled tears.

"My lady?" I ask, confused. Scared.

Her lip quivers as she takes my bandaged hand and turns it palm up. "Please don't apologize to me. You've done nothing wrong. If anything, we should be…" She quiets and traces warm fingers along the deep bruises on my wrist, staring intently at the damaged skin.

I flinch from the sting, but don't pull away. I wouldn't dare, as I'm suddenly as fascinated by her as she seems to be by me.

"I've wanted to touch you since the moment I saw you," she whispers, and my blood goes cold.

There it is. The truth. She's just another admirer here to take what she thinks she's owed.

My shield snaps back into place as I brace for what comes next. I know this script well. It was the rest of our interaction that threw me.

"What's it like?" she murmurs in a wistful tone.

Old anger burns hot as I follow her gaze to the mottled wounds on my arm. I'm used to these intrusive interrogations before they take what they want, so I don't understand why her morbid curiosity hurts more than usual.

"I don't understand your question," I recite in a flat tone. "What *what's* like?"

"Being you," she says softly. "A gladiator."

Jaw clenched, I swallow a bitter laugh. "Which part? Being chained? Beaten? Whipped? Starved? Burned? Raped?"

I regret my harsh response when her throat catches and her eyes fill with tears. I force in a calming breath. She didn't deserve that. Whatever she wants from me is her right after all.

"I'm sorry," I say sincerely. "I shouldn't have responded like that. It's not my place, and you are probably good to your slaves. Danae thinks very highly of you."

Her anger is all over her face. It should be. I was out of line.

"My lady, please. I'm sorry. Truly. However you wish to—"

"For the tenth time, I said stop! Do *not* apologize," she snaps. "I'm the one who's sorry."

Surprised, I go numb as her light brown eyes search mine. There's a deep pain in her gaze, fierce compassion that tugs at me, and I shudder through a warm surge of feelings I don't recognize.

Now, I'm even more confused about what she wants from me.

"You've endured all those things?" she asks, blinking back more emotion.

I don't know what to say, and so I study the floor. "A slave's life, my lady."

"Not all of them."

I shake my head, uncomfortable with everything about this conversation. None of it's making sense. She shouldn't even be here, let alone discussing such intimate topics with me.

She definitely shouldn't be touching me with anything besides anger or lust, but the way her thumb gently strokes my wrist doesn't feel carnal. It feels…kind.

"I didn't get to finish my statement earlier about wanting to touch you," she says in a firm tone, shifting closer.

A shiver runs through me as she brushes her fingertips over my arm. I don't remember ever being touched like this. So soft and innocent.

"I've wanted to touch you since the moment I saw you, because you looked like stone on the sand that day. I wanted to feel that you were alive. Real."

Stunned, I scan her sad, thoughtful expression.

"Jason, I know what you're used to. What others have…"

Voices echo behind the door.

Mallia drops my hand, and—*am I actually disappointed?* My skin tingles from her touch.

Telemon pushes into the room and stops abruptly. "Oh, hello, my lady. What a surprise."

"Good afternoon," Mallia replies with a weak smile, pushing to her feet.

"Sorry for not being here when you arrived. General Severus said he wasn't feeling well, but I could find no signs of illness. How can I help you, my lady?"

Mallia's smile seems forced as she straightens her gown, as if she might be disappointed our meeting was cut short as well.

"Actually, I was just about to leave. I was only checking on the patient."

"Ah. Well, he certainly gets a lot of visitors," Telemon replies with a chuckle as he takes a seat at his desk.

Mallia maintains her smile until he's engrossed in a scroll and then turns one last saturated look on me.

My gaze fixes on her, my entire essence, really, and I can't tear it away. When she reaches the door, she casts a final discreet glance over her shoulder before disappearing into the corridor.

I glance down at my wrist, still buzzing from her touch.

MALLIA

"What is your game, Legatus?" I stalk through Severus's study toward his desk. "You *wanted* me to befriend Jason, didn't you? You set all this up, even faking an illness, so we'd be alone. Why?"

His crafty smile as he looks up from the wax tablet only agitates me further. I cross my arms with impatience while he dismisses his attendants.

"Are you not interested in his friendship?" he asks once we're alone. "Wasn't it you who came to *me* about visiting him?"

"Well, yes, but I'm also interested to know why you're so interested!"

"Ah. You are a conspiracy theorist, then."

He rubs his chin with dramatic flair, and I narrow my eyes at him. "Only when there clearly is one. First, you manipulate me to admire him, feel sympathy for him, and now befriend him. Out with it, General! Enough games. What's going on? Who is he that we should all be connected to a slave?"

His smile spreads into a grin, and my scowl deepens. I can't imagine why any of this is funny.

"Have a seat," he says, motioning toward a chair near his desk.

With a huff, I drop to the edge of the red cushion. My sandaled heel taps a frantic cadence on the tiled floor.

"Mallia, what do you know about how our Emperor came into power?"

I shake my head with a glare. "I'm not here to talk politics."

"Everything is politics, my lady. Everything."

I return a challenging look and make it clear I'm not accepting any more cryptic responses.

With a deep sigh, he pushes up from his desk and drags a chair close to mine. Lowering to the seat, he clears the humor from his face. "Look, I don't like politics either. I've served Rome my entire life. I've won wars, counseled multiple emperors, and remain virtually immune to execution by staying as invisible as possible. I survive by *avoiding* politics. Yet that doesn't mean I deny the power of the political game and the role it plays in every aspect of our lives.

"Whether you like it or not, your very existence depends entirely on politics. Mine, too, even though I've done everything in my power to leverage that reality into the appearance of the opposite."

I must look as impatient as I feel, because the general clasps his hands and leans forward as if finally getting to his point.

"The current Princeps is a good man and a rightful monarch, but ruling Rome is a near-certain death sentence in these violent times. It is the most dangerous position in the Empire. More so than a legionary who has the advantage of numbers and anonymity to protect him. More so than the gladiators who are prepared for an attack and know when it's coming."

He pauses and knits his brows in somber reflection. "As you know, the previous two emperors were murdered after terms of less than three years. One by members of his own Praetorian Guard! May Mars strike me down if I let that happen to this one. It's time to stop ignoring the chaos and fight for peace, for stability."

Severus sits back slowly, allowing his words to permeate the space between us.

"You're forming a coalition to protect the Emperor," I conclude, my heart racing.

He nods and taps his fingertips on his knee. "In a sense. By protecting the Emperor, we protect Rome. I've recruited the elite. The best of the best. The most capable, skilled, and talented warriors in our Empire. Three men I will trust with his life and who will be fully committed to protecting him and the very foundation of Rome at all costs. They will not be a public presence. In fact, the fewer who know about their existence, the better. They will be warrior ghosts."

I squint at him. "You're expanding the Praetorian Guard?"

He shakes his head. "No. Something entirely different."

A shudder runs through me at the finality in his tone.

"Why are you telling me this?" I ask, searching his face. "Why expose such a secret? And what does this have to do with Jason? Is he one of these *warriors?*"

"Jason is a born warrior. In more ways than you know."

I tilt my head with a shrug. "So what? I'm not."

"No, not in the traditional sense. Women are often overlooked as allies, despite the strength and ingenuity they possess. It's an unfortunate weakness of past efforts at intelligence."

My heart pounds as he scans the shadows. My fingertips press into my thighs.

"Mallia, you have access to people and information my men and I could only dream of obtaining."

A tremor of excitement moves through me beneath his intense stare. "Because I'm a woman or because I'm the daughter of a senator?"

"Both. As we speak, there is a threat mounting against the Empire. A threat that will evolve directly from the Senate."

My heart lurches in my chest.

"So that's what this is about?" I ask, shifting forward. "You've been getting close to me because you want to use my father and his connections to investigate this alleged threat? You want me to be your spy?"

He shakes his head. "No, I want more than that. I want you to join us, Mallia. I want you to help us protect the Emperor, to save Rome."

"To help the ghost warriors?"

"To *be* a ghost warrior."

Time stops. Sound, light…it all seems to siphon away as his heavy confession echoes around me, but the words don't make sense. I must be misunderstanding something.

"I've never even held a sword," I say in a bewildered tone, but he only smiles.

"We each have a role. Yours will not be fighting."

"But…" I shake my head, still struggling to piece this together. "What if I refuse?"

He shrugs and settles back in his seat. "I am not demanding anything, Mallia Justa. I am begging, as much as a retired legatus knows how to beg. We need you. I trust you and hope you will trust me in time. Will you join us? Will you help protect your king?"

"I…" My mind races with a thought. "Is that why you've been watching Jason so closely? Is he important to this cause?"

Severus searches my gaze for several seconds and returns a slow nod. "He doesn't know, but yes, once he's been tested, he will be our foundation, the core of our unit. Like you, I trust him a lot more than he trusts me. I only hope to earn his trust as well."

"You saved his life."

"He will save mine."

"What you're asking is extremely dangerous."

A wry smile twists his lips. "That fact alone weeds out most. We will not consider cowards."

I raise my brows in a defiant look. "You barely know me. How do you know I'm not a coward?"

He smirks. "You're forced to endure more time with Aurelia than anyone on earth and still you show up at the palace each day. You might just be the bravest person in the Empire."

My grin breaks, and I snort a laugh while he chuckles to himself.

Our humor quickly fades as the gravity of his declaration settles in. For several moments, I sit in silence, working through my turbulent thoughts. It seems so absurd, and yet everything in his demeanor and delivery is sincere.

I've always felt out of place in my privileged world, disillusioned by the rampant injustice and hollow veneer. My life is pageantry and pretense with pockets of cruelty so disgusting I can barely stand to watch it.

Deep down, I've been yearning for an escape, a chance to break free of the gilded chains. I may not be a soldier, but I've been "fighting" in my own way for as long as I can remember.

Could this be my chance to pursue something greater? To be an agent of change instead of a victim of circumstance?

Heart pounding, I draw in a long breath and fix my gaze on Severus. "If I do this, would you teach me to hold a sword?"

His piercing gray eyes sear into mine. "Mallia, if you join us, I will teach you to lead an army."

Chapter VI

TACITUS

"*Caenum*. Another hot one." Argus wipes sweat from his forehead and shifts against the chipped plaster façade of our client's storehouse.

Stationed a few paces away, I squint against the sun and adjust the gladius at my left hip, a habit from my centurion days.

Shoddy buildings rise up on either side of us, each appearing to be a violent sneeze away from collapse. More stained, graffiti-covered buildings form the opposite barrier of the narrow alleyway in Hades Hand, closing us in on all sides. I never thought I'd be grateful for the claustrophobic reality of Rome's poorest neighborhoods, but right now the decaying walls are the only thing blocking the brutal sun from making this thankless job completely unbearable.

High-pitched shrieks erupt from the insulae building to our left, and we jump back to avoid a burst of children rounding the corner and flying past.

"Hey! Watch it!" Argus barks after them.

I'm more forgiving as the small bodies fade from sight. That near collision might be the highlight of the day.

Streets typically crammed with activity are relatively bare as the heat traps many at home or at the baths. Boredom is threatening to drive us mad, especially combined with the foul odor of baking waste rising up from the ground.

"What I wouldn't do for an afternoon at the baths right now," I mutter, fanning the collar of my sweat-soaked tunic.

"What I wouldn't do for an afternoon at the brothel," Argus returns.

I cringe and rest my head against the wall. "Too hot for that."

"The tavern then."

We exchange a half-smile.

"The tavern," we echo in unison.

Laughter once again draws our attention toward the end of the alley, but this time it's deeper and more menacing. I go rigid when the boisterous shadows materialize into a cluster of Ursus's men.

"*Frax…*" Argus grunts, straightening from the wall.

"Here we go," I mumble, tightening my grip on the gladius.

"Well! If it isn't Rome's most celebrated storehouse guards!" one of the men taunts as they approach.

The five bodyguards stare us down with smug disdain, and I can't help but wonder if they've come looking for a fight. There are a lot of alleys in Rome, but only one holds Argus and me captive six days a week.

"Well, if it isn't Ursus's most celebrated peacocks," Argus quips in a languid tone.

The man returns a cruel smile. "Better Ursus's peacock than a warehouse nursemaid. But I suppose there aren't many options for disgraced soldiers kicked out of their legion. Is it true your commissions were replaced by teenage freed slaves?"

"Is it true Ursus chose you for how pretty you look in those uniforms?" Argus returns.

I wince while suppressing a snort at the same time.

"Careful," the man's hand flies to his own weapon.

"Or what?" Argus taunts through a droll smirk. "Do you even know how to draw that sword, or is it just a prop for his fantasies?"

The man whips the gladius from his belt.

Bestia filius…

"There are five of them," I mutter under my breath.

Ursus's man grins. "You should listen to your girlfriend, Argus."

His snide look clears when he collapses from the hilt of my gladius.

"Did I say five?" I direct at Argus. "I meant four."

Argus grins and draws his blade just as the remaining guards advance.

ARGUS

I groan and throw an arm over my head. Morning has come too early after a night of drinking away the pain of our skirmish with Ursus's men.

Tacitus fared better than I did, but he was always the smarter of the two of us. I rush in and get clobbered. He always seems to make his way through to the other side with casual grace. Although we both came away with injuries, we both survived—more than all of Ursus's men could say.

"You're bloody. You need a bath."

I bolt up in bed, staring in the direction of the unexpected voice.

A small shadow hovers in the far corner of the room, its head cocked at an inquisitive angle.

"What happened to you?" it chirps. "Are you a gambler? I think gamblers are bloody a lot."

"What are you doing in my house?" I cry, throwing off the blanket and tossing my legs over the edge of the bed.

"You're angry," the shadow says, though it seems unmoved by that fact.

"You're in my flat!"

It shrugs and scrambles toward the open window.

"Hey! Where are you going? Hey!"

I jump to my feet and catch the intruder before they reach the opening. In the late-morning light, I'm able to see that the squirming ghost is a little girl. Six, maybe seven? Tight curls cascade over her head, and the weight of her slight frame barely registers in my arms, despite the violent thrashing.

"I'm sorry! I'm sorry!" she squeals, flailing in my grasp. "I'll go! Don't hurt me!"

"I'm not gonna—*ow!*" I grunt from a pointy elbow in my side and gently set her down. "I'm not going to hurt you, just..."

I motion a warning for her to stay put. If this is my thief, we're going to settle the mystery right here, right now.

"Have you been breaking into my house? Stealing my food?" I ask with a stern look.

She shrinks slightly, but doesn't look as terrified as I'd expect. I've made hardened soldiers cower with less than the look I'm giving her now. This little one just seems annoyed I've thwarted her plans.

"I like your house," she explains, scanning the room. "You have lots of nice stuff."

I gape at her sincere expression.

"Do I now," I say, choking back a laugh. She'd be the first to ever think so.

"Yup. Like that. That's nice."

I can't help myself and follow her finger to the sword lying on the small chest at the foot of my bed.

"That's a gladius. Don't touch it."

"I won't." She skirts around me and approaches the blade at a tentative angle. "It has lots of carvings," she observes, bending close. Her tiny hands remain tightly clasped behind her as if keeping them from betraying her with a forbidden touch.

"It was given to me by a great legatus when I fought with him in the Fourth," I explain, moving toward the shelf of provisions. I inspect the loaf of bread I bought yesterday. Slightly stale, but not moldy. It's too late to go to the market today for fresh food.

Cursed tavern.

"Which legatus?" she asked squinting at the worn hilt.

"Severus."

"Why'd he give it to you?"

"Because I was a good soldier."

"Did you ever save his life?"

"Once."

"Did he ever save yours?"

"Many times. Look, kid…" I twist back to her. "Once again, what are you doing in my flat?"

She lifts her bony shoulders and scans me with wide, curious brown eyes. "I see you a lot. You looked nice."

"I looked nice?" She'd be the first to think *that* as well.

She returns an emphatic nod. "Yes. You looked nice. Are you still a soldier?"

"Sort of, just not the official kind."

"Do you fight the rebels and bandits?"

I shake my head and tear off a chunk of the stale loaf. The little girl's inquisitive expression fades as her hungry gaze follows the path of the bread to my mouth.

"Ah, *frax,*" I mumble.

She frowns. "You shouldn't say those kinds of words."

"Why not? It's my house."

"Vesta wouldn't like it."

"Vesta doesn't care, believe me."

"What if she does?"

"I don't suppose you'd like some." I lift the bread in her direction. Anything to get her to stop talking. The girl is by my side before I even lower my arm. I hand her a chunk, and she devours it. I pass her the rest of the loaf.

"Where are your parents?"

"I don't know," she garbles through a mouthful of food.

"You don't know? Do they leave you alone a lot?"

She nods. "All the time."

"Did they tell you where they went?"

"Yes, but they're probably not there anymore."

"Why do you say that?"

"It was over a year ago."

I go still as she continues working on the stale bread.

"They abandoned you? Where do you live now?"

She shrugs again. "Wherever I can. The bad man wants me to live with him, but I don't want to. So I told him I live here."

I almost choke on the dusty air. "You told him you live here?"

"Yes. He stopped chasing me after that."

"Who's the bad man?"

"I don't know his name. He has a lot of boys and girls in his big villas."

"Lepidus," I hiss, and her gaze snaps to mine.

"Yes, I think that's it. He scares me. He says things, but they don't seem true. I don't like his smile."

I grunt and mutter another curse. "No, I don't either, kid. Is that why you've been breaking into my house? To make it look like you lived here so the bad man wouldn't get you?"

She pauses and lowers the bread from her mouth. "Are you mad?"

"Have you been stealing my food?"

Tears glisten in her giant brown eyes when they lift to mine. The orbs are so impossibly huge in her scrawny face.

"You *are* mad," she says quietly. "I'm sorry. I was so hungry and…are you going to tell the bad man I lied? Will I have to go live with him?"

My stomach curdles from more than old alcohol at the thought.

Lepidus. I'd put a gladius through "the bad man's" skull if I thought I could get away with it.

"No, I won't tell him." Even as I say the next words, I can't believe they're coming out of my mouth. "And if he's looking for you, you should probably just stay here from now on."

Her big eyes test the limits of their sockets. "Stay with you for real?"

Clearing a strange burst of emotion from my throat, I turn to the shelf with a shrug. "I'm not around much, anyway. This place is usually empty. Just don't touch my stuff when I'm gone."

The scamper of feet flies toward me, and I twist back just as tiny arms cinch around my waist.

"I told you, you looked nice."

TACITUS

The lazy smile of a middle-aged widow hovers inches from my face when my burning eyes flicker open. Light streams in through the open shutters, illuminating a large, opulent bedroom. Birds scream from the nearby garden of the peristyle as hazy memories of yesterday's fight, followed by too many drinks at the tavern, come crawling back.

"Good morning," I mumble to Sentia in a hoarse voice.

"Welcome to the new day, my love." Propped up on her right arm, she reaches with the left to brush soft fingers over the bruise on my cheek. "Explain to me again why getting ambushed by a bunch of criminals was cause for celebration last night."

I suppress a groan as I sink into the soft linens of her bed. "Because there were five of them and two of us, and they look the same this morning." I add a late grin that draws an exasperated head shake from her.

She chuckles softly before leaning in for a lingering kiss. Her breath tastes of dates and honey from a morning snack, which means it must be later than I thought. Curse Argus for goading me to stay until Carbo refused to serve another drink.

When she pulls away, light brown eyes search mine with disturbing intensity. It's a look I've seen too many times in situations like this. A look that cares too much. A look that serves as a death sentence for the casual arrangement Sentia and I had.

"I hate how reckless you've been lately," she says in a tender voice that confirms my fears.

I bark a bitter laugh at the irony. "Reckless? I've been a soldier since I was seventeen. Up until six months ago, anyway." I shift to my back and scowl at the ceiling. "*Everything* is a reckless affair when you're in the frontier. I was more likely to lose a limb eating a meal than anything I do now."

A frown deepens the lines of her pretty face when I glance over. "Yes, and you're free now. Why risk your life for no reason?"

"Free?" I spit out, angling back to her. "I'm not free. I've never been more trapped. I belong on the battlefield."

She stiffens, brown eyes narrowing at me. "Oh? Well, I'm sorry for chaining you to this miserable life."

When I don't respond, she pushes up and snatches a blanket from the bed to wrap around her body.

I sigh and reach for her arm to pull her back. "That's not what I meant, and you know it. It's just been difficult since my discharge. I lost everything. If not for Severus, we wouldn't even be having this conversation. I'd be off in some distant province working the mines with the slaves."

She scans me for several long seconds before dropping to the edge of the bed again. "I know. But it hurts to hear you say these things. You won't even tell me the truth about what happened." Her eyes move over my face, bare chest, and then down to the blanket pooled at my waist. "I know everything about your body, and nothing about *you*."

Dread trickles through my limbs at the possessive way she's looking at me. There's permanence in her expression. Expectation.

"I'm falling in love with you, Tacitus." Her soft words land like a gut punch. "I don't like the fact that I have to wonder every time we part if I'll see you again. You carry so many secrets. I worry for you."

Her gaze climbs back to mine, pleading for any reassuring lie. I know what she wants to hear, what she's really asking. It's the same question I've gotten so many times in so many ways from civilians who can't understand I no longer belong in their world.

And like all the other times, the truth is the same. As much as I enjoy her company, the only time I really feel alive is when I'm in battle.

Now, without access to real ones, I've been forced to create my own. Ursus's "criminal soldiers" included.

Argus feels it, too. Despite our varied backgrounds and being a decade apart, we're now living the same life. We've become inseparable since our mutual disgrace.

As soldiers, our paths were on opposite trajectories. Argus ran his mouth off and earned the ire of several officers, while I'd done nothing but excel as an ambitious centurion on the rise toward greatness. Many expected me to be legatus one day, despite being of equestrian blood, a step below the revered senatorial class. My father certainly did, but I would've been content with any appointment that kept me in the heart of the action.

All it took was one command, one decision, to crush generations of dreams and expectations.

Severus always says I was lucky I'd only been flogged and not executed for what I did, but there are plenty of days when I'm not so sure. Ursus's men struck a nerve with their taunting. I can't think of anything worse than a born officer falling from one of Rome's top legions to a warehouse guard detail.

It almost *is* a fate worse than death.

"Tacitus?"

I drag myself back to Sentia's imploring stare.

"Do you love me?" she asks.

I flinch, weighing the truth and the fantasy. I've never been much of a dreamer.

"Sentia, you know I value you and enjoy our time together."

She winces and averts her gaze to the floor. "That's what I thought."

With a heavy sigh, I gather my strength for the inevitable separation. It always ends this way. Now that I've become a scarred shell of a man, it always will.

"I'm sorry," I say quietly. "Truly. But I don't make promises for a reason. Besides, you'd have no future with someone like me."

"I know. It's just..." She lets out a breath and shakes her head. "If only I were a gladius," she mutters.

CHAPTER VII

MALLIA

THE YOUNG WOMAN'S LIPS ARE MOVING. SHE'S GIGGLING, POINTING WITH HER EYES, gossiping about something. I blink and try to focus on my companion, but her words keep floating up and getting lost in the frenzied din hovering around us.

This wedding banquet has been going on for hours. The bright colors, the dancing, the lewd jokes, the endless flow of wine and food—it's all becoming muddled chaos in my head. Like so many of these events, I don't know the bride or the groom, but as the daughter of one of Rome's top politicians, my presence is always required for posterity.

Tonight's festivities are no different, except for my unusually high level of distraction and the constant tension in my chest.

"Mallia! Are you listening? Did you hear what I said about Cornelia?"

I force my attention toward accusatory arched brows and a dainty frown.

"The consul's wife?" I ask.

"Yes! I just told you the whole story about what happened at the baths last week."

"Oh. I…I'm sorry. I'm not feeling well." I press the back of my hand to my spinning head.

Her cosmetic-tinged features droop in concern. "Oh? Well, why didn't you say something?"

Because I didn't think of the excuse until now.

I force a weak smile and smooth a crease in my dark red silk gown. "I didn't want to interrupt. Actually, I think I'll go for some air, if you don't mind."

I push up from the couch and wave off a slave who moves to assist me. I miss Danae. Father thought it best we leave our own attendants at home since the host, Senator Varro, went through great lengths to stock his villa with a fresh shipment of expensive slaves.

"Would you like me to come with you?" the other girl—Julia, I think—asks, searching my face.

Gods, no.

I shake my head. "Thank you, but I wouldn't dream of taking you away from your cousin's wedding celebration. I'll find you when I feel better."

Julia sags to the cushion when I take my leave, and I can't tell if she's concerned about my well-being or losing her high-status companion. The way she ambushed me the second we arrived and has talked incessantly about Aurelia and Cornelia made me think she's much more interested in my connections than my friendship.

I slip from the banquet hall without interruption. Even my father is too caught up in an animated discussion with other senators to notice. Although I've never been to Varro's estate, I know the layout of these lavish villas well. My goal is the gardens, my favorite place in any home.

The crowd thins the further I venture from the epicenter of the celebration. Senator Varro's home is magnificent, to say the least, comparable to my own. Fitting, considering he and my father seem evenly matched in every other measure of status as well. Although they're fierce rivals in the Senate, it isn't uncommon for the men to feign civility at these types of events.

Enemies, friends, it makes no difference when displays of wealth are involved.

I pass through several colonnades, following what seem to be telltale signs of a path to the giant peristyle. I can almost smell the evening air, and can't wait to soothe away the turbulence of these last couple of weeks with a cool breeze and gurgling fountain or two.

A heated whisper through a slightly open door to a sitting room stops me in my tracks. It isn't the words that grab me, since I can't make them out. It's the tone, laced with urgency. I creep toward the sliver of an opening and press against the stone wall for a better read.

"You're sure you can get this done?" a man grits out.

"Ursus, you're family now," another man soothes in a slick tone. I almost gasp at the familiar voice of our prestigious host. "As long as you keep up your end of the arrangement, I will hold to mine. I can deliver at least half the Senate. The rest is details."

"And what of Justus and his influence? He will never allow such a thing to happen."

I go numb at the mention of my father and tilt closer to the door.

"He won't know until it's too late."

"Yes, but—"

"I've already turned one of his key allies against him without his knowledge."

My fingers curl into fists at my side.

"And you swear Legatus Nepos will shift his allegiance."

"I swear. It's already been confirmed."

"So that's it, then. It's done?"

"It's done."

I duck behind a column to hide as the pair disperses. As feared, the fathers of the bride and groom slip from the room and stalk in the direction of the party. Their footsteps clap along the tiled floor, clashing with the echo of their cryptic words still flitting through my head.

Dangerous. Confusing.

Ursus and Senator Varro are clearly plotting something. Combined with the ambiguous threat to my father and the reference to Legatus Nepos, I have no idea what to make of it.

My legs tense with the urge to run to my father. I have to tell him what I've heard. It's my duty as his daughter to warn him.

But as I consider the report and play through the events, another part of my soul calls for caution. After all, what do I really know? The sketchy information could put my father in even more danger when he begins investigating this unknown threat. Asking questions, raising suspicions…

Still, I have to do *something* with the volatile information. If only…

General Severus!

This is what he meant and why he was so interested in "sparking a friendship and opening the lines of communication."

Maybe, I'm glad that line has been opened.

MALLIA

Severus stares at me with a grave expression as I recount as many details of the conversation between Varro and Ursus as I can remember.

I tracked the general down in his office at the palace as soon as I arrived the following day. Aurelia doesn't even know I'm here yet.

"And you're sure of the conspirators," he says, scratching at his stubble. "You're sure it was Ursus and Senator Varro."

"Of course. We were there to celebrate the marriage of their children, Arata and Lurio."

Severus nods and massages his temples. "Yes, we were aware of the event. The Emperor was invited but had to decline for health reasons."

I straighten in alarm. "Health reasons? He's not ill, is he?"

"No, and we want to keep it that way."

A chill runs through me. The threat is real.

"What should I do now? Should I tell my father what I heard?"

Severus shakes his head as he shuffles some scrolls on his desk. "No, your instinct was correct. He's already in danger. Making him aware would only spark premature confrontations, which wouldn't benefit anyone."

He softens at my distress. "Because of you, we have an advantage. We suspected Ursus and Senator Varro were working on something, but we didn't know for sure, and we certainly had no links to Legatus Nepos until now. Thank you, Mallia. Thank you for your courage and for trusting me with this. I will not betray your trust, and we'll do everything we can to protect your family."

I try to smile, to be strong, but the threat is now real on many levels. What if I'm not the "warrior" he thinks I am?

My thoughts turn to Jason, standing tall on the arena floor. Alone. Scared. Facing three armed men and a certain death. To Severus and his soldiers, facing the violence of war with every breath.

You can do this.

"Please let me know how to protect my father."

Severus nods. "Of course. It will be difficult, but try to act like nothing's wrong. I will discuss your information with my trusted agents and determine what needs to be done."

SEVERUS

I curse at the battered condition of my "trusted agents" when I meet them at Tacitus's two-bedroom flat in the middle-class Brick District. Although his residence isn't the luxurious urban villa he would have been accustomed to growing up, the clean, sturdy brick apartment building is much nicer than Argus's plebeian insula in Crassus Pass.

"So, it's true then. You idiots clashed with Ursus's clowns," I grunt, waving a finger between them.

Argus and Tacitus exchange a commiserating glance.

"They challenged us," Argus mumbles.

"Challenged or taunted?"

"There's no difference," Argus returns.

"For you, no." I lean forward with a stern look. "You must be more careful. I need you to remain in the shadows. Especially now."

Tacitus's brown eyes flash with immediate understanding, and I swallow a twinge of loss at what this talented young man could have been. If I have my way, he will soon have another chance at greatness—even if only a few will ever know.

"You have news," he concludes.

I nod and cast a quick glance at the shuttered window. "Two days ago, Ursus married his son to Senator Marcus Aratus Varro's daughter."

The soldiers let out a slow breath as the revelation sinks in.

"Then, it's official," Tacitus observes darkly. "It's begun."

Despite the noise drifting up from the busy street, the air around us goes still.

"There's more," I say, breaking the long silence. "You remember Mallia, Senator Justus's daughter? She's provided some critical information."

SEVERUS

"Legatus Nepos? Of Legio Six in Britannia? You're certain?" The Emperor casts me a distracted glance before squinting into the shadowed gardens below his balcony.

A chill runs through me at the glimpse of his anxious expression before he turned. I've served this man as a trusted advisor and confidant for over a year now, and never once have I seen him display fear in another's presence.

Since seizing power after the assassination of the previous Emperor, he's led with integrity and compassion—at least, as much as a person in his position can demonstrate. With each passing day, each new crisis, he's proven to be a rare gem shining from the depths of the muddy cesspool of elite politics.

It's why I've come to serve and protect him so fiercely.

"Where did this intelligence come from? Who gave you this information?" he asks in a measured tone, studying the darkness below.

"The daughter of Senator Justus. I'd hoped she would decide to help us, and she has."

He snaps a look at me. "Mallia. Aurelia's friend."

I return a quick nod. "She's a valuable ally. Strong, intelligent, and compassionate."

"So it seems."

When he turns back to the night air, I scan the contents of the desk beside me. Several lamps illuminate the scattered documents, but one scroll stands out. Its weathered condition reveals its age. The careful binding represents its importance.

I know it well. Just months ago, we stood in this very spot discussing the magnitude of the secrets it contains.

Septem Fideles. The Faithful Seven.

"Did I tell you I found that scroll shortly after the acclamatio a year ago?" he asks solemnly. I look up to find his gaze locked on me. "I spent the first few days of my reign poring through the libraries and records of my predecessors. I found it buried in an alcove behind a stack of military records. Literally. As if it was never meant to be found."

It probably wasn't, so when his vile predecessors let it die in their quest to pervert their sacred duty into selfish ambitions, so did the secret weapon for Good.

The Emperor returns to the balcony and grips the marble balustrade. After weeks of excruciating heat, the gods have finally granted a day of relief. It seems like a very fitting hour for the birth of an era.

My heart pounds as the magnitude of what's happening rips through my head and pulses through my veins.

"We don't have a choice anymore, do we?" he says gravely.

"I don't believe so, Caesar. This threat is legitimate and fully active. It's time," I say, joining him on the balcony. "Are you ready to recommission *Septem Fideles*?"

He casts a look at me, dark eyes searing into mine. "More than that. I want to *transform* it. We will restore this covert unit and convert it into the greatest threat against corruption this Empire has ever seen. Evil has reigned for far too long. It's time to fight back."

A shiver runs over my skin as I force in a steadying breath. The somber atmosphere from a moment ago now crackles with tense anticipation.

"How soon can you make this happen?" he asks, turning back to the gardens.

"I've already put the pieces in place. The players are assembled."

His brows knit in thought. "Including the gladiator?"

"Not yet, but say the word and I will begin the transformation."

With a grave nod, he tightens his grip on the marble rail of the balcony.

"Do it," he commands. "I want *Septem Fideles* recommissioned before Nepos expands his northern campaign."

Chapter VIII

MALLIA

On most days, I can tolerate Aurelia. At the very least, I've learned to numb myself to her petty outbursts. In the company of the Consul's wife, where their snobbery often turns downright cruel, I can barely stomach a single conversation, let alone an entire afternoon.

It didn't take long for the lavish exedra where Aurelia entertains friends to feel more like a prison. Opulent couches line two of the three walls of the vaulted sitting room, anchored by bronze incense burners and small marble tables. Detailed frescoes of her favorite deities decorate the floors and walls, including the curved wall behind us. Immaculate marble columns form the fourth barrier of the room, opening to the luxurious gardens of her private peristyle, where she and I typically spend our days.

Despite the inviting sunshine, fragrant scent of blooming flowers, and pleasing birdsongs cascading through the sheer linen curtains, an ominous current slithers throughout the tranquil retreat. There's something about Cornelia's scheming demeanor today that's making my skin crawl.

Her brunette hair is twisted in ringlets and braids more suitable for a formal banquet than a casual afternoon with friends. The intricate gold trim of her rose-colored silk stola seems just a bit too much for the occasion. The thin gold bands around her upper arms are one too many. As the wife of the consul, she has nothing to prove, so I can't guess why she'd be trying so hard to impress for this visit.

To make matters worse, Cornelia brought her obnoxious social-climbing protégé, the youngest son of Senator Gaius Numerius Ovidus. This is my first encounter with the entitled young man, but when he brutally berated a slave for not pouring his wine at the correct angle, I grew wary of him.

Once the gossip turns to a woman I don't even know, I stop paying attention and get lost in the relaxing cadence of the wafting curtains. If I'd known Cornelia and Numerius were visiting today, I would have come up with an excuse to regretfully decline my own invitation.

"What a lovely afternoon," Aurelia announces with a wistful sigh. "Shall I summon a musician?" She motions toward the lyre on a bronze stand. "Or a poet, perhaps?"

Cornelia and Numerius exchange a conspiratorial glance before Cornelia shifts on her couch toward Aurelia. "Actually…we were hoping…is it true *Jason the Fearless Murmillo* is here? In the palace?"

I just about choke on a sip of wine. Danae goes rigid beside me.

Is that what brought them here today?

Dread trickles through my stomach and spreads into my limbs. Although I haven't dared to visit the gladiator since that initial meeting, I've thought about him a lot. Worrying, wondering, wishing, as if he's a longtime friend, not someone I spoke to once.

Danae still visits him as often as possible, and her updates have become an anticipated part of my day. According to her latest report, he's doing well and seems to be in good spirits. Although not fully healed, he's mobile again and has been moved from the infirmary to the slaves' quarters to complete his recovery with light duty. It's been almost a month since he first showed up on the palace grounds, and I don't like how that time has done nothing to tame my strange fascination with the man.

I *really* don't like the idea of these opportunistic parasites showing any interest in him.

Aurelia selects a date from a tray and examines it with a coy expression. "It's true. My uncle purchased him from the ludus where he'd been training."

With a glib clap, Cornelia leans forward. "The gods have smiled on you, then. Tell us everything!"

I sense Danae's concern behind me and fix a hard stare on a fresco of Diana inlaid on the floor. There's nothing I like about the direction of this conversation. There's also nothing I can do to stop it.

Aurelia shrugs and nibbles on the edge of the date. "Well, there's not much to tell, really."

"How could that be?" Cornelia huffs, narrowing her eyes at her. "You own

Rome's Champion, yours to command at will, and there's nothing to tell? Secrets don't suit you, Aurelia."

Aurelia bites her lip, shooting an anxious glance toward the curtained wall leading to the peristyle. "The truth is, I haven't seen him since his arrival."

"*What?*" Cornelia cries, straightening on her couch.

"You can't be serious," Numerius scoffs.

"He was severely injured when he was brought here," Aurelia defends with a pout. "He was in no state to be of use to me."

Cornelia scrunches her prim nose and settles back into the cushions. "Well, that's a shame."

She traces a finger along the rim of her amber glass cup. My blood runs cold when a mischievous smile breaks on her painted red lips.

"And now?" she asks in a sly tone. "Is he still *useless*?"

Aurelia frowns. "What do you mean?"

"She means, is he too injured to play?" Numerius adds with a grin, placing his glass on a nearby table.

My fists clench in my lap. Tight knots form in my stomach.

Aurelia's expression ignites with excitement, and I think I'm going to be sick. "I don't know, to tell the truth. It's been weeks since my last inquiry."

I take a long swallow of my diluted wine, longing to be anywhere else. The air thins when Aurelia turns her attention to me.

"You've been sending your maid. What news?" she demands.

Trapped, my fingers clench around the cup as I glance at Danae. Her pale face means she's as concerned as I am.

"Well, out with it! How is the gladiator progressing?" Aurelia insists.

We don't have a choice. He's not even my slave to protect.

"Tell her what you know," I direct at Danae in a gentle tone.

My maid stares at the floor, jaw set. I silently will her to betray her friend for her own sake. For all our sakes.

"Jason is much improved, my lady," she recites without emotion. "He's been released from the infirmary and now serves your house."

"Really! Well, that's excellent news." Aurelia claps her hands once like Cornelia did earlier. "Fausta, find him and bring him to us. We wish to see him."

A cold sweat breaks over me when the slave girl moves toward the exit, and I don't know why. I shouldn't have any opinion on this situation, shouldn't be feeling anything other than a reprieve from boredom like the others. Aurelia's intentions for her slave are none of my business. He's her property, hers to do with as she wishes.

But telling myself that does nothing to soothe the nausea clawing through my gut.

Danae's pleading gaze burns into me, but I can't meet it. There's no way out of this. I shouldn't even be looking for one.

By the time Fausta returns with Jason, my nerves have taken on a will of their own, however. My rational head is completely at odds with my heart, and when his hypnotic hazel eyes brush mine, I can't breathe. I wish I could dissolve into the cushions and disappear forever into another time and place where horrible situations like this don't happen.

Should I leave? It's a tempting thought, until I remember General Severus's strange confidence in me. He said he admired my strength. What would he do in this situation? I know he wouldn't run and hide. None of them would.

Jason *can't.*

I force my gaze back to the young gladiator, and an ache forms in my chest. Severus would never leave him alone without a friend or ally, even if that friend was powerless to intervene. I still don't know exactly what a "ghost warrior" is, but I know they wouldn't abandon a brother in a time of crisis.

Nothing in me wants to stay, but I anchor myself to the couch.

In the tense silence, Jason's powerful presence seems to fill the room. Though still weak, his proud bearing makes that fact almost unnoticeable to the untrained eye as he stands quietly on display.

But I'm not fooled. I see how he favors his left side and how his hands behind his back don't curl into full fists. Remnants of bruises still litter his body, giving testimony to his unfinished recovery, and I wonder how many of the marks will be permanent.

Still, his progress is remarkable. I'd be grateful for Telemon's skill and the gods' mercy if it hadn't landed him in this position.

The other nobles squirm in their seats as he towers over them, scanning his body with a mix of awe and lust. I swallow a growl of frustration when I notice his clenched jaw and icy expression.

He knows why he's here too.

"I was so happy to hear of your recovery," Aurelia says, studying him intently. "I have not yet had the chance to welcome you to our home."

"Thank you, my lady," he responds without emotion. The walking void in front of me contains no trace of the shy smile and gentle humor I encountered in Telemon's lab that day.

"I trust you are comfortable and healing well?" she continues in a flat tone.

"Yes, my lady."

"We wish to see the evidence," Cornelia interrupts, impatient with her friend's hesitant approach. "Remove your covering. We wish to inspect your wounds."

Jason's gaze shoots to his mistress, and Aurelia nods.

"Well? Do as she said," Aurelia confirms with a flippant wave.

My nails gouge into my palms when he has no choice but to obey.

With casual movements, he frees the leather cord around his waist. A collective inhale works through the audience when he pulls his tunic over his head to reveal a flawless form, artistically sculpted from head to toe.

Gods, he's breathtaking up close, a broken masterpiece that plunges the room into a disturbing silence. Standing there, tall and chiseled, he could have been another marble statue in the imperial palace or the temple itself. Beautiful. Cold. It's only the many scars and recent injuries that harshly remind us he's human.

And a slave.

He remains motionless as he grips his uniform and awaits his fate with an unreadable expression. I hold my breath when the others rise from their couches and approach him, clearly mesmerized by the object before them.

Because with each passing second, it's sickeningly clear that's all he is to them. An ornament, a toy for their afternoon amusement. They don't care about his weeks of agony in the infirmary or the litany of unspeakable abuses he's probably endured up to this point. They don't care about his character or his honor or his intelligence or any of the reasons he earned the attention of the Emperor himself.

They certainly don't notice his clenched jaw or distant expression that indicates he's separated his mind from his body. They only see themselves. How the erotic trinket they own will please them like the rare gems they'd purchased at the market earlier this morning.

Severus's critique screams through my head as I witness the ugly truth unfold right before me.

"Tell us about this one," Aurelia murmurs, tracing a gash on his ribs. Her fingers glide up his chest, and I wonder if she'll even hear his response. Her thoughts are obviously elsewhere. An alarming smile plays on her lips when Cornelia and Numerius join her.

I can't watch their humiliating exam, so I focus on his face instead. I'm both fascinated and disturbed by the change from the last time we talked in Telemon's study. His enchanting smile, the depth in his eyes that drew me in, has completely disappeared. His expression is now vacant, a stony mask that tugs at something inside me. This entire encounter may disgust me, but it clearly isn't new to him.

Gods have mercy, how often does this happen?

"You still haven't answered our question," Aurelia chides in a playful tone. She raises her other hand to trace his cheek, his jaw, his lips. "Explain your wounds."

Jason remains completely still through it all.

"Opius Plinius chained me to a post and had each of my brothers take a turn with a weapon of their choice. The wound in question was from Ino."

A deep chill runs through me. I scan him again, each bruise, gash, and scar suddenly taking on a life of its own. What would it be like to suffer the creative cruelty of trained killers? To be at the mercy of limitless power and hatred? To constantly live under the shadow of death?

My heart constricts when I can't imagine it, even as I watch it happen right in front of me.

Emotion burns in my throat, threatening to spill over when Jason's eyes land on mine again. The slightest flicker of life returns to his face, and I want to reach out, to do something, anything, to show him the same strength and mercy he demonstrated in the arena that day.

But I can't. I can't fight Aurelia and Cornelia, and this ancient system that has turned an atrocity into a right. He seems to understand. He isn't expecting a savior, just a friend.

An ally.

I bite my lip to keep from lashing out and do everything I can to convey that he has one.

Even if she has to be a ghost for now.

"And this one?" Cornelia asks, spreading her palm along his lower abdomen.

"Hector."

"And these?"

They circle him like vultures, breathing in his pain like a drug. Their hands explore him, their animal under inspection for slaughter.

"Beautiful," Cornelia muses. "He's perfect, despite the marring," she adds in a conversational tone. "And tamed, I presume?"

"I suppose we'll find out," Aurelia laughs. "Fausta, go fetch three of my uncle's men in case he's not."

A furious protest rises in my throat at the insult, but somehow, I manage to contain it. Jason's knuckles are white from his grip on his tunic, eyes blazing. Even worse, I make the mistake of glancing at Danae, who is stiff and pale. She isn't watching, clearly fighting emotion as well. It makes my own battle nearly impossible.

None of my anger makes sense. How many times have I seen this? My entire life is run by slaves, and although my father's household isn't cruel to them by any means, I've seen plenty that are. It's bothered me, of course, but never enraged me until this moment.

This person.

"Mallia is a virgin. Very inexperienced," Aurelia blurts out, drawing me back into the horrible scene. "Come, girl. See what you've been missing."

Anger transforms into fear as blood pounds in my ears.

"Come! Don't be such a child."

My hands shake as I stare at the others in numb silence. There's no way I'll be able to join them, parading around like predators preparing for a kill. Subjecting the man I've come to care about to such open abuse, even if he is practically a stranger…and a slave.

I also can't imagine the consequences if I don't.

What would a ghost warrior do?

My trembling legs barely support my weight as I move forward. I try to avoid his gaze, but it becomes harder as I approach. When I lose the battle, my body goes cold and then hot.

In that split second, our souls connect, and somehow it makes this moment harder and easier at the same time.

"Go ahead. He's yours," Aurelia says, vacating her place so I can have access to his body.

I look up at his face instead, trying once more to read his thoughts. This time, there's something more there. Forgiveness, maybe. Understanding. He gives what almost appears to be a slight nod. It makes the whole thing more nauseating.

I try to return an unspoken apology, but what silent message is strong enough for this offense?

Even worse, I feel the attention of everyone else. It's suffocating—the anticipation, the gloating, the lust…the betrayal radiating from Danae, who's silently screaming at me to stop this. But I don't know what else to do except reach out a shaky hand and follow the script.

I slide my fingers from his wrist to his shoulder and across his chest. Solid, warm, exactly how I've imagined. A body carved by suffering, beautiful and devastating. I wish more than anything that we were alone, free of prying, filthy eyes.

Because in this moment, the truth comes into sharp focus. I don't want his body. I want the stories that created it. To understand the soul that fills it. There's a profound mystery about Jason, a depth that seduces me more than the chiseled form and handsome face. I sensed it from the moment we met, attracted by what I hadn't seen as much as by what I had.

And here I am, inches from the captivating puzzle, yet somehow further than ever. It makes me incredibly sad, yet ignites a terrible longing as well.

Lost in these thoughts, I almost forget our audience for a brief moment. A snort of laughter returns me to the present, however, and I blush at the circle of triumphant grins surrounding us.

Embarrassed, I pull away and take a step back.

"See? What did we tell you?" Aurelia is clearly enjoying her role as mentor. "It gets much better. Believe me."

My disgust must be all over my face when they laugh.

"You've shocked your little friend," Cornelia says with a snicker.

"It's not a difficult task, trust me," Aurelia quips.

Humiliated and helpless, I find Jason's eyes again. Like the other times I searched those hazel irises, I'm overcome by the hidden layers forced away by years of trials and abuse. Severus believes this man is special, different. I'm starting to believe it, too, but that only makes me more uncertain, more resentful of my weakness. Severus would know how to extricate us from this mess. Me? I have no idea what to do.

Guilt nearly crushes me when I leave him alone and return to my couch.

"I pity your future husband," Cornelia taunts. "You do realize what it takes to produce an heir, correct?"

I ignore her as I sink back to my seat, ashamed and furious. At them. At myself.

I'm already aching inside when I feel a hand on my shoulder. I glance up to meet Danae's haunted eyes. Her gaze speaks volumes, a silent plea begging me to intervene. I'd forgotten how close Danae and Jason must have become after weeks together in the infirmary, but I've never felt as helpless as I do now.

I shake my head and pull my gaze away.

As the action escalates, I fight back tears, cowering on my couch, too afraid to interfere, but more afraid of the prospect of facing my conscience when it's over. I hear Danae's silent screams behind me. My own brain echoes them, but I can't get it to produce anything helpful.

What would a ghost warrior do?!

Just when I think I can't take any more, Aurelia claps her hands in excitement.

"I have an idea!" she exclaims. "We have our very own gladiator. We should have a match. Right here!"

"Yes!" Numerius cries. "Excellent idea."

"Three-on-one, just like that glorious showing at the primus," Cornelia says. "I'll be the murmillo. What was his name?"

"Basinus, I think," says Numerius. "I'll be the secutor."

"I suppose that makes me the retiarius," Aurelia sighs. She perks up when she focuses on Jason again.

"What do you say?" she asks him. "Wouldn't you like a rematch? Show us your skill on a more intimate level?"

His expression darkens. He's clearly aware of what she's really suggesting.

Enough!

I can't take it anymore.

"I'm sure Jason has a lot of work to do," I interrupt. "We've detained him long enough, don't you think?"

Their startled looks make it clear they forgot about me. But any relief I feel for finally interfering fades at their leering grins.

Cornelia shifts toward me and raises her brows. "Why, Aurelia, I believe your friend is uncomfortable with your idea."

Aurelia smirks. "Should we be surprised?"

Jason's gaze settles on me, and the warning in his eyes is enough to make tears burn hot in my chest. It's almost like he doesn't want me to help him, even though I can see how much he's hurting.

Aurelia sighs. "You're about to be married, Mallia. It's time for you to see the real world and stop being a child. I've said it before, but now it's downright embarrassing. You're too sheltered."

"I'm not! I just don't think this is right. We—"

"Not right?" Cornelia snaps with a frigid stare. "Not right, is it? You know what, Aurelia? I think you have a bigger problem. Look at her. She's about to cry. And look at her maid."

My heart pounds as Cornelia stalks a few steps toward us. She glances back and forth between Jason and me with narrowed eyes. A deadly silence falls over the room when her expression darkens and turns cruel.

"She's not just sheltered. It's worse than that," she hisses. "Little Mallia actually cares about this slave. Are you in love with him?"

"What?" I choke out. "Of course not. I just don't agree with mistreating them."

"Oh? We're *mistreating* him now? You have a lot of nerve for a little mouse! Where did you find this child, Aurelia?"

Aurelia blushes at the harsh critique and shifts her weight.

"She's just young and inexperienced," Aurelia defends in a meek voice.

"Enough of this!" Cornelia growls. "On your knees, slave!"

I flinch when she slaps Jason hard across the face.

"Aurelia, please!" I say before I can stop myself.

Aurelia fires a venomous look at me. "Cornelia is right. Your deference to a slave is embarrassing, Mallia. You're lucky I don't have all of them flogged right this second!"

Cornelia's scowl turns hostile. "Actually, I think that's a good idea. She needs a lesson. You should start with her maid! Guards!"

"Wait! My lady, please," Jason interrupts, and I watch in horror as he submits. His eyes lock on mine, silently begging me to stay quiet. It makes me want to scream. Throw things. Rip hair from scalps with a fury I've never felt before.

"Finally," Cornelia mutters. "I was beginning to think you were too stupid to understand the instructions."

She's only trying to get a rise out of him, probably enjoying her power over someone so powerful. But Jason ignores her, retreating once again to that far-off place where he can obey without murder.

My chest is so tight I wouldn't be able to protest anyway, as the others find their "weapons." A blanket for Aurelia's net and a candlestick for Basinus' short sword. But Cornelia's dagger is real, and nausea swirls in my stomach when they surround him.

He remains eerily motionless throughout the assault, completely absent from the scene. As the minutes drag into what feels like eternity, it's as if he's disappeared, stopped existing. He's powerless…no, not even that. Incredibly powerful, but forced to be powerless. I have no doubt he could kill us with barely a breath, but instead we'll be the ones who send him to Hades one day. We're the ones who can break him and bend him to our will. The others are clearly drunk on the same reality.

And I hate them. Hate how they tear at him, savoring his inability to fight back. Trapping him in their cruel fantasies and stealing whatever they want for their own pleasure. I hate how he's forced to let them, to suppress everything he is and accept it with a silent dignity no one will ever see.

But I do. I watch it all, and when Cornelia's blade slices across his chest for no other reason than her desire to watch him bleed, I'm done.

"Stop!" I say, jumping to my feet.

They go still, their gazes cutting to me in shock. Inside, I'm terrified and shaking, but outside, I force a calm façade.

"I've changed my mind," I say, moving toward them. "I want a turn as well."

Aurelia's surprise melts into a smug grin. "Well, then. Maybe our little mouse is becoming a lioness after all. Choose a weapon and join us."

I shake my head. "No, alone. I want him to myself."

Cornelia snorts a laugh while Numerius tosses himself on his couch like he's about to witness a show.

"Really?" Aurelia asks, tilting her head. "You didn't even want to touch him a moment ago."

"I was embarrassed because I'm so inexperienced, as you said. Please, Aurelia?"

"Will she even know what to do on her own?" Cornelia quips.

I swallow a wave of bile when the horrible woman has to cleanse Jason's blood from her hands before she can select a snack from the tray beside her.

"This should be fun. I say yes," Numerius coos.

Aurelia scans the room and then steps back with another smile.

"Fine. Go ahead." She waves toward him. "He's yours."

I adopt the most shy, embarrassed look I can manage. "I…well, I meant in a private room."

Aurelia scrunches her nose as the others burst into laughter.

"Of course she did," Cornelia mumbles.

I ignore her and focus my efforts on Aurelia. "Please, Aurelia. Just this once. It's my first time."

That's not a lie. This entire day has been a nightmare of firsts.

After an interminable wait, Aurelia sighs. "Fine. Use one of my private retreats. But you must share every detail."

"Of course." I even manage a tight smile.

I start toward the corridor that leads to Aurelia's private chambers.

"Come," I say to Jason, and then motion to Danae to follow as well.

"You're sure you're not afraid to be alone with a gladiator?" Cornelia calls after me. "They're animals, you know."

I cringe and somehow suppress my retort. Pretty sure the *animals* are still cackling over their wine and gossip.

MALLIA

Jason and Danae follow me into the furthest sitting room of Aurelia's private suite. I look around to make sure we're alone and then close the door.

We're far enough from the others that they won't be able to hear us, but we still need to be careful. There are plenty of guards and household staff who could cause trouble for us.

I turn to address my companions, but freeze at the look on Jason's face. His expression is still blank and unreadable. Does he not realize what I just risked for him?

"What position would you prefer, my lady?" he says in an even voice.

My heart stops.

Is he…? I search his face in disbelief.

"*Pluto's chains*, you're serious," I breathe out.

A startled look flashes over his features before he can hide it.

"I didn't bring you here to use you," I hiss, disgusted that I even have to spell that out. "Danae, go find supplies to clean his wounds."

I catch my maid's gratitude and relief before she leaves on her errand.

My heart breaks when I turn back to Jason and see how confused he is. He really thought…

He can't even comprehend kindness, can he?

My head aches, my chest, everything hurts as I absorb the blow.

I massage my sore temples.

"What do you intend to do with me then?" he asks quietly.

"*Do* with you?"

I wince from my tone when he lowers his gaze.

"Sorry," I say. "That anger wasn't meant for you."

I pull in a deep breath and approach him slowly. I want to touch him, just to offer the slightest gesture of reassurance, but after what just happened, the last thing he probably wants are my hands anywhere near him.

"I don't intend to do anything with you," I say, softening my tone. "I brought you here to get you away from *them*. To give us time to think and figure this out."

"Figure what out?"

Gods, his world is so warped he can't even recognize a small act of mercy, either.

I release a frustrated breath.

"I'm not letting them hurt you anymore. That's what we need to figure out. How to keep you away from them."

His eyes narrow in confusion. "I don't mean any disrespect, my lady. But how exactly would you prevent that?"

His meaning is clear, and I swallow the fresh nausea rising in my stomach. He doesn't belong to me. He doesn't belong to himself.

I chew on my lip, trying to think. "Maybe we tell them your injuries are more severe than we thought. You had to return to Telemon for treatment."

His jaw ticks, indicating he has a response.

"Speak," I command.

He averts his gaze again, and I wince at what I just did.

"I'm sorry," I say gently. "I shouldn't have said it like that. I only mean, you're not a slave when you're with me. You may speak your mind. I know how intelligent and strategic you are, and I need your help with this situation. If you have thoughts, I want to hear them."

He searches my face with suspicion, as if this is all some kind of trap, maybe another cruel game.

I can't blame him for not trusting me after what I just saw. Is that what he sees when he looks at *me*? Aurelia and her leering grin? Numerius and his insatiable lust? Cornelia and her sadistic pleasures? Am I the next attack he's bracing to endure?

My throat closes up. It all seems wrong. How was I so conditioned to think anyone has a right to treat another person like an object?

"Please." My tone is pleading now. "Tell me what you were going to say."

He clears his throat, still looking uncomfortable. "Only that…" He stops, and maybe his expression softens slightly as well. "Thank you for your kindness, my lady, but there is nothing you can do. There is no injury that can replace a master's will. Often, the injury *is* their will."

My teeth sink into my lip as my heart cracks open.

"So what do we do?" I ask in a shaky voice.

His fingers twitch at his side in an unnatural movement, almost like…

I reach out slowly, hesitating as I read his reactions so I can stop if necessary. But when he moves his hand *toward* mine instead of away, heat washes through me.

It's almost a feeling of relief when I touch his fingers again. So warm and strong despite the injuries. Rough and calloused. I never want to stop holding them. I turn his palm up and trace the ugly wound marring the center of it.

"What should we do?" I repeat faintly.

His fingers close around mine as much as they can, and I hold my breath.

"Nothing. We should do nothing," he says quietly. "I can't claim an injury, but you can, my lady. It would be best for both of us if you went home when I go back."

MALLIA

Alone in my room, I cling to Danae as she releases the emotion she's been holding onto since we left the palace.

"It's not fair!" she cries into the fabric of my gown.

"I know."

Danae shakes her head and pulls away, the horror on her face so vivid I shudder.

"Do you, my lady? Do you really? How can you?!"

My heart hurts at the accusation in her tone. "I'm trying, Danae, really."

"How could you understand what it's like to become an object?" she continues, gripping the edge of my shawl. "To bury your soul and pray for death! I saw his eyes, my lady. For those horrible moments, he was dead. His body was alive, but his soul was dead!"

"And what was I supposed to do?" I return with a hard look. "Tell Aurelia not to touch her slave? Run to the Emperor? Fight them off myself? And then what? Who do you think would have faced the consequences for my interference? You saw what happened every time I tried to speak up! They were ready to have all of us punished."

I shake my head, trying to piece all the broken shards together. "Such is our world, their right. My father doesn't believe in using slaves, but he is of the minority. You know this!"

"But we just left him there!" she cries, eyes wide with grief. "We ran away and just *left him.* We…" She buries her face in her hands as the sobs take over.

"It's what he wanted," I say in a weak tone. "He asked me to go home."

It's the truth, but it still feels like a betrayal. I wrap my arms around my stomach as the ache in my chest spreads throughout my entire body.

Danae only shakes her head again, crying into her hands.

Silence settles around us as I wipe my own eyes with the edge of my wrap. The truth is, I'm haunted by the same questions. That's the real travesty, the real force behind my argument. My words may be true, but I don't accept a single one of them.

Danae lifts her head, blasting me with a flood of desperation. "And despite it all, he's still beautiful, my lady. In here." She presses her fist against her chest. "If you only knew…but it doesn't matter. It never matters. They will never even know the man they're destroying."

I close my eyes to steady my emotions. "I suspect they did not succeed in destroying him. We may have been shocked by the encounter, but he clearly wasn't. He's accustomed to that life." I regret my words the second they come out.

"And therefore he doesn't bleed?" she fires back. "He doesn't feel? He's not in pain now, trying to piece himself back together after being ripped apart?"

I soften at her obvious distress. "That's not what I'm saying, and you know it. And you also know I would never let anything like that happen to you."

She flinches at my attempt to comfort her. "So, who looks after him? Who's going to make sure his life is worth more than an animal's?"

Tears spill down my cheeks as the horrific events replay in my head. Details I want to forget, even though I know I never will.

"I don't know who looks after him," I say in a shaky voice. "I don't know."

No one. No one does.

He walks through the shadows completely alone.

"I would have killed them if I could," she hisses with venom I've never heard from the mild-mannered servant. "May they be cursed with all the fire of the gods!"

I have no more words. No more defenses or explanations. All I can do is pull her close again as I shatter under the weight of a truth too heavy to carry.

"He bleeds, my lady. Inside. He doesn't show it, but I know he does."

Her arms tighten around me, as if she knows it's her turn to comfort me.

CHAPTER IX

ARGUS

I THROW THE DICE ON THE WORN PINE TABLE AND UTTER A CURSE WHEN THEY SEEM TO curse *me*, yet again.

A roar of laughter erupts from the crowd of soldiers packed into the small tavern in Hades Hand.

"When will you come to terms with your terrible fortune, my friend?" Geminus teases with a snicker.

"When you come to terms with your hideous face," I mumble, scooping the dice off the stained surface.

Geminus returns a wide grin as he slides the mound of coins toward himself. "I can name plenty of women who would disagree with you."

"Good, then maybe you should be tormenting them instead." I toss back a gulp of spiced wine, mostly so I don't have to watch him sort his bounty.

"You're a sore loser." He chuckles, dropping a few coins on the table for the wine.

I bite back a smile as he shoves the rest of his coins in a pouch, and I scan the unfamiliar tavern for potential threats. I don't usually come this far east, but I heard this particular establishment is a favorite among veterans and soldiers. My real gamble paid off when I ran into Geminus, a ghost from my past who was always a good man and even better soldier.

The truth is, he'll probably steward those coins with more wisdom than I would have. Giving him a hard time is part of my veteran status, but I'd serve beside him again in a heartbeat if I could.

He runs a hand over thinning, close-cropped black hair. "Another game?" he asks with a crooked smile.

"You took it all," I grunt. "How about you buy me another drink with my stolen coin instead?"

Geminus laughs and signals the server. "Fair enough."

While we settle onto the wooden bench to wait, the audience disperses in favor of more exciting tables in the busy tavern.

"How's Tacitus?" my friend asks, fanning his off-duty tunic against the stuffy heat. "If memory serves, you were discharged together. Is he in Rome as well?"

"He's fine. Adjusting to civilian life, like I am. I heard you were being transferred again."

His thick brows crease as he nods. "I report in two days. Since Legatus Severus disbanded the Fourth, I've been getting passed all over the Empire. I just got back from Cappadocia, and now they're sending me to Legatus Nepos to enlist with the Sixth."

Despite the sweat coating my neck and back, a cold shiver runs through me. Violent memories rush from the shadows, and I force them back into the vault.

"The Sixth? Wow."

Geminus nods and takes a swig from his freshly filled cup. "Apparently, Nepos has requested more men for his Britannia Campaign and is levying a new legion."

I go completely cold. It takes a measured breath to keep the alarm from my face. "A new legion? And the Emperor agreed to this?"

Geminus shrugs. "So it would appear. I don't know. I don't ask questions."

No, which is why he'll have a long, successful career and won't ever find himself guarding a warehouse like Tacitus and I do.

I force a casual stretch, even as my mind spirals. "Well, good luck to you. If you see Celetus, tell him Argus said to eat ashes."

Geminus offers a weak smile that quickly turns into pity. "I wish you and Tacitus were coming with me. I don't believe the rumors about what happened."

Ah, yes. The *rumors*.

"Oh? And what are the rumors these days?"

Geminus tips his head back, eyeing me with a curious look. "Word is you stole Legatus Nepos's seal."

I nearly spit out a mouthful of wine. "Really, now? Stole the general's seal? That's a new one."

My friend lifts his brows, relief flickering over his features. "So it's not true?"

I return a wry look. "I wouldn't even know where to start planning a heist like that."

"No, but Tacitus would. He was always a genius at that sort of thing."

"So it's Tacitus, the brilliant thief, now?"

"The brilliant strategist."

I let out a quick breath. That part is true. "He may be a brilliant strategist, but I assure you he's no thief."

Geminus rubs his clean-shaven chin. "So why the missio ignominiosa? I confess, I still don't understand why you were even allowed to return to Rome."

My mouth clamps shut as I study his sincere expression. It's a fair question, especially from a former legion brother. I have no reason to suspect anything other than genuine concern, but I'm not sure how to respond. What happened to Tacitus isn't a nice story, nor is it mine to tell.

I have no desire to relive it, anyway.

"You know me and my mouth," I deflect with a late grin.

Geminus barks a laugh, tension easing from his shoulders. "True. I've seen the vine stick on you plenty of times. It's a wonder you weren't executed."

"Probably would have been if not for Legatus Severus. Nepos would've loved to see our heads on a stick, but not if it meant making an enemy of the Emperor and his favorite advisor."

Geminus releases a sly grin. "He would've had to get in line, anyway."

I snort and drain my cup. "True enough. I could name a hundred men who would be happy to see me dead."

"Still…" His forehead creases as his lips sag into a frown. "What of Tacitus? He doesn't have your temper. He's still young. An incredible officer, from what I understand. I don't believe he was discharged for insolence."

My muscles tense as I stare into the empty cup. That's a harder battlefield to navigate.

"Tacitus may be too brilliant for his own good," I mutter. "Nepos never liked me, but he always feared him."

"Feared him? Why?"

I wince at my slip. We're getting dangerously close to the truth.

With a dismissive wave, I rest an elbow on the sticky table. "Nepos had it out for him since the beginning. Everyone in our cohort knew it. Maybe Nepos's wife gave him too many glances. The kid isn't as sorry to look at as we are."

"True enough," Geminus chuckles. "It doesn't seem fair, though. No wonder he's bitter."

You don't know the half of it.

Images of my friend's brutal flogging stream through my head like it happened yesterday.

"His family renounced him after the discharge," I say in a dark tone. "Just left him in the dust with nothing but a bloody back."

More memories threaten the silence, and I block them with a dry laugh. "But enough of that! I'm here to get drunk, not whine about the past. What do you say? Another round on you, Primus Pilus?"

Geminus relaxes with a smirk. "Primus Pilus? I'll be lucky to return to my rank as centurion."

JASON

Mallia shifts nervously on her sandaled feet when I find her in a secluded corridor just outside the servants' quarters. I was surprised by the summons, and grow more concerned when she motions for me to follow deeper into the shadows.

"You asked to see me, my lady?" I say evenly once we're tucked behind a column.

Inside, my pulse races with terrible possibilities about what she could want. Anything would be better than what I fear most—that this odd interview is somehow related to yesterday's events in the exedra. Mallia was trying to help, but only made things worse. She's too good, too pure and honorable to understand the dark dynamics of sadistic cravings—how easy it is to fuel pleasure into torture.

And I love that about her. Her innocent kindness is refreshing in my ugly, violent world, and it's something I've clung to more than I should since our first meeting. I still think about her gentle touch. Her thumb on my wrist, and how, for a brief moment, I felt…cherished. I'd never felt that before.

"You…" She quiets, her light brown eyes narrowing as she studies me. "Your face."

She reaches up, and I instinctively duck out of reach.

I glance around in alarm, relieved at the empty shadows.

"I'm fine, my lady."

She looks hurt at the rejection, but I don't regret it. Her compassion is sweet, but it's going to get us in trouble.

"Did you…tell anyone about what happened?" she asks in a hesitant voice.

Confused, I stare back, trying to read into her strange question. "Who would I tell? *What* would I tell?"

She winces and averts her gaze. "Right. Sorry. Of course."

Her teeth sink into her lip as she tugs on a cluster of brunette braids hanging over her shoulder. Pale blue silk cascades around her slight form, showing off smooth, unblemished skin so foreign to my marred existence. A strange urge to shield her from every evil steels through me.

With a resigned sigh, I lean closer. "Look, I know that was upsetting for you, but you can rest with a clear conscience. I don't hold any resentment toward you. I know you're not like them."

She snaps her head up, and I wince when her surprised look transforms into distress.

"You think that's why I'm here? To absolve my conscience?"

"No," I rush out, blood pounding. "Of course not. I just meant…I'm so sorry, my lady. Of course you wouldn't apolo—"

"Stop. Talking," she hisses. Anger blazes in her fierce brown eyes, but I'm not entirely certain it's aimed at me.

Confused by the sudden shift in tone, I lower my gaze as a fresh wave of anxiety swirls in my stomach.

Maybe she changed her mind and wants a private demonstration after all. I force in a shaky breath and brace myself for what comes next.

The din of activity in the slaves' quarters drifts toward us, igniting a fresh sense of urgency. Just down the hall, dinner preparations are being made, linens are being laundered, and a host of other slaves are seconds away from seeing us together. I'm about to ask to be dismissed when her entire demeanor hardens.

"I heard what happened after I left." Her bitter tone locks me in place. "I heard what they did to you after you went back."

I go numb. My insides twist at the rage in her narrowed gaze.

"And after they finished, they callously dismissed you like a dog, didn't they?" She spits the words like they cut her tongue. "But did you tell anyone? No. You couldn't. Like you said, who would you tell? *What* would you tell, because nothing happened, right? It was just another afternoon of aristocrats playing with their toy. So next, you did what? What did you do after that?"

I blink at her, having no idea what she wants me to say.

"Go on. Tell me." She motions for me to speak. Dark brows arch in challenge as she crosses her arms.

When I don't respond, her eyes grow hot with anger, but it doesn't feel directed at me.

"I…"

"What did you do, Jason? You don't even understand my question, do you? Tell me what you did after they finished with you."

"I don't…" I shake my head in confusion. "Nothing. I went back to my quarters."

With an emphatic nod, she drops her arms. A pained look spreads over her delicate features. "Precisely. Alone, right? Abandoned. You rinsed the blood from your body and prayed for sleep. But you don't even get peace *there,* do you? No, the Fates wouldn't grant you such a mercy. They certainly haven't given a worm's rot about you so far."

I flinch. A sharp sting, typically reserved for my body, slices through my soul.

Her eyes land on mine and fill with bitter tears. "I didn't come here to tell you I'm sorry for what happened." Her harsh tone softens into gentle determination. "I came to say it *shouldn't* have happened. It wasn't nothing, and it wasn't okay. I came to tell you someone was thinking about you all night and praying to the gods they'd show you an ounce of mercy."

She takes my hands and tugs once, forcing me to look at her.

"This isn't about my honor," she continues, searching my face with heartfelt intensity. "I'm here on your behalf. To defend *you*. You don't deserve this life. You don't deserve to be treated that way—no one does—and I was embarrassed that I didn't do more to stop it. I hated what happened to you. I hated myself for not doing anything to protect you."

Her wide, innocent gaze exposes her pain—for me, for us—but it changes nothing. That's what she doesn't understand. Compassion, kindness, *words* do absolutely nothing. She has the luxury of philosophy and choosing between right and wrong. I have a choice between obedience and death.

At the end of the day, I have to walk back into the lion's den and let them tear me apart. Every single time.

I pull away and clasp my hands behind my back where they belong. "You speak as though we live in the same world, my lady."

"We do live in the same world," she argues with an earnest step toward me. "We're both here, in this moment, together. And despite your status, I can tell every time I look in your eyes that your spirit runs as deep as your scars. I can tell there's so much more to you."

A litany of protests rises in my throat. So many things I could say to illustrate the dark truth she doesn't want to believe. Horrors she can't imagine, evil that would keep her awake at night.

She thinks she understands, but she doesn't. She can't, and I don't want her to. I *like* the idea that there's one person in this world who's not poisoned by the stain of violence and depravity. If anything, I'd accept more pain to protect her precious innocence, because I need to know it exists, even if I can't see it or touch it.

But I also need her to understand enough of our reality that she doesn't get us killed. I hate what I'm about to do, but I don't know how else to steer her from this dangerous, futile path. What she's saying is treason. Worse than that. It's hope.

And hope is a death sentence.

With a deep breath, I fix my gaze on the stone floor beneath our feet.

"Can I tell you a story, my lady?" I don't wait for a response before continuing. "Before I was sold to the ludus, I spent many years as one of Fabius Lepidus's boys. It was hades, but it was all I knew."

I sense her shock and distress and force myself on without looking at her. There's no other way to tell these stories.

"When I was sixteen, a wealthy family came to him. They said they wanted to adopt me, to take me away from my life of horror and give me a better one. They said they could tell I wasn't like the other boys, that despite my difficult circumstances, I had strong character and would rise up if given the chance. I heard the whole conversation. Lepidus made sure of it. They even offered to buy me from him and fully compensate his future losses."

I stop, shuddering through the memory. The pain slices into me fresh and raw like it did that day.

Hope. That's what hope is: staring into the face of something better while it's being ripped away.

"Jason?"

I blink back to the present and shift my gaze to hers.

"You know what Lepidus did? He threw them out and said the world had enough great men. My role was to be their reward. He sold me to the ludus the next day."

Her expression wilts, but I don't regret telling her the story. This tragedy is just a grain of sand in the arena of what I could share about what I've lived and seen, and that's my point. She will never understand my world. She can't and she shouldn't.

I don't want her to.

Neither of us speaks as my fractured words settle around us. Her broken heart and dashed ideals stream through the wounded look on her face. I didn't want to hurt her, but she has to know there's no justice for some. No comfort or peace. There is survival, and there is pain.

We don't live in the same world.

"Is there anything else you needed, my lady?" I ask gently.

It was a loaded question. And a pointless one. I can't give her what she wants, just like she has nothing for me.

Her lips press together as she shakes her head.

"Have a pleasant afternoon, my lady."

I offer a weak smile and leave her to her pleasant life.

MALLIA

"Good to see you, Mallia," Severus greets from his desk as I march into his study.

I'm trying to stay calm, but my anger has been festering too long already. After my disastrous conversation with Jason, I requested an audience with Severus, but he couldn't see me until hours later. By then, my anger had morphed into rage.

"I thought you said Jason was important," I snap, stalking toward him. "You made it sound like he was your key warrior ghost or whatever you called them. You *need* him for some great calling."

The welcoming smile drains from his face as he lowers the silver stylus in his hand. "He is. What's your grievance?"

My *grievance?!*

It will be a miracle if I survive this conversation without throwing something.

I clench my fists at my side. "You told me you brought him here to protect him from that lanista, Opius Plinius. He was supposed to save Rome and the Emperor. He's *noble, extraordinary,* with vision and strength and a whole list of attributes I was supposed to admire. You made it seem like he was an equal to any great senator, yet instead, you've left him as just one more slave for Aurelia's bed!"

Severus's surprised look would make me feel better if I wasn't still haunted by every detail of the entire incident.

"What have you heard?" he asks with a frown.

"*Heard*? I had to participate in it! You say he's special, and yet banish him to the slaves' quarters to be treated like a whore! So, which is it? You rescue him from one horror to throw him into another? Where does that fit in this brilliant plan?"

Afternoon sunlight streams in through the large window to his left, illuminating the creases around his gray eyes and somber lips. This man has been tested by war, violent politics, and the burden of running an entire empire. I'm overstepping in every way imaginable, but I'm too angry to filter my words, too hurt to care. Most wouldn't dare to reprimand one of the most powerful men in Rome, especially over the treatment of a slave that isn't theirs and a situation that has nothing to do with them.

I'm dangerously close to being treasonous, but I have no stomach for hypocrisy, especially if he expects me to align with his precious cause.

He meticulously places the stylus beside the wax tablet and leans back in his chair. I search his face for any clue to his thoughts, but his patient expression bears the mark of a carefully curated façade.

It reminds me of another man who can become unreadable when he needs to be.

"I'm sorry for your distress regarding whatever it is you saw," he says in an even tone. "I can understand how something like that could be upsetting for you—"

"Upsetting for *me*?" I spit out, pressing a fist to my heart. "That's the problem, isn't it? It's all about us! All about—"

"Jason is still a slave, Mallia," he cuts in with a stern look. "Plans are being put into place, but we can't move forward until he's fully healed and the timing is right. We must be patient."

Furious, I let my eyes reflect his betrayal right back at him.

"Well, guess what? He *had* been healed! But while you're planning and being patient, your noble savior is being assaulted by Aurelia and her friends!"

Satisfied I made my point, I spin on my heels and rush from the room before I end up in prison.

JASON

With a deep breath, I approach Legatus Severus's private study near the Emperor's imperial suite. The general is engrossed in a pile of documents at his desk, so I wait quietly in the open doorway.

It's my understanding that the retired legatus has his own estate somewhere in the city, but spends most of his time at the palace to be more actively involved in the Empire's affairs.

The more I learned of his busy schedule and heavy governing responsibilities, the more confused I became about why he rescued me from Opius Plinius. What importance could a common slave have to a man such as the revered general?

I haven't seen him since he stopped visiting the infirmary once he was satisfied with my progress toward a full recovery. I thought he'd forgotten about me, which only increased my bewilderment about why he'd taken an interest in the first place.

Tonight's abrupt summons to his private rooms solved the mystery. I hadn't taken the man for the type to use slaves, but it wouldn't be the first time I've misjudged someone, though it's rare these days. Hopefully, his appetite will be easily satisfied.

When he finally glances up from his work, I force down the mounting dread.

"Good. You're here. Come." He waves me toward him.

Lamplight flickers over the angles of his face, making him look harsher than I remember. Or maybe it's the anxiety churning in my gut as I cover the distance to his desk. No matter how many times I go through this humiliation, it doesn't get easier. I just get better at walling off the pain.

I steel myself as Severus dismisses the other servants. Outwardly, I show nothing, staring at the marble floor, praying this will be quick.

"You look much improved since the last time I saw you," he says in a conversational tone. "How are you feeling?"

I sense his rapt attention and clench my fists behind my back.

"I am well, my lord."

A long pause is followed by a rustle as he rises from his desk. "Jason, look at me."

With a careful breath, I lift my head and meet his fixed gaze.

"I'm not being polite. I want the truth. How are you really? Some of your wounds look fresh."

I swallow hard, rocked by the strange question. He can't possibly want the truth. They never do. They want *their* truth. The honest answer would be too complicated to explain anyway.

"I'm truly much better, my lord. Telemon says I'd be able to train again in a couple of weeks if you choose to send me back to the ludus."

A small burst of fear explodes in my chest at the thought.

Severus grunts with a dark look. "You will resume training, but it will not be at the ludus, I can assure you."

He saunters to a bronze table below a shuttered window and pours himself a cup of wine. With deliberate movements, he pivots on his heel to face me again.

"You still haven't answered my question. With your background, I imagine adjusting to life as a house slave has been a challenge."

My gaze shoots to his before I can stop it. I quickly lower my eyes, but the damage is done. My heart races in the tense silence. Was there a complaint against me? Are they not sending me back because they have a worse fate planned?

Mallia…

Alarm spikes through my veins.

Did someone hear us speaking this morning?

"My lord, if I've done something wrong—"

"No," he interrupts in a cold tone. "You're here because of what's been done to you."

I glance up in confusion, and his hard stare softens as he searches my face.

"I…don't understand, my lord."

After a short pause, he sighs and motions toward a couch. "No, I don't suppose you would understand, given your experiences. Sit."

I swallow a familiar wave of nausea as I obey, but I'm surprised again when he takes a separate chair instead of joining me.

He places his glass on a table and leans forward.

"A friend of yours has informed me there's been some confusion among the members of this house about your role here. I wish to clarify that. Look at me, son."

I force my gaze up to meet an unexpected expression. There's nothing of the violence or lust I'm accustomed to, just…concern?

He shifts, allowing candlelight to illuminate the sincerity etched into his face. "If you're willing, I'd like you to serve as my personal bodyguard and valet. I can assure you the Emperor has agreed to the terms and hopes you will accept the position as much as I do."

Stunned, I blink slowly. Is this a game? Some kind of test? My gaze darts to the door as if the real threat will materialize at any second.

But when nothing happens, my focus returns to his patient countenance. "You weren't expecting that, were you?" he says, a smile flickering over his lips.

I shake my head, still in disbelief. "No, my lord."

"Well, I'd ask you to think about it, but I need your assistance immediately, so if you could kindly accept the offer now, I'd greatly appreciate it." Even in the dim light, his eyes dance with gentle humor.

I search his face for missing clues. I've been mocked plenty of times in a similar manner, but there's no sign of sarcasm or deceit.

He's serious. A rare tug lifts the corners of my mouth.

"Hmm. I'm not sure I've ever seen that before." He rubs his chin in exaggerated thought. "Is that a smile?"

Another smile works its way to my face as a burst of warmth explodes through me.

"So may I interpret your response as a yes?" he prods with a soft chuckle.

"Of course, my lord. I'd be honored."

I dare another look, stunned when his eyes soften with affection.

He rises from his chair, bidding me to do the same. He clasps my shoulder with a calloused hand and squeezes before letting go.

"Excellent. Then please see the steward about being fitted with a uniform. I have very stringent standards for my men. From this point forward, you will shadow me at all times. I'll make sure the rest of the palace understands the terms of this arrangement. You are to answer only to the Emperor and me. If anyone challenges you on the matter, you can direct them to me. Is that clear?"

I manage an even expression as I nod. "Very clear, my lord."

"Good. Now do as I said, but return quickly. We have a lot to review."

Chapter X

ARGUS

"Tacitus, I'd like you to meet Seia."

Standing in the entrance of my flat, my friend bows with all the grace of an equestrian officer.

"Gaius Atius Tacitus, at your service, my lady," he says in a faux formal tone. "It's a pleasure to meet you."

The little girl giggles and bounces on her toes. "You're the one who fights bandits with Argus," she announces with pride.

Tacitus flickers an amused glance at me.

"She's not wrong," I say with a shrug.

"She's not." He smirks before crouching to be eye-level with her. "So, Seia, Argus tells me you're going to be staying here and taking care of him. Is that true?"

Her wild curls flutter in a vigorous nod. "Yep. He's letting me stay so the bad man doesn't take me."

"The bad man?" Tacitus's concerned look snaps to me.

"Lepidus," I mumble.

Disgust washes over his face, and we silently agree not to finish the conversation in front of the girl. That monster isn't a suitable topic for any decent human being.

"Well, I think that's great, Seia," he tells her in a lighter tone. "Argus could definitely use some help around here. I mean, look at this dirt." He slides his finger along the dusty floor.

"*Porca.*" My muttered slur at Tacitus earns an amused smirk from my friend and a disapproving glower from Seia.

"That wasn't nice," she scolds. "Say sorry to him!"

"Sorry," I grunt toward Tacitus, who's straight-up snickering.

"Now, I will clean!" She darts through the open doorway of the flat and clambers down the stairs on a mission—I assume in search of cleaning supplies.

Good luck with that, little one.

"Lepidus is recruiting from *your* neighborhood now?" Tacitus hisses, pushing to his feet.

"Got me, but it appears so." I peer out the window for a glimpse of Seia. Her determined little steps march down the alley, but I can't guess what's going on in that precocious head.

"I've seen him hovering around a few times," I continue, still observing the little girl. Okay, fine—*guarding*. "His lair is over in the Fountain District by the Antius Baths, but maybe he's moving."

"Maybe he's franchising," Tacitus growls.

"*Frax…*"

"Exactly." Tacitus joins me at the window, squinting in the direction of my tiny roommate. "How old is she?"

"She wasn't sure. I'm going to guess about six?"

Tacitus frowns as we watch her turn the corner out of view. His gaze slices back to me, saturated with concern. "If Lepidus was really after her, you're doing the right thing."

My focus drifts toward the small straw pallet by my bed that we made for her. She hasn't even formally been here a month, and already she's turned this dreary flat into a vibrant home bursting with energy. I shudder at how close she came to a very different fate.

"How much do you know about Lepidus and his operation?" I ask, pivoting back to the window to watch for her.

"Not much. And I took pride in that fact until now," he huffs.

I nod, feeling the same. Some evil is beyond comprehension.

A mop of dark curls flutters around the corner of the neighboring building, stirring a rush of concerned affection. Seia's little hands are clasped around what looks like scraps of fabric, and the triumphant grin on her face sends a fierce wave of protectiveness through me.

"As much as it pains me, we might not have the luxury of ignorance anymore," I say. "We need to know what he's up to."

"Agreed," Tacitus says with firm resolve. His brows knit as he absently watches the progress of our new little friend. "And if the rumors are true, I think we have access to someone who knows everything."

MALLIA

Commotion in the atrium draws my attention as I pass, and I divert toward the grand entrance to our villa. Peeking through the line of ancestral busts, I see my father rinsing his hands in a bowl held by an attendant. He's back from the baths early, a fact that doesn't concern me until I see the worn expression on his face.

"Are you alright, Father?" I ask, entering the large formal hall.

Sunlight streams through the open rectangle in the ceiling, glistening off a thin layer of rainwater collected in the pool below. The woody, citrus-tinged bite of freshly burned frankincense drifts from the shrine on the far wall, filling the imposing space with its recent offering. Servants have already swapped his robes and sandals for lighter, more casual attire. He accepts a cup of watered wine from a slave boy, while his groom dabs scented oil on his neck and arms.

A trip to the baths should have been a relaxing experience, but the creases in his forehead and stiff posture hint otherwise.

"I'm fine, my dear," he lies with a tired smile.

He waves off the attendants and motions for me to wait while he checks in with his secretary in the attached tablinum.

I chew on my lip as they review the day's correspondence in the small office opening into the atrium. If he wants me to wait, there must be news beyond the short messages and dictations he exchanges with his scribe. By the time they finish and he leads me deeper into the house, my insides have twisted into knots.

"Did you enjoy the wedding ceremony last week?" he asks in a conversational tone as we enter the peristyle.

I search for clues in his mannerisms, but come up empty.

"Yes, although I must say, I'm still not fully recovered. I understand why we must attend such events, but they can be exhausting."

He tosses a weak smile and waves toward a bench beneath an olive tree in our private garden. "You didn't enjoy yourself? Even with all the food and entertainment?"

I adjust my thin home palla to sit on the cool marble surface. "If by entertainment you mean listening to Julia go on for hours about Arata's bridal gown and veil, then no, I didn't enjoy it."

"Varro's niece, Julia? She's a sweet girl."

"She is. Just terribly dull."

Another forced smile barely disrupts the flat line of his mouth as he joins me on the bench. "I'd imagine so, especially compared to your adventures at the palace with Aurelia."

I flinch, still raw from the recent one.

"Exactly," I say, forcing a weak smile. "I wish the Ursus and Varro families all the best in their union. I just don't like witnessing it for three days straight."

His features twist into a grimace that lands in my stomach.

"It was a bit lavish, even for them," he says in a distracted tone.

"The bride and groom are well?" I ask casually.

"From what I understand."

"That's good to hear."

My father crosses his gaze toward the rustling of a bird in a neighboring laurel tree. Something's wrong, and I suspect whatever it is needs to get to Severus.

"You don't look well, Father. Is everything okay?"

He releases a heavy sigh and takes my hand. "I need to talk to you about something."

Air sieves from my lungs. When his expression sags from discomfort to distress, my chest constricts with fear.

"What is it? What's wrong?"

He rests his gaze on my face, and in that brief moment, I see his love for me. I love him too. He's all I have left after my mother's death four years ago—a tragedy also responsible for the fact that I'm not already married. As much as my father feigns otherwise, his selectiveness over a suitable match has been about not wanting to lose me more than any issue with the offer. The Pius family must have made quite a proposal for my father to finally accept.

"The truth is, everything isn't fine," he says, releasing my hand. "I have some news that will be difficult for you to hear."

Alarm slices through me. Does he know about the conspiracy involving Varro and Ursus?

I brace for news of death threats and betrayal. Ejection from the Senate. Maybe General Nepos is marching his legions home to slaughter us all as we speak!

My father draws in a deep breath and mutters a curse. "Gods help me, this is harder than I thought. I'll just be out with it." He inhales deeply again and twists toward me on the bench. "I met with Placidius Pius last week and again today. He informed me that he's no longer agreeing to the terms of your marriage to Primus. Apparently, the oracles are portending disaster for both families. I'm so sorry, Mallia, but you are no longer betrothed."

The engagement is off?

His eyes fill with such pain for me, I swallow my laugh of relief. Somehow, I manage a pensive look instead.

"I see," I say, biting back a snort.

He curses again and massages his forehead. "I know I should have told you sooner, but I was hoping to change his mind at today's meeting at the baths. He wouldn't move on the matter. And then you spoke of the Varro-Ursus union with such delight, obviously envisioning your own wedding. I couldn't bear to keep it from you any longer. I'm truly sorry, Mallia. The man is a fool."

I suck in my lips to keep my amusement in check.

So the big secret is that I'm free of the pretentious fiancé I had no interest in marrying? Severus was right about my investigative prowess.

I wait until my father pulls me into a comforting embrace to free the relieved grin from my soul.

JASON

I have a lot to learn about being a personal valet. Until now, I've known body slaves as the ones who deliver the demands of their masters, or stand by quietly while they feast and get drunk. They hold the bowls when their owners vomit and wipe the spit from their faces. They summon other servants and then dutifully watch while their masters rape and beat them.

Fortunately, Severus has plenty of patience for training me, and so far, it seems like my main duty involves serving as a shadow to the powerful man. After a lifetime of horror, I'm still having trouble accepting this abrupt new chapter.

"You're quiet today," Severus observes, glancing up from the scrolls on his desk.

My concerned gaze darts to his. "I'm sorry, my lord. Should I be doing something else? I wasn't sure of my duties while you work."

Understanding warms his eyes as he smiles. "No, that's not what I meant. Come over here."

I do as instructed and wait as he spreads open what appears to be a map.

It's still early enough in the day that sunlight from the open window illuminates the lines and letters etched into the parchment.

Severus rises from his chair and mirrors my position on the other side of the desk. He leans in and runs his fingers across the scroll in deliberate paths.

"Rome is here, and the Empire stretches from here to here to here," he explains in a coaching tone. "Legatus Nepos reports that he's conquered this region here."

I follow his movements, confused by the trajectory of his outline. "I'm sorry, my lord, but I can't read. What is this region he says he's conquered?"

"Northern Britannia."

Surprised, I squint at the lines and curves. "And you're certain the legatus claims to have conquered all of this Northern Britannia?"

Severus straightens and scans me with a curious look. "That news surprises you. Why?"

I clear my throat and fidget with the wide leather belt of my new uniform. A deep green thigh-length tunic and soft leather sandals complete the ensemble. I've never worn such fine wool, and without the simple wristband marking me as a slave, it would be hard to distinguish my status from the free plebeians on the streets.

All this fancy uniform has done, though, is make me more uncertain. More out of place in a role I was taught to regard completely differently than the way Severus is watching me now. His look of expectation—almost respect—has me questioning everything.

I shift on my feet, trying to determine how to respond. He can't possibly be interested in my opinion, and yet that's what—

"Jason, if I didn't want to hear your thoughts, I wouldn't have asked," he says in a stern voice, drawing my gaze. "Why does it surprise you that Nepos has conquered Britannia? Well, besides the fact that he was never appointed legate of that province." A shadow filters over his face that he seems to shake off. "That's a story for another day."

I avert my focus back to the map, gathering the courage to speak. How is it that I can stand firm in the face of certain death in the arena but can't bring myself to discuss politics in a private study?

"It means nothing, I'm sure," I begin hesitantly. He shifts his weight with impatience, and I force the words out.

"Right before my last fight, Opius Plinius brought in a new shipment of slaves, prisoners-of-war mostly." Confidence builds when Severus leans forward with intense concentration. "Two were Britons, clansmen from the north, surrendered as hostages. They didn't speak much Greek or Latin, and I certainly didn't speak their language, but…"

I stop, suddenly hit with the full reality of what I'm about to do. Am I really going to question a claim of one of Rome's top generals?

"But what? Speak, boy!" Severus commands.

I stare at the map again, mustering the courage. It's not in my nature to back down from a fight, but this isn't a battleground I understand. Using a sword is completely different than wielding a tongue. Gladiator games are not political games.

Soft wool brushes my skin, reminding me my loyalties belong to Severus now.

I stand tall and meet his penetrating gaze. "They said their tribe was one of only three to surrender hostages to the Roman legions north of the wall. That, in fact, the native tribes had pushed Nepos almost to the cliffs at the water's edge. According to them, all three legions in Britannia were on their heels."

His eyes go wide, and I draw in a deep breath. "My lord, they boasted that Nepos is *losing* ground, not gaining it."

Severus stills as an ominous look spreads over his features. I remain stoic, despite the hammering of my pulse. I've been punished for much less than implying one of the most celebrated generals of Rome is a liar.

"Of course, that could all mean nothing," I hedge quickly. "What do they know? Petty officers who see only their small piece of the campaign, handed over to their enemies as slaves, so vindictive and bitter besides."

Severus still doesn't speak, his severe gaze locked on the map. He's clearly disturbed, though I can't tell if it's from fear, concern, or rage. Maybe all three.

I shouldn't have spoken. If I've learned anything, it's that silence fuels survival infinitely better than words.

"How much do slaves talk?" he asks in a dark tone.

I wince and instinctively step back from the desk. "Please, my lord. I didn't mean to implicate others. Any punishment must fall on me. I—"

"Son, listen to me." He grips my arm, tugging me to face him. His gaze locks on mine, revealing a sliver of the complex man before me. "Your information has proven incredibly valuable. I only wondered how much more you have."

A wave of relief washes through me. I take a full breath for the first time in a while.

"My lord, slaves talk all the time. So do their masters when they consider them nothing more than a stool in their dressing room."

Chapter XI

MALLIA

The Emperor's palace is buzzing about the sudden promotion of the injured gladiator to esteemed personal attendant. The conversion of a revered death machine into a house slave is strange enough. Stranger still that it puts that death machine in the heart of Rome's elite.

While Severus and Jason seem numb to the open attention, Aurelia hasn't stopped complaining since we reclined for the evening meal in the Emperor's private dining room.

The small triclinium just off the Imperator's private peristyle boasts a much more tranquil atmosphere than the lavish banquet hall of the palace's public reception area. Severus and the Emperor recline on one of the three long couches circling a large central table piled high with gourmet delicacies. Aurelia and I whisper to each other on another couch.

Beneath the hum of a lyre, slaves replenish our glasses with pear and citrus-infused wine, while we help ourselves to the honey-glazed roasted lamb, milk-fattened snails, stuffed dormice, and a variety of richly seasoned sides.

I had my fill long ago, and I now pick at the remains of asparagus drenched in olive oil and garum.

"I don't understand why my uncle would do such a thing," Aurelia whines, eyeing the couch on the far side of the table. "It's such a waste!"

I follow her gaze to where Jason stands at attention behind his new master, and my pulse picks up like it did when we first entered the room. He makes a fine figure in his new uniform—tall, sculpted, and dressed in a dark green military-style tunic, studded belt, and sandals. But even if he were barefoot and wearing the drab off-white tunic of the other house slaves, he'd stand out.

It's not surprising he resembles a bodyguard more than a valet, given his talents. Severus didn't conscript a decorated warrior because he needed help getting dressed in the morning. A smile threatens my lips when I consider my role in the development. No doubt my tongue-lashing of General Severus contributed to Jason's abrupt reassignment.

Very few people would be confused by the former gladiator's new position, but unfortunately, one of those few is lounging beside me. Her obsession with Jason means her complaint is likely coming from between her thighs, not her head.

"Severus is an accomplished legatus," I say, wiping my sticky fingers on a linen napkin. "Who better to serve as his right hand than another accomplished warrior?"

Aurelia crinkles her nose as she plucks a snail from the tray in front of us. "Well, it's not right. I know my uncle loves the man, but to make such a gift is absurd."

"How do you know it was a gift? Maybe General Severus purchased him outright. It was he who found him in the first place, wasn't it? Obviously, he recognized his value."

Aurelia's scowl indicates I'm approaching my threshold for defiance. Being the established voice of reason only grants me so much immunity, and I'm already on shaky ground after my interference the other day.

"Really, Mallia, whose side are you on, anyway? Maybe Cornelia was right about you and that gladiator."

I flutter a dismissive laugh. "I didn't realize there were sides. I'm just trying to soothe your disappointment."

"Disappointment? Over a slave? Please." She tosses a cascade of blonde curls and braids over her shoulder.

I take a long sip of wine, seeing no point in challenging her over the lie.

"I heard your engagement was called off," she quips with the cruel glint of retaliation. "Is it true?"

I think I do a good job pretending to be injured as I swirl the remaining liquid in my glass. "It's true. Terms could not be worked out."

Satisfied with her retribution, Aurelia sighs and places a jeweled hand on my arm. "There now, you are better off. I said from the beginning that silly man was no match for you."

"Perhaps, you're right." I play along with a weak smile.

"Of course I'm right. What happened? Did he explain?"

She lifts her glass for more wine, and a slave rushes over to fill it.

"All my father said was that the family no longer agreed to the terms of our marriage due to bad omens. I don't know the specifics."

"Sounds like an excuse to me. Do you think Primus found another woman?" she asks, lifting higher on her elbow.

I almost laugh at her lust for a scandal. As if she doesn't cause enough of her own.

"I don't know. Maybe but I doubt it. Probably something silly like a dowry dispute."

"Dowry dispute? How in the name of Jupiter could a merchant give up a chance to marry into a Roman title? They must be mad. I know a dozen families who would kill for a union with the Justus family. I will speak to my uncle."

"Oh no, my lady," I rush out. "There's no need to trouble yourself with such things. I know how busy you are. My father will take care of finding another match."

Aurelia quickly relaxes into the cushion, making me fairly certain she had no intention of interceding.

"Well, you're probably right." She selects a chunk of bread from the tray and swirls it over her plate to sop up the decadent sauces from the meal. "One day you will make a stunning bride. I'm sure of it."

Maybe, but right now I'm more consumed by an overwhelming urge for another conversation with Severus.

TACITUS

I wave Severus into the vestibulum of my two-bedroom flat, surprised by the late-night visit. I'm even more surprised to see Argus enter behind him.

"Are you alone?" Severus asks, glancing past me into the darkened space—most likely in search of a mistress.

"I am," I reply, suppressing the sting of the subtle rebuke. "What is it?"

"Light another lamp. Let's sit."

Argus saunters past him toward the folding stools leaning against the wall behind my small desk.

As I ignite a lamp on a bronze stand in the center of the room, Severus shutters the window, and Argus sets up the stools at the meal table.

"Sir, before we get started, Argus and I would like to ask you a question," I say while we work. "Actually, it's for Jason when you next see him."

Severus shoves the edge of his cloak behind him in irritation but returns a curt nod. "Fine. What is it?"

I cast a quick glance at Argus before focusing back on the general. "We have concerns about Lepidus and his operations."

"Lepidus? What of that swine?" Severus grunts, yanking one of the stools from the table. He drops into it with an impatient look.

I wince at the added tension, regretting my timing for this topic. Argus pretends to fidget with the hinge of another stool.

"Well, sir," I force out. "We think he might be spreading his business to other districts."

"*My* district," Argus spits out, coming to attention. "I've seen him around Crassus Pass. He's been harassing one of my neighbor girls."

Severus curses and rubs at his dusted chin. "That *porca* is a monster. Actually, no, worse than that, but he's not our problem right now. We have bigger things to worry about."

"Of course, sir," I cut in. "We're not looking to eliminate him…yet. We just need information, and there are rumors…" I stop at the severe look hardening over the general's face.

"Rumors?" he echoes in a cold tone. His gaze passes between us in a silent warning.

Too late to stop now.

Argus tugs at his beard and clears his throat. "We were, uh, hoping Jason would know something about Lepidus's operation that could help us."

"No," Severus snaps.

We shrink at his murderous glare.

"Just a few questions!" Argus persists. "We'd only—"

"I said no! You will not put that boy through any more trauma, understood? Now, are you interested in why I've called you together or not?"

We swallow the rest of our protests and nod.

"Good. Then, sit."

I take a stool, but Argus hovers in the background, arms crossed.

"I don't have much time, and now I have even less, so let's not be delicate," Severus says in a matter-of-fact tone. "Tacitus, you were included in many strategic conversations with Legatus Nepos and his officers prior to your discharge. What can you tell me about his plans for Britannia?"

"Britannia?" I ask, straightening on the stool. "Isn't he there now?"

"He is."

I sink back and search my memory. My stomach aches as I sift through graphic, painful images of my last days with the Sixth.

"We were still on our way north when I left," I say, squinting toward the lamp. "I don't know much. Only that he had orders to assist Titullus and take the region at all costs."

"Orders from whom?" Severus asks. "Britannia already had a legate in Titullus. Why was Nepos even headed there?"

Confused by the question, I glance from Severus to Argus and back to Severus. I'm usually one step ahead of those around me, but I can't guess where he's going with this. Ignorance isn't something I tolerate well.

"I assume the Emperor," I reply. "It would be up to him to commission campaigns and appoint provincial governors for imperial provinces, correct?"

"Of course," Severus agrees, ever more cryptic.

I dart a look between them again. "What is it? What's wrong?"

Severus leans forward with a grave expression. Even Argus's usual humor has been shaded by a heavy brow.

"It's time to act," Severus says in a low voice. "There's a threat forming, a serious one, and we can no longer afford to wait."

"A threat involving Legatus Nepos?" I ask. "In addition to the alliance of Senator Varro and Ursus?"

"Maybe *included* with the alliance of Varro and Ursus. We can't rule out the possibility they're all connected."

Air leaves my lungs in a sharp exhale. A plot like that would be… catastrophic.

"We don't know the specifics yet," Severus continues. "But we do know that our enemies are advancing. As their offensive grows, so must ours. Where's your cooking brazier?"

I blink in surprise, but Severus' stern look allows for no discussion. Pushing to my feet, I swallow my questions and lead him through a doorway to the culina, my small kitchen nook.

"Excellent. Ignite it and then meet us back at the table while the fire burns hot."

"Sir, it's—"

He lifts a hand, silencing my protest. I cast another look toward Argus, who shrugs.

With the charcoal embers still smoldering from the evening meal, it doesn't take long to bring the fire back to a healthy flame.

While the brazier heats, I rejoin Argus and Severus standing in silence near the table. Severus scans each of us slowly, as though considering every aspect of our being.

I swallow hard, breathing in the abrasive scent of scorched charcoal.

After a long pause, he pulls a small bronze seal from the red lining of his cloak and heads to the culina. Using a pair of tongs, he shoves the seal among the burning embers.

My heart beats wildly as I watch the bronze disc turn an angry red.

"Argus, Tacitus, you have been chosen for a purpose greater than the common pursuits of men," he begins in a grave tone. "A duty marked as a great honor, and a greater curse. A burden that, should you accept, will follow you even unto death."

He twists back to face us, eyes blazing as hot as the flame-lit seal.

"Men, are you ready to accept the seal of *Septem Fideles*?"

Excitement explodes in my chest. Argus and I exchange a surprised, eager look.

"We are," we reply in unison.

"Good. Then do you swear on your life and the supreme gods to protect the Emperor and remain loyal to your calling?"

"We do."

Blood pounds in my ears. My hands tingle with nerves and excitement.

"Do you swear on your life and the supreme gods to forsake all other earthly pursuits and devote yourself solely to the service and values of *Septem Fideles*?"

"We do."

Severus nods, scanning us slowly with a somber expression. "Then come forward and present yourselves. From this day forward, you no longer exist as individuals. You are now *Septem Fideles*, Ghost Warriors, Servants of Rome."

We remove our tunics, and Severus withdraws the seal from the embers. He uses a folded cloth to grip the handle and approaches me first.

I take a deep breath, bracing myself as he presses the scalding emblem into the bare skin just above my right hip. Pain sears through me. The smell of burnt flesh fills the room in a macabre incense to honor this sacred pact.

I absorb the agony with stoic poise like every time I've borne such pain. Only this time, I wear the permanent scar with honor.

"Long live the Emperor," Severus says, offering a firm salute.

"Long live the Emperor," I echo, returning it.

Air moves back into my lungs. Tension releases from my shoulders.

Finally.

I can breathe with a purpose again.

Argus grins and bumps me out of the way. "My turn."

MALLIA

I search for Severus in his study at the palace on my next visit to Aurelia. It's funny how the frequent social calls that were once a burden have become a necessity.

It's also becoming clear why Severus recruited someone with my connections for whatever it is he's orchestrating. I may have been hesitant about betraying my own circles at first, but after what happened to Jason at the hands of "the elite," I'm ready to burn this whole cursed system to the ground.

Maybe one day we will.

I freeze in the entryway of Severus's study at the sight of Jason, still unaccustomed to his constant presence. His hazel eyes flash with just enough emotion to send a streak of fire through me when they collide with mine. Has he forgiven me for my blundering attempts to help him? Does he think about me as I think constantly of him? Does he wonder what it would be like to taste my lips, run his hands over…

Stop, Mallia.

Of course not. And nor should I.

He doesn't acknowledge me after the initial spark of recognition, and I do my best to do the same. While everything in me wants to cross the room, take his hands, and explore his warm skin again, I force myself to ignore his presence altogether.

"What can I do for you, my lady?" Severus asks with something between a sigh and a smile.

"You can answer a question." I lower myself to my favorite chair in front of his desk.

"Which is?"

"My engagement to Pius's son fell through."

I watch closely for a reaction. The slight widening of his eyes and crease in his forehead resemble legitimate surprise.

"Is that so? Sorry to hear it."

I narrow my gaze at him, fighting the urge to flicker a glance at Jason. "You wouldn't happen to know anything about that, would you?"

He studies me in that careful, pensive way he does. "Is that your question?"

I cross my arms over my light blue palla, making it clear I'm not leaving until he gives me answers. His heavy exhale borders on a resigned sigh.

To be fair, he should be used to me by now.

He scoops a sealed scroll from the desk and holds it out to Jason. "Make sure this letter gets filed with today's dispatches. I need it delivered as soon as possible."

Jason takes the document and bows. His gaze brushes me briefly on his way out, and I suck in a quick breath, annoyed by my body's scalding reaction to his attention. Is it always going to be like this? How are we supposed to work together to save the world when my insides burn up every time he's close?

Severus follows my stare to the empty doorway. "He makes quite a figure in that uniform, doesn't he?" His mischievous tone only irritates me more.

I hope my glare covers my blush.

"Don't change the subject," I fire back. "What is Pius's objection to my family?"

"You were so in love with the man?" he asks dryly.

"That's irrelevant," I quip. "Did you have a hand in his rejection or not?"

Severus pushes up from his desk and comes around to take a chair near mine. "I must confess that the dissolution of your engagement is news to me."

Frowning, I search his face for signs of deception. "So, you knew nothing of this? This wasn't some *Septem Fideles* interference? A way to keep me in Senator Justus's home so I could spy?"

All humor drains from his face as he adjusts in his seat. "You think we'd manipulate your life to such an extent without your knowledge? Without your consent?"

My resolve wavers as I consider his words. "I would hope not, but…"

He slides his chair closer and clasps his hands in front of him. The gold signet ring on his left hand catches a glint of sunlight from the open window. I never noticed the griffin, the sacred emblem of his former command, etched into it.

"Mallia, while I can't say I'm saddened to hear you will not be removed from your very helpful position so you can marry a man you don't even like, I assure you we would never do such a thing without your consent. If you had asked, we would have helped. If we thought it must be done, we would have asked."

He leans back with a grave nod. "Pius acted on his own."

"So, if it wasn't *Septem Fideles,* what happened to change his mind? The excuses they gave don't ring true."

He shakes his head and rises, returning to his desk. "I don't know, but I know this proves one thing."

"What's that?"

His gaze drifts to me. "You're as important as we thought."

The room goes cold and then hot. My stomach twists as I scan his sincere expression in the filtered sunlight. "As who thought? Important to what?"

He remains silent, scouring me in a way that sends a shiver over my skin. I'm glad I harbor no secrets.

Just the one.

Then again, based on his earlier joke, my crush on his valet might not be a secret anymore. I need to be more careful.

"It's time, Mallia," he says in a somber tone. "*Septem Fideles* needs you as much as any skilled warrior. We don't just want your help. We want you to join us. We want you to become one of us."

My heart hammers behind my ribs. Excitement rushes from limb to limb.

"Last night two were commissioned, and now it's time for the third."

He retrieves a small object from a pouch on his desk and holds it up in the stream of dusty sunlight.

"Mallia Justa, will you accept the seal of *Septem Fideles*?"

Chapter XII

TACITUS

Captain Cassius Drusus Atticus evaluates me with casual authority in the atrium of Senator Varro's lavish urban villa. I maintain a stoic expression throughout the appraisal, though inside I'm burning with anticipation at my first assignment as a member of *Septem Fideles*.

It wasn't hard for Severus to convince me to take up arms again, even if my new "legion" is a small private security detail protecting a corrupt senator. Captain Atticus had been a respected soldier in his day, reaching the rank of *pilus prior* before losing a hand in Gaul. The seasoned man has done well for himself in the private sector by acquiring a good reputation for providing quality, skilled bodyguards.

I also have the advantage of coming highly recommended by General Severus.

"Severus assures me your discharge from the Sixth was not due to an issue I need to worry about," he says in a crisp warning.

"No, Captain. It was a personal dispute."

The man raises his brows while rubbing at a scar near the cleft of his clean-shaven chin. "Well, you have an impressive look about you, and Severus swears you are a smart, capable fighter."

He pauses again, and I hold my breath through another quick scan. Finally, he motions for me to follow. "Well, then, let's see what you can do."

Atticus leads me through the house toward an exit into a walled garden annex at the back of the villa. A wave of familiarity washes through me when we reach a small patch of sandy terrain, complete with a rack of weapons and target posts for training. Even better is the inviting clash of iron and steel from the men paired up on the sand. I've missed the pungent smell of sweat and sun from soldiers exerting themselves.

The clanging fizzles out at the appearance of Captain Atticus and his unknown companion. I feel the eyes of the other men, assessing me like I am them. I count ten, ranging from a few years younger than I am to older than Severus. Most appear to be of lower classes, though they bear arms with a comfort that indicates likely involvement with the legion auxiliaries.

"Helveticus! Messor! Glabrio! Step up."

Three men stride from their places around the sand, weapons swaying in a lazy tempo at their sides. Captain Atticus must not be wasting any time with his "test."

I study my soon-to-be opponents as they approach.

Helveticus is tall and lanky, which would give him a long reach. He also moves with a slight limp and will most likely favor his right side.

Messor's shorter stature is offset by thick, burly arms and a confident sneer. He holds a dagger in his left hand, but the muscles in his right arm are larger and more defined. He may be training with his left, but only to develop the same skill he will demonstrate with his right.

Glabrio stands several inches shorter than I, but he twirls his gladius in an absentminded flurry of steel. His speed will be matched by his enthusiasm based on the eager glint in his dark brown eyes.

"I was assured this man is a worthy opponent for any warrior," Captain Atticus announces. "Shall we test this claim?"

The onlookers clear a circle on the sand, buzzing with zeal for a fight. Would they kill me just to prove a point?

"Glabrio, you first," the captain says.

I relax when I realize they won't be attacking as one unit. This is an interview, after all, not an execution.

Glabrio advances with several quick steps. His gladius seems to fire in multiple directions at once, and I barely have time to draw my own before dodging to avoid a hole in my gut. At first, it's all I can do to deflect the rapid blows, but his frantic dance begins to show signs of a steady pattern. I watch his feet and quickly adapt to partner him.

The shift allows me to repel his sword with a force that sends the smaller man back a few paces. I reset into a solid stance, subtly taunting him with my patience.

The scowl that spreads over his face means he isn't accustomed to retreating, nor does he appreciate my relaxed approach. I take note of his quick temper and decide to leverage it into frustration, which will lead to an easy slide into defeat.

Glabrio comes forward again, his feet clapping the sand and sending sprays of dust around us. I see an opening for a strike, but don't take it, choosing instead to defend against a few more from him. My patience is rewarded when he lets out the telltale grunt of a man who knows he's facing an opponent who's holding back. He swings again, this time with tremendous force that weakens his accuracy. I easily spin away from the thrust, and Glabrio barely keeps his footing as his arm circles around from the overzealous swing, nearly throwing him down.

While he resets, my gaze flickers to the other opponents waiting for their turn. I need to end this and move on.

Glabrio lunges again, and I smash the capulus of my gladius into his side. He falls with a groan, but jumps back up. His second angry run yields another collision with the hilt of my sword, and Captain Atticus steps in to grab the man's arm before he can further injure his ribs.

"Okay. A gallant effort, my friend, but I think we've seen what we needed. Helveticus and Messor, you're up."

I grip my sword, bracing for the next trial. I can't tell if Atticus always intended to pair the final two, or if my effortless dismantling of Glabrio resulted in a change of plans. Either way, I'll have to show more vulnerability if I'm going to convince these men I belong with them.

Two opponents prove to be more of a challenge anyway.

Messor presents with a left-handed attack, but I prepare for a spontaneous shift to the right. Likewise, I'm not fooled by Helveticus's sloppy lunge at my chest when I realize he's balancing on his bad leg. These men are tested and know better than to display their best before they've gauged their opponent.

Unfortunately for them, Glabrio's weak showing hadn't allowed for many clues, and their read of me isn't nearly as strong as mine is of them. To be fair, I don't have many weaknesses to identify. Growing up in a prestigious military family means I've been training since the day I was born.

Messor has traded his practice dagger for the standard gladius and flexes his wrist in a low motion as he paces to my left. Helveticus roams along the right, his longer spatha rigid in his tightly clenched fist.

I've noticed the increased popularity of the spatha over the last few months. It's becoming the weapon of choice for trained fighters, even some gladiators. The infantry in my legion cohort hadn't yet adopted the longer sword before my departure, although a few cavalry auxiliaries supporting the Sixth had abandoned the gladius in favor of the extended blade. Personally, I prefer the tighter control of the shorter weapon in close combat, but wouldn't be surprised if I found a spatha in my hand at some point soon.

Maybe even today, based on the way Helveticus clings to it like a lethal limb extension.

Helveticus charges first, but only a fraction of a second before Messor. I arch from right to left, deflecting both blows before jumping back to regain my stance. The challengers don't allow much grace and advance again with a joint attack that forces me to choose which limb to preserve. I block the spatha, but end up with a shallow gash from the Messor's gladius.

A cheer erupts from the audience at the first drawing of blood by their man. I let the insult fuel my resolve.

After several more lunges and deflections, I realize my opponents still haven't shown their strong sides. They're toying with me, as I did with Glabrio, waiting for the moment when I'll equal their weak advances, so they can switch and easily dispose of me. They've probably played this game with their prey many times before, which will work to my advantage if it breeds overconfidence and routine movements.

It's obvious I won't be able to beat them two-on-one by sheer strength. My best maneuver will be to play along.

At the next parry, I stumble on purpose, grunting as Messor's foot crashes into my ribs. Helveticus launches a kick of his own, grinning from the easy victory.

While everyone focuses on the feet smashing into a stranger who seems to have surrendered, I ignore the laughter and taunts and focus instead on my opponents' faces.

The two men are snickering, exchanging jeers as they bear down, incredulous that this supposedly skilled soldier has fallen like a new recruit.

Sure enough, a few seconds later, I spot the puffs of easy victory I've been waiting for. They consider this battle all but over.

I wait until they're distracted by their own arrogance to roll hard into their shins, knocking them to the ground.

Jumping up, I grab Messor's left arm and Helveticus's right at the same time and smash them together. They yelp and drop their weapons, which I recover, while leaping to my feet.

It all happens so quickly, the audience is left stunned to see their companions sprawled out on the sand with their own blades at their throats.

Silence gives way to shocked murmurs, followed by a sudden burst of furious laughter from Captain Atticus.

He raises his hand in approval, stalking toward us with a grin. "Well done! *Thunder of Jupiter,* that was the most entertaining match I've seen in months!"

He laughs again and reaches down to help Messor to his feet while I assist Helveticus. The men stagger a few steps, nursing their bruised wrists, but the look in their eyes is respect, not resentment.

"Well played, my friend," Messor says, extending his good hand.

"And a good fight to you," I reply. "I wouldn't have bested you in skill…at least, not if you had switched to your strong hand."

The man looks surprised and then grins. "Perhaps you're right."

I return it. "Perhaps."

ARGUS

"Drunk again, I see!"

I lift my head from the grimy tavern table to find Livianus hovering over me—right on time, like all good former centurions.

"Is there another state to be in at this hour?" I mutter.

Livianus snickers and drops to the bench across from me with his cup. "It seems not much has changed since your legion days."

I huff a laugh and take another swallow of my drink. "Not much has happened to warrant it."

Livianus smirks and finishes off the remnants of his own. "True enough."

"What about you? How's retired life?" I ask, blinking away the spinning room.

The other man shrugs and signals for another cup. "Not what I thought. Never would've guessed I'd miss serving under that arrogant *porca*, Nepos, but here we are."

I nod my agreement. "Here…we are," I slur out.

Livianus curses and runs a hand over his tightly cropped dark hair. "You know, the worst part about being back isn't even the city itself. It's the ignorant swine who live here. They have no idea what it's like out there. How good they have it."

"Out where? In Britannia?"

"Gods, everywhere," he mumbles.

He grabs the server's arm after she refills his cup so she can't leave. After inhaling the fresh pour, he holds it up for a refill.

"It's the Roman way," I grunt, scowling into my drink once we're alone again. "Death by indulgence."

Livianus grunts. "Makes me sick."

"And so we drink."

"Yeah, true patriots, I guess."

I snort a laugh. "You know me. Patriot through and through. So, tell me about Britannia. I got kicked out before we made it up there."

Livianus's humor fades as he picks at a scratch on the table. "Vah, it's a total disaster up there. As much as I hate being back here, it's better than that cursed frontier."

"Yeah? Why's that?" I take another gulp of my drink.

Livianus shrugs with a distant look toward the serving area opening to the street. "Place is barbaric above the wall. Cold. So many different enemies—it's like a game trying to guess what monster is going to try to slit your throat next. Tribes are like swarms of insects. Always there, stinging 'til you bleed and then dissolving into those cursed rocks and fog. Don't even get me started on the channel and its impossible cliffs."

"Nepos seems intent on conquering it."

"Intent? Try obsessed." He quiets and glances around the crowded tavern before leaning close. "The man is a lunatic. A *verrux* fool."

I raise my eyebrows. "Really? How so?"

Livianus shrugs, disturbed by whatever memories are haunting him at the moment. "You wouldn't believe me if I told you."

"I'd believe a lot more now than I would have a few months ago. That's for sure."

He quiets, staring into his cup in a trancelike state. A loud cheer erupts from a neighboring table, jerking him back to the present. He shakes off the waking nightmare with a wave of his hand.

"Vah! There I go again. Listen to us. Two drunken soldiers whining about the old times." But the way his eyes shift makes it clear there's more. A lot more.

Unfortunately, Livianus isn't drunk enough yet.

I force a laugh and call for more wine. Livianus will need it, and I'll make sure he's well-supplied.

Despite all appearances to the contrary, I haven't had a drop of liquor in days as I prepare to execute my first assignment.

Chapter XIII

MALLIA

The burn has mostly healed, but I still feel the small mark on my hip as I float through the halls of the palace toward Aurelia's private rooms.

Severus waited a week to issue my first assignment, and although I'd been impatient to begin, I understood his rationale. I may be valuable, but I'm also young and inexperienced. He trained me for hours these past few days, prepping me on expectations and equipping me with basic skills for gaining intelligence. I haven't met the other members of *Septem Fideles*—who are already deeply embedded in their own missions—but Severus promised I would soon.

A smile flutters over my lips as I consider how my brand gives me equality with the other great soldiers. I'm also a ghost warrior, maybe not as strong in body, but certainly of the same value. Otherwise, I wouldn't have been honored with the seal that joins us in a permanent bond.

Excitement mixes with a touch of anxiety as I enter the private triclinium for the evening cena and my first assignment: convincing Aurelia we need to make a new friend.

"Mallia! Darling, I've hardly seen you in days!" Aurelia cries, reclined on one of three large couches connected in a U-shape around a central table. Each is designed to accommodate up to three guests, but I recline on another, since it appears it will just be the two of us this evening. The table is already covered in snacks, and a slave pads over to hand me a glass of diluted wine.

"I'm sorry for being distant, but with the dissolved engagement, my family thought it best to remain private for a time."

"Of course! You poor creature." She plucks a date stuffed with nuts and honey from a tray and takes a dainty bite.

While Aurelia nibbles, I use the opportunity to sip my wine and search for any clues about her state of mind. She's dressed less formally than usual, and the simple braids of her hair make it clear she hasn't had other visitors today, nor is she planning to receive any.

"Well, it's for the best, I'm sure," I say in a resigned tone. "I'll find a way to recover."

Aurelia lets out an indignant breath. "Of course it is! You are well above his station. It infuriates me that they would dare to insult your family."

"Thank you, my lady. It means a lot to hear you say it." I fake interest in the tray of dried fruit. "Speaking of weddings," I say casually. "I didn't see you at the Varro-Ursus union."

Aurelia's dismissive huff sounds as forced as I hoped. I glance over to see a crease in her chalk-dusted pale forehead.

"Yes, well, my uncle refused to attend, and I could hardly go without him—could I?" She flips her hair behind her and selects another date from the tray.

"Of course," I say, mirroring her action. "It's a shame, though. It was quite a celebration."

A pout slides over her face. "Vibius Acilius Ursus is known for putting on a show."

"He certainly spared no expense to celebrate the marriage of his son. And Senator Varro's daughter looked stunning. She wore the latest jewels and silk from her new father-in-law's vast store of imports."

Aurelia's chewing slows as her dark blonde eyebrows knit. "Really? They were of quality?"

"The finest." I pretend to search for the perfect olive on another tray. "I've never seen anything like it. I can only imagine the collection Arata must have at her villas with a father-in-law who owns half the ships in the Empire."

Aurelia sags on the couch, her jealous mind already working furiously. I see the scheme I've planted forming in her head.

"Well, then, I'm very disappointed I wasn't present to show my support to the happy couple. I suppose I have no choice but to invite Arata to accompany us and offer my congratulations in person. She must be terribly bored now that she's married. I'm sure she'd appreciate new friends."

I bite into the olive to hide my grin. She's so predictable. "Of course, my lady. I'm sure Arata would be grateful for your kindness."

Aurelia nods and pushes up on her elbow, satisfied with her charitable plan.

Maybe this ghost warrior role will be easier than I thought.

ARGUS

Severus is already waiting in Tacitus's flat when I burst inside for our meeting. I shut the door and stalk toward the table where they're seated on stools. The other men study me in amusement as I drop to the empty one.

"You clearly have the most urgent update, so you begin," Severus says.

"I will, but only because you're right." I lean forward, scanning their shadowed faces. "I just left the tavern after an evening with our old friend Livianus, a recently retired centurion from Nepos's Legio Six. Remember him?" I direct at Tacitus.

"I do," he says, scratching at his temple. "Pilus Prior of the Eighth Cohort. Excellent soldier."

I nod and adjust onto my elbows. My bouncing knee crashes into the underside of the short table, and I force it still.

"I got him very drunk and learned some interesting information. Apparently, many of the officers are starting to worry Nepos has lost his mind."

"Really? How so?" Severus asks, all humor draining from his face.

My focus shifts between them. "It's said he refuses to admit defeat, even after it's apparent he's lost."

Severus sinks back in his stool. "And? That only proves he's brave and persistent, essential qualities in any good legatus."

I shake my head. "No, that's not what I mean. I'm talking *in actual form*. After the battle—after the enemy has left with their spoils, as the legionaries lie dying on the battlefield—the great Legatus Nepos calls his remaining officers to the praetorium to celebrate with food and drink, as though he has won a great victory!"

An eerie silence spreads over the room. It makes me sick to think of a commander feasting while his men's corpses rot nearby. Shadows from the lamp etch deep lines into my companions' faces as well.

"You're certain?" Severus asks after a long pause. "Livianus has seen this with his own eyes?"

"On several occasions." I take a deep breath. "And that's only the beginning. According to Livianus, Nepos refuses to adapt his strategy and forces the men to keep traditional formations—even over the cliffs and rocky terrain where it's impossible. Almost an entire century was lost in one battle when the ground gave way beneath them."

"What?" Tacitus cries, pounding the table.

"Wait, it gets worse. Livianus said of the three legions Nepos commands in Britannia, the equivalent of an entire legion and its auxiliaries are gone—destroyed by the local tribes in guerrilla battles as he keeps pushing them further north into hostile territory."

Tacitus jumps to his feet. "An entire legion! That can't be true. They're not even supposed to be fighting a war in Britannia. Nepos told us we were only going to restore order at the request of the provincial governor, Titullus."

I shrug and rub at my close-cropped beard. "How would we know the truth? The only formal information we have is from Nepos and his officers' dispatches to Rome. Besides, I didn't say a legion was lost—just the equivalent of a legion. According to Livianus, what remained of the Sixth, Twelfth, and Second was incorporated into the Sixth and Second. Titullus's Legio Twelve has been completely disbanded."

"Only two are left? That explains why Nepos is trying to raise another," Tacitus growls, eyes blazing.

We quiet in somber agreement.

"So he lied to the Emperor and Senate," Severus says in a harsh tone. "Nepos claimed the new legion was needed to maintain stability in the province after the death of Titullus."

"The legate of Britannia is dead?" Tacitus asks, eyes wide.

Severus returns a solemn nod. "Reportedly killed in battle shortly after Nepos arrived. Not sure which is more surprising: Titullus's death or the fact that he was supposedly on a battlefield while all reports had him holding assizes on the other side of the province."

Tacitus exhales sharply with a slow shake of his head. "Well, his death would certainly be a convenient twist for someone intent on writing their own history."

I smirk and angle toward my friend. "Why, Tacitus, are you implying our great Legatus Nepos isn't just a liar but also a murderer?"

Tacitus returns a morbid smile. "At the very least, it appears our man is something other than a 'great legatus.' But I could have told you that before any of this," he adds under his breath.

I shudder through a dark memory and turn to Severus. "So now what?"

He rubs his chin, his hard gaze fixed on the flickering oil lamp. "Now we find out who else is involved and why."

JASON

I follow Severus and the Emperor at a respectful distance as they stroll through the immaculate palace gardens. A seemingly endless variety of trees, flowers, and plants weave around ornate marble columns, elaborate fountains, and shaded pergolas. Intermittent birdsongs mix with hushed human voices as the occasional peacock carelessly struts across the stone path.

Although it's been over two weeks since my promotion, I still wake every morning in disbelief at fortune's favorable hand. How I went from constant chains, beatings, and starvation to wandering stately gardens with Rome's elite is still a mystery to me. Even more inexplicable is how Severus treats me more like a son than a slave. He educates me with patience in all his activities, showing me respect I'm not accustomed to. It's been strange being exposed to the beauty of a world I've only known as ugly until now. For the first time in my life, I don't meet the sun of a new day with fear, but with anticipation.

I wish I could say the same of my restless nights.

The Emperor's brow sags in thought as Severus speaks to him in muted tones. I can't hear their words, but their body language conveys an intense subject. The Emperor nods and replies with an equally severe look.

We round a bend in the path, headed east toward a spectacular cluster of fountains.

Without warning, four armed men burst from the vegetation and rush toward the Emperor with clear intent. Cold dread sweeps through me as I draw my dagger and charge forward.

Screams erupt from the Emperor's party, but I barely hear them as I spring toward the attackers with a cry intended to draw the enemy's attention away from their targets. The intruders spin toward me, giving me a clear view of their peasant dress and legion-grade weapons. It's a strange combination, but there's no time for investigation.

Instead, I easily avoid the weak lunge of one man and send him to the ground with an elbow to his back. After retrieving his gladius, I dispatch two of the three remaining men in just a few strokes. The final man trembles before me, barely holding his weapon in front of him. Abject fear burns in his eyes, confusing me as much as why an untrained, destitute freedman would have a professional sword.

The Praetorian Guard has launched into action behind me, but I don't need their assistance. These assailants aren't seasoned warriors, but armed civilians, most likely zealots engaging in a poorly constructed act of political or religious aggression.

I'm already eliminating the final threat by the time the first member of the

Guard even reaches the scene. The terrified intruder swings a few haphazard thrusts before joining his comrades on the ground, blood pouring from his chest and throat.

While the other soldiers finish them off, I stalk back to my master's side.

"Are you okay, my lord? Imperator?" I scan them with concern.

The men nod while absently surveying the bloody scene, but don't appear as shaken as I expect.

"We need to get you to safety," I continue in an urgent tone. "There are probably others. Judging by their weak showing, this was likely a decoy to lower our defenses. The real threat must still be coming."

"Yes, thank you, Jason," the Emperor says, distracted. I watch in surprise as he returns to the carnage to address Verus Falco, the captain of his Praetorian Guard.

"But Imperator!" I call out after him. "My lord, please, you must..."

Severus places a firm hand on my arm.

"Walk with me, Jason."

"My lord?"

The general squeezes my elbow and pulls me further down the path, away from the others. "We are not in danger. Leave the weapon and walk with me. I'll explain everything."

I glance back at the retreating crowd, now concerned *and* confused. Reluctantly, I lay down the blood-soaked gladius and follow.

Severus leads us through a maze of fountains toward a secluded grove of olive trees. He lowers to a stone bench and motions for me to join him.

Once we're seated, he shifts to face me. "The men you killed were not assassins but convicted criminals in line for execution. There were several hidden snipers, armed with bows, stationed around the garden in case they got too close to the Emperor."

I squint at him, replaying the events in my head. "How do you know?"

Severus settles a grim look on my face. "Because I arranged it. On behalf of the Emperor."

My chest goes tight. A cold shiver runs over me. "I don't understand. Why would he arrange an attempt on his own life, and then contract snipers to stop it?"

"He didn't," Severus says with a quick twist of his lips. "He arranged a test for you."

"A test for what?"

His gray eyes sift over my face, searching, probing. Distant shouts remind us of the violent events that just occurred.

"What you just saw may not have been real, but it's a very real possibility that could occur at any moment," Severus explains in a solemn tone. "The Emperor faces constant threats to his life. Some trivial, others serious."

He leans forward and looks me in the eyes. "There's a severe one brewing that could change the course of Rome if we don't stop it—a threat so great we don't even know the depths of its scale and power yet."

He relaxes slightly and fixes a preoccupied look on the geometric design near our feet. "We have many enemies, Jason. More than you know—more than *we* know. What we need now are allies."

I remain quiet, still not sure what any of this has to do with me. Is he selling me to someone else? Sending me back to the ludus after all? I don't even know if I passed or failed "the test."

Severus's dour expression transforms into almost paternal concern as he slides his attention back to me.

"I'm sorry for the deception," he says. "If there had been another way, we would've done it, but we had to see your heart and where your true loyalties lie. Now we know."

An icy rush floods through me. "You know what?"

"That we can trust you. That your values align with ours. That your instinct is to protect the Emperor at the risk of your own life."

The hair bristles on my arms despite the warm breeze ruffling the vegetation around us.

He twists toward me, his eyes filling with a mixture of affection and resolve. "And now that we know, it's time for you to know about *Septem Fideles*."

MALLIA

"Oh, Arata, we're so happy you could join us!" Aurelia coos as we settle in her private exedra. "I've been lamenting for weeks that I was unable to attend your wedding. Wasn't I, Mallia?"

I force a tight smile at the lie. "It's all she talked about."

Our guest clasps her petite hands in her lap, amber eyes warm with gratitude. "Of course, my lady! I was honored by your invitation to visit today."

I hadn't been sure what to expect of Senator Varro's daughter. Even at her wedding, she was so swarmed by constant attention, I didn't speak more than five words to her. Now, dressed with casual elegance in a pale rose stola and yellow shawl, it's becoming clear she holds none of the pretense common in our circles. While Aurelia spent hours decorating herself and plotting to impress the wealthy young woman, Arata has shown nothing but grace and humility.

My mission is to convince Arata to accept me as a new friend. It's fortuitous that I might actually like her.

"I was fortunate enough to attend," I say with a genuine smile. "You looked magnificent, Arata."

Pink splotches color her cheeks, surprising me again. Modest too?

"That's sweet," she says through a soft laugh. "I'm sure you will be just as lovely in your own upcoming ceremony. I heard about your engagement to the eldest son of Placidius Pius."

"Oh, we don't discuss that," Aurelia says in a conspiratorial whisper. "The engagement is off."

Arata shifts toward me on her couch. "Oh? I'm sorry." Like everything else, the frown on her pretty face looks sincere.

"It's for the best," I reply. "I can only trust the Fates on the matter."

"Well, of course you're right," Arata agrees. "Pius is a friend of my father's. I've met his son Primus a few times. You may be more comfortable without him."

I snort a laugh at her wry grin.

A warm breeze filters through the curtains forming the open wall to the peristyle. I breathe in the sweet, exotic scent of jasmine.

"How's married life?" I ask Arata, redirecting the conversation to something more helpful.

Her serene expression hardens ever-so-slightly, and the tight smile appears more forced than the others. "Well enough, I suppose. Lurio travels a lot, so I rarely see him. I spend most of my time at my father's house."

I swallow a surge of excitement. Tacitus has been assigned to her father's guard detail. If she's there a lot, that could prove very opportune for our mission.

"I'd do the same," I say, sipping my chilled mint water. "I'd much rather spend time with my family than be alone in a new villa."

Arata's smooth skin flushes again. "Yes, I suppose. Time with family is always a blessing."

She exchanges a suggestive look with Aurelia, who bursts out laughing.

"Who is he?" Aurelia cries, straightening on her couch. "You must tell us!"

Arata's eyes crinkle with innocent mischief. "I'm not sure what you mean, my lady. I'm a married woman."

Aurelia laughs. "Your lover is a slave then," she guesses, but Arata shakes her head.

"No." She twists her hands in the soft silk of her stola, biting her lip. "He's one of my father's bodyguards, but you mustn't say anything!"

Aurelia claps in delight. "You scandalous woman!" A grin stretches across her face.

Arata continues chewing her lip, her embarrassed gaze running over the floor. "Really, it's nothing. Just the fantasy of a bored socialite. I haven't even spoken to him." She flutters a dismissive laugh. "It's nothing more than a silly crush, but it makes visits to my father's home much more…enjoyable."

Aurelia sags back to the cushion, probably disappointed the "scandal" is so dull, but I'm fascinated. Our married target has a crush on one of her father's bodyguards? There must be something in this we can use.

"Well, his name at least," Aurelia says, boredom seeping back into her demeanor as she sifts through a tray of honey cakes.

"I don't know his full name, but the other men refer to him as Tacitus."

I nearly choke on a swallow of water.

Tacitus? *Our* Tacitus? Was that his mission? To seduce Lurio's wife?

"He's different than the others," she continues in a wistful tone. Her shy smile sends a trickle of dread through me. "Based on his bearing, he must come from a family of quality. It's said he was a former officer. He is quite skilled."

"In arms or in bed?" Aurelia snickers.

Arata inhales sharply, pressing a hand to her warm cheek. "In arms, of course. I wouldn't know of the other."

"Is he handsome at least?" Aurelia mumbles through a bite of pastry.

Arata squirms, a timid smile playing on her lips. "Very. I'm not the only one with a crush. He's become the talk of the household."

Aurelia releases a dramatic sigh. "Well, we look forward to hearing more once you've actually *spoken* with this Tacitus," she says in a droll tone. "Fausta," she calls to her maid. "Fetch my amethyst necklace. The new one freshly arrived from Egypt. You have never seen gemstones like these," she boasts to us.

While Aurelia quizzes Arata about her own taste in jewelry, I file every detail of what just happened in my head.

I'm not sure if our new friend recognized Aurelia's insulting challenge about Tacitus, but I did. Will Arata pursue her interest in the former centurion? If this is a *Septem Fideles* ploy, I hope Tacitus and Severus know what they're doing. By all accounts, Vibius Acilius Ursus and Senator Varro are not men to be toyed with.

My stomach flutters in anticipation for my next meeting with Severus.

Chapter XIV

MALLIA

The opportunity to share the latest information comes just over a week later when the esteemed General Severus asks the esteemed Senator Justus to escort his daughter to the palace for the Emperor's birthday celebration.

My father was honored by the request, and I had to suppress a grin when he shared the surprising news with an air of wonder. I'm sure Severus omitted the part where the journey would include a stop at a small flat in the impoverished district of Crassus Pass, in the opposite direction of the palace.

The morning of the banquet, there's a great deal of fussing over my hair, jewelry, and attire, none of which will matter when Aurelia sees me and disapproves.

"They're excited for you, my lady," Danae says as she helps pin the shoulder of a deep blue silk palla draped over my embroidered ivory tunic. "This is an honor for our household. And escorted by General Severus, no less!"

She steps back and hands me the polished bronze mirror. I knit my brows at the strange reflection staring back at me. Lined with black kohl, my light brown eyes appear huge and innocent. Braided hair extensions interwoven with a sprinkle of rare pearls are piled high on my head in an elaborate style that took the hairdresser hours to complete. The rouge tinting my cheeks feels like too much, the blue powdered azurite on my eyelids too thick. I'm not accustomed to parading around in such finery, but Danae assured me it wasn't too much and was necessary for my mission.

I need to fit in now more than ever.

"Yes, well, they don't know this is *Septem Fideles* business," I whisper, placing the mirror back on the marble-topped vanity table.

Danae gently grips my shoulders and turns me toward her. "I'm proud of you, my lady. It's a very brave thing you're doing. I'll help in any way I can."

Warmth floods through me as I search her dark brown eyes. "I know you will. You already have. But my father can't know about this. No one can, do you understand?"

She nods with a quick smile of her own and releases me. "Of course, my lady."

She'll keep my secret. Severus also trusts her and, in some ways, included her first.

"Good. Then let's go see what our next adventure will bring."

JASON

Our footsteps echo off the high marble walls and rectangular ceiling of the atrium as an usher leads us into Senator Justus's villa. I knew from the moment we approached the imposing double doors of the external gate that the estate embedded in the elite neighborhood of The Laurels would be impressive.

Striking is a better word. The majestic receiving hall of Mallia's home rivals any I've seen in the great villas of the city.

While Severus and Senator Justus exchange pleasantries, I take in my surroundings, fascinated by this glimpse into Mallia's life. A rectangular cut-out in the roof of the atrium leaks air and light into the vast space, illuminating a shallow pool below. Stately busts of revered familial ancestors watch from various niches and architectural shelves. Geometric frescos painted in rich reds, blues, and greens coat the walls, punctuated by corridors to other rooms and wings of the house.

But it's not the tasteful display of extravagance that has my attention. As a favorite plaything of the wealthy, fancy halls and expensive furnishings are not new to me. It's the peek into Mallia's world that has me captivated. My thoughts should be on the coming meeting in Crassus Pass, my recent commissioning into *Septem Fideles*, and all the many threats constantly surrounding me—but all I can think about is Mallia.

This is her home—and I'm about to see her again.

When Severus said Mallia was our fourth "brother," nothing about that surprised me. In fact, it helped explain her strange behavior since the day we met. She must have known of my importance to the cause, so of course she'd take a professional concern in my treatment.

If only I could convince my pounding heart that's all it was.

The din of polite conversation stalls when Mallia and Danae enter the room. I keep my expression neutral, but inside, my pulse erupts at the sight of the walking goddess before us. Heat sears through me as Mallia glides across the tiled floor, completely mesmerizing in her palace-worthy finery. Streaks of sunlight dance over her flawless form, reflecting the gold accents in her gown and subtle red highlights shimmering through her dark hair.

When her intense brown eyes seek mine before anyone else's, something stirs deep inside me. I don't react openly, but I can't help staring long after I should. My sin becomes more egregious when her gaze remains locked on me as well.

For several haunting seconds, it's just the two of us in the room.

We haven't spoken since the day she tried to apologize for all of society's ills, though I've seen her often, typically from a distance. The look in her eyes is always the same, though. Innocent curiosity. Awe. She's fascinated by me, which isn't new, but the genuine compassion that accompanies her interest turns it into something dangerous.

I'm just as fascinated by her—this woman, barely more than girl, who possesses a character worthy of General Severus's admiration and the seal of *Septem Fideles*.

My value is clear. Same for the other former soldiers I met in the infirmary. But Mallia. Whatever she is, she must be far greater than mere muscle and skill. I've glimpsed what makes her so special a few times now, each leaving another indelible impression on my battered soul. Her strange apology, as absurd as it was, haunted me long after we parted. I hadn't been able to accept it because it wasn't hers to give, but the fact that she felt the need to try chipped sharply at the heavy armor around my heart.

After a lifetime of betrayal and abuse, I don't have friends—I can't—but this girl keeps piercing my resistance with each unexpected action that spits in the face of what I've come to understand about her class.

Mallia Justa may not understand me, but I find her just as much of a mystery.

"Mallia, you look lovely!" Severus greets, stretching out his right hand.

She clasps it gently before letting go. "Thank you. I'm looking forward to the festivities."

"As you should. I have it on good authority it will be quite the spectacle." He adjusts the ornamental chest plate fitted around his torso and pivots toward Senator Justus. "I'll take good care of her, Senator."

"I know you will." The politician casts an adoring glance at his daughter, filled with respect and affection. It's clear he loves her, but does he know of her involvement with *Septem Fideles?* "Thank you again, Legatus Severus. We're honored by your invitation."

"The Emperor wouldn't dream of celebrating his birthday without his niece's closest friend," Severus says. "I'm sorry to be brief, but we must go. Shall we?" he asks Mallia.

She returns a polite smile and accepts a kiss on the cheek from her father.

With great ceremony, General Severus leads us from the atrium through the outer vestibulum to the front gate. The doorkeeper opens it, revealing a two-person litter carried by eight slaves waiting along the street.

"Is that really necessary?" Mallia asks, wrinkling her nose at the vehicle.

Severus quirks a fleeting smile, probably amused like I am by the latest surprise from the privileged noble. Would she really prefer to walk through the crowded, muck-filled streets? She'd be the only patrician I've ever encountered who would.

"Jason is a worthy bodyguard, but there's no reason to put him to the test every time I travel," he says, casting a knowing glance at me. "Besides, our first stop is some distance away."

I fight a smile as I pull back the curtain of the litter and hold out a hand to help Mallia inside.

"My lady," I say, bowing my head.

Her gaze cuts into me as she slides her small, warm palm into mine. Soft fingers brush my calloused skin, reminding me of the time they innocently explored my body. Her touch was different than what I'm used to: filled with intrigue and questions instead of selfish desire. It lingered on the scars, not the parts of me every man has, but the parts unique to my story.

For one of the first times I can remember, I hadn't hated those few seconds of the show. I hadn't been an object to her, but a man, a soul. For a brief moment, I allowed the unexpected connection to seep into me, transforming what was usually pain into an ache of pleasure. It was a strange feeling, addictive even, and it wasn't until I'd been forced to resume my role as slave that the encounter went dark again.

That whole afternoon has become a conflicting memory, to say the least.

My hand feels cold when she releases it and settles onto the cushioned seat in the small vehicle. Severus climbs in after her, and I step back so the eight litter carriers can hoist the two long poles lining the vehicle to their shoulders.

Danae and I follow beside them at a steady pace, but our progress slows considerably once we leave the wealthy residential area and move into the packed streets of the upscale commercial district. Merchants clamor from shops and stalls on all sides, while our party fights through a mass of carts, citizens, slaves, and animals. The litter bearers carry their load with an expertise that disguises the obstacles from the precious cargo inside, but Danae and I don't have the same experience as we push through the sea of odors and flesh.

I keep watch as we walk, my hand always a flinch away from drawing my gladius at the first sign of trouble.

"How are you, Jason? It's been a while since we last spoke," Danae asks after a long silence. Sandwiched between me and the litter, her clean, fitted tunic, green shawl, narrow leather belt, and thick brunette braid wrapped in a bun at the back of her head make her look every bit the beloved servant of an important noble.

"I'm well. I miss our conversations." I add a fleeting smile before focusing back on the surrounding chaos.

"I miss them as well. I'm glad to see you seem mostly healed."

"Thanks in large part to you."

Her kind, sincere smile reminds me a lot of her mistress. "I was so happy about your promotion as well. General Severus is lucky to have you as a confidant."

A rush of friendly affection moves through me. "Thank you. Just as Lady Mallia is lucky to have you."

She tugs the faded green shawl over her head as a hood against the sun. "Lady Mallia is my friend as much as my mistress. You will find the same with your master in time."

"I hope so. He's a great man."

"He is. I look—ah!" Danae yelps when a vendor carrying a basket of fruit sends her stumbling into me.

"Hey! Watch it!" I shout after him while helping her straighten. "Are you hurt?"

She brushes off her tunic with a frown. "No, but I can't say the same for my palla."

I glance at the small dark stain on her shawl before tugging her forward to catch up with the litter. We need to stay even closer now that we're leaving the relative safety of The Laurels for the middle-class Brick District.

"It doesn't look bad. I'm sure we can secure a replacement when we arrive at the palace," I say while surveying the large brick insulae building to my right. I wonder if Tacitus lives in one of these apartments. Severus said he lived in the Brick District, while Argus occupies a small flat in Crassus Pass to which we're headed.

Danae's brow sinks as she squints around the crowded streets. "About that, aren't we going in the wrong direction?"

"Yes. General Severus and Mallia have some business to attend to first," I explain in a cryptic tone. Another quick glance reveals her nod of understanding, which means she must know about *Septem Fideles*. As Mallia's constant shadow, it's almost a necessity.

We're silent for the next few blocks as we inch along the packed thoroughfares, each lost in our own thoughts. I hate that mine keep turning to the woman in the litter. Is she comfortable? Nervous about what's coming? Is Severus giving her additional information? Is she sharing any with him?

We've just crossed into the plebeian neighborhood of Crassus Pass when Severus gives the command to stop at an alley beside a busy bakery.

He reaches through the opening and waves for me to approach.

"We'll disembark here and walk the rest of the way," he says in a low voice. "The litter won't fit down the alleys anyway. Help Mallia, please."

Something flutters in my stomach as I offer my hand, surging when she takes it with a shy smile. Her grip tightens just beyond what's required for the formal exchange, and I hold on longer than necessary to ensure she's gained her footing. She pretends to need the extra support as she adjusts her delicate shawl with the other hand.

Once again, she seems as reluctant to let go as I am. Her fingers drift over mine in an intentional caress when she finally pulls away, sending a shiver through me.

"Wait for us here. We will return shortly," Severus says to the litter bearers. "Danae, you may wait inside the litter and take a break from the sun."

"Thank you, my lord," she says, bowing her head.

The rest of us continue on foot, drawing stares from the locals unaccustomed to elite citizens traveling through this part of the city. I study each gawker we pass, instinctively evaluating threats and constructing an escape plan for Severus and Mallia, if necessary.

The stench of the main thoroughfares is bad enough, but the small passageways in these districts make the central roads seem like gardens. I grew up in this filth, and my blood chills as the well-known smells take me back to a time I'd do anything to forget. I can't help but wonder how my privileged companions are adjusting to the seediest parts of Rome.

My heart rate picks up as our familiar path triggers memory after memory. It's been seven years since Lepidus sold me to the ludus. Four since we last crossed paths. With his base of operations several blocks away in the Fountain District, that monster shouldn't be close but something feels off. It's like I can sense the man's foul presence lurking nearby.

I glance at Mallia, expecting to find a look of disgust on her face, but there's only genuine curiosity. She doesn't even gag at the piles of human, animal, and food waste frequently blocking our path, just lifts the hem of her tunic and skirts around it with grace that catches me off guard.

She's too beautiful to be in this ugly place. I'm not happy that Severus brought her here. There had to be another, more suitable location to meet. But the longer I watch her take in the unfamiliar surroundings, the more I understand. He *wants* her to experience our world—to live and breathe the unfamiliar—just as we experience hers.

We turn down another narrow alley shaded by rundown buildings, and I grip the handle of my gladius in preparation.

I didn't think I'd need it so soon.

Air leaves my lungs when I spot the demon before he sees me. Paralyzed, I stare at the man who haunts my dreams standing just a few steps away. Severus, ever-observant, follows my startled gaze and utters a curse.

"*By Pluto's chains,* Jason, I'm sorry. I didn't even consider…"

I clench my jaw, trying to calm the violent storm raging inside. I feel Mallia's intense stare and can only wonder what she's thinking.

The horrible man turns our way and his thin lips spread into a vicious grin.

"*Bestia filius!* You've returned," Lepidus sneers, stalking toward me.

I tense and duck out of his reach.

"You have no business with him. Move aside," Severus barks, eyes blazing.

Lepidus unleashes a bitter laugh. "No, I suppose not. I see he's done well for himself. Went from servicing lonely merchants to fancy patricians, huh, Jason?"

I scowl at him, wanting nothing more than to plunge my dagger through those cold demon eyes. I'd do it right now if it didn't mean I'd have to move closer to him—and put the others in danger.

"You're blocking our path," I growl instead.

Lepidus snickers. "Am I now? Apologies, *my lord*."

Despite his mocking tone, he flattens against the wall of the neighboring apartment building so we can pass.

Mustering every bit of strength, I compel myself forward, following instead of leading this time. The narrow street barely gives us space to clear another person, and we file awkwardly toward the light at the end of the alleyway.

Despite the sticky heat, my body goes cold when my turn comes up. Lepidus does nothing to make my path easier. Heart racing, I slide past, his familiar scent sending a wave of repulsion through me. Our tunics brush in the exchange, and panic erupts inside me when he lunges forward and forces me into the wall.

"You turned into quite a masterpiece, you know," he purrs, running his hands over me. "I've kept an eye on you."

I shove him away, drawing my gladius. It provides an additional barrier between us as I back toward the others. Lepidus leans against the building, grinning like the monster he is.

"Ignore that swine," Severus growls, firing a glare at the disgusting man. "He's not even worth the spit."

Lepidus only laughs. "It's a pity I sold you when I did. Not a day goes by that I don't regret it. You'd be worth a fortune to me now. Clients these days want quality over quantity. Come, good sir, name your price!"

I swallow the nausea rocking in my stomach. Would Severus sell me? I've lived with that threat every day of my life. There's no security in a slave's existence. Every second could be worse than the last. For me, it often is.

But Severus looks murderous, not tempted, as he takes my arm and leads me away.

"He's in the past. He can't hurt you now," he hisses.

I nod, but the darkness has already settled in. My body still burns from the recent assault, as if it's been branded by a past I'll never escape. My head knows Severus is right, but it doesn't stop the trembling in my soul. This is who I am. *What* I am, and—

Sudden warmth on my arm draws my gaze to slender, jeweled fingers circling my wrist. Mallia's thumb caresses my skin like it did the day we met, soothing away the horror of the previous moment.

I meet her eyes and I'm blasted with unrelenting compassion, pain she can't possibly understand but is trying so hard to absorb anyway. Holding her gaze, I allow the unexpected salve to piece me back together.

With a weak smile, I gently pull away before anyone else notices her transgression. She twists a soft smile of her own and tugs the edge of her palla around her.

Neither of us speaks as we finish the journey, but we don't have to.

We both know something just shifted between us.

Chapter XV

MALLIA

After shimmying down another passageway and enduring the curious—sometimes hostile—gawking of the locals, we finally stop before a shabby apartment building that looks a few strong wind gusts away from collapse.

A fire burns in a sliver of open space just outside, surrounded by drying laundry and remnants of abandoned household items. Rodents scurry through stacks of furniture and earthenware, belonging to everyone and no one. A woman bent over the flames with a pot glances up as we approach, first in surprise and then in suspicion.

The insulae building itself rises up in a jagged irregular block behind her. Rickety stairs provide access to the upper levels, where linens wave in the doorways that can't afford actual doors. Closer inspection reveals evidence of the previous building constructed on that lot, destroyed by fire and rebuilt in the same shoddy manner. I wonder how many times that cycle has resulted in the erection of the same building.

Voices and activity echo from the tightly packed apartments as we climb the hazardous steps toward Argus's flat on the first floor, and my thoughts quickly return to Jason.

I watch him carefully in the dim light, still concerned after the encounter with that horrible man. I don't know who the stranger was, but he's clearly a ghost from Jason's past.

Studying my friend's tall, confident stride now, I wouldn't have known he was troubled by the confrontation. The fixed concentration that's replaced the typical fire burning in his eyes is the only indication something's wrong. It's his fight *not* to display his pain that serves as its greatest clue. I hate that I can't comfort him or offer even a kind word as he battles his demons in silence.

"This is the home of your brother, Argus," Severus says as we reach a narrow landing on the first floor. Several doorways line the short corridor, and he motions toward one of only two wooden doors in the series. "Argus fought beside me for many years in the Fourth and is one of the finest soldiers to serve Rome. It's likely your other brother, Tacitus, has already arrived as well."

Despite the humble surroundings, I don't question Severus's assessment of these men. After all, Jason stands as evidence that greatness is not forged by wealth and status.

I'm eager to meet Arata's crush, Tacitus, as well.

"Follow me." Severus knocks briskly on the door and pushes inside without waiting for a response.

Two startled men reach for their weapons and then relax when they recognize us. They both straighten to their full height in unison. Their coordinated response is even more amusing since they couldn't be more different in appearance.

The older of the two is burly and gruff with auburn, curly hair. Flickers of sunlight from the open door and one window reveal silver strands littered throughout, almost giving his head the appearance of a bronze helmet. He hasn't shaved for days, if not weeks, producing a short beard slightly darker than his hair. The silver has penetrated the hair on his face as well, splotching the thick mass from ear to ear. His wide grin when he greets Severus reveals a gap in his teeth, and I don't need an introduction to know this is Argus, the seasoned legionary feared by allies as much as enemies.

The other must be Tacitus.

I study the younger soldier with more interest. Even at first glance, it's not hard to understand Arata's secret admiration. I can't help but agree that he looks striking in a military-style uniform designed to intimidate potential threats while also conforming to the elegant expectation of a wealthy senator's status. A short-sleeved slate blue tunic shows off powerful, sculpted arms, while the studded belt inlaid with faded insignia adds an air of refined strength. The gladius strapped to his hip completes the menacing image.

In contrast to Argus's thick, round muscles and brute force, Tacitus has a relaxed intelligence in his expression that further increases his appeal. Medium-length brown hair slopes away from his tanned face in natural waves, while deep brown eyes sparkle with wry amusement that would easily captivate the bored daughter of a senator.

He's the archetype of a Roman hero—handsome, intelligent, dangerous—and everything a noble would want in a secret lover.

Tacitus and Severus will have quite a challenge navigating this situation with Arata.

Argus lets out a low whistle as he scans me. "Please tell me this is our *brother*, Mallia," he teases. "I'd be happy to train her for you, General."

Tacitus narrows his pretty eyes at him. "It's only the women you pay who pretend to appreciate your insults, Argus." He sends me an apologetic look. "I'm sorry for my friend here. He only speaks the language of soldier vulgarity."

"*Eat ashes,* Tacitus! It was a compliment!"

Tacitus twists toward him with an exasperated squint. "In what universe?"

"All of them! I was trying to be helpful!" Argus throws up his hands.

"Did I mention these two never stop bickering?" Severus mutters. "Yes, this is Mallia, daughter of Senator Justus. And now that everything is official, may I also once again present Jason: a champion gladiator and my personal attendant and bodyguard."

The mood in the room sobers abruptly. A subtle tension thickens the air as the three stranger-brothers assess each other.

Jason's stoic scan gives nothing away, even though I know he's reading every detail. The others evaluate him as well but with less restraint.

"Good to see you on your feet," Tacitus says, his dark brows furrowed. "We watched your fight in the arena against the three opponents. It was a display of beauty."

"*Frax,* yes! A work of art!" Argus exclaims and then cowers at Tacitus's critical look at the use of profanity. "*Caenum*. Sorry, my lady. I mean…*bollax*."

Tacitus smacks his arm, and he shuts up.

"What he means to say is that we were impressed," Tacitus continues in a dry tone. "We're glad to see you recovered and we're honored to join you in the brother—and sister—hood of *Septem Fideles*. We hope to prove ourselves just as worthy to you."

Jason's hard expression softens in surprise, and I melt a little at the near-smile on his face. "Thank you. It was an honor to be chosen," he says with a short nod.

"Same for me," I cut in, not about to be left out of the bonding.

Argus glances over in amusement. "And what's your specialty, darling? Let me guess—the net and trident?"

"Keeping arrogant warriors in line," I fire back, drawing laughter from the others. Even Jason finally cracks a full smile. The rare sight lands hard in my chest.

Beautiful.

Argus grins and holds up his hands in surrender. "I don't doubt it, my lady. My sincerest apologies."

"Light a lamp and close the shutters," Severus commands, securing the door behind us. "Where's the girl?"

"Seia? I sent her on an errand. She won't be back for a while."

"Do you have a daughter?" I ask Argus.

He grunts as he strikes a spark with a piece of iron and flint and ignites the tinder. "Not one I chose. She chose me."

"Seia was abandoned by her family," Tacitus explains, pulling the shutters closed. "Argus allows her to live here since Lepidus was preying on her."

Jason goes deathly still. "Lepidus is recruiting here?" he asks.

We freeze, watching a shadow move over his face as the lamp flickers to life.

"Tacitus," Severus warns. "We talked about this."

Tacitus bows his head. "Sorry, sir." He casts a concerned look at Jason, and I shiver at the blank, stony look that's settled over the gladiator. It's like his soul has vanished.

"Who's Lepidus?" I ask, glancing between them.

"It doesn't matter. That's not why we're here," Severus answers in a gruff voice.

"The man in the alleyway," Jason replies, his jaw set in its typical hard resolve.

"Wait, he's hovering around again?" Argus cries.

"We think he might be expanding his business," Tacitus explains to Jason.

"He already has if he's interested in girls," Jason mutters.

An uncomfortable silence settles over the room as Severus lays a hand on his arm.

Nausea sweeps through me when the truth crashes in. The vile man in the alley. The horrible story Jason told me the day I tried to apologize. The little girl in Argus's apartment. Was that man the villain from his childhood? If that's true, that means…

I feel sick. No wonder Jason reacted the way he did.

My chest hurts. I try to meet his gaze, but he won't look at me. He won't look at anyone as he stares at the floor, clearly somewhere else. Gods, I hope it's not there.

"Enough distractions," Severus says, pulling us back from the painful silence. "This is a very important meeting, and we have a lot to cover. You've all begun your assignments separately. I thought it time you meet and finally understand how you're working together."

We stand around the small table, staring into the eerie shadows of flickering faces as the weight of our calling settles over us.

In a grave tone, he continues, "*Septem Fideles* was formed generations ago with one mission: to protect the Empire at all costs. Over time, as our rulers became obsessed with personal glory and power, the secret unit tasked with fighting for the greater good fell into oblivion. Rampant corruption replaced the principles of justice. Greed and entitlement trampled on the very subjects our leaders were sworn to protect. Depravity has polluted every crevice of our city from the highest palace hall to the lowliest street corner in the slums of Hades Hand."

My gaze creeps to Jason, whose intense stare remains fixed on the floor. I can't guess where his head is, but I suspect he's seen more of what Severus is describing than any of us.

"Evil runs unrestrained," Severus continues, "but the tides are turning. While new enemies are rising, so is the force for good. The current Emperor is different than his predecessors, a rare servant leader willing to stand for justice and honor. He has re-commissioned *Septem Fideles* because we can no longer ignore the insidious war raging in the shadows. It's time to fight back. To seek out the threats and be the aggressor against the evil poisoning our Empire. As a sanctioned covert unit, our permissions are endless, our resources limitless. We will accomplish our goals with cunning and ingenuity as much as violence and force."

He leans forward and braces his arms on the table, his long black cloak fluttering behind him. "Though originally seven members, *Septem Fideles* has been recommissioned with just four. Only those of you standing in this room were deemed worthy of the seal. Separately, you are exceptional, but together you will be invincible. You have a sworn duty to each other as much as to Rome. Over time you will see the other three as extensions of yourself."

He takes a deep breath and scans each of us in the dancing lamplight. "On the surface, you four couldn't be more different. I know your pasts. I know how some of you have suffered." His gaze rests on Jason, and a muscle tightens in the young warrior's jaw.

"But your slates are clean as of this moment. You are no longer slave, child, or disgraced soldier. You are ghost warriors, more important to the Empire than anyone in the palace, though no one will ever know. On pain of torture and death, you are never to reveal the existence of *Septem Fideles* and the true nature of your non-severable relationship with each other. You will take on many identities, possibly even relinquishing your previous lives."

Air rushes from my lungs when his penetrating gaze lands on me.

"But through it all, you will be serving a cause greater than all of us, greater than the Emperor himself. You will be saving its people—this civilization—from threats most of its subjects could never imagine, let alone defeat. There will be times when you four are the only thing that stand between peace and chaos."

He straightens and eyes us sternly. "Now that I've laid it out, I give you one last chance to withdraw without disgrace."

Silence rings loudly as his words echo through the thick air around us. No one moves. No one seems to breathe as we lock stares in a quiet linking of souls. Shrieks and bangs from the surrounding apartments penetrate the heavy moment, but it feels foreign. Something is happening in this small room. A cosmic shift greater than any one of us.

When no one heads for the exit, Severus clears his throat and straightens to attention. Ruffling his cloak behind him, he officially calls the meeting to order.

MALLIA

"With that settled, we'll start with updates on each of your assignments," Severus continues in a pragmatic tone. "Argus, you've been tasked with gathering intelligence on Legatus Nepos's role in the plot against the Emperor. What do you have for us?"

Argus nods and launches into a detailed recounting of the information he gleaned from former Centurion Livianus.

"He said Nepos celebrates defeats like victories?" Jason asks when he finishes.

"What are you thinking?" Severus directs the question at him.

Jason squints into the shadows, as if trying to pull together pieces of distant memories.

"I've seen that same behavior before. Often, actually." He drags his focus back to us. "Battles don't always have clear victors, particularly in the arena. Sure, at the end, one of us stands with an arm raised while the other looks on from the sand, but usually it's nearly impossible to tell which side suffered bigger losses. Sometimes, the winner fared much worse than the loser, he just got lucky in the final clash and held the sword at the end of the contest. A simple mistake could be the difference between victory and defeat."

He pauses, still working the theory through his head. "Winning in the arena is as much a mental game as a physical one. After a defeat on the sand, you never carry it back to the cell. You grow bolder. You laugh at the victor's injuries. You call for his blood and hunger for revenge. You convince the others that your loss was barely a loss at all. No one wants to be the first man to face a gladiator who has just been defeated."

"What are you saying?" Argus asks, rubbing his beard.

Jason shifts his gaze to him. "A person only loses when they let others believe they've lost. Controlling perceptions is more important than the truth."

Argus smirks. "So, you don't think Legatus Nepos knows he's losing his tunic up there?"

Jason shakes his head. "I'm saying he needs his men to *believe* he's not. He needs *us* to believe he's not. He's acting like he's winning because he has to make everyone believe a lie. Let me ask you, what does he stand to gain if he delivers Britannia? What does he stand to lose if he doesn't?"

Tacitus's eyes widen as he taps his knuckles on the table. "He's right. If Nepos returns to Rome as the man who conquered northern Britannia where no one else could, he would be lauded as a hero."

"Why though? There's no value to those *verrux* cliffs," Argus mutters. "A total waste of resources."

"Yes, but a victory would bring pride, which appeals to the people," Tacitus argues. "He'd be capable of raising whatever troops and resources he wanted if he had their favor."

"A solid foundation to commit treason," Severus hisses.

Jason nods with a grave expression. "Exactly. So we're asking the wrong question. It's not why Nepos is trying to make us think he's winning when he's losing. That's obvious. The question is, what would he have to do to validate the lie? That's where you should be looking for the evidence that will expose him, as well as who or what is in the crosshairs of his deadly game."

Severus leans back on his heels, the lines of his face deep in the sparse flashes of light. "There it is, Argus. Your next mission. If Nepos is lying about his campaign in Britannia, we need to find out what he's done to perpetuate the lie, who's supporting his claims, and who's disputing them."

"I'd start with who's been discharged, living and dead," Tacitus suggests.

"You mean collect reports from veterans like Livianus?" Argus asks, concerned.

Tacitus nods. "Exactly. We should also find out more about the fate of the previous governor, Titullus. Did he really invite Nepos to Britannia to assist with uprisings?"

"And is he really dead?" Argus adds. "What were the circumstances, if he is?"

"Find out what you can," Severus instructs him. "Reach out to all the veterans you know. See if any refute the claims. You also need the testimonies of active legionaries. Jason and I will have more luck with the politicians. The popular opinion in the top circles is that Nepos has been successful. We need to find out why they believe that and understand the lie before we can investigate the truth."

Argus nods while Severus turns his attention to Tacitus. "What about you? You were accepted into Senator Varro's unit of bodyguards. Have you gotten close to him yet?"

Tacitus shakes his head. "Not yet. Since I'm new, I rarely interact with the Senator. I'm trying to find a way into his confidence without being obvious."

"I may have an idea," I say, drawing their attention.

Tacitus locks his gaze on me, and I warm beneath the intense strength of his perceptive stare. Arata will have her hands full with this one.

"Well, what is it?" Severus encourages.

I swallow my nerves and force the words out. "You should know that Tacitus's name came up in one of my visits with Aurelia and a new friend."

Tacitus's brows knit in confusion. "How is that possible? I've never met Lady Aurelia."

"No. Nor has her friend met you, though you have quite an admirer in her, apparently." A smile weaves over my lips at the memory. "The woman is Arata Varra, Senator Varro's daughter, and she's very…shall we say…approving of your service to her father."

Tacitus releases a sharp exhale while Argus barks a laugh and pounds his friend on the shoulder. "Of course she is. Just like all the other noblewomen of Rome," Argus quips.

Tacitus glares at him. "I'm glad you think this is funny."

By the troubled concentration spreading around the room, this "seduction" of Arata wasn't planned.

"What's everyone so anxious about? This is great news," Argus says. "Imagine how much Tacitus could learn from an interview in her bed."

"A bed that belongs to Vibius Acilius Lurio," Tacitus fires back.

Argus winces and scratches his beard. "Ah, right. I see the dilemma."

"Thank you for the warning, Mallia. That's extremely important information," Severus says before turning to Tacitus. "You need to play this very carefully, son. A scorned lover can prove just as dangerous as an amorous one."

"And the elite are accustomed to getting what they want from their inferiors," Jason adds. A twinge cuts through me at the subtext of his reminder.

Tacitus massages his temples. "What do you want me to do, sir? Pursue the lead or diffuse it?"

"Pursue it for now," Severus replies. "You have to, but only to the edge of propriety. Your flirtation with Varro's daughter must be without reproach.

Deflect her without offending her. At least we can be prepared for the challenge and use it to our advantage, thanks to Mallia."

Brow furrowed, Tacitus nods slowly, clearly conflicted by his new assignment.

"If it helps, she seems genuine," I say. "She's not spoiled and petty like a lot of the nobles in my circles. She may actually prove to be helpful on some level."

"Thanks, Mallia. I'll keep that in mind," Tacitus replies in a resigned tone. "If you learn anything else I can use, I'd appreciate the assistance."

I offer a reassuring nod, and Severus focuses back on me. "Your information is proving to be very valuable, yet again. Continue ingratiating yourself with Aurelia and her friends. Also, keep learning what you can from your father's acquaintances and activities. You're on the front lines of this and have easy access to people and information the rest of us will never have. You already possess the confidence of the elite."

A rock lodges in my stomach, and I lower my gaze to the stained wood floor.

"I know it's hard for you," he continues gently. "I know the values of that world don't always align with your own, but you must become one of them, Mallia. You are a patrician with access to some of the most influential circles in Rome. You are invited to tables from which even your father is excluded. You must play the part and join them. You don't have to agree with their behavior, but you must swallow your disgust and accept it. For now, your assignment isn't to fight your peers but to be trusted as one of them." He follows my pained look toward Jason. "No matter what it takes."

I bite my lip as I study Jason's hard expression across the table. He's avoiding my gaze, no doubt caught in the same memory tearing at me. The encounter with Aurelia and Cornelia hangs heavily between us.

What Severus is asking of me seems impossible. He can't actually expect me to condone what happened, or even worse, participate. I'd never be able to do what they did. To force his body to act against his will. To strike him with a fury that draws blood. Even if he allowed it, even if he *understood*, I wouldn't be able to hurt him, or anyone else, for that matter.

Jason must be tormented by the same subject, but, as usual, he says nothing.

"I will try," I mumble.

"No! You will succeed!" Severus snaps, pounding a fist on the table.

His paternal expression hardens into a stern warning. "It's time we discussed this openly. Mallia, you witnessed something reprehensible that happens every day in half the buildings across this city. It shook you, infuriated you, as it should. It's evil, appalling, and one of the many ills we will fight at some point, but that is not our battle now. It's certainly not your battle."

My stomach twists in agony, but his harsh speech is not without an element of truth.

He pivots toward Jason, his expression still severe but not cruel. "You've been a slave most of your life. Was that the first time you were assaulted?"

Jason flinches and shakes his head. "No, my lord," he replies quietly.

"No? The second then?"

Jason's stare burns into the table, his hand flexing absently at his side. My soul aches for him, even as I'm beginning to understand.

"No, my lord."

"Okay, the third then. The fourth? How many times? How many times have you been beaten, raped, tortured?"

Jason's shocked gaze darts to him before landing on the floor. We watch helplessly as he struggles under the weight of a truth the rest of us have spent our lives trying to ignore.

But Severus refuses to let us hide. I get it now. How he's forcing us to confront the darkest reaches of our broken world.

"Tell us! Make us understand. How many times?"

Flustered, the younger man swallows and shakes his head. "I don't know, my lord."

"You don't know? Guess. A hundred? A thousand?"

Jason closes his eyes, shrinking, and my heart shatters. The crushing darkness nearly suffocates me.

Severus lets the thought penetrate deep before turning back to me. "It's disgusting what you saw. It's disgusting what happens on the battlefield, in brothels, in temples, in the ludus, in homes of the rich and poor. We live in disgusting times, but we are not going to fix anything by hiding from it. You cannot fight that which you don't see. Our first step is exposing the evil. We drag it from the whispered shadows into the light. Then we fight by committing to each other and sacrificing everything for a priceless end that, at times, will require accepting horrific means."

He focuses on the group again, finished with his painful illustration. "You're all here, not because you're strong of body, but because you're strong of heart, mind, and will. You're not heroes—you're soldiers who believe in good, but understand that you have to face the evil in order to defeat it. You will do what saints can't, what heroes won't. As members of *Septem Fideles*, you will have to make decisions that will haunt you, torment you, if you have any hope of winning the war for Good."

Severus turns back to Jason and grasps his arm with a strong, calloused hand. "I know you understand that truth better than anyone. I know what you've seen, even though none of us can imagine the depths of the horror this world has inflicted on you. I know the pain you hide, how it courses through you. I know what Lepidus, Opius Plinius, Lady Aurelia, and countless others have done to you. I know your pain, Jason, and it hurts me. It crushes me. Just as it will now crush them." He points an emphatic finger at the rest of us. "But I can't stop it. I can't even promise it won't happen again. In fact, it probably will, but I can promise you this: you will no longer face it alone."

He releases his hold and addresses all of us. "You are one now. You will experience each other's joys and sorrows. You will laugh and cry together, and when one of you is forced into the fires of Hades, it's up to the rest to rescue them from it, to stop the bleeding and soothe the pain. Together you will burn, but not be consumed."

Heavy silence envelops us. His piercing gaze passes from one to the next, branding our souls in the same way his seal branded our bodies.

Together you will burn, but not be consumed.

I rub at the scar through my tunic, understanding the full magnitude of what it means for the first time. Would I follow these men into Hades to save them? Would I suffer the flames to save millions of strangers who will never know?

My gaze lands on Jason. Tacitus. Argus.

They're watching me.

After stripping our souls raw and exposing them to each other, Severus marches from the flat without a word.

MALLIA

"I'm sorry I had to be so harsh with you and Jason, but you understand now, don't you?" Severus says once we're back in the litter on our way to the palace.

I fidget with the amethyst ring on my finger, my stomach still grinding from what just happened. "I do. It's just hard to accept. If all you said about him is true, how does he go on? How can he still be the person he is?" I glance up again, silently pleading with him to understand.

Severus quiets and casts a distracted glance at the billowing curtain of the vehicle.

"Many would say it's the life of a slave," he begins in a distant tone. "It's his duty to go on. That he doesn't have a soul. That he has no right to quit."

His pained gaze crawls back to me. "They would say it's not possible to abuse such an object, that there are no moral boundaries that apply. He has been taught nothing else since he was a child."

Chills run over my skin, but he isn't finished.

"I am not one of those people, Mallia. I've seen a lot over the years. I've seen men broken by a fraction of what Jason has endured. He goes on because he has a strength of character unmatched by anyone I've ever encountered. He goes on because he's somehow been able to separate what happens to him from who he is. But even he has limits."

He shifts on the cushioned seat to face me. "The lad is so accustomed to enduring his prison alone, to ingesting the pain until it hardens inside him, that he will not be easy to love, but I need you to persevere. You are incredibly valuable to *Septem Fideles* for your skills, character, and connections. I would have selected you for those reasons alone, but your most important mission isn't in a palace. He's walking beside us."

Stunned, my throat closes as hot blood pounds in my veins.

"I don't mean in a romantic way, lest your father dismember me," Severus rushes out with a fleeting smile. "I mean, the love of a friend. More than that. You must be Jason's anchor, Mallia. You are uniquely suited for that difficult task, and it will take strength and compassion even I don't have. Despite what I said, I don't understand half the burden that young man carries with each breath, and I'm not sure I could. He's seen a side of the world you and I can't imagine. That revolting man in the alley..."

He shakes off a thought, and an icy shiver collides with the burn of anger inside me.

There's a clash around my heart ready to erupt. Nothing fills me with rage like the thought of what's been done to Jason. Nothing stirs my will like the challenge of getting past his walls. Nothing squeezes my soul like the longing to see him smile, and maybe that's what Severus means. Maybe it's not freedom Jason needs most, but unconditional love.

"That monster had some kind of power over him," I recall darkly. "Jason didn't show it, but I could tell he was terrified."

Severus nods and draws in a deep breath. "Jason doesn't show much. He is a bronze statue, but in order for him to survive, someone will have to share his burden. Someone will have to reach into the abyss of his soul and pull him out."

He turns and locks determined gray eyes on mine. "He will not allow it, Mallia. You will have to force it from him. Do you understand?"

His haunting tone shakes me to the core. I'm not sure I do understand. I'm not sure I can.

"What if I'm not strong enough?" I ask, gripping the fabric of my silk palla. "What if I can't get through his walls?"

Severus sighs with grief that seeps into my soul. "Then we will lose him."

Chapter XVI

MALLIA

Our arrival at the palace is a welcome distraction from the somber ride to its walls.

After moving through the imperial gate, the litter bearers lower the vehicle to stone slabs in a private receiving courtyard lined with guards and palace attendants. Jason pulls back the curtain and holds out his hand to assist, but it feels entirely different than the last time I slid my palm into his. Gone is the subtle spark of our previous contact, replaced by the formal stiffness of duty. I search his face as he helps me to the stone block for disembarking passengers, cringing when his fleeting acknowledgement is nothing more than a slave to his mistress. I hate that reaction even more than if he had ignored me outright.

Danae is quickly at my side to make adjustments to my hair and garments, reviving a sense of normalcy.

A praetorian guard verifies our status and turns us over to an usher, who leads us through the colonnaded halls of the spectacular palace. Music from a smattering of musicians mixes with the echoes of voices from other arriving dignitaries. Strategically placed braziers eject wafts of incense through the air to drift among the hanging flowers and garland.

We enter a majestic atrium where we greet the Emperor and join the crowd of guests. Festive music plays and honeyed wine flows along with the din of polite conversation. Even though I've been to the palace countless times, most of my visits involve intimate encounters with Aurelia in her private rooms.

Rarely have I been afforded the privilege of state dinners in the grandest public halls.

When the ushers escort us into the main banquet hall, my breath catches at the sight.

Endless rows of couches line the marble floors and walls of the cavernous room, surrounding a raised dais constructed for the Emperor. Gilded beams run across the ceiling, while more ornate garland twists around columns and furniture. Hundreds of oil lamps in silver stands cast a warm glow over the pristine, polished surfaces.

It's a spectacular sight that makes even my privileged existence feel inferior.

As one of the Emperor's closest friends, Severus is given a place of honor on the couch closest to the Imperator. While he reclines beside a high-ranked senator, I'm shown to a cushioned chair nearby. Aurelia spots me from her own chair near her uncle's prominent platform and waves with an excited smile. I return it, still in awe at the extravagance around me.

As we wait for everyone to be positioned, the mouthwatering scent of roasted meats entwines with the sweet spice of burning incense in an enticing invitation of what's to come. Flute and lyre music filters through the buzz of conversation, crafting jovial melodies for troupes of choreographed dancers.

Danae takes her place behind me while Jason stands at attention behind Severus a few paces away. He resembles a statue even more than usual with his hard, vacant expression and chiseled body covered in a tailored dark green tunic, bronze-accented leather belt, and short black and crimson cloak mirroring Severus's more elaborate version. His entire being seems sculpted in living marble, and I stare for several seconds before Severus casts me a warning look. Heat spreads up my neck, and I force my attention back toward the dancers.

Seconds later, a line of slaves files in carrying polished silver trays of pickled eggs, an array of olives and cheeses, exotic fruits, and an assortment of vegetables dressed with oil and honey. I select my fill of sticky treats from the offered trays, grateful for the additional slaves circulating with basins of scented water and perfumed towels.

Throughout the lavish meal, I mostly pick at the food, using the opportunity to observe while the guests are conveniently organized in order of importance. Later, when the formal ceremony descends into drunken revelry, the real games of intrigue will begin.

Partway through the next course, Severus motions to Jason, who bends close. The general speaks hushed words I can't hear, but I follow their gazes to a nearby couch. A cold feeling sweeps through me when I recognize Senator Varro and another politician from the wedding a few weeks prior. Even more alarming, their covetous gazes are fixed openly on Jason.

What is Severus up to?

Severus finishes his message, and Jason returns to impassive attention behind him as if unaware that two powerful and dangerous men are gawking at him.

"What's going on?" I whisper to Severus while we wait for the main course. I plaster a demure smile on my face for the benefit of any onlookers.

"Nothing you need to worry about," he says, wiping his fingers on his napkin.

I motion with my eyes toward the other couch and Severus's hard stare flashes with warning.

"Mallia." He silences me with a severe look, and I sink back into my chair. He relaxes slightly and angles toward me. "When the meal ends, and the real festivities begin, we will part ways. Find Aurelia and go about your evening as planned. For now, pretend to enjoy the feast."

Enjoy the feast? That will be hard when the little I've eaten has already soured in my stomach.

Each course has been more elaborate than the previous one, so I'm not surprised when the main course is delivered with dramatic fanfare. A chorus of oohs and ahhs ripples around the room when platters of stuffed meats, exotic birds, and whole fish are presented to the Emperor for approval before being distributed on smaller platters to the guests. Honeyed wine flows freely from a web of nearly naked slaves, while talk of politics, business, and gossip flows more freely.

With no acquaintances positioned nearby, I mostly keep to myself, watching and taking mental notes. I'm only too glad when the drawn-out meal ends and the Emperor invites us to enjoy the rest of the evening in a more casual atmosphere.

As the guests rise from the couches to disperse throughout the neighboring rooms, Severus and I also part ways with a brief word of encouragement.

I start toward the dais where Aurelia was sitting, but in the ensuing commotion of scattering guests, I quickly lose sight of her. Squinting through the crowds, I catch a glimpse of her deep purple gown. My relief fades when I realize she's being led away by Cornelia.

The sick feeling in my stomach returns.

This may be my mission, but I'm not sure I'm ready to face her and Cornelia and whoever else they rope into their conniving circle of sadistic pleasures. I need to prepare myself for such a trial and determine to find them later.

For now, I wander in the opposite direction toward a large peristyle for a breath of fresh air. Once I regain my composure, I'll continue my quest.

"Aurelia is probably headed toward her private rooms," Danae says, coming up beside me.

"Most likely. I need to let my food settle first."

A smile skims her lips as she nods and falls in step behind me.

My plan to clear my head fails when we reach the lush courtyard. The party has already spread to my quiet escape, transforming what's typically a serene oasis of flowers, trees, and trickling fountains into a raucous celebration.

Slaves from the furthest reaches of the Empire dance in sensuous homages to their homelands along the pathways. Music and laughter swell from the benches, pergolas, and surrounding sitting rooms. More slaves distribute trays of snacks and endless pitchers of wine, while the sea of guests consumes until they vomit into designated bowls to make room for more.

Typically, these demonstrations of excess disgust me, reminding me more of a dizzying nightmare than a fantasy. But right now, the promise of a distraction becomes an irresistible temptation. Gutted by my recent confrontation with a world I'm not sure I'll ever understand, I find myself eager for escape.

I accept a glass of wine. Then another. By the third, I'm fascinated by a troop of acrobats, naked except for the paint on their sculpted bodies. They twist and contort in ways I never thought possible.

"They're magnificent!" I shout to Danae as I lift the glass to my lips.

"Perhaps you've had enough, my lady," she says gently, blocking the wine's path.

I shoot a hazy glare at her. "Perhaps, you should mind your own business. It's probably time to find Aurelia, anyway. Go find out where she is."

Danae hesitates, clearly not wanting to leave me alone, but that's exactly why I sent her on the errand. I need a break from the heaviness that's become my constant companion. To feel light and free just for a few precious seconds. To forget.

"I'll be fine," I assure her. "Go! Don't return until you find her."

She lowers her head and finally starts away.

I watch to make sure she's following orders and then take a step in the opposite direction.

My intention was to go on the hunt for Aurelia as well, but the wine has had more of an effect than I anticipated. Lack of food and rapid consumption leave me on unsteady feet, like many other patrons.

Severus told me to fit in. He should be proud.

I smirk to myself as I shuffle along the wall, leaning heavily on it for support. Blurry faces offer a constant string of greetings on my wobbly journey. Some I recognize, others I don't. The rooms blend together in spinning clouds of color, sound, light, and smells.

It doesn't take long until I've forgotten my mission, along with everything else. Dizziness overwhelms me, and I close my eyes to regain my balance, but that just makes it worse. The cold, smooth marble of a column beside an open doorway soothes my skin as I press my forehead against it.

"Why, General Severus, I must say I was intrigued by your choice of valet. The news made quite a stir. I wouldn't be surprised if you've begun a fad of purchasing gladiators as personal attendants."

Despite the mist in my head, I perk up at the familiar name and peek into the room.

The sight of Severus and Jason has a sobering effect. When I recognize several of the other occupants, I grip the wall through a wave of anxiety.

Once I steady myself, I dare another look. Ursus reclines on a couch along with another man I don't know. Their attendants wait dutifully behind them. More strangers occupy another couch, looking just as drunk and frighteningly intrigued as Ursus.

Concerned, I adjust to a better vantage point and suck in my breath when my gaze lands on Jason again. He's so beautiful in his crisp uniform, standing tall and fierce beside Severus's couch. So haunted and inaccessible in the one way I want him. In my wine-fueled state, the longing to be alone with him is almost unbearable.

Ursus has his eyes fixed on him as well, leering with a hunger I've seen many times now. That raw fascination mingled with an open craving to possess.

It disturbs me, makes me burn with rage, and I watch Jason's jaw set against whatever instinctive response is rising up within him as well.

"He's been quite an asset and worth every denarius," Severus says, raising his glass for a refill. A slave rushes over with a pitcher, and I marvel at the general's poise. He appears as calm and steady as ever, even though he must be aware of the fire he's stoking.

Ursus nods, continuing his appraisal. "I've no doubt." He places his glass on a short bronze table and rises from the couch. "May I?" he asks, motioning toward Jason.

Severus lifts a hand with a smile. "Of course." He flicks his head at Jason, motioning him to the center of the circle.

I clench my fists, horrified that Severus would betray him so easily. After everything he's said, everything he's promised, how can he throw our friend to the lions like every other entitled rich man?

Jason's back is to me now, but I don't miss the tension in his shoulders as he stands rigid, transformed once again into the statue that rips at my heart.

"Remarkable," Ursus whispers, circling him slowly. His probing stare crawls over every inch of the gladiator, but he doesn't touch him.

"I was there, you know," Ursus tells Severus as he takes his seat again.

Severus motions for Jason to return to his side.

"At the munera," Ursus continues. "I saw the fight. It was breathtaking." His gaze traces Jason in another intense appraisal. "He must have cost you a fortune. I'm surprised Opius Plinius parted with him."

Severus shrugs, easing back on the cushion. "Everyone has a price."

Ursus raises his glass in agreement. "True enough," he laughs. "I take it the Emperor agreed to the arrangement?"

"Of course. He sees the value of having a warrior so close."

Ursus furrows his brows. "Assuming he's been tamed, of course."

A smug look spreads over Severus's face as he rises from the couch.

"Come," he commands Jason.

Jason moves forward and faces his master, head bowed. The audience goes still when Severus draws the ceremonial dagger from his belt.

"May I borrow yours?" Severus asks a senator on another couch.

The man perks up and draws his weapon. He holds it out to Severus, and the onlookers gasp when the general hands it to Jason.

I swallow a surge of panic. *What is he doing?*

"Hold the blade before you and give me your other hand," Severus commands Jason in a stern tone.

Again, Jason does as he's told. The room crackles with excitement when Severus steps forward, aligning his neck with his valet's blade. He reaches for Jason's empty hand and pulls it taut, turning it so the soft flesh of the wrist and forearm is face up. With little ceremony, he drags his own blade across Jason's arm, leaving a healthy stream of blood in its wake. Jason barely flinches, remaining stoic as the crimson stain runs down his skin, dripping onto the patterned marble floor.

After what seems like an endless pause, Severus nods, and Jason returns the borrowed dagger to its owner with a bow. Severus hands him a cloth, and Jason applies it to his wound.

"Go clean yourself up," he commands.

Jason nods and starts for the door as the audience looks on in awe.

"Extraordinary," Ursus mumbles. The look in his eyes sends a surge of fear through me.

JASON

I nearly crash into Mallia as I leave the exedra after our demonstration. When she tilts her head up, my stomach drops at the look on her face.

How much of that did she see? By her expression, too much.

"What are you doing here?" I hiss, dragging her away from the exit. She's lucky no one caught her spying on us.

"What am I doing? What are *you* doing?" she shoots back, her eyes wide with horror. "How could Severus do that? Did he not see what—"

I clamp my hand over her mouth and pull her further into the shadows behind a myrtle tree.

"Quiet!" I snap.

She sways in my arms and I have to steady her as the strong scent of wine drifts toward me.

"Are you drunk?"

She stiffens at the accusation, but her indignation fades into intrigue the longer we stand connected. Her grip tightens on my tunic, her eyes searching with an earnestness that ignites those strange sparks I don't understand.

We clearly need to talk before I can release her back into the chaos around us. She could use a chance to sober up as well. The stakes are too high to let wine make our decisions.

I scan our surroundings for a private meeting place of our own.

"This way."

We pass other guests, but the drunken revelers give little notice to one more slave and young patrician snaking through the crowds. I tuck my injured arm against my body to hide the blood-soaked cloth. The wound stings, but I'm so used to such injuries, I barely notice.

By the time we find an unoccupied annex deep within the halls of the palace, Mallia seems to be walking straighter and thinking clearer. I let her go, and she steps back, her glare cutting into me.

I ignore her ire and sink to a cushioned bench, suddenly feeling lightheaded. Her intended reprimand stalls on her tongue when her gaze drops to the saturated cloth on my arm.

"*Thunder of Jupiter,* it's still gushing," she mutters, rushing forward and kneeling in front of me.

I yank my arm away and try to raise her up with my good hand. "I brought you here to sober you and get you back on task, not to nurse me. You can't go traipsing around with blood on your gown."

She fires another glare. "I'm not going to watch you bleed to death."

"I won't bl…never mind," I mumble when it's obvious she's not listening.

She's already on her feet, retrieving linen napkins from a refreshment table against the wall, along with a basin of water and a cup of wine.

"My lady, please," I say in a tone somewhere between a plea and a threat.

"Please, what? Let you die? No."

"My lady…"

"Don't make me command you to be still!" she snaps, placing the items on a marble table beside us.

She squares her petite shoulders to intimidate me, and I bite back a smile. She'd make any gladiator tremble.

"I apologize, my lady. I'm not trying to disobey you."

"No? Could have fooled me."

"I swear. I just—"

She grips my chin and tilts my face up to her. "Explain to me why Severus is allowed to slice you open, but I'm not allowed to put you back together?"

My smile breaks at her adorable indignation. She softens and gently spreads her palm over my cheek.

"You did your part. Let me do mine," she says quietly.

My pulse pounds as her touch lingers on my skin. Warm. Gentle. The way she looks at me, like there's something deep inside she's trying to find, has my heart pumping a foreign heat through every inch of my body.

She fills my head with so many questions, my body with so many sensations. As I stare back, my rebellious hand lifts in search of her soft skin.

Horrified, I stop abruptly and duck away from her.

"I'm so sorry, my lady. I shouldn't have—"

"Jason, stop. Stop." She traps my face in her palms. "You are not a slave when you're with me. You're a man. My friend. You're…"

Her fingertips finish the thought as they glide along my cheek, down my jawline, to the scar still visible through the stubble of my unshaven chin.

"This one," she says softly, tracing the jagged mark. "How did this one happen?"

My blood runs cold, and I stare at the relief of Mars on the wall beside us.

"It's not a suitable story for a lady."

Her thumb runs over the scar, drawing me back, and I close my eyes to avoid the pleading look in her gaze. I don't know what to do with this, with *her*. It's so different from anything I've encountered before. So dangerous and enticing.

I open my eyes and capture her hand to lower it, but I can't bring myself to let go. We remain like that for too long. Too many unspoken words, too many confusing feelings and desires.

With what seems like incredible effort, she finally pulls away with a faint sigh.

"I suppose we should finish up with your arm before we're missed." Her voice comes out hoarse, and she clears her throat as she retrieves the cup of wine from the table. "Drink this. It will help with the pain."

The pain I can handle. It's the rest of what's happening between us that has me taking the cup and consuming the contents in a few desperate gulps. I need to get her out of my head, to center myself back in reality.

Peeling back the blood-soaked cloth helps with that, and she curses as she examines the wound.

"The cut is deep."

"It had to look authentic."

Her eyes shoot to mine in my alarm. "Wait. That entire scene was staged?"

"Of course."

Her grip tightens on my arm as she wrestles with a thought. "But so deep?"

"It wasn't intentional. He was in an awkward position to be precise."

I wince when she presses a clean wet cloth into the gash. She chews on her lip, as I've seen her do many times when she's nervous. Is it me or the situation that has her on edge?

"So you were *intentionally* targeting Ursus?" she asks, dabbing at the wound. "Did you not see the way he was looking at you?"

My gaze brushes hers before dropping to the floor again.

"I did. That was our goal."

"To make him lust for you?" Irritation is back in her tone. Anger.

I nod while surveying my arm. Satisfied with the condition, I pull away and finish wrapping the makeshift bandage myself.

"It's part of the game."

"It's a dangerous game."

"It's our only play."

She crosses her arms with a scowl, and I sink back to the cushion in frustration. "We have eyes on Senator Varro, paths to Nepos, and you can access almost anyone in the palace and Senate," I explain. "What we don't have is a door to Ursus. His men hate Tacitus and Argus and would never accept them into their circles. He doesn't trust Severus, who is close to the Emperor. That leaves me, the one thing he wants but can't have."

The scheme is so simple and obvious. I don't understand why she doesn't see it.

"Ursus is a fan of the games," I continue, willing her to understand. "He's trained with gladiators many times as a visitor. So is Senator Varro. They're obsessed with us. Who better to get close to them than their living, breathing fantasy?"

Her skeptical look sinks into anger. "So, what? Severus is going to give you to him? Is that the brilliant plan?"

"Not give. Just lend me," I reason.

"*Lend you?* You can't be serious. Lend you how?"

I shrug and look away. "I don't know. However Ursus wishes."

"No," she hisses, stomping her foot. "No! That's unacceptable. I'll speak to Severus. There's no way—"

"Not permanently," I counter. "I still have my duties to Severus. He'd just let them use me for a social event or two. To impress Ursus's friends. If I had to guess, to impress Varro himself."

"And how exactly does that help our cause?" she snaps.

"How does it *not*?" I fight the rising exasperation at her constant challenges. "I'd be in the heart of their affairs. Interacting with their acquaintances, eavesdropping on their conversations, and gaining the trust of their slaves."

It makes perfect sense. Logical, calculated, clinical. I have no idea why she's upset. How can a person as intelligent as her not see the value?

"But at what cost?" she cries.

"What do you mean?"

Pain flickers in her eyes before she closes them and takes a deep breath.

"My lady?"

"Mallia," she corrects in a wounded voice. "Please, call me Mallia."

Her gaze locks on mine again, searching, pleading. Why is she making this so difficult? Our roles aren't confusing. At least, they're not supposed to be.

"My lady, I don't…"

She looks away and takes a shaky breath. "And you think they'll trust you? You're Severus's man."

I shake my head. "I'm not a man to them. I'm a slave. I'm nothing."

She flinches, and I hate that I'm hurting her, but I don't understand why. All I'm doing is answering her questions.

"We're expecting him to use me for his own schemes," I continue, trying to explain. I need her to understand. I need her to stop looking at me like I'm crushing her. This entire ploy is going to be hard enough without her disapproval weighing on me.

"What kind of schemes?" Her voice is more controlled now, as if she's buried whatever was bothering her.

I shift on the bench, applying more pressure to the injury. The wound throbs, and I focus on the steady beat to calm myself down.

"We think they'll want to use me to get to Severus and the Emperor somehow. It'll be a game of wills and wits between us, but I have the heavy advantage of being underestimated and aware of their schemes."

Mallia doesn't respond this time. She searches my face until the apprehension melts into something softer. Something hypnotic that makes my heart race and my body warm.

"I understand the strategy, Jason, but there was evil in his eyes," she says in a haunted voice. "When he looked at you, it was like..." She blinks through a visible shudder. "What if he wants more from you than Severus anticipates?"

I sigh, finally understanding her concern. But she still doesn't understand mine.

"Remember the conversation in Argus's flat? I've endured such things a hundred times. A thousand. At least this time it will serve a purpose."

My reassurance has the opposite effect when she stiffens in anger.

"No! Not good enough," she snaps. She takes my face in her hands again and locks her stare on mine. "No."

She holds me there, forcing me to confront her compassion, her distress.

Something shifts inside me. The thing I can't touch or control. It's an internal struggle, a battle for something, but I don't know what.

Her thumb runs over my lips, calming one storm and igniting another.

"Don't let them hurt you," she whispers. "Please, Jason. I'm begging you. Make Severus swear they won't hurt you."

Her desperate eyes are breaking every rule I know. Her soft touch.

Speechless, I force in a heavy breath. I hate denying her, but there's no way I can promise what she wants. My body is all I have to offer.

"Thank you for your concern, my lady," I reply, gently pulling away.

I feel her anxious gaze as I rise and brush past her to the exit.

ARGUS

No one can believe my luck. A disgraced legionary appointed to the Praetorian Guard? Most lose their citizen rights after a missio ignominiosa, and here I am—an imperial employee. But the Emperor had insisted, at Severus's urging. Since it was his neck on the line, Praetorian Prefect Verus Falco couldn't exactly refuse a recruit.

The other members of his cohort seem to be accepting me easily enough. Severus hadn't been kidding about the key to their affections. It only took a few rounds of drinks and gruesome war stories to win their favor.

"You say the women rode naked?" Eustacius asks, tugging at the collar of his tunic.

"Naked as the day they were born," I snort. It might be a *slight* exaggeration, but my audience doesn't seem to mind. The enemy forces did have women fighting among them.

"*Caenum*, how I'd love to see that," he murmurs.

"You'd love to see any woman naked," Decien snickers.

"Yes, well, at least my goals are more attainable," Eustacius retorts. "This lad thinks he will one day grace Lady Aurelia's bed."

"*Eat ashes*, Eustacius. She touched me once!"

"Touched you?" I laugh out.

"Right here," Decien says, slapping his backside.

I bark a laugh as Eustacius erupts. "I'm surprised you're not already married after that encounter!" he snorts.

Decien fires a glare at him. "Laugh all you want, but you would bed her in a second if she'd have you. We all would."

"And then be shackled in the arena to be ripped apart by lions. No thanks," Eustacius quips.

I can't argue that. A likely end to any fantasy involving the Emperor's niece.

"Have you ever seen action against the Emperor?" I ask, changing the subject. I already know more about Aurelia's twisted desires than I care to.

"Many times, my friend," Decien says, taking a long swig from his cup. "I hope you are as brave as they say."

"Just a few weeks ago, there was an attack right in the Emperor's own gardens," Eustacius boasts, shifting forward on the bench. "Four aggressors. Came out of nowhere."

"Really?" I ask, feigning surprise. "Was anyone hurt?"

"Only the intruders when we gutted them," Eustacius brags with a smug smile. "They barely put up a fight. It was quite a disappointment, really."

I'm sure it was, since it was Jason's sword that felled them. My companions don't seem to have any intention of crediting the slave, however. No surprise there.

"Wow. His own gardens? I didn't realize the threats could hit even on palace grounds."

Decien grunts and rolls his cup in his palms. "They're everywhere. We stand watch every hour of the day throughout the city."

"Yeah, don't ever cross Falco or you'll be assigned to arena crowd control," Eustacius warns. "I'd take an entire cohort of rogue legionaries over wrestling drunk spectators from their seats."

I toss a wry grin and pretend to take another swallow of my drink. "I don't doubt it."

Eustacius stretches with a heavy sigh. "Speaking of which, we should be getting back. Our shift begins at dawn."

I slump back in my stool and wave a hand. "Fair enough. I'll see you then."

While they weave through the tavern toward the exit, I pretend to ignore them in favor of finishing my drink. Once they're on the street, I drop a handful of sesterces on the table and follow.

Chapter XVII

TACITUS

I strain forward from my position at the perimeter of Senator Varro's peristyle to hear pieces of the conversation in the attached exedra. After wasting days clearing paths through crowds, securing space at the baths, and pretending to learn combat techniques from men half as skilled as I, there's finally an event of interest.

Ursus is visiting Varro this morning, joined by an unknown man dressed in embellished fabrics and a ceremonial cloak well-beyond what's appropriate for such a casual visit. He must be a wealthy social climber and recent addition to the equestrian class, not yet skilled at blending in with the etiquette of the elite.

They joined Senator Varro for an early lunch before reclining for a more in-depth conversation in the curved sitting room off the peristyle. Although I can't see them clearly from my place beside an ornate column, I can hear enough to know this conversation could be of grave importance to our mission. I don't recognize the stranger, but Severus or Mallia might.

From my brief glimpse upon arrival, I noted the visitor is short and heavy-set, with a face that appears younger than the rest of him. Bright red cheeks and a bulbous nose give him a look of eternal youth and the appearance of being on the verge of laughter even though he rarely seems to indulge. I haven't gotten a name yet, but—

Footsteps clap toward me from the left, and I turn to find Captain Atticus motioning for me to approach. I leave my post to meet him in the neighboring corridor.

"Sir?"

"Lady Arata requires an escort this afternoon. Protect her like you would her father."

My stomach drops. He can't be serious. My thoughts dart back to the exedra several paces away and then collide with a more alarming reality.

"Everything okay, soldier?" Atticus asks, adjusting the gladius at his hip.

"Yes, sir. Of course."

"Good. She'll meet you in the atrium." The captain waves me on before continuing his patrol.

While I march through the corridor toward the front of the house, Mallia's warning about Arata's interest echoes with each step.

My shock at her report was genuine, but that doesn't mean I hadn't noticed the young woman since my tenure at Varro's house began. Arata's stunning amber eyes and generous smile are impossible to ignore, and will be especially problematic now that I know the coy glances are intentional. It's fair to say my thoughts about the daughter of my employer haven't always been entirely appropriate.

And now I have to spend an entire afternoon alone with her.

I doubt she'd be bold enough to request my service directly, which means this assignment is the misfortune of being the newest recruit. No seasoned soldier wants to be sentenced to an afternoon of merchant shops and public baths.

My suspicions are confirmed by Glabrio's snicker when I pass his post at the edge of the atrium.

"Enjoy the perfumes, pendants, and baubles, *recruit*," he whispers.

I glare at him, but don't respond as I continue past the family shrine, ceremonial pool, and graphic mosaic of the flaying of Marsyas on the wall that made me shudder the first time I saw it.

This reassignment also means I'm missing the crucial meeting between Varro, Ursus, and the mystery man. I should be gathering critical intel, not traipsing around Rome doing the boring things nobles do when they're not scheming to take down an empire. The sinister plot we've feared could be forming mere paces away, and I have to miss it to watch a rich girl shop.

It's everything I can do to keep from grunting in frustration when I take my place in the atrium to wait for my charge. Just a few minutes later, Arata glides into the room wearing a light blue tunic, cream stola clasped at the shoulders, and a pale gold palla. Her maid follows close behind, but no other attendants join them.

She hesitates when she sees me, her eyes widening enough to confirm my theory that this isn't a planned seduction that will end with my head on a spike. The shy, pleased smile and full-body scan *after* the surprise confirms Mallia's.

"Shall we go?" she says, drawing the golden palla over her head in a loose hood. When she glances up at me, I can't help but notice how the gold tone accents her amber eyes.

"Would you like me to call for a litter, my lady?" I ask, leading her toward the vestibulum.

"No, I feel like walking today. It's lovely, and I don't wish for a full entourage. Hence, my request for one of my father's men."

I cringe and cast a concerned look back at her. "I'm sure your husband and father would be more comfortable with a full entourage."

"Them or you?" she quips, a disarming glint in her eyes.

"I only meant…"

Her brows lift in challenge. "I'm not an idiot. I know my father's men. You're probably bitter that Captain Atticus assigned you, the fiercest of Mars' warriors, to babysit a woman while she shops. Don't take it personally. It's the burden of all new guards." She steps into the vestibulum and squints into the sunlight. "Besides, why would you want to stand in a stuffy hall listening to my father jabber about boring politics, when you could be enjoying the afternoon sun with a beautiful woman?"

I return a tight smile. Pretty sure she wouldn't like my answer to that question.

"Where are we headed, my lady?" I ask as we walk the stone path through the forecourt toward the villa gate. I nod to the doorkeeper, who opens it and lets us pass.

Arata twists a grin up at me. "Right down to business, aren't you? A true professional. You are Tacitus, correct?"

I scan the street before motioning for her to leave the safety of her estate. "I'm not trying to be rude, my lady, I just don't think your father would appreciate his defense coffers being wasted on conversation."

"No? He'd rather fund a hallway of living statues while his obnoxious friends consume his best wine?"

A wry smile threatens my lips, despite my sour mood. Mallia might also be right about this woman's wit. Beautiful and smart? Confident and brave?

Based on the pounding in my chest, I'm in deep trouble.

"Obnoxious friends, huh?" I say as we start down the street. "Isn't one of them your father-in-law?"

She scoffs and keeps pace beside me. "I fail to see how that fact changes the composition of his personality."

My grin widens, and yeah…she's going to be a dangerous temptation.

"Why Tacitus, did I actually draw a smile from that brooding face?"

"I apologize, my lady. Smiles make poor masks for bodyguards."

She shoots me a mischievous look. "Perhaps, but they suit you well."

Not sure how to respond, I shake my head and let an easy silence settle over us. Her maid follows behind by several paces, but the lack of a litter and other attendants has me very uncomfortable.

"Entertain me while we walk," she says in a conversational tone. "Tell me about yourself. Who is *Gaius Atius Tacitus*?"

I glance at her in surprise. "You know my name?"

"Yes, but learning it took some effort."

A rush of heat mixes with swift unease as I turn my attention back to the busy street. We're a block from where the wealthy residential district of The Laurels transitions into the upscale markets.

"Do you always take an interest in your father's men?" I ask, deflecting.

"Only the interesting ones. Atticus says you're former military, but there's a refinement about you. If I had to guess—a centurion?"

Stunned, I can't help another quick glance in her direction. When those hypnotic amber eyes lock on mine, I quickly focus back on searching for threats. "Good guess. Legio Six."

"So, you're not a freedman like most of the others."

"No," I say through a short laugh. "I was born into an equestrian military family. My grandfather served as Camp Prefect in the Ninth, and my father determined his second son would follow in his footsteps. My family owns a villa in the Amethyst Hill neighborhood, and a farm just outside Rome's walls where they employ as many former soldiers as possible. Well, the ones who can't claim, or keep, their own land after retirement."

I sense her surprise, but don't dare another look. "Oh? You can't be more than thirty. How is it a young centurion with such a military pedigree ended up escorting a married woman to the marketplace?"

The gods themselves couldn't make me answer that question honestly.

"What are you implying?" I return with a flash of humor. "I thought this mission was the highest honor?"

She bites back a grin as she surveys my face in slow perusal. Another surge of heat sears through me, and I do my best to ignore it.

"You're a mysterious man, Centurion," she murmurs.

"Lucky for you, I'm also adept at carrying packages."

Her laugh breezes over me, piercing my guard almost as much as the light in her eyes. Budding warmth mixes with a growing stab of concern that we may have uncovered a flower among the weeds of our enemies. My mission regarding Arata has suddenly gotten even more complicated.

"I bet it's harder than people think being the daughter of a senator," I say, daring another brief peek in her direction.

She narrows her eyes at me. "Are you mocking me?"

"Not at all. Just speaking from observation."

She seems to relax as she falls into a thoughtful state. "Maybe. But I'd never admit such a thing."

"Why's that?"

She cocks her head toward me. "You're a soldier. You've seen death, blood, hunger, pain, and cold. Do you really think I'd try to gain sympathy for the fact that I find my life frightfully boring? Can you imagine complaining about endless days of shopping and lounging at the baths?"

I shrug with a smirk. "Depending on the company, that sounds horrifying."

Her radiant smile returns, and it bothers me how much I want to keep it there.

"Present company excluded," she teases.

"Thank you," I chuckle. "But in all seriousness, you clearly have a complex mind. I can see how it would be hard to force it to remain idle."

Her silence is longer this time as we walk. I notice that our pace has slowed, despite the clear path in front of us.

"As do you, Tacitus," she says quietly. "Are you really content standing around watching my father eat and talk all day? I think you understand more of what I'm saying than you'd dare to admit. Besides, it wouldn't matter anyway. I'm a woman. Married to a man I only see for a few days a month. Even when he's home, he has little interest in anything except producing an heir."

"He's a fool then," I mumble before I can stop it.

Frax.

Arata raises her brows. "A brave thing to say about your employer's son-in-law."

I clench my jaw and bow my head. "Apologies, my lady. I shouldn't have."

She tortures me with a lengthy pause and then lets a smile slip out. "Maybe not, but I'm glad you did. He *is* a fool, though no one admits to it. Certainly not our fathers who have become the best of friends."

"They seem an unlikely pair."

"Why do you say that?"

My pulse picks up at the direction of this conversation. Lines of merchant stalls loom ahead, meaning I only have a few more moments before she's distracted.

"Your father is a patrician and highly regarded senator. Ursus is a merchant of the equestrian class. It just seems like a mismatched union."

She readjusts the golden hood over her hair to block the afternoon sun.

"Ursus is inexcusably wealthy. He owns more ships than the Emperor. He's also a huge fan of the games like my father. Did you know my father leases gladiators from a ludus in Rome? He's a well-known patron."

"No, I didn't."

As hoped, this conversation is quickly getting more interesting. Maybe today's excursion won't be a waste after all.

She shrugs and fixes an absent gaze on something ahead. "It's true, and it's an expensive business, let me tell you. Ursus's money could come in handy for this and other pursuits."

"What kind of pursuits?" I try to keep an even tone through the spike of adrenaline.

She laughs and waves her hand. "Who knows? That would be the subject of those boring conversations from which I rescued you. All I know is that if you're a senator with high aspirations, you need unlimited funds. And if you're an equestrian merchant with unlimited funds, you would be wise to share them with an aspiring senator."

"Especially if they're both fans of the games."

She nods. "I can tell you one thing. My father would love nothing more than to sponsor lavish munera, eclipsing anything Rome has seen in decades."

My limbs go numb. I swallow my shock. "He wants to host games? In whose honor?"

Arata shrugs, resuming her casual pace. "Probably my grandfather, who died a year ago. Maybe my mother, who passed when I was eleven? Does it matter? It's all a political farce anyway."

I force a nod, my mind spinning. "Do you know when he plans to sponsor these games?"

"Why? Don't tell me you're obsessed with them as well. And here I thought I've finally found a civilized friend."

I flicker a tight smile. "No, I'm just curious. After all, an event like that would require heavy involvement from its sponsor's bodyguards."

She relaxes with a soft sigh. "True enough, but no, I'm sorry. I've only heard brief discussions about it. I don't know any more details than what I've told you."

The first merchant booth is just a few paces away. I'm out of time.

"I have an acquaintance who's interested in patronage," I say, grasping for anything. "Do you happen to know the lanista from whom your father leases his gladiators?"

She pauses, knitting her brows as she thinks. "I've never met him, but his gladiators were among those used by the Emperor for this past munera. I believe it is the House of Opius Plinius."

TACITUS

"We have a problem," I say as soon as Argus joins me at the table in Carbo's tavern. "Where's Severus?"

Argus shrugs, glancing behind him toward the opening to the main room. "No idea. I couldn't find him and came as soon as I could. Your message seemed urgent. I'm supposed to be asleep right now."

I grunt in frustration. "I am, too, but this can't wait. Remember Arata?"

"Varro's daughter."

I nod, leaning toward him. "I had a very interesting conversation with her today. Her father also has ties to Opius Plinius."

Argus stares at me with a blank expression.

"The lanista?" I remind him.

Argus shrugs, scratching his beard in irritation. "And?"

"The lanista who supplied the gladiators for the Emperor's games. Jason's former owner."

His eyes go wide as he sinks back on the stool. *"Frax..."* he breathes out. Seconds tick by while he processes the news. "Do you think Severus knows?"

I fix a distracted gaze on the lewd graffiti painted on the far wall. "I have no idea. What I do know is that it seems like Varro is using Ursus to raise funds to sponsor munera in honor of his deceased father."

His alarmed look darts to me. "When?"

I shake my head. "I don't know, but there's only one reason I can think of why a powerful senator would need an army, an unlimited purse, and the favor of the masses."

Argus breathes another violent curse. "We need to find Severus."

Chapter XVIII

Jason

I force away the cold sweep of simmering dread as I present myself to the steward of Ursus's house. The servant tells me to wait in the small tablinum attached to the atrium as he sends for the dominus.

It's been two weeks since the staged encounter with Ursus at the Emperor's birthday celebration, and we weren't surprised the merchant took Severus up on his generous offer so soon after the invitation. Supposedly, tonight's private event will be stocked with curiosities and unusual entertainment brought in from around the Empire.

Of course, it required the presence of elite gladiators.

It's surprising and unsettling to be received in the master's office like an honored guest instead of a borrowed slave. Severus warned me to stay on my guard, that the elite play games and embrace with one arm while stabbing with the other, though I didn't need the reminder.

I know such duplicity better than anyone.

"Jason! So good to see you!" Ursus cries, shuffling into the room and clapping my arm.

I bow my head in a deferential greeting. "Thank you, my lord. How may I be of service?"

His boisterous laugh echoes through the stark walls of the atrium and reeks of forced humor. "I did not realize you had talents besides limitless bravery and ferocious combat, neither of which will be necessary at the moment. No, I only need you to make a fine figure for my guests. Has Silenus presented you with your armor yet?"

I shake my head, uneasy. "My armor?"

Ursus rubs a hand over his balding head in irritation. "He hasn't. The idiot. Yes! I have procured the most glorious adornment for you. I hope it fits. I have reason to believe it will."

I manage a weak smile despite the churning in my stomach. His cryptic words only add to the ominous feel of his strained joviality. "Of course, my lord. Whatever you require."

Ursus clasps his hands, showing off several gaudy rings on his long, bony fingers. His pretentious robes and jewelry remind me so much of my former master Plinius. Both are plagued by the irony of hubris—when exaggerated pride leads to brazen flaunting of their own humiliation.

"Excellent," he says, fluttering his embellished crimson cloak behind him. "Now, if you'll excuse me, I still have much to attend to prior to the arrival of my guests. We have quite a night planned!"

Good. Severus and I are counting on it.

MALLIA

The surprise invitation from Arata to attend a banquet at her father-in-law's estate left me both concerned and intrigued. I hadn't realized I made an impression on the woman, but I can't say I'm displeased. Aurelia received an invitation as well, although the Emperor's niece had no intention of degrading herself by attending such an event.

I'm relieved her snobbery freed me to further my investigation without distraction.

Fear and anticipation ripple through me as an usher leads me through the opulent corridors of Ursus's villa toward a richly decorated triclinium. Not only will this be my first direct engagement behind enemy lines, but I didn't have time to strategize with Severus beforehand, which means I'm operating on my own.

Danae and I exchange a surprised glance as we enter the dining room. While there are more than the typical three couches for nine guests, the total space couldn't accommodate more than twenty. Despite the sparse guest list, we passed several tables stocked with refreshments on the journey from the atrium to the peristyle and encountered an army of slaves wandering the grounds serving beverages and assisting arriving guests.

Who are these people, and what's the true purpose of this event?

Arata finds me stalled in the entrance and grabs my hands.

"You came!" she says, squeezing lightly before letting go. Her light brown hair frames her head in tasteful braids. A simple string of pearls graces her pale neck, and the fine silk of her green stola gives it a chic flair without crossing into gaudiness. In short, she's dressed in the married version of my own simple elegance.

"I was so afraid you wouldn't come," she says, amber eyes saturated with relief. "I wasn't sure how you and Aurelia reacted to my visit. I fear she didn't like me much."

I offer a sincere smile. "Don't worry about Aurelia. She's always that way. And of course, I came. I was happy for the invitation."

Arata leans close, scowling at the cluttered room. Every inch of space is draped in food and decoration. "Don't be fooled by the grand décor. It's the only interesting aspect of my father-in-law's feasts."

"Noted," I say with a chuckle. "And where's your husband this evening?"

Arata's subtle flinch catches me off guard, and she quickly covers it with an indifferent shrug. "Somewhere in this house talking about something boring. He allowed me to invite friends to keep me out of the way more than anything. Come! I'll show you around. I remember you saying you love a home's gardens the most."

While pleased she remembered that detail, I'm even more grateful for a tour and the opportunity to gather intelligence. She takes me through the peristyle, pointing out rooms and other guests as we encounter them. Most of the names I don't recognize, although I try to preserve them to memory. These must be people outside my father's typical circles.

Arata drags me through a wall of flowing sheer linens into a giant exedra.

"You can help yourself," she says, waving over a spread of pre-feast snacks tucked against a side wall. "The main meal won't be served for quite some time yet."

I barely hear her. I'm not even sure I'm breathing.

All sights and sounds dissolve when my gaze locks on the imposing statue beside the table. My mind and body scream a response when his hazel eyes brush mine and then return to staring absently like the ornament he's supposed to be.

"He's a gladiator," Arata explains in an absent tone, noting my interest. "Well, he was. Don't ask me why he's here except to impress my father, I suppose. Apparently, this one is quite famous and has a distinguished reputation. An actual champion. You can touch him if you'd like. He won't hurt you. He's not even armed."

A dangerous combination of resentment and desire floods through me at her offer. Jason doesn't react, even though he must have heard. Dark memories of a similar situation in a palace exedra flood my head.

"No, thank you. I'm not much for the games," I force out in a stiff tone.

"Good," Arata huffs, scanning the table of snacks. "Neither am I. Now these honey cakes, on the other hand…" She holds up a delicate pastry with a grin.

I select one as well, knowing I won't be able to swallow it. I cast another discreet look at Jason, but his jaw is set in its distant display of indifference. I know I can't acknowledge him, but it feels traitorous to carry on like he's nothing—ironic, considering his powerful presence has taken over my entire awareness.

"What will they do with him?" I ask as casually as possible. I take a small bite to keep my mouth from screaming.

Arata shrugs. "Nothing, if my father-in-law has any sense, but more than likely, he plans to cap off the evening entertainment with an exhibition. You'll notice he's collected several gladiators from a ludus in Rome tonight."

Alarm fires through me. My body feels cold as I fight the urge to meet Jason's gaze again. All I want to do is shout a protest that this particular slave is no longer a gladiator, nor does he belong to our host for his perversions.

I manage to swallow the objection along with the pastry at Jason's silent warning. He wouldn't want me to get involved and risk our mission or make the situation worse. What happened before comes screeching back, and now the stakes are even higher. I understand, but it pains me to choke down my anger. I feel Danae's strong reaction behind me as well.

"Where is your father?" I ask, changing the subject before I lose the battle with myself. "You mentioned the gladiators were acquired to impress him, but I don't recall seeing him."

Arata nods with a bored expression. "Who knows? Somewhere being fawned over and adored, I'm sure." Her eyes light up as she twists toward me. "Oh! You must come see the gardens behind the villa. They're even more impressive than the peristyle."

I can't help another quick glance at Jason as she drags me away, and his subtle nod of reassurance has no effect on my troubled heart. He and Severus might be fine with all of this, but I'm not.

I'm pretty sure I will never be.

JASON

Relief flushes through me as I watch Mallia leave the exedra. Her obvious concern is sweet but dangerous.

I'm accustomed to difficult battles, but not within myself, and certainly not the ones I face every time she's close. She confuses and distracts me, two things I can't afford if I have any hope of completing my mission—and surviving the night.

I force her out of my mind as I shift in the uncomfortable armor Ursus provided.

He was correct about the fit, but nothing else. The ornamental bronze cuirass with its chiseled abs and pectoral impressions looks as ridiculous on my chest as the embellished helmet flowing with dyed horsehair covering my head. An embossed shin guard features the same laurel and lion motif as the rest of the armor, while a useless decorative leather sword belt does everything except hold an actual sword. Even the crimson, thigh-length tunic feels wrong for actual combat when I'd typically fight in nothing but a soft leather loincloth.

This whole get up is clearly designed for aesthetics, not functionality. It's heavy and impractical, solid where it should flex, decorated where it should be bare. I wouldn't be able to handle a weapon effectively with the shifting weight of these pieces throwing off my balance.

I'd laugh at the thought of trying to fight in this costume if it wasn't a likely possibility. I've spent most of my time beside this table thinking of strategies to overcome the heavy disadvantage I'd face in battle. The second they positioned me in this prominent location, I knew I'd be sparring an opponent at some point in the evening.

Now, I have to prepare for the possibility that Ursus will make me do it while wearing his "generous gift."

"...but you heard the report about Legatus Titullus, correct?" a man says to his friend as they enter the exedra and approach the refreshment table.

"The Governor of Britannia?" His companion wears a tunic with the distinguishing purple stripes of a senator.

The man nods and glances around. Seeing no one but a slave statue, he leans close. "The legate is dead. Supposedly killed in battle."

The senator stiffens, his hand stalling above the tray of chilled oysters. "Supposedly?"

"I have it on good authority Titullus wasn't even at the battle that supposedly killed him," his friend whispers with a conspiratorial look.

The senator turns to him, brow furrowed. "You think he was murdered then?"

"I think it would be very hard to die in a battle in which you didn't participate."

"But the report! I told you what was read to the Senate."

The other guest shrugs and surveys the table. He reaches for a pickled egg. "You know this game. What are reports but one man's word?"

"What you're implying is treason."

"No, simply interpretation," he garbles through a bite. They make their way back toward the peristyle. "Besides, I didn't say murder. You..."

I can't hear the rest as they disappear through the curtains with their snacks.

Interesting. I add that piece of helpful information to the long list I've already collected tonight.

TACITUS

After completing my sweep of Ursus's estate, I draw up beside Captain Atticus just outside the triclinium to deliver the report.

"I count seventeen guests. Two have their own detail, for a total of seven armed men. The main entrance would be too conspicuous for a threat, and the side entrance is nearly blocked with extra provisions for tonight's festivities. There's a small gate that exits to the cross street through the far north wall behind a garden annex. It's guarded, but only by a house slave who appears unarmed. If we need an escape route, that would be it."

Atticus nods. "Good work. Let's hope we don't."

I set my jaw as my hand instinctively adjusts the gladius at my hip. "Have you ever been forced to evacuate the senator?"

"Twice, that I can recall," Atticus replies in a distracted tone while scanning the large atrium. "Once, when a celebration was interrupted by a rival of the event's host. He sent ten men to wreak havoc, but most of the damage was to the food and furniture. We got Senator Varro home without even a drop of wine on his robes."

"And the other time? You said you had to act twice."

Atticus's lips spread into a wry grin as he flickers a quick glance at me. "The other time was from his own country estate when his late wife caught him exercising his marital rights with another woman."

I snort a laugh. "His wife must have been quite a woman to strike such fear in her husband."

"She was, and her daughter has every bit of her wit and fire. Watch out for that one. I've had to let more than a few of my men go when they became too enamored with Arata's charms. Not that she does anything to encourage them. She just happens to be a beautiful girl who possesses a dangerous combination of intelligence, beauty, and passion for any lonely soldier."

From my own interactions, I understand exactly what he means. Add her reported interest in me, and I'm in the perfect position to be dismissed. Or gutted. I'll have to be very delicate with this situation.

Finished with the report, we spread out to patrol the festivities. While roaming the house and watching for threats, I also absorb as much as I can, searching faces, eavesdropping on conversations, and evaluating each scene I encounter. Who sits where, who is drunk, who takes advantage of what type of entertainment.

I'm surprised to encounter Mallia at one point, but we don't acknowledge each other except for a brief second of eye contact. I'm also concerned when a statue beside an hors d'oeuvres table in the exedra turns out to be Jason. I know Severus isn't in attendance, which makes Jason's presence more unsettling.

I wait several paces away, pretending to stand watch, until the room clears.

"I'm surprised to see you here," I say quietly.

"Ursus and Varro are fans of the games," my friend replies in an even tone.

I eye his absurd armor with a smirk. "Clearly."

He returns it before growing serious.

"Jason, you need to know something," I whisper, moving closer. "I've learned from Varro's daughter that he and Ursus have ties to Opius Plinius. It's likely your former lanista will be in attendance tonight. This whole thing could be some kind of setup."

Jason glances at me in alarm. "Plinius is here? You're sure?"

"Just a guess, but Senator Varro leases gladiators from Plinius and is intending to do so again in the near future. I'm sure he had his eyes on you before Severus took you from the ludus. As a freedman, he wouldn't be welcomed for dinner, but he could show up later for an exhibition. It's a possibility you should prepare for."

A muscle moves in his cheek as he directs a hard stare at the far wall. "Does Severus know any of this?" he asks in an agitated tone.

"Do you think you'd be here if he did? I haven't had the opportunity to tell him. I wasn't expecting to see you tonight."

Jason doesn't respond as his fist clenches tightly at his side.

I search his troubled expression, my stance firm but sympathetic. "I can't help you if it comes to it. You understand that, right?"

His gaze cuts to mine before darting back to the wall. He nods once, and I sigh in frustration. "Don't get me wrong. It would take all my strength to stand down. I promise you, I will get this information to Severus as quickly as possible so he can act, if necessary."

"Mallia," he says suddenly.

"Mallia?"

"She's here." He turns an urgent look on me. "Protect her at least? She's a noble. You can do that without raising suspicions, right?"

I furrow my brow. "It would be natural for the host's bodyguard to protect a guest, but it shouldn't be necessary. I don't see how she'd be in any danger from this development."

Jason shakes his head. "That's not what I mean. I meant, keep her from defending me."

My stomach drops when I realize what he's saying.

Don't let her intervene while they rip him apart. Protect her from *herself.*

Pluto's chains, that would be brutal. Let's hope we're wrong.

Concern and admiration stir inside me as I watch him bury his emotions again.

"Of course I will, my friend."

Jason nods in gratitude. "There's something else you should know in case I don't have the chance to share it later. We have confirmation that the Governor of Britannia is likely dead. We also have more reason to believe it wasn't an accident."

MALLIA

It feels strange that Tacitus positions himself so closely to me as the guests assemble for the highlight of the evening's entertainment in the grand hall of the atrium after the meal.

He and I crossed paths several times throughout the evening, and it always seemed as though he wanted to say something. Circumstances never allowed it, however, and now it's too late as we're surrounded by our enemies.

"Ladies and gentlemen! Honored guests!" Ursus shouts, waving his arms above his head like an editor of the games. His booming voice echoes over the marble walls and high, rectangular ceiling. He glances around, acknowledging the "honored guests" standing in curious clusters near the shallow pool.

"I hope you've been enjoying the food, drink, and entertainment so far this evening," he says in a theatrical tone. "You've all been invited as friends, not only of mine, but also my co-host, Senator Marcus Aratus Varro. It is his generosity that brings you tonight's main event, along with Rome's favorite lanista, Opius Plinius, who so kindly contributed some of his men."

He steps back and bows with dramatic flair. "Let the games begin!"

I tense when a small, overly dressed man emerges from the shadows, leading a line of four gladiators. My breath releases when none appear to be Jason. I cast a quick glance at Tacitus, and my relief fades at the hard set of his jaw.

He must know something. Is that what he's been wanting to tell me all night?

"May I present four of my best!" the stranger boasts to a round of polite applause. "Now, for your entertainment, please enjoy a private demonstration of their skill."

The staged battles that follow quickly dispel some of my fears. Each "match" is well-rehearsed and carried out with practice weapons that wouldn't harm a civilian, let alone a warrior. Still, the crowd oohs and ahhs as though they're watching a clash of the gods themselves.

I'm relieved to be bored but eager for an end to the evening. As much as I enjoy Arata's company, this night has been taxing. I'm ready to go home and document everything I can remember.

Tacitus's increasing tension as the exhibition wears on unnerves me, however. His employer doesn't appear to be in any danger, nor do any of the patrons. Yet his rigid stance, constant clench of the fist, and rapid scan of the room has me on edge. Something's wrong.

It's not until the pretend performances end and Ursus once again takes the stage that I learn what it is.

Chapter XIX

Jason

"What a show!" Ursus cries as the final staged match comes to a close. I can't see much from the shadowed corridor where they've kept me hidden, but I've experienced enough of these events to know what's happening. "We look forward to the next opportunity to witness the real thing in the arena."

He moves into view of where I'm standing, and a chilling grin spreads over his lips. "Now, I have a special surprise for all of you."

The nudge of a vine stick into my back presses me forward. I step into the light and ignore the gasps of the crowd as I follow a parting pathway through them. When Opius Plinius steps into place at the end, old anger mixes with a touch of fear. His hard expression morphs into a cruel smile, churning my stomach.

"May I present, Jason, one of the most decorated gladiators of our time!" Ursus announces to a chorus of awed applause.

"How did you get him back?" Opius Plinius hisses to Ursus under his breath.

Ursus returns a sly smile. "What do you mean? Do you know this gladiator?"

"Everyone knows he was my champion, stolen from my house!" the lanista growls.

"Stolen?" Ursus feigns surprise as he motions for Opius Plinius to follow him behind a marble column for a private conversation.

While the crowd buzzes with conspiratorial murmurs, I force in steadying breaths and try to discern what they've plotted. I don't believe for a second any of this charade is real. Nor do I believe Severus was a willing accomplice. He assumed what I did, that I'd attend tonight's festivities as an ornament and possible actor in a pretend match.

There's no way he'd betray me.

I scan the crowd, relieved to find Tacitus hovering near Mallia. Her stunned look slices through my stoic resolve. When our eyes lock, distress floods her face. I tear my gaze away from her silent pleas, praying Tacitus will get her out of here.

Ursus and Plinius return from their staged conference, drawing my attention back to the present nightmare.

"Ladies and gentlemen, I have just learned an interesting fact," Ursus declares with theatrical gravity. "It appears there's a dispute over the ownership of this slave. Some claim he is now an imperial servant in the Emperor's Palace. Others claim he was unjustly pilfered from his owner—this man here."

He takes a deep breath and clasps his hands, further confirming this circus is planned. "We've determined to resolve this the way a gladiator resolves any dispute…with a *real* fight!"

Cheers erupt from the crowd as my blood runs cold. When he turns and presents me with a small wooden sword, I see the truth in his devious smile. None of this is an accident. He's known all along that the finale of his spectacle was going to be more than a casual exhibition.

"Your weapon, *champion*," he says with a sneer. "You will also remove your armor. It would be a shame to damage it."

I ignore the subtle insult, secretly relieved to rid myself of the stupid suit. My short tunic will be much less impressive, but it will give me a fighting chance to survive whatever's coming.

I hand over the helmet and cast a quick glance at Tacitus as I loosen the cuirass. His concerned expression offers some comfort until I shift my attention to Mallia.

My heart seizes in my chest when I see she's on the cusp of rage. I shake my head, willing her not to react. Tacitus must understand and whispers something to her. She responds with a plea of her own, but further words from Tacitus end with him leading her away from the scene.

Thank the gods.

"Who will be first?" Ursus asks the crowd once I'm down to nothing but the thin tunic and wooden sword. "Senator?"

Senator Varro shakes his head and holds up his hands in feigned humility. "I couldn't. I'm no match for such a champion."

"Oh, come! Your modesty is admirable, my lord, but we all know of your tremendous skill."

The crowd applauds, and Varro furrows his brow in obligatory hesitation before giving in. He makes a great show of selecting his weapon and chooses a gleaming spatha from the buffet of choices.

A real one.

Frax…

So, this is the game, then. Noble versus slave. Armed versus unarmed.

I'll be their opponent, but I won't be allowed to fight back. There's a line of guards and trained gladiators prepared to stop me if I try. *Jupiter's thunder*, this sentence is worse than what I faced at the ludus after the fight. It's certainly more humiliating.

My pulse pounds at the hopeless battles ahead. At least Mallia won't be here to witness this farce.

"Shall we begin?" Ursus asks, signaling his friend.

Senator Varro lunges without warning, and I easily deflect the blow with my small weapon. The next advance results in a similar reaction, and so it goes: attack, defend, attack, defend.

"Fight back!" Varro spits, slashing again.

I stare at him, paralyzed by the impossible command.

"My lord?" I ask, glancing between him and Ursus.

"Fight back, you beast! What joke is this?" Varro growls at Plinius. "Will you let your slave insult me?"

"Of course not, my lord!" Plinius says, signaling his men. I spin around to face four of my former gladiator brothers, including my good friend Ino. The man's stony mask gives little away, but I read the apology deep in his brown eyes. It's good to see he is alive and well, at least.

A sudden chill in my thigh draws me back to the present horror. The wound becomes hot, then wet, and then burns. I turn back to Senator Varro, who wears a cocky sneer.

"Now I have your attention, don't I?" he taunts.

I glance down at the gash on my leg and clench my teeth in frustration. When Varro charges again, I finally strike with an intentionally weak thrust that he blocks.

"Come now. That's the reaction of a schoolboy, not a gladiator. You're still not trying!"

My fingers tighten around the handle of the gladius as I survey the scene, still not sure what to do.

A sudden blow to the back sends me sprawling to the floor.

"Fight, you animal!" Plinius roars. I look up to see Ino standing above me, flexing his fist with a tormented expression. His eyes scream the truth his mouth cannot. That he's sorry, indignant on my behalf. That we're both victims of this charade.

I push myself up, staggering a bit to retrieve the toy sword. This time, when Varro lunges, I not only deflect but land a light blow of my own.

The crowd gasps as the senator grunts and gingerly rubs at his bicep, where he was hit.

The silence hangs heavily.

My veins run ice cold as visions of imminent punishment tear through my head.

The entire room is imagining the same…until the man's shock spreads into a grin.

An audible sigh lifts from the audience.

"There he is. Finally," Varro says, charging forward.

I block the spatha and come around to deliver another hit to the topside of my opponent's carrying hand. The long blade falls from his grip, clattering to the floor in a dramatic testimony to the senator's clear inferiority.

I step back, a cold sweat breaking over my body. Holding my breath, I wait in silence, still confused by the challenge of obeying conflicting orders.

Varro recovers his sword and hovers several paces away. With the weapon hanging loosely at his side, he studies me intently, scanning my face, my body, and the scene around us. After an interminable wait, he laughs and relaxes his stance.

"Well done!" He waves a hand and returns the spatha to the table. "Well done."

My relief only lasts a second when a line of eager guests begins to form.

TACITUS

After finding Helveticus to escort Mallia home, I return to the festivities as quickly as I can.

Mallia was distraught when I helped her and Danae into the litter, but I refused to share the depths of my fears. For a brief moment, I considered sending her to Severus with a message, but there was no point. If General Severus loaned Jason for the evening, there's nothing he can do to intervene without causing a scandal. It's no accident that Ursus determined to resolve the "ownership dispute" with theatrics instead of a formal legal claim. As cruel as the events may seem, none of what's happening is outside the realm of possibility for an evening like this.

Besides, Severus would never risk our mission. Not even for Jason.

I'm furious that we didn't see this coming. We're supposed to be the elite, one step ahead of our enemies, and now we're fighting for survival after a botched plan of our own design.

I almost wish I'd abandoned my post and escorted Mallia home myself when I return to the atrium to find Jason limping through yet another battle. Only a few minutes into the unfair mismatches, his breathing is already labored from exhaustion and pain. His current abuser is a wealthy cousin of Ursus, his weapon of choice a large club.

I flinch along with several other guests when the heavy mass lands on Jason's abdomen, forcing out whatever air is left in his lungs. He doubles over, catching his weight with his hands to keep from crashing into the floor. He doesn't even bother recovering the useless toy sword they gave him as the man laughs and cheers, arms raised in victory.

A polite applause floats around us, but it's pitiful compared to the pure reverence after a magnificent clash in the arena. I'm not surprised, given the laughable nature of this circus. It's everything I can do to keep the scowl from my face.

"This coward said he preferred no blood drawn," Messor whispers as I draw up beside him. "What a joke. Poor slave just has to stand there while these *porcae* beat him."

I swallow my anger as Jason spits blood from his mouth and tries to gather his strength for the next "match." A slave girl hands him a flask of water, and he drinks deeply, coughing from the effort. My heart goes out to my friend, but I have no idea how to help without exposing our alliance.

This must be what Severus warned us about. We won't be able to stop the destruction, only help collect the pieces after it's over.

Ursus's son, Lurio, steps forward next, and my pulse picks up at the appearance of Arata's husband. The man is striking at first glance—tall with artistic, chiseled features, similar to his father. He has a refinement about him, an ingrained air of privilege. But closer inspection exposes a darkness in his eyes that puts me on edge. I instinctively glance at Arata, who clutches the shawl around her shoulders and shrinks back a few steps into the crowd.

Is she afraid of him?

"Lurio, my boy! What will it be?" Ursus asks, spreading his hands over the display of weapons. "You've always shown promise with the gladius."

Lurio shakes his head and holds out his arms while a slave unclasps the cloak at his shoulder. "They've seen enough of that. It's time for a real show. I think a flagrum would liven things up."

I stiffen in alarm, certain I must have heard incorrectly. Even these monsters wouldn't use that nasty scourge against an innocent man. Ursus's wiry brows pinch as he smooths his palms over his tunic in agitation.

The host clears his throat with an uncomfortable smile. "An interesting choice. I didn't think to include a flagrum. Still, there are so many other exciting options right here."

Lurio directs an icy stare at his father, challenging him to deny his request in front of their audience. Ursus's eyes shift around the room. Awkward silence thickens the air.

I glance at Jason, not surprised that his expression remains flat as he waits for the verdict, despite the fact that his mind must be screaming obscenities.

"Here, you can use mine," Opius Plinius interrupts, stepping forward with the ghastly weapon in hand. "It was for show tonight, but there's no reason it can't make an actual appearance."

He hands the modified whip to Lurio, who examines it with unsettling delight. Several leather straps lined with razor-edged shards of glass, metal, and bone hang from a sturdy handle, resembling the tail of a demon horse. This is a weapon designed for one purpose: ripping the flesh off criminals. It has no business in hand-to-hand combat.

It's especially offensive for something that's supposed to be an exhibition.

I shoot a concerned glance at Atticus. Eyes blazing, my captain's fist is clenched tightly around the hilt of his sword. By the direction of his murderous stare, it's not Jason he's desperate to gut.

Even Senator Varro shifts uncomfortably from the cushioned bench just beyond the action.

"This will do," Lurio quips just before flinging the deadly whip into Jason's left side. Lurio rips it away, shredding Jason's tunic and leaving crimson streaks of blood in its wake.

Jason jumps back in shock, staring at the man with a rare, bewildered expression. Lurio quickly lunges again, forcing Jason into a forward roll on the floor. The gladiator comes up out of reach, and I sense the growing tension around me.

Lurio charges once more, and this time Jason has no choice but to raise his forearm to block the blow. The appendages of the flagrum slice into his arm, tearing at the flesh and muscle when Lurio yanks it away.

Jason gasps and studies his torn limb in disbelief.

We all do.

An unexpected touch on my hand pulls me from the gruesome scene.

When I look over, Arata's angry tears glisten back at me.

"It's disgusting," she hisses. "I want to leave. Take me to my father's estate. Now!"

I look to Captain Atticus, who presses his lips together and nods. With one last glance at my brother, I shudder through the thought that I might be the last of our unit to see him alive.

If so, I swear to any deity that's listening, I will avenge him. No one deserves this, least of all a proven champion who's done nothing but honor his calling.

This mission just got extremely personal.

Leaving my friend to his fate is excruciating, but I have no choice as I escort Arata from the atrium and into the cool evening air.

"That's entertainment? Watching a man get tortured for no reason?" Arata spits once we're through the gate onto the street.

As usual, she refused the litter, insisting her drunk husband will need it more when he's had his fill of butchery. I suspect her real motivation is a need to release her disgust at what we just witnessed, and I secretly welcome the long walk for the same reason.

"I'm sorry you had to see that, my lady," I say, holding up an oil lamp to light our path.

When she turns to me, I catch the sheen in her eyes.

"What's the point of it?" she snaps in a harsh tone. "Tell me that. Robbing a man of his life for what? Simply because you can?"

I swallow my own anger and force myself forward.

"You agree with me," she continues, falling into step beside me. "I can tell you do. You were just as disgusted as I."

"Maybe, but how do we stop it?"

"That's a question I ask often." She grabs my arm and pulls me around.

Surprised, I don't move as she tugs at the shoulder of her tunic. My blood runs cold and then hot when I see the ugly bruise.

"How do we stop it?" she echoes in a haunted voice.

"Did Lurio do this to you?" I seethe, furious at the thought. She returns her sleeve to its place and continues walking.

Moonlight reflects the white stone path, offering some support to the oil lamp in my left hand. My right is now eager to draw a gladius and start slashing.

"Violence, blood, love, lust. It's all the same these days, isn't it?" she muses in a far-off voice. "We've combined love with hate, fury with compassion."

I catch her arm and gently turn her toward me. "No. It's not the same. It's not supposed to be."

Her eyes soften as she stares into my face. "You're not like the others. I could tell from our first conversation. Who are you really?"

I force a thick swallow as my mouth goes dry. "I told you, a former soldier and current bodyguard."

"No, you're more than that. You're too good of a fighter, too intelligent, too compassionate to be one of them." She places a hand on my arm, her probing gaze searing into me. "So, who are you, *Gaius Atius Tacitus*? Why are you really here?"

Panic rises within me the longer she waits for a response. I'd been prepared for an entirely different kind of dilemma when it came to her. I know how to navigate matters of the heart. I'm clueless when it comes to the linking of souls.

"You can't tell me, can you?" she concludes, releasing my arm with a resigned sigh. "Don't worry. Your secret is safe. I may not know what you're up to, but I trust the fact that whatever you're doing is for good."

Stunned, all I can do is bow deeply, my heart pounding in my chest.

"I am, and always will be, your servant, my lady," I say sincerely.

A genuine smile lifts her beautiful lips. "Then, maybe at least one positive has come out of tonight's horror."

JASON

I manage to avoid Lurio's next two swings of the flagrum, but the effort throws me off balance. My position on the floor leaves me exposed as an easy target, and the deadly straps crash into my back.

I bite back a shocked cry at the searing pain. Another direct strike forces my cheek against the cold stone tile.

I can't fight anymore. I'm too weak to defend, too exhausted to think. I've faced plenty of battles before, but I have no idea how to fight one I'm commanded to lose. They've left me with no choice except to give them what they seem to want: complete surrender.

Pushing myself to my knees, I close my eyes and accept my brutal fate. It goes against everything in my nature, but strangely, facing death with my head held high feels like a victory.

Lurio raises his arm, and I brace for a devastating blow to the face.

Time stops. I feel the collective inhalation of everyone in the room.

A life in the arena has made me an expert at reading crowds, and I sensed this one turning against the vicious attacker a while ago. No one seems to be enjoying this farce except the one holding the weapon.

Now, they'll get the inevitable end they've been bracing for…

Except the collision never comes.

The clap of flesh-on-flesh echoes off the high walls, and I open my eyes to see Senator Varro's fist clamped tightly around his son-in-law's wrist.

"That's enough," the senator growls.

Lurio appears just as shocked at the intrusion. His arm strains against Varro's punishing grip.

"I said, *enough*," Varro repeats, bending Lurio's wrist until he drops the weapon.

Varro releases the younger man with a slight shove, and a deadly glare stains Lurio's face as he massages his sore wrist. He scans the scene in frigid silence before shoving through the guests toward the exit.

All eyes turn to Senator Varro, who straightens his cloak and clears his throat. "Well, then, an eventful evening, to be sure!" he says with forced cheer. "Please! Continue to enjoy the rest of the food and wine. There is plenty!"

He signals the musicians waiting along the far wall, and jovial instruments pierce the awkward silence. Dancers quickly flood the atrium from neighboring rooms along with slaves carrying trays of food and pitchers of wine.

Once the activity swells to safe levels of distraction, hands slide beneath my arms to help me up. I turn to see two of Ursus's slaves, along with Varro himself.

The senator sets his jaw and guides our unlikely party toward an empty corridor.

Chapter XX

TACITUS

Arata leads me into the atrium of her father's house, and I wait as she issues commands and dismisses the servants.

Our conversation flowed the entire walk home, natural, easy—and now, dangerous since it's clear we're both reluctant to re-enter the reality of our situation.

"Is there anything else I can do for you, my lady?" I ask once we're alone.

Her soft smile lodges in my chest as she shakes her head. "No. You've already been wonderful. I really appreciate everything you've done."

A slight flush blooms over her skin when our eyes meet, triggering a rush of forbidden heat through my body.

Her dark lashes fan over stunning amber irises before she diverts her focus to the geometric design on the floor. "I noticed you escorted Mallia from the event as well. She said she wasn't a fan of the games, so I'm not surprised."

I suppress a wince through the fresh sting of the night's events. "She didn't look well and asked to go home. I made sure she got off safely."

"That was kind of you."

Her intense gaze drifts back to me, now burning with something else. Heat. Desire. She scans my face, tracing my body, and then lingers on my eyes in an unspoken plea. Tension builds between us as her mind works through something. I fear it's the same forbidden fantasy tormenting me.

"I'm tired," she says in a strained voice. "I should retire for the night."

I clench my jaw and bow. While disappointed, I'm also grateful. The spark between us is becoming impossible to control.

"Of course. Please let me know if you need anything else. I'll be in the guard barracks."

She nods, but doesn't move. I wait, my heart pounding while she hesitates a few steps away. "Actually, there's one more—"

Heavy footsteps storm into the atrium.

"There you are!" a male voice roars from the shadows.

I stiffen when Lurio staggers toward us, murder in his stride. Dark circles sag below his eyes, and I nearly choke at the flecks of dark blood accenting the fine wool of his blue tunic.

Jason's blood.

I whisper a quick prayer that my friend is still alive.

Raw hatred for this vile man spreads through me, and I force it below the surface. Right now, my top priority is Arata's safety. We'll deal with his other crimes later.

"How did I know you'd go to your father's house instead of mine?" he sneers at her.

"You're drunk, Lurio," Arata hisses, her eyes narrowing in disdain.

He releases a bitter laugh and stumbles a few steps closer. "Am I now?"

She backs away and crosses her arms, but I see the way her fingertips dig into her skin. My own nails cut into my palms.

"Come, my dear. Is that any way to treat your husband?"

Muted rage simmers in his eyes, and my muscles instinctively brace for a fight.

I step forward to block Lurio's path to Arata.

"Your wife is tired and not feeling well, my lord. Is there something I can do for you? I would be happy to arrange transportation for you to your own villa."

Lurio aims a violent glare at me. "This is between me and my wife, slave," he growls.

I level a hard return stare, unfazed.

"I am not a slave. I'm a former centurion employed by your father-in-law to maintain order and protect those in this house. As I said, may I prepare your litter to return home?"

"I'm not going anywhere without my wife!" he cries, lunging for Arata.

I jump forward and catch the drunken man's arm to hold him back.

"My lord, I would ask you to seriously consider how you treat the daughter of Senator Varro in his own home," I say in an even voice.

"How dare you?" Lurio shrieks, launching his other fist at my face.

Stunned by the blow, I momentarily lose my grip but quickly recover before he can reach Arata. A glance in her direction reveals her fear, and I burn at the memory of the fresh bruise hidden beneath her stola. It's going to take restraint I'm not sure I possess to keep from killing this pig.

"I won't let you hurt her," I warn, blocking another advance.

Lurio swings again, connecting with my cheek, but I stand my ground.

I'm a free man, following orders from my employer. As long as I don't engage in my own assault of Varro's son-in-law, Lurio has no power over me.

By now, other slaves have gathered in the doorways and alcoves, drawn by the commotion involving the man they've probably come to despise. Off-duty members of Varro's guard have entered the room as well. We make eye contact, and they cautiously survey the scene in preparation for a battle.

Violence blazes in Lurio's deadly irises. It's a hatred I've only seen a few times before, even in a career dedicated to confronting enemy soldiers.

He scans the audience with cold precision, probably evaluating his odds should he choose to act on his anger.

His gaze rests back on me, and I feel his hot, foul breath as he leans close.

"You chose poorly," he spits out. "I will make sure you are dismissed and never work again. You will rot in the slums where you belong!" With that, he spins on his heel and marches toward the exit.

A collective sigh releases from the room.

After he's gone, I debrief the guards, while Arata sends the servants back to their duties. It isn't until we're alone again that the color drains from her face and violent trembling takes hold of her.

I rush forward and secure her in my arms.

"I'm sorry," she whispers, burrowing against my chest. Her fingers twist into my wool tunic at my back. "I'm so sorry."

I pull her close as she breaks down, absorbing her fear, her distress. I don't understand why she would apologize. What I witnessed was incredible strength and bravery in the face of a terrifying situation. I can't imagine what it would be like to stand alone against that monster every day. No wonder she spends so much time at her father's house.

I feel sick when the horrifying pieces snap into place.

She pretends it's boredom—I've heard the excuses often enough—but now I shudder in the face of the truth. I'm angry with myself for not seeing it sooner, and even more frustrated that there's nothing I could have done. It's not my duty to intervene. In fact, social norms would dictate I'd be the one in the wrong for interfering in a man's treatment of his wife, but to Hades with protocol.

There's no way I will let this go now that I know.

"I can't imagine what you think of me," Arata murmurs with a harsh laugh as she pulls away. She swats at her eyes, looking everywhere but at me. "A silly woman, I'm sure."

I shake my head and brush her cheek, drawing her back. "Not even close. And I'm not going to let him hurt you anymore."

She averts her gaze again, chewing on her lip. "Thank you, but it's not your burden to carry. You work for my father."

"Maybe, but I'm your friend."

Her focus slips back to my face, and a frown settles over her mouth. "He hurt you." Her fingers glide over the swelling mark around my eye.

I don't respond as I marvel at the soothing nature of her touch. I want to close my eyes and imagine those soft hands moving over the rest of my body, healing years of pain and scars. I want to feel the heat of her skin, the pressure of her curves against me.

But I force away the dangerous fantasy. This story will only end in tragedy.

It takes every bit of willpower I have to lower her wrist and remove her touch from my face. I squeeze gently as I pull away.

"Who are you, Tacitus? Who are you really?" she asks again earnestly, and I force down the twisting in my gut.

"I told you. A former centurion, nothing more."

"No, a lot more. You are everything a legatus could ask for in an officer, yet here you are, discharged at a young age."

"We all make choices."

"And you made a bad one?"

I clench my jaw, aiming a hard stare at the floor. The instinctive deflection I've recited dozens of times rises in my throat. It's balanced on my tongue, but I can't bring myself to release it this time. I want her to know me. I just want someone to know the truth.

I look up and meet her open gaze.

"No, I made the *only* one."

Her eyes soften as she studies me. "Tell me."

"It's not a nice story."

"Maybe, but I want to understand it. To understand *you*."

I hesitate as months of anguish rock against the recesses of my soul. I don't know how to tell this story, but I also don't know how to deny the request of her sweet, sincere soul.

I drop to a bench facing the shallow pool, just as rain begins to tumble through the cut-out in the roof above it. The steady drops pebble the water below in a soothing pattern. She lowers herself beside me and waits patiently while I stare into the ripples and scrape dark memories from their tomb. I've never shared this story openly…except that first time.

Then I watched my father choose pride over his son.

"You were right about a lot of things related to me," I begin in a reflective tone. Some parts of this confession will come easier than others. "I was born into the equestrian class as a member of an esteemed military family. Highly educated, groomed to marry up and possibly lead my own legion one day. But instead of serving as tribune like most young men from our circles, my father insisted I earn my honor as a centurion."

I huff a laugh at an old memory. "My grandfather always considered the *tribuni angusticlavii* nothing but spoiled children, so when I was seventeen, I enlisted as a low-ranking legionary to earn my own way through valiant service, not my name. And I did."

I cast a fleeting glance in her direction and twist a weak smile. "I made it all the way to the first cohort by my own right after just a few years, and finally reached the rank of centurion. I was drawn into the inner circles, entrusted with commands far beyond what someone of my age and experience level should have been given."

"How old are you now?" she asks. My gaze remains fixed on the water, but I feel her eyes on me, the heat of her body as she shifts closer on the bench.

"Twenty-six."

With a deep breath, I nervously adjust the gladius at my hip. Now comes the hard part. "It was already dark and very cold the night my cohort camped near a village during one of our patrols. I was told some of the local youths had been responsible for the theft of a few animals from our livestock herds. My tribune commanded me to take a unit of men to find the thieves and bring them to justice."

As dark memories pound the recesses of my skull, I close my eyes, terrified of what might escape my carefully constructed barrier.

"Tacitus?" Arata's soft voice pierces the void and draws me back.

"I had a plan," I continue in a distant tone. "A good one, but Legatus Nepos grew impatient and had my unit wake the entire sleeping village. Crashing into their homes, dragging the residents into the streets. Our soldiers collected all the boys and young men and lined them up in front of their parents, siblings, and wives."

A lump congeals in my chest, pressing hard against my lungs and making it difficult to breathe, let alone speak. Arata takes my hand, firing a burst of warmth through the ice around my heart. I squeeze back, holding on to anchor myself in the present.

"I was preparing to interview the boys," I continue, urgency seeping into my voice. "I needed to determine who was responsible for the theft and if it would be possible to retrieve the contraband. Then, my orders came directly from Nepos."

I stop. Tears press hard on my throat, burn behind my eyes. I thought I'd buried these feelings, the pain of the memories.

Arata's grip tightens on my hand, and I draw in a ragged breath.

"There would be no investigation, he said. No trial. No justice. I was ordered to slaughter all of them. Every male child from infant to young adult. We were going to send a message to the other villages in the region."

Arata gasps, her hands flying to her mouth. Horror fills her eyes, and I look away, wiping at my cheeks with a rough hand.

"I couldn't do it," I say in a fractured voice, shaking my head. "I *wouldn't*, and Legatus Nepos forced me to watch as others carried out his orders. Forced me to listen as mothers screamed and fathers were beaten when they tried to interfere. He butchered them. Every last one and then had me flogged right in front of the wailing villagers, stretched out among the line of bloody corpses. Stripped me and beat me until I thought I would die."

I close my eyes, afraid the images burning in my mind will somehow seep into the present. I hate this story, everything about that night. Every cursed nightmare that presses against the wall around the shadows of my head.

I especially hate the secret truth behind the event no one will ever know except the man who's haunted my every breath since.

"Tacitus."

Arata's call is so soft, so gentle. It sucks me back from the terror of that day.

Her fingers drift up my arm, along my neck, my jaw. Every touch transforms the pain into something else. Something hot, forbidden, and so incredibly necessary.

She leans in, her tentative lips just a breath away.

Impossible.

But I can't play the sacrificial martyr anymore. I need something pure and beautiful. I need to feel alive again.

With raindrops pinging a serene melody beside us, I lose the battle with myself.

My soul broken and bleeding, I lean in and allow just the softest brush of my lips against hers. Just one kiss to soothe the pain.

But the pull of two fractured souls finding healing in each other is too strong.

Her quiet whimper when our lips connect is a knife to my will, and I tangle my fingers in her silky hair to drag her closer. Our mouths wrestle for the same air. Our tongues battle and stroke in a desperate hunger that can't be satisfied.

She slides her palms over my chest and up my neck, locking us together as her sweet, warm breath drags me into submission. The scent of lavender teases my senses while the soft curves of her body rub against my hard planes with each hungry kiss.

"Come to my room. Please," she breathes, her fingers working at the clasp of my belt. "I want this. I have since that first day."

My gladius clatters to the floor, and soon she's loosening the brooch fastening my cloak at the shoulder. That, too, flutters to the floor, and I feel the strain of her delicate muscles against my rigid body as she fights for me.

I close my eyes again, dizzy from the war of duty and desire raging through me.

"Just this once. I will never ask again, I promise." She tugs at the fabric of my tunic, and I help pull it over my head.

Her breath catches as she surveys my body, tracing each detail with her eyes and then her eager touch. When she grazes the scars on my back, tears obscure her irises.

"You keep startling me. In so many ways," she whispers, brushing her lips over mine.

I drag her close again, punishing her compassion with a violent kiss.

She moans as she grips my hair and arches into me. Her mouth is an addiction, intoxicating in its passion, its plea. I want her just as much, more than anything. Every part of me is hers to command.

Her other hand runs down my chest, over my hip, and between my legs, forcing my breath into a tortured groan. Her own labored breathing mingles with the sound of the trickling water behind us.

"Please, Tacitus," she pleads again, taking my mouth once more.

I have to stop this. For so many reasons.

But my arms pull her onto my lap instead of pushing her away. She straddles me on the bench, her tunic dangerously close to exposing her center in an impossible invitation. She's breathtaking, inside and out. Rare, precious—perfectly forbidden.

"Arata, wait," I gasp out.

I clasp her wrist, torn between guiding her hand further and pulling it away.

My eyes slip closed as I force air into my burning lungs.

"What is it? Do you not want me too?"

I meet her gaze again, crushed by the devastated look on her face. She's still so close I could taste her lips again if I were a weaker man. The gods know I want that more than the breath in my lungs.

"Of course I do, but I won't do this to you. I won't put you in danger."

She huffs a bitter laugh. "Danger? I'm married to a sadistic beast. My life is nothing but danger."

I grit my teeth and push a hand through my hair. "Exactly. He wouldn't hesitate to destroy you for unfaithfulness. I won't be responsible for that."

Her expression deflates into troubled concentration, mirroring my own. We sit in silence for a long time, both considering what is, what should be, and what we want. Forbidden fantasies and harsh truths.

My mind is a mess. My body is in complete mutiny.

I remember Severus's warning regarding scorned lovers. What if I've misjudged her? She could do plenty of damage to someone like me. But it's more than that.

It isn't fear of retribution that's holding me captive—it's fear of myself, of my own weakness when it comes to her.

The rain pouring into the room thins into a calm mist. We watch it billow in the moonlight for several long seconds. Finally, with a heavy sigh, Arata flattens her palm along my cheek and searches my eyes.

"A selfless warrior with principles and compassion," she murmurs. "Where in the realm of the gods did my father find you?"

Her weak smile as she shakes her head eases some of the tension in my chest.

"I'm sorry, Arata. Truly. I just…"

She holds up her hand to silence me. "You are something of a treasure, Gaius Atius Tacitus. I couldn't ask for a better protector. A better *friend*."

With a light kiss on the cheek, she climbs off my lap and pushes to her feet. Her gaze lingers on me for another moment, testing my resolve.

I don't dare make a single movement. I can't. If I do, I'll make another decision that will destroy my life…

And this time I will have chosen wrong.

JASON

"Tend to his wounds," Senator Varro barks at the slaves holding my arms when we enter an empty sitting room.

I grimace as they lower me to a stool, blood leaking everywhere. My torn tunic is saturated. My skin looks just as bad. I suck in a breath at the ribbons of damaged flesh cutting across my forearm.

"*To the lions with you,* Ursus! When will you figure out how to control your son?" Varro growls.

Ursus flinches and takes a step back, nervously wrapping his fingers in his cloak. "He may show poor judgment on occasion, but—"

"Poor judgment? Look at him!" Varro roars, waving at me. "That slave belongs to the Emperor! What are we supposed to do now? He was on loan. A lure to tempt our guests for the upcoming games! Don't you think Severus will be upset when we return him in such a state? He's a *palace* slave, for Jupiter's sake!"

Ursus clears his throat. "I'm sure he will recover. He is strong—"

"I care nothing for his health! I care about the fact that twenty of the most influential citizens of Rome just watched your son act like an appalling animal! Tonight was supposed to be about securing allies. I need their respect, Ursus, not their disapproval. Certainly not their disgust!"

He throws up his hands as he launches into violent pacing, his dark blue cloak fanning behind him with each step. Ursus twists a gold signet ring in nervous circles around his finger.

Despite the intense pain and nausea, I'm doing everything I can to focus on their conversation.

"You're worrying too much. Lurio's actions will not reflect on you," Ursus soothes, but the tremor in his voice undermines his attempt at reassurance.

"No? He's my son-in-law," Varro fires back, turning on him. "Do you think the people will accept a leader who can't control his own family?"

Both men pause in a silent standoff, but it's no secret who will win. This war was over before it began.

"Get a handle on him," Varro spits finally. "We are too close to lose it all over your son's unbridled perversions. And if I ever find out he's displayed similar cruelty to my daughter, I swear on the spear of Mars, this entire city will watch jackals feast on Lurio's mangled flesh."

Varro spins away from him with a flick of his hand. "Give us a moment," he barks, dismissing Ursus along with the slaves in a final insult.

Once they're gone, I'm shocked when the proud senator takes a stool beside me.

He mutters a violent curse as he examines my wounds and runs a hand over his close-cropped salt-and-pepper hair.

"Tonight's exhibition went too far," he says in a grave tone. "Your master will be upset, and I don't blame him. Know that he will be compensated for the damages, and you have my deepest apologies." His brown eyes flicker toward the open doorway and then land back on me. "I wish to make it up to you."

I remain still, scanning his face in confusion.

"I know gladiators well," he continues, adjusting to face me. "I can't imagine a fierce warrior such as yourself is satisfied holding your master's robes at the baths and washing the dust from his feet."

His brows sink into concentration as if carefully considering his next sentence. "In less than a month, I will be hosting a magnificent spectacle of games. I would be honored if you'd accept the primus match and fight as my champion."

Stunned, all I can do is stare as he pushes back to his feet.

He smooths out his robes and then surveys me with a stern expression. "If you agree to my terms, I will make arrangements with your master and ensure you are rewarded beyond anything you can imagine. The purse will be enormous. Honor me with your loyalty and a good fight…" He casts another quick glance at the door. "Well, let's just say, if all goes well, I will soon be in a position to secure your freedom."

I freeze in place. His words hover around me in visceral detail, but I can't make sense of them. He's offering my freedom?

"My lord…"

Varro holds up his hand. "No need to answer right now, but you have my offer. Wealth, status, and freedom for your loyalty. That's all I ask."

My pulse pounds as my grip tightens around my injured arm. "Thank you, my lord. I don't know what to say."

"There's no need to thank me. It's an even exchange. Just keep this between us for now."

He delivers a tight smile, but there's something unsettling about the veiled look in his deep-set eyes. Combined with his severe cheekbones and thin lips, he resembles a figure from the underworld more than a living being in the hazy lamplight. Even without the ghastly transformation, I would never trust his words. Men like him have used me and lied to me my entire life.

After a short pause, he seems to clear a thought from his mind. "Well then, I'll let them finish cleaning you up."

His sharp slap on my shoulder triggers a stab of pain, reminding me of the truth about why we're here.

Chapter XXI

MALLIA

I'm relieved to find Severus in his palace study the following morning.

Last night's sleepless waiting was torture as I stared into the dark, counting the seconds until I could "visit Aurelia" the following day and learn Jason's fate. Tacitus refused to say much about what was happening when he escorted me from the banquet, but I understood enough to know there was a reason he and Jason didn't want me there. I only agreed to leave because I didn't trust myself to stay in character any more than they did.

"How is he?" I ask the second Severus dismisses his attendants.

My heart sinks at his look of confusion.

"What do you mean?" he asks, rising from the chair.

Gods, he doesn't even know?!

"Jason! When I left Ursus's banquet last night, they were about to use him for sport. Tacitus sent me away beforehand, and I can only imagine why."

Severus leans forward, pressing his fists into the desk with a grave expression. "You were at Ursus's banquet?"

"Yes. Arata invited me." My voice is thick with fear. "He hasn't returned then," I whisper.

"No, but that's not unusual."

"Did you know Opius Plinius would be there? The lanista laid claim to him in front of the entire gathering! Declared Jason was stolen from him. You don't think…" I can't even finish the thought.

Severus levels a stern look at me. "Jason was not sent to the ludus. Ursus might be foolish enough to make such a mistake, but not Varro. The senator wouldn't risk making an enemy of the Emperor in favor of a simple lanista like Opius Plinius. Not now."

I want to believe him. I want to accept that there are a dozen benign reasons Jason hasn't returned to his post. I chew on my thumbnail, my sandal tapping the marble floor. The soft linen of my finely woven tunic suddenly feels rough and scratchy against my skin.

"He's a smart boy, Mallia. Strong. He's okay," the general soothes, but how am I supposed to accept that when he doesn't even know what happened to his valet or where he is?

I take an earnest step toward the desk. "Yes, he's strong, but you said it yourself, we live in a world where attributes like that don't matter for him. He's still a slave. His strength means nothing while chained to the whims of this cruel world."

Severus's brow sinks into a troubled crease, his lips flattening into a firm line. I feel no victory in winning this debate.

A messenger interrupts the somber silence with an urgent approach.

"Yes? What is it?" Severus barks at him.

The slave bows. "I'm sorry to disturb you, my lord, but Senator Marcus Varro is here to see you."

Severus stiffens in surprise. "Varro?"

The senator is here? My heart pounds against my ribs.

Severus stalks out from behind his desk, fluttering his black cloak behind him. Burgundy streaks from the lining peek through the folds as he strides forward.

"When did he arrive?" Severus demands.

"Just now. He waits in the atrium, my lord," the page says. "Shall I take you to him?"

Severus frowns and casts a quick glance at me. "I'll go on my own. Please escort Lady Mallia to Lady Aurelia instead. We've finished our discussion."

I shoot a startled glance at the general, fists clenched. I can't believe he'd dismiss me when the answer to my question just arrived! Severus ignores my silent protest as I storm out of the room.

The journey from the Emperor's suite to Aurelia's seems much longer than usual. Instinctively, I strain for a glimpse of Senator Varro as we move through the corridor connecting the private wings of the palace despite the fact that Severus would never meet Varro in such an intimate setting. He's probably on his way to the public side of the massive building now.

My tormented heart finally accepts defeat when the usher leaves me with

Aurelia's attendants. When her slave guides me to her bedroom instead of the exedra, my concern takes a new turn.

"Oh, my dear! You've finally come," Aurelia croaks, pushing up on the pillows of her bed. Limp blonde hair hangs around her petite shoulders, making her appear even paler than usual against the ivory linens. The deep purple embroidery of her bedding reflects her imperial status, but right now, she looks anything but regal.

"It's been such a terrible night," she whispers, dropping back to the pillows.

I nod in rare agreement with the woman. "You don't look well, my lady," I say, moving toward her.

Aurelia exhales and pats the edge of the bed for me to sit. "I don't look well because I've hardly slept. I can't eat. I can't think."

"Is something wrong? Are you ill?" I scan her face, concerned by the heavy rings beneath her eyes.

"I'm miserable, Mallia. My head, my stomach. I've had Telemon here five times, and he still can't find a cure for my suffering."

I shift toward her on the bed, tucking one leg beneath me. For all of Aurelia's typical melodrama, she does seem significantly more drained than usual. I can't remember the last time I've seen the vain woman without cosmetics and full regalia. Lines I've never noticed crease the corners of her eyes and lips. She resembles a tortured ghost more than a woman, and maybe I almost feel bad for her.

Almost.

Jason probably didn't sleep well after they were finished with him either.

I exchange a look with Danae, who watches from her position near the wall. My maid's dark brows crease with worry, but I suspect it's for me more than Aurelia.

"Shall I send for Telemon again?" I ask.

Aurelia shakes her head and presses the back of her hand to her cheek. "He's already said there's nothing he can do. The gods are punishing me! I just know they are!"

"Nonsense. You'll be fine in a day or two."

Haunted blue eyes search mine. "What have I done, Mallia? Tell me! Why do they punish me?"

I wince and avert my gaze. Graphic images of Jason, bloody and kneeling on the floor just down the hall, assault the silence between us. Maybe the gods are indeed just, but Aurelia would never accept that conclusion. All she wants to hear is what I've said.

Fresh anger rises within me at the injustice of it all, and I force a tight smile.

"I'll let you rest," I say, sliding off the edge of the bed.

Aurelia relaxes with a heavy sigh. "Perhaps that's best. Check on me later?"

I return a stiff nod, unable to look at her again as I move toward the door.

SEVERUS

"General Severus, thank you for speaking with me," Senator Varro says when I join him in a private receiving room off the atrium. His valet and two bodyguards stand behind him, but neither man is Tacitus.

I nod a polite greeting, despite the churning in my stomach. "How can I help you, Senator?"

Varro clears his throat, and his obvious discomfort unsettles me further. Seasoned politicians like Varro rarely show emotion and never weakness. If he's nervous, maybe Mallia was right to be concerned.

"I just wanted to personally thank you for your generosity in loaning us your slave. The gladiator was well-received." Varro produces a pouch of coins from a pocket in his cloak and holds it out to me. "The first of many, I hope."

I stare at the offering in alarm. "Thank you, but that's not necessary. I've already been compensated."

Varro twists a tight smile and shakes the pouch for emphasis. "I assure you it is. Your slave is of strong character. He is well-worth the additional gift. Please, I insist."

Ignoring the coins, I study his agitated movements instead. His other hand absently runs over the hilt of a ceremonial dagger tucked into his belt.

"He has returned then?" I ask.

Varro smiles, but there's no conviction in the weak attempt. "He has. We look forward to his next visit."

After a short pause, he drops the pouch on a bronze table beside a chair.

"I'll be in touch." He motions to his attendants who follow him from the room.

I stare after them in silence, considering the strange encounter. Concerned, I signal the usher waiting in the corridor.

"I heard my valet has returned to the palace," I say. "Where is Jason? Why did he not report for duty?"

The slave frowns and lowers his head. "Forgive me, my lord, your valet has indeed returned. But given his state, the steward first sent him to the physician."

ARGUS

"Senator Varro just delivered his ultimatum," Eustacius hisses at Decien. They hover near the bend in the corridor intersecting with mine. I shrink against the wall and inch closer to the corner to listen. Their hushed tones make it clear this news is not meant for anyone else.

"When? *How?"* Decien whispers back.

"Just now. Tracked me down while he was here visiting General Severus. Are you in or out, Decien? It's time to decide. He's demanding an answer."

My fingertips press into the cool stone behind my back. I've been secretly following them all morning, waiting for a moment like this. Too bad I chose to follow Decien instead of Eustacius. I wasn't sure which was the ringleader, but now I know.

"I'm in," Decien says. "You know that, but—"

"Then there are no buts! There can be no hesitation. No wavering!"

"It's not that, it's…well…"

"It's what, you fool? You're lucky Varro isn't here to witness you acting like a *bracca*. He would withdraw his offer and then celebrate with your head on a platter."

"*Eat ashes*, Eustacius!"

"It's my head at stake as much as yours! I vouched for you. You're my responsibility. You screw this up, we'll both eat ashes!"

"I'm not saying—"

"In or out?!"

Decien mumbles another curse. "In. Of course I'm in."

"But?"

"No buts."

"Good."

JASON

Motion in the doorway draws my gaze. I glance over from my seat on the exam table to see Severus duck into the infirmary.

"Give me a moment with my valet," he says to Telemon.

The physician pauses his stitching on my arm, a scowl settling over his face. With unveiled irritation, he places his supplies on a nearby table.

"Let me know when it's okay to return, my lord. Don't move that arm," he directs at me.

Severus waits until we're alone and then takes the stool vacated by Telemon. I remain still as the other man does a slow survey of my state. Deep lines form in his brow. Growing anger simmers in his eyes.

"Those aren't gladius wounds," he observes coldly.

I shake my head and study the series of long, jagged tears on my forearm. No, but they could prove to be tremendously valuable.

"Varro made me an offer," I say after a tense pause. "A good one." I meet his gaze, reading every tweak of his expression.

"I'm sure he did, given the price he made you pay."

"Lurio was responsible for the worst of it."

He straightens on his stool, the troubled look returning. "Ursus's son?"

I nod. "Varro was furious. He stopped the attack in front of all the guests and then privately chastised Ursus for letting it happen."

Eyes narrowed in concentration, Severus leans forward and motions for me to continue.

"Varro seemed very concerned with his image and how it would look if they couldn't control Ursus's son. It was then that he made his offer, and I realized why I was there in the first place."

My gaze locks on his, and I release all the concern in my heart. "He admitted to sponsoring games in a month. He wants me to fight in his primus and promised me enormous wealth." I take a deep breath. "He offered me my freedom, my lord."

Severus inhales sharply, his eyes going wide. We sit in silence as my words haunt the air around us.

"Varro isn't your master," he mutters in a grave tone. "There's only one way he could have the power to make such a declaration. There is no doubt now."

Jaw clenched, I brace through a surge of resolve. "I can confirm that within the next few weeks Senator Varro intends to be Emperor. And that's just the beginning of his plan."

TACITUS

It's been a quiet morning. Boring, even. After returning from a brief visit to the palace, Varro is now hosting yet another donor. This is the same round, cherub-faced, over-dressed man who had been visiting with Varro and Ursus the day I escorted Arata to the shops.

This time, I was able to learn the man's name is Quintus Placidius Pius.

I was annoyed by the assignment that day but would do anything for an afternoon alone with Arata now. I haven't seen her since our encounter after Ursus's party, and I suffer under a constant weight of concern. Maybe she's been avoiding me, but I fear a worse fate. A man like Lurio would think nothing of holding his wife prisoner at their estate.

The lack of fallout from my confrontation with Lurio unsettled me. I can only assume he determined his story would gain little sympathy and his best course was to keep silent. For all his faults, Senator Varro seems to genuinely admire, if not love, his daughter, and I doubt reports of her abuse would go over well. At the very least, the proud senator would see it as a grave insult to his family that would need to be addressed.

My worry for Arata is beginning to overwhelm me, however. As the hours drag into days, it's become a constant fight to resist the urge to mount a dramatic rescue from her own home, her own husband. An absurd thought, of course. I have no right to interfere, and I'm confident Severus wouldn't support such a rash act that would compromise everything we've been working for.

Still, it's constant torment to think about her in the hands of that monster. Once this is over, there will be justice at any cost. I'd consider it an honor and gladly take an afternoon with the lions to plunge the sword into his neck myself.

"And if I support you?" Pius asks Varro in an oily tone.

"I thought I made that clear," Varro clips back. "You would see a return on your investment ten times what you put in."

The man taps his fingers on the rim of an aqua-tinted wine glass. "No, I mean, your empire, your reign. If I support you, what is the Rome I'm buying?"

"Ah," Varro says, plucking an olive from a tray. "A visionary. I like that."

Pius takes a smug sip of wine, preening at the compliment. "Wealth is only an asset in a desirable State, Senator."

Varro nods, chewing slowly. "Well said, my friend. I couldn't agree more. That's why our first order of business will be to clean up Rome."

Pius sags on his elbow. Bushy eyebrows arch in quiet skepticism. "Clean up Rome? You're proposing more impotent laws, then."

Varro levels an intense stare at his guest. "No. There is nothing impotent about the coming changes. We have plenty of laws. It's time to focus on enforcement."

Pius tilts his head in thought, scratching at his rosy, clean-shaven cheek.

"You are a successful merchant," Varro continues. "How would you like the entire Hades Hand block to sell your wares? I have no reports of bidders yet, so it could be yours for quite the bargain."

The man recoils with a grimace. "You're offering me a shop in the slums? That place is crawling with thieves and prostitutes."

Varro barks a dry laugh. "No, my good man. I'm offering you the entire district. After it's razed and rebuilt to your specifications."

My stomach drops. My entire body goes cold. I can't believe what I just heard.

Pius inches forward on his couch, eyes wide. Except, the surprise on his face is delight, not horror. "You're going to tear down the entire district?"

"Every last stone and plank." Varro's eyes flash with eager malice as he sifts through the tray for another olive. "It will be the first of many renovation projects in an effort to clean up the filth that contaminates this great city."

Pius shakes his head in wonder. "Brilliant. But what about the people living there?"

A slow, conspiratorial smile slithers over Varro's face. "When I'm emperor, you can let *me* worry about the details. If you support us, all you need to do is draw up your building plans."

MALLIA

I stifle a cry of relief when Danae leads Jason toward my secluded bench in the gardens. I forget all about potential witnesses, social propriety—everything—as I jump to my feet and throw my arms around him.

He flinches, hesitating for a moment before sliding one hand up my back to hold me close while the other grips my arm as if intent on pushing me away. Despite the conflicted embrace, I melt into the contact, grateful for the warm, living breath on my hair.

"Severus gave permission for me to meet with you," he says quietly. "He said you were worried."

"I was more than worried," I murmur, settling against his hard chest. I was scared. *Terrified.*

His hold tightens briefly and then relaxes. "I'm okay, my lady. Nothing that won't heal."

I force myself to pull away, shuddering when the late morning breeze brushes through the trees. I tuck my shawl around my shoulders, but my relief fades into a scowl the longer I study him.

"I see why Tacitus sent me away," I mumble, frowning at a cut above his eye, his cheek, the bandage on his arm. While not nearly as bad as the first time I saw him in Telemon's study all those weeks ago, I fear he's more injured than he's letting on. I hate that he's so used to being in this state that he's accepted it as normal.

"It's nothing. I'm fine," he deflects, as expected.

"Of course it is. You're always fine, aren't you?"

"You're angry," he says, frowning.

His concerned gaze sifts over my face, and I fight to calm the rising storm.

"Not at you," I sigh out. "Injustice makes me angry. How many times does this have to happen?"

His slow smile draws one from me.

"What?" I ask, warming beneath his humored gaze. "What's so funny?"

"Nothing, my lady. Just getting used to a patrician with compassion for slaves, that's all."

Shining pools of hazel threaten to unravel me as I absorb his rare smile.

"Well, *I'm* still getting used to a champion gladiator who isn't vain and arrogant."

His soft laugh almost hurts, and I can't help but take his hand, not ready to let him go. He resists slightly when I tug him toward the bench, but quickly gives in. Based on his anxious look around, his hesitation is more about witnesses and etiquette than not wanting to sit with me.

"Would you give us a moment, Danae?"

My maid fires a warning glance at me before reluctantly disappearing down the path. I wait until she's gone before pulling Jason down to the marble bench beside me. I'm fully aware she's not happy about this, but I don't care.

I also know these elaborate gardens like my own villa. No one wanders this far into the maze of intricate paths and exotic vegetation. Jason wouldn't even have found me without Danae's guidance.

"It was nice of Severus to release you to reassure me," I say, tucking a stray lock of hair behind my ear.

Another stunning smile skims Jason's lips. "He said you were…'insistent' in your concern and didn't think you'd accept his word on its own."

"He's a wise man."

Jason shakes his head with another shy grin. I collect the priceless image like a gift from the gods and file it into my memory.

"He is very wise. And generous," Jason says. "If you are satisfied, then I should get back to him."

"And if I'm not?" I lift a brow in mock challenge. "If I'd like a few more moments of *reassurance?"*

His conflicted gaze snaps to mine before darting back to the ground. "You make it seem as though it's easy for us to be friends, my lady."

Another frown settles over his face as he stares hard at the mosaic beneath our feet.

Frustration hardens inside me. It *is* easy, I want to say, but that's a lie. It's a lie for so many reasons and he knows that better than anyone.

With too many useless words swirling around my head, I take his hand to trace the bandage on his arm instead. Blood has seeped through the rough linen, screaming its reddish-brown testimony to an evening gone awry.

"Flagrum," he explains quietly, answering the question I couldn't bring myself to ask.

I wince as gruesome images replace the sweet ones from a moment ago. I don't know what to do except squeeze his hand tighter.

"There will be justice one day," I whisper. "There has to be."

I glance up, and my pleading gaze collides with his haunted stare. For several seconds, I get lost in the dark green depths flecked with brown. So beautiful. So full of sorrow, pain, strength…open affection.

My breath catches at the new emotion I see for the first time.

Pulse pounding, I can't resist the urge to reach up and graze his cheek. The unshaven surface is rough but perfectly formed, like every other deceptive inch of him. A breathtaking shell hiding a deeply battered and scarred soul.

Longing simmers low in my belly and spreads throughout the rest of me. Gaze locked on his, I fan my palm along his cheek in a firmer grip. I run my thumb over his soft lips, watching the slow indent graze the deep red arches with fascination.

Juno's breath, I want to taste them.

My gaze crashes into his again, and I swear I see a flash of heat as I inch closer. Then…

Eruption.

I'm not sure who initiates the kiss. Maybe neither of us. Maybe Fate intervenes in its first show of mercy to the young gladiator, but the connection is swift and strong.

The first kiss is gentle, like the faint brush of a leaf hanging over a path in the garden.

But it isn't enough for my starved body and ravenous soul. Not when I've been suffering the constant burn of forbidden attraction I'm just beginning to accept.

The second kiss is more intentional.

I slide my arms around his neck, forcing him to confront every bit of the truth about my feelings as we mold together. I want him. Not his body, not an experience. *Him.* Every dark, disfigured, broken, frightening inch of the story that created the magnificent man in my arms.

A soft moan escapes me as the kiss deepens. His firm hands slide down my back, over my hips, and along the outside of my thighs. I can't breathe through the searing rush I've never felt before. It surges through every part of me, pooling low and hot in forbidden places. I don't want it to stop. I never want it to stop. The ache, the insatiable hunger for something only this one person can give me.

I drag him down on top of me as I recline to my back on the bench. The cool marble does nothing to soothe the consuming flames as his hard body stretches over me. My fingers sink into his short, dark hair, gripping hard.

"Jason," I breathe, pressing into him as he spreads soft kisses along my jaw, my neck. I can't get close enough to satisfy the hunger. It's taking over, devouring me.

His mouth on my skin, his hands roaming my curves—every touch so thrilling, so dangerous in the way it never satiates, only makes me crave more.

My thoughts have become a complete blur, obscured by sensation. Touch. Taste. Smell.

Breathing hard, I guide his hand over me, melting into the searing precision of targeted pressure.

"Is this okay?" I gasp out. "You're okay?"

"Of course, my lady. Whatever you want. You just have to tell me."

My hot blood goes ice cold.

The ache of tears is already forming in my chest as I shove him away and struggle to my feet.

His devastated, confused expression only cuts deeper. Of course, he's confused. I can't breathe. Gods, how stupid am I?!

"I'm sorry, my lady," he rushes out, dropping to his knees. "Did I do something wrong? I didn't—"

"Stop. Just stop," I rasp out, holding up my hand, fighting for a breath.

He obeys. He always obeys. I nearly choke.

Hot liquid fills my eyes. I try to blink it away, but it just tumbles down my cheeks.

"My lady, I'm sorry. I'm so sorry."

He tilts his head up, grief-stricken as he searches my face. "I thought that's what you wanted. I never would have…"

I cut him off again, still unable to speak, and now sick to my stomach. I'm heartbroken, horrified, so full of remorse and compassion. There's so much I want to say, but my clamped lungs won't release the words.

His tortured expression is killing me.

I cup his face and lose myself in those infinite eyes.

"You have nothing to be sorry about," I manage finally. "I wanted that. I wanted you."

He only stares, confused.

I sigh and gently guide him up, willing him to understand. I never want him on his knees. Not for anyone, but especially not me. Not until it's *his* choice.

It's so simple and so impossibly complex. I have no idea how to explain love to someone who's never experienced it.

"If that's what you wanted, why did you stop it? Why are you crying?" he asks.

I swallow hard and step back, resisting the urge to kiss him again and confuse him more. "Because I don't want you to please me. I want to please *you.* I want to make *you* happy. To warm *you* inside. Not the body, but here." I place my hand on his chest near his heart.

I take his hand and brush my lips over his knuckles. "What Lepidus said is wrong, Jason. You're not a reward. You're a gift. A miracle. I don't want you until you want me just as much. And not because you're grateful, but because you don't think you can live without me. *That's* what I want."

His brows sink in concentration before settling into the flat, unreadable void his face so often is. I'm not sure if he's angry, hurt, confused, or touched as he stands tall, silently evaluating the situation, measuring the stakes, and forming this unexpected turn of events into a survival plan. I see it now more than ever. Watching as the statue breathes.

It breaks my heart, but I understand.

I always did, and all I can do is hope that love can melt stone.

Chapter XXII

MALLIA

It's a rare meeting with all five members of *Septem Fideles* in Tacitus's second-floor flat in the Brick District. His multi-room apartment is considerably nicer than Argus's, although it's not nearly what he'd be accustomed to growing up in a wealthy equestrian family. I don't know much about his story, but it must be full of intriguing twists.

"We have a lot to discuss and not much time, so let's make this a frank conversation," Severus says from where he stands at the head of the table. Several oil lamps cast a warm glow over the plaster-coated walls and wood floor. A simple fresco of Achilles handing his armor to Patroclus decorates the far side of the room behind a small writing desk.

"Pieces are pouring in, and we need to take a moment to assemble them." Severus waves toward where I'm seated on a stool at the table. "Mallia, please begin with your update."

I straighten in my stool as three sets of flame-soaked eyes rest on me. Only Jason continues a hard stare at nothing.

"Aurelia is ill," I begin, ignoring the sting of his snub. "At first, it seemed like a minor affliction, but she degrades more each day. Her hair is falling out, and her skin is littered with lesions." I take a deep breath, my thoughts racing like they have since my suspicions first developed. "What do you know about Cornelia Dura?"

"She's a noblewoman of the senatorial class," Tacitus says, brows furrowed. "Married to Consul Gnaeus Livius Matho."

Argus smirks. "And there's nothing *noble* about her, according to her reputation. Or her husband."

I glance at Jason, who leans against the wall behind Argus. As usual, his blank expression reveals nothing. Grisly rows of jagged stitches line his muscular forearm, currently crossed with the other over a dark green tunic. His bruised face, typically a rainbow of purples, yellows, and blues in the sunlight, appears eerily shadowed in the flickering lamplight. He looks spectral, a powerful ghost warrior come back from the dead to avenge his enemies.

And suddenly, all I can think about is our encounter in the garden a few days ago.

I'm still buzzing from the passionate moment. No matter how hard I try, I can't erase the feel of his heat, the firm pressure of his body. Memories of the sweet kisses take my breath away even now.

We've barely spoken since, and I fear he's been avoiding me.

"Why do you ask about Cornelia?" Severus directs at me, drawing me back.

Jason's gaze finally drifts to me as well.

I swallow the blistering effect of his hazel stare and focus on Severus. "According to a maid, Cornelia was the last visitor Aurelia had before the sickness took over. She's continued to visit daily and sends all the attendants away while she's there. Aurelia's maid insists the woman is a witch and cursed Aurelia."

Argus grunts in flippant dismissal, but Severus seems more concerned as he rubs his jaw.

"What do you think, Mallia? Based on your interactions with the woman, do you think Cornelia is capable of that?"

"Of cursing Aurelia?"

"Of poisoning her."

I cringe at hearing it out loud. The theory seemed absurd when it first crossed my mind. They've been friends for years. Well, acquaintances. No, not even that.

Accomplices.

Images of that horrible afternoon with Jason haunt me every time I see her. The taunting, the violence, the blood, the lust. The hunger. What happened to Jason was new to me, but not to them.

Would *accomplices* poison each other? Maybe.

Are they capable of it? Definitely.

"She's capable, yes."

A disturbing silence falls over us.

Street noises from below drift up through the shuttered window. Two neighbors shout at each other in a foreign language from an adjacent flat. Rhythmic thumping pounds the floor above us. Life goes on for a million people in this bustling city, none of whom have any knowledge of the secret war brewing in their midst. I used to live in that ignorance, but now that I know the truth, I can't imagine continuing on in casual indifference.

"Okay, so she's capable and had the opportunity," Severus says. "What would be her motive?"

"Jealousy. Envy," Jason states in a distracted tone.

We turn to him, only to see his vacant stare has no intention of elaborating.

"Come, son. We know you have a theory. What is it?" Severus encourages.

Jason shifts on his feet, clearly uncomfortable beneath our expectant gazes. It must be difficult for him to go against a lifetime of being forced to stay silent.

"I don't have evidence," he says, fixing an absent look on the table. "I just know people. Well, those kinds of people. They weren't partners or friends that day in Aurelia's exedra, they were competitors."

Argus and Tacitus squint in confusion. Severus seems pensive. I feel sick.

"*That day?* What day?" Argus asks, glancing between us.

"The day they assaulted him," I spit out, still angry over the whole thing. "I guess we left that event off the official *Septem Fideles* record?"

My resentment softens slightly when my gaze settles on Jason. As disgusted as I am about what happened, it also fascinates me that he could be so perceptive in the face of such trauma. I've always wondered what goes through his mind when he shuts it off. Does he disappear entirely or does he evaluate, absorb, and plan like every other situation he encounters?

Argus and Tacitus exchange a hard look as Severus frowns.

"But is Cornelia's envy of Aurelia enough for murder?" Severus asks, adjusting his cloak behind him. "You need to get more information, Mallia. Find out what goes on when Cornelia visits Aurelia. Make sure you're present for the next one."

"They prefer to be alone. Cornelia wouldn't even let me see her last time I tried to visit."

Severus shakes his head with a stern look. "You are Aurelia's closest friend, whether you want that title or not. She will side with you if you press the issue. Use whatever means you have to discern the truth."

"If you can't get to them, I can," Jason says evenly.

I fire a glare at him. "Not a chance," I snap before focusing back on Severus. "I'll find out what's going on. If it's related to our mission, we'll know soon."

Severus returns an emphatic nod. "Good. Even if it's not related, we have a duty to protect Aurelia." He motions toward Jason. "Your turn. Share your report with the group."

Jason straightens from the wall, wearing the same flat expression he's had since we entered the apartment. It's starting to worry me. He's being distant, even for him.

"I've learned several things from Ursus's banquet last week," he says. "First, it appears our suspicions were correct. The death of Britannia's legate Lucius Marius Titullus was not an accident. I overheard two guests discussing a theory of murder. Like we thought, the legate wasn't even at the battle that killed him."

Argus pounds a fist into the table. "So, it's true! That *bracca* Nepos covered his tracks by murdering the most influential witness who could counter his lies."

Jason absently runs a hand over the dagger at his right hip. "It appears so. I also got direct confirmation that Senator Varro is intending to sponsor munera in less than a month in order to curry the favor of the people. He's as much as said he plans to be emperor."

Shock ripples through the rest of us.

"You're certain?" Tacitus asks, leaning forward with an urgent expression. "You've had direct confirmation?"

Jason settles his cool gaze on him. "He offered me the primus, along with my freedom if I triumph."

"Pluto's chains!" Argus mutters. "That supports my update as well. It all makes sense now." Flames blaze in his eyes, compounded by the glint of the lamplight. "At least two of the Emperor's guards are in on the conspiracy. After Varro's visit to the palace yesterday, I overheard Eustacius and Decien discussing an ultimatum regarding their involvement in something Varro cooked up. The details weren't part of the conversation, but something big is happening. I'd bet the little I have that it's an assassination."

Air siphons from the room. Grim silence sinks over our cluster as the threat hangs heavy with each breath.

"You have to get those details, Argus," Severus commands in a severe tone. "If the Praetorian Guard is involved in an assassination attempt, you're our best hope of learning where and when."

Argus returns a solemn nod. "Already on it, sir. What about the captain, Prefect Falco? If there's a coup in the works involving The Guard, the captain would have to be complicit, no?"

Severus clenches his eyes shut, massaging his temples. "Logic says yes, but not necessarily." After a short pause, his gaze finds Argus again. "Do you have any evidence of his involvement?"

Argus shakes his head. "His name hasn't been mentioned."

"But it's possible, if not likely, right, sir?" Tacitus cuts in. "As Praetorian

Prefect, he's officially the Emperor's military advisor, even if it's you the Emperor trusts. What's your read of Falco, sir?"

Severus fixes a hard stare on the fresco of Achilles. "I have no reason to suspect him, but I will certainly investigate. You're right. It's hard to believe two guardsmen could plot something like this without the knowledge of their captain. Senator Varro would try to get Falco's support if he could."

Argus shoves to his feet, muscles tense for a fight. "We should take the guards out now. Why take the risk?"

Severus levels a firm look at him. "No. We can't alert Varro and Ursus we're onto them. Clearly, their claws go deep, their influence far-reaching. They need to think they're invincible. If we thwart a small piece too early, we'll lose our advantage and possibly the war. We must wait until we know the depth of what we face, especially if Falco is involved." He turns to Tacitus. "What do you have?"

Tacitus exhales with a grimace. "It's not good news."

"It never is," Argus mutters, sinking back to the stool.

"I learned one of our mystery investors is Quintus Placidius Pius."

I almost choke and exchange an alarmed look with Severus.

"What is it?" Tacitus asks, glancing between us.

"I was briefly engaged to his son," I explain, shuddering at the thought of being married to the enemy. Maybe I have a new appreciation for Arata's difficult situation. "But the family called it off for unknown reasons."

"I guess they're known now," Argus quips with a smirk.

I fire a wry glare before turning back to Tacitus. "Pius is yet another merchant, like Ursus, who is incredibly wealthy but without noble blood or political influence. Why are they involved in all of this? I can understand why Senator Varro wants the funding, but what do the merchants stand to gain?"

Tacitus's hard gaze turns cold. "Rome."

Severus furrows his brows. "What do you mean?"

"Based on what I heard, I believe once they're in power, they intend to raze what they deem the undesirable parts of the city and claim them for themselves. They're auctioning off the various districts to the highest bidders. They called it 'cleaning up'." He spits the words with all the venom they deserve.

"What about the people who live there?" I cry in horror.

"Yeah, people like *me*," Argus growls. "What about innocent children like Seia?"

Tacitus clenches his jaw, running a hand through his dark hair in agitation. "From the sounds of it, they'd suffer the same fate as their homes."

My stomach churns, my body rigid on the stool. I feel like running, screaming, and punching something all at once. "They would never be able to pull that off. Not without an army," I argue.

"They have one," Jason reminds us flatly.

"Okay, but we're talking about killing civilians. Women and children," I return. "Is Nepos really capable of such slaughter?"

"Yes," Tacitus spits without hesitation. "He's more than capable."

I glance at him, surprised by his vehemence. He's typically so composed. I'm even more shocked when Argus lays a hand on his friend's shoulder to calm him. No.

To *comfort* him.

There must be a story there.

Severus watches the interaction with a creased brow before turning to Jason. "If Tacitus is correct, and I believe he is, the stakes are catastrophic now. You may be our most valuable agent at this point. Varro not only trusts you, but he is pursuing you."

I straighten in alarm. "Pursuing him? What do you mean?"

"He wants me to fight," Jason explains.

"I know that, but…"

Severus silences me with a warning look. "If Jason agrees to fight for Varro, he would need to resume his training as a gladiator."

Dread sinks through my stomach. I stare at him in disbelief. "You're returning him to the ludus? To Opius Plinius?"

Severus and Jason exchange a long glance that makes me want to scream.

"Maybe," Severus replies in a solemn tone. "It would be up to his master." He inhales deeply and turns to Jason. "Right now, that person is me, through the Emperor. You couldn't fight unless he allowed it, and he can't do that. You understand the politics involved, right?"

A muscle moves in Jason's cheek as he nods.

"Let me do it, my lord," Jason says, his expression set in firm resolve. "We can't let those people die."

"I know, son," Severus says, gravel in his voice. Pain coats his face as he scans his valet with a mix of sadness and respect.

I shake my head and lean forward, pressing my fists into the table. "You just said you *can't* let him fight!"

Jason turns a patient look on me. It's the first real emotion he's shown, and I fight the urge to grunt in frustration.

"He can't as my master," he says. "That's why he can no longer be my master."

I stare at them in horror. They can't mean…*no!*

No! No! No!

Severus settles a firm but compassionate look on Jason. His jaw is tight, eyes conflicted, as if the words in his heart don't match the words in his head. Like he doesn't want to say what he's about to.

So, don't. Please don't!

"I'm not going to force this on you, son. I won't even ask it of you. It's your decision alone," he says finally.

Gaze fierce, Jason clenches his fist and pushes away from the wall. "Contact Senator Varro. He will agree to any price."

Chapter XXIII

JASON

"Thank you for coming to my home, Mallia," Severus says as we greet the young aristocrat in the atrium.

Mallia's expression is hard as she glances from Severus to me.

"You asked. I came. That's what we signed up for, right?" she quips.

Severus's brows knit in irritation, but he suppresses any rebuke. He must know she's scared about what's coming. The gods know I am too.

"I invited you here to say goodbye," he says evenly, leading us toward the empty tablinum. "It's unlikely the two of you will have a chance to interact again. I'll give you a few minutes alone, but it must be quick. Varro's men will be here any minute. Danae, you can come with me."

Heavy silence settles over Mallia and me once we're alone.

I study her beautiful, stern face, not sure where to begin. I can't blame her for being upset about the arrangement. It's dangerous, an incredible risk, and yet I've never been so sure about any of my steps since joining *Septem Fideles.* I just need her to understand.

She brushes her long, brunette hair behind her back. Unlike the typical elaborate updo women of her class wear, only a few braids adorn her silky locks today. Her ivory tunic and blue palla are unembellished, yet perfectly elegant as well. Even in her most casual state, her refined beauty is so far beyond my scarred existence that we don't belong in the same realm, let alone the same room. Our vastly different classes pulse in the tension between us. I will never understand what she sees in me.

"I want to beg you not to do this. But you already know that," she begins in a flat tone.

I meet her gaze, mesmerized by the dark lashes blinking over her vibrant brown irises. "And you know I have to."

The gentle arches of her lips press together as she tears her gaze away.

"We can't let this happen, my lady," I continue, clenching my fist. "We can't let Varro and Ursus play gods with this city. We can't let them demolish districts of innocent people."

"I know."

"We're running out of time to stop this. Every time we follow a lead, we learn the poison runs deeper, more deadly."

Old anger for this world's rampant injustice ignites deep within me. Memories of what I've seen…experienced…fought and lost…burn hot with renewed vengeance. "Maybe there *is* a lot of crime and evil in the poor districts, but no more than you'll find in the palaces. No more than I've faced in every mansion and villa owned by the elite. And what about the innocents whose only crime is being poor? I will not let those monsters slaughter them for circumstances they can't control!"

"Jason—"

"How long do I have to sit here and accept injustice?" I step toward her with strange urgency. "How long do I have to do nothing while these beasts rape and pillage just because they can? It has to stop, my lady! We have to stop it!"

"Hey." She grabs my hands, pulling me back to the present.

I swallow and look at her, embarrassed by my rare outburst. I can't remember the last time I lost my composure in the presence of another. Emotion is death for me, but my strict walls weaken with Mallia for some reason. It's the way she looks at me, her essence. Even now, instead of the resentment I expect, her eyes have softened with compassion.

"I know," she says quietly, squeezing my fingers. "I hate it, but I understand."

I draw in a deep breath and let the warmth of her touch seep into me. It feels good, soothing away some of the fear that's been simmering just beneath the surface since I agreed to this.

But there's another sensation plaguing me, an ache in the pit of my stomach I've never felt before.

For the first time in my life, I have something to lose.

Our gazes lock as we stand in silence, both aware that this is more than goodbye. This could be the end of a beautiful connection I've been too afraid to start.

"I'm sorry, my lady. I'm sorry for everything." I'm not even sure what I'm apologizing for. She nods and laces our fingers, somehow reading me anyway. Her palm is so soft and small against mine, but I feel the underlying strength in her confident grip.

"You don't deserve your fate," she says, searching my eyes. "I know why you have to fight the injustice. All the pain, all the suffering you've endured. You need to make it mean something. To redeem it. I do understand."

I clench my jaw, afraid emotion will soon invade my resolve, and I can't afford such weakness. "It's not just my own fate—my own redemption—at stake, my lady. We fight for all the oppressed. It doesn't matter if it's a war we can't win. We fight because of who *we* are. Because we accepted the seal and pledged ourselves to something greater than ourselves."

"I know that too." The corners of her mouth turn up in a sad smile, while her hold tightens on my hands. "Just do me one favor before you go? It's the only thing I'll ask of you."

I scan her face, taking in every detail and scorching her image on my heart for when I need it later. A flicker of light in the darkest shadows. Hope when all else is lost.

Based on what's coming, this could be the last time I see her this side of Hades.

"Anything, my lady."

She reaches up and molds her palm over my cheek. Wide brown eyes make a quiet plea as they scour mine. "Call me Mallia? Let us be equals for just a moment?"

Mallia.

Our strength.

Our hope.

Our greatest warrior no one will ever see coming.

My lips twitch with a gentle smile. "May the gods be with you…*Mallia.*"

Her grin slices into me, coating every inch with warmth. She brushes her thumb over my skin, blinking back a stray tear.

"Thank you," she whispers. "And Jason…may the gods finally bless you with all the beauty you deserve."

JASON

Senator Varro and Vibius Acilius Ursus seem quite pleased with their acquisition when I'm delivered to Varro's home. According to their discussion in the atrium, the price is high but fair.

"I'm thrilled that you accepted my offer," the senator says, approaching me. He makes a quick scan of my green tunic, studded belt, and leather sandals. Severus thought it best I leave my dagger with him and give Varro the option to arm me however he sees fit.

"It is the Emperor who agreed to the sale, my lord. It is he you should credit."

Varro waves his hand. "Of course, of course. You know what I mean."

"First thing's first. Your armor!" Ursus claps in excitement while I suppress a cringe. Every pound and pinch of that uncomfortable monstrosity is still seared into my memory. I'd prefer to walk around naked.

"My lord, perhaps we should save it for special occasions," I suggest with a bow. "Ceremonial displays and such. I would not want to see it damaged during my training."

Ursus taps his chin as he surveys me. The heat in his gaze churns my stomach, but Varro's impatient look quickly ends the debate.

"Agreed," Varro interjects. "Also, we considered contacting Opius Plinius and resuming your training at his ludus, but Severus warned me about your history with the man. Given your value to me, I'm hesitant to trust his care. You shall train here, on my own grounds, with my men. I'll bring in whatever you need."

I school my features to hide my relief.

"Yes, my lord. I understand."

Varro nods. "Good. I hope you also understand the importance of your role as our champion."

"Of course, my lord."

"You represent us now."

His biting gaze cuts into me, demanding I meet it. When I do, the intense warning blazing from his irises sends a wave of anxiety through me.

You are mine, his silent message shrieks.

"You probably still have concerns after that nasty encounter with Lurio," he continues in a deceptively softer tone. "It's understandable, but I can assure you that as long as you do your duty, nothing like that will happen again."

"I understand, my lord. I will train hard and stay focused."

The senator releases a curt smile that stops well-short of his eyes. "I know you will, my boy. I know you will."

MALLIA

"He's going to be fine. Jason knows that world much better than ours."

I reward Argus's poor attempt at comforting me with a tight smile. Now that we're both on assignment at the palace, he must feel an additional obligation to check in with me whenever possible. Based on my extensive experience with palace politics, it should probably be the other way around. Based on his complete lack of tact, it should *definitely* be the other way around.

"Thanks, Argus. I know if anyone can handle this situation, it's Jason. I'm just worried about his safety. At least when he belonged to Severus, we had some means of protecting him."

Argus's scarred face scrunches into something akin to a frown. "He's a slave. There is no protection for him. He knows that better than anyone, believe me."

I wince and slide my gaze to a statue at the end of the corridor. I felt better about the whole thing *before* Argus tracked me down to reassure me.

"Have you learned anything new about the Praetorian Guard plot?" I whisper, angling back to him.

He scans the deserted hall and shakes his head. "Not yet, but I haven't been alone with Eustacius and Decien since I overheard the initial conversation. I'm hoping to get more information after our shift. What about Aurelia? Any updates on her condition?"

"I'm headed to her now. As of yesterday, she is still deteriorating."

His coarse beard tickles my skin when he leans close to my ear. "Do you suspect Cornelia?"

"Jason does, and that's enough to initiate an investigation," I whisper back. "I'm not going to let them send me away when Cornelia visits today."

"Good." He straightens again and offers a stiff salute. "Well, back to work then, soldier. Keep Aurelia alive," he teases, green eyes dancing.

He's much better at playful mockery than sympathy.

"I will. And you keep the Emperor alive," I fire back with a grin.

MALLIA

My humor dissolves when I reach Aurelia's room, only to discover Cornelia already at her side.

Irritated, I plaster a smile on my face and join them. Not only have I missed potential clues to the poisoning, but I've also lost any hope of strengthening my position with Aurelia before Cornelia could exert her insidious influence.

"How are you feeling?" I ask, reaching for Aurelia's outstretched hands.

"Mallia!" Tears spring to her eyes as she pulls me down to the bed beside her. "The gods are cursing me! There is no longer any doubt!"

"Don't be ridiculous," Cornelia scoffs from a chair nearby. "You're simply suffering from an imbalance of fluids."

"An imbalance of fluids?" I ask, casting a glance between them. Cornelia's sharp brows knit in warning while her painted red lips purse in a scowl.

Aurelia blinks terrified blue eyes up at me. "Yes. Cornelia is so talented with medicines and herbs. She's been nothing short of a goddess through all of this." She tosses her friend a grateful look before focusing back on me. "She's hardly left my side and has been doing everything she can to help me."

"Oh?" I force out. "I assume the physician has been involved as well?"

"Telemon?" Aurelia grumbles, releasing my hands. "He's been completely useless. I've told him to stop bothering me with all his pointless treatments that only do more harm than good. If not for Cornelia, I'd already be dead. I'm sure of it."

A chill runs through me as I flutter another concerned look at the visitor's smug expression. Beside her, a bronze table lined with tinctures and tiny clay pots further confirms my fears.

"The gift of healing has run in my family for many generations," Cornelia explains with fake humility. Her targeted glare warns me not to challenge her.

I decide not to only because it would do nothing but turn Aurelia against me.

"Well, I'm sorry for not visiting as often as I should have," I say, shifting closer to Aurelia on the bed. "I assure you that will change. I want to be here as much as possible from now on." I cast an adoring glance at Cornelia. "In fact, I'm sure poor Cornelia could use some rest herself. Your own home must be in need of supervision after such an absence."

I add a sickly sweet smile for the older woman. Cornelia's expression darkens as she shifts uncomfortably in her chair.

"Mallia is right, my dear," Aurelia says with a frown. "You've been wonderful, but you must be exhausted. Why don't you go home and rest?"

"Thank you for your concern, but it's not necessary," Cornelia clips out. "There's nowhere I'd rather be than by your side in this time of crisis."

Aurelia chews on her dry, cracked lower lip, and I grab her cold hand again in support.

"Aurelia will be fine," I say brightly. "I've already informed my father I intend to stay with Aurelia at the palace until she returns to full health. If you'd like, you can show me her medicines, and I would be happy to administer them myself." I include an innocent wave over the spread of poisons for good measure.

"Yes! Excellent idea," Aurelia says, squeezing my hand. "You can leave the herbs, Cornelia. Between Mallia and Telemon, we should be able to take care of the treatments on our own. Just show her what to do."

I detect the slightest scowl on Cornelia's face before she covers it with a stiff smile.

"Well, I suppose some rest would do me good," she mutters, tracing the gold trim of her rose-colored stola. "As for your treatments, the current dose should be enough until I return. I'd hate for you to have to bother with all of that while I'm gone. It can be tricky to administer."

My fierce gaze burns into Cornelia as she rises from the chair. She pretends not to notice and busies herself with packing the "herbs" in a small basket.

"I'll be back as soon as I can," she says to Aurelia with a tight smile.

She adjusts the basket in her arms, hesitating for another moment before finally taking her leave.

I'm only too glad to see her go. The air feels infinitely lighter and more breathable without her.

Aurelia closes her eyes, taxed by the whole exchange. She appears even more depleted than the last time I saw her, like life itself is being drained out of her. What has the consul's wife been doing to her?

"Why don't you rest, my lady?" I say gently. "I'll stay close and make arrangements for nourishment to be brought for you when you wake."

Aurelia nods without opening her eyes. "Thank you," she whispers, giving my hand a weak squeeze. "I'm so glad you're here."

I stare down at the shrunken figure on the bed, almost feeling sorry for her.

Almost.

Chapter XXIV

TACITUS

"The Captain wants to see you," Glabrio announces as he breezes into the barracks.

"Me?" I ask as I finish securing my belt.

Glabrio shrugs. "If you're still Tacitus."

I shoot an irritated look and fasten my gladius to my hip. "Where?"

"Report to the training grounds."

"Did he say what he wants?"

"Got me. Another high-priority shopping trip, maybe?" He snickers at his joke, but I ignore it and move past him.

Voices drift toward me as I approach the training grounds embedded deep within the exterior gardens of Varro's estate. I nearly stumble a step when I see Captain Atticus showing Jason our collection of weapons and equipment.

"Ah, Tacitus! Finally. Come over here. There's someone you have to meet."

I force a blank expression as I close the distance.

"Tacitus, this is Jason, Senator Varro's champion gladiator. Jason, this is one of my top men, Gaius Atius Tacitus."

I glance at Atticus, surprised by the accolade, but appreciative if it got me involved in whatever this is with Jason.

"Yes, I remember him from Ursus's banquet the other night," I say, scanning my friend with the appropriate level of expected intrigue.

Jason returns a polite nod and does the same.

"I'm sure you're wondering what's going on," Atticus says to me. He adjusts his cloak and straightens with an air of authority. "Jason was recently purchased from the Emperor in order to take part in a magnificent contest sponsored by our great Senator Varro."

I manage a surprised look at what should be news to me.

"I see." I continue evaluating Jason as any good fighter would. "How can I assist?"

Atticus seems pleased with my reaction and motions between us. "As you can imagine, Jason is very valuable to the senator, who's trusted us with his training here at the villa rather than sending him to a ludus. We can't take any risks before his appearance in the Aratus Munera."

This time, my surprise is genuine, and I cast a glance at Jason before focusing back on Atticus. "Interesting. Are we equipped for such training? Defending against street attacks is very different than surviving the arena."

Atticus's blue eyes spark with humor as he shoots a knowing grin. "True. But something tells me your skill runs deeper than defending against street attacks. Am I right, *Centurion*?"

A return smile teases my lips. "It's possible."

"Good. Then, grab a weapon and get acquainted. You two will be spending a lot of time together over the next few weeks."

He stalks off, confident his instructions will be heeded.

And they will. Gladly.

Jason and I wait until Atticus disappears to drop our guard and exchange an amused grin.

"What do you think, gladiator? You ready to train?" I say with a smirk.

Jason returns it, eyes warm with rare mirth. "Don't worry. I'll be easy on you."

ARGUS

I wait until the laughter dies down and the next round of drinks is consumed to evaluate my fellow guards. They're happy, but not drunk, so I don't dare to bring up the topic yet.

"Tell us more about naked warrior women!" Decien snorts, pounding the table.

Wine sloshes out of the cups, adding fresh embellishments to the sticky mural of stains on the pine planks.

I force away my growing impatience and signal the tavern slave for another round.

"I haven't encountered any new ones since our last conversation," I say dryly, drawing a laugh from Eustacius.

"You have to forgive my friend here," Eustacius sneers. "He knows nothing of women. All he has are stories."

Decien glares at him. "*Eat ashes!* I've been with plenty of women!"

"Whores don't count," Eustacius quips, draining his cup. Decien does the same, and I add another drink for each to my mental tally. Five for Eustacius and six for Decien. How are they not drunk yet?

"Leave him alone," I say with mock compassion. "Women are expensive. Well, the right women, anyway. My friend spends a fortune on his mistresses."

"What about you, Argus? Who sucks the coins from your purse?"

I grunt with a bitter wave. "Vah, I'm done with women for a while, thanks to my ex-wife."

"Bad breakup?"

"She left me and ended up in Ephesus."

They burst into laughter and raise their fresh drinks in salute. "Ephesus! It must have been quite the fight to send her across the empire," Eustacius snorts.

I shrug and force a grin. "It didn't take as much as you'd think, trust me."

Their eyes turn glassy as their laughter grows to an inappropriate level for the weak joke. I glance at the half-empty cups the slave just delivered and decide my window is approaching.

Too drunk won't work either.

"I ran into Senator Varro at the palace the other day," I say, taking a fake sip from my own cup.

The men exchange a quick glance. Excellent.

"Is that so?" Eustacius says in a distracted tone.

I nod, cataloging every movement of their faces, every gesture of their bodies. "I was surprised to see him," I continue casually. "I didn't realize senators spent a lot of time at the palace, especially such prestigious ones."

It's a ridiculous comment, but I need to get them talking.

"There are senators at the palace all the time," Eustacius laughs. "Senator Varro is there often."

I return a dismissive shrug. "Oh, well, I guess I'm still getting used to rubbing elbows with the elite. If only some of their obscene wealth would rub off on me in return."

The others burst into more wild laughter at my bad joke.

"Then maybe you could afford a new woman!" Eustacius cries, slapping my back.

"Ha! Maybe. Do you ever get any side jobs out of your position?"

"Side jobs?" Decien asks, scratching at his short blond hair.

I shrug again through a swig of my drink. "I've done all kinds of jobs since my discharge, guarding storehouses and such. I know of other former soldiers who now serve as private bodyguards in the elite houses. With all these rich patricians walking around, there have to be other opportunities for us." I force a quick laugh and lean close. "Here's a story for you. I once had a merchant pay me sixteen denarii to follow his wife and find out who she was sleeping with."

Their eyes go wide as their heads loll toward me. "Really? Sixteen?"

"Yup, and the best part? Turned out to be no one! She'd been going to the Temple of Vesta to pray for children. Guy was just a jealous *porca*, but I still got my money."

The other guards laugh and exchange another much less discreet look.

Perfect.

"Anyway, I'm not trying to jump in on anything you've got going," I continue in a relaxed tone. "Just, you know, if you hear of something or are looking for another man, I'm always interested in making a little extra. This commission is way better than legionary pay, but come on. These people have so much coin they don't even know what to do with it."

They grunt a curse and glower at the table.

"Oh, we know," Decien grumbles. "Working for the Emperor is supposed to be the top of the line for soldiers like us, but the pay is *bollax* compared to what it should be."

"Really? You obviously haven't seen a disgraced legionary's purse," I joke, drawing smirks.

"It's not bad," Eustacius corrects. "But like you said, it's nothing compared to what those useless politicians have."

I scowl into my cup with appropriate indignation. "Makes me sick to think about it."

"We put our lives on the line so they can roll around stuffing their faces," Eustacius hisses.

"Yeah, well, I guess that's the cursed lot we drew," I mutter, waving my hand in disgust.

Once again, the men aim targeted glances at each other. The wine has completely eliminated the art of subtlety from their reactions.

"Don't get me wrong," I add, reading them closely. "I was happy to get this post, believe me. Disgraced soldier redeems himself as an elite palace guard? It's the stuff of legends. But, well…" I sigh out a bitter oath. "*Vah!* There I go again. Running my mouth off."

Eustacius drains his cup and smacks it on the table. "No, we get it."

The silent message they share is long this time. And *definitely* good news for me.

MALLIA

After leaving Aurelia to rest, I go in search of Severus, only to learn he's away on an errand. The wait for his return is excruciating, and I quickly run out of tasks to keep me occupied. There are only so many times one can circle the grounds and walk the gardens, even at a massive palace.

I'm almost ready to hunt the streets of Rome for the man when I finally get word he's returned.

Severus hasn't even finished his refreshing routine when I demand an audience from his secretary and wait impatiently outside his study. His new valet finally meets me in the peristyle and ushers me into the private room.

"His name is Clement," Severus says of the new attendant once we're alone. "He's capable, for the most part."

I instinctively glance in the direction the young slave just left and wince from sudden pressure in my chest. I'm still having trouble accepting Jason's absence.

"He's experienced, at least," I say with a weak smile.

Severus nods and chuckles to himself. "That he is. He's certainly a much better valet than Jason was."

I try and fail at another smile. Severus sighs and motions for me to sit.

"I miss him, too, Mallia. You understand why he had to do this. I know you do."

I look away as I take the cushioned chair, having no desire to finish this conversation. Not now. Not again if I can help it. That's not why I'm here anyway.

"We were right about Cornelia," I say instead. Severus's expression grows serious as he lowers himself to a chair beside me. "She was with Aurelia when I arrived this morning and got extremely defensive when I tried to separate them. Apparently, she's been 'treating' Aurelia's 'ailments' herself."

Severus stiffens in his seat, his brow sinking in concern. "Does Telemon know about this? The Emperor?"

I shrug and fiddle with the silk of my light blue palla. "I don't know, but you will probably have better luck discerning that than I will. I do know that Cornelia refused to let anyone else administer her 'treatment' for Aurelia and was very secretive about it."

Severus's expression sinks further as he settles a hard look on the wall. Light streams in through the open window, casting inviting streaks on piles of scrolls on his desk. I wonder how many of those documents could make or break an empire.

"It seems likely that Jason was right then." His grave observation slices through the long silence. "Cornelia may be poisoning her."

A shiver runs over me at the image of her sinister expression only a few hours ago.

"I just don't understand it," I say, squinting toward the window. "Why would she do this? I understand Jason's point about jealousy, which could certainly be a contributing factor, but enough for murder? I don't know if I can believe that."

"If we're right, then it's more than that." He leans back in the chair, his gray gaze shrouded in thought. "Jealousy may be the reason Cornelia agreed to carry out her role in a bigger plan."

My stare cuts back to him. "What are you saying?"

"I'm saying the more I've thought about the threat to Aurelia, the more I'm convinced it's related to everything else. It's too much of a coincidence that an attack is being carried out on the Emperor's only close relative while we're also investigating a plot for a major coup. It has to be connected."

Air releases from my lungs. I sink into the cushion, my mind jumping into a frantic review of the last few weeks. As much as I hate it, I even let myself consider the horror of the afternoon with Jason. What had he said about their motivations? They weren't friends. They were competitors.

I bolt to attention in my seat. "Who would take power if something happened to the Emperor?"

Severus lands a surprised look on me. "With no male heirs, it would be a messy situation. Some would campaign for a high-ranking senator. Others would campaign for Aurelia as a relation of noble blood."

"What about the consul? Would he be considered?"

Eyes narrowed in thought, Severus scratches at the scruff on his cheek. "As much as anyone else in our current turbulent state. Things aren't what they used to be. For all the laws and structure we've put into place over the last century, very little is respected. We re-commissioned *Septem Fideles* because we can no longer trust our system. It's a free-for-all in the fight for power."

"So, if Aurelia was out of the way and the Emperor was assassinated…" I let my words trail into dire possibilities.

Severus arches forward with a concerned expression. "The field narrows considerably."

"Exactly. And Consul Matho, Cornelia's husband, leads the pack of remaining candidates."

My gaze locks on Severus's as all color drains from the room.

"Jason was right," I murmur quietly, thinking out loud. "I didn't truly understand what he was saying at the time. When he said the motive was jealousy, I thought he meant over him, but I don't think he'd put himself on such a pedestal. Cornelia envies Aurelia's entire existence. It's not driving her to murder out of vengeance, but out of anticipation. If the Emperor is killed, there's a very good possibility Cornelia will have the life Aurelia has. The life she clearly wants at any cost."

"Thunder of Jupiter…" Severus breathes out. "So, you're saying the consul is aligning with Varro and Ursus at the moment, but will betray them and make a play for Emperor once he's gone?"

I cringe at the frank portrayal of the harsh truth. "They all need each other for now, but like you said, the elite live in a world of self-interest. If I've learned anything watching the strain of my father's term in the senate, it's that fellow conspirators make terrible friends."

"Pluto's chains…" Severus mumbles to himself.

I exhale sharply as the new theory crashes around us. We've just exposed another tentacle of this burgeoning plot. Now, we have to figure out what to do with it.

After a long silence, Severus clears his throat and steels himself with resolve.

"This is a serious threat, but Cornelia is still the consul's wife," he says in a stern voice. "We have to be very careful how we approach this situation. We're not even absolutely certain of Cornelia's guilt, or the Consul's connection to Senator Varro. The Emperor can't make accusations without evidence. He can't risk that kind of backlash. We have to remember that, while this threat consumes our lives, it's unknown to anyone else. We'd make many enemies if we attacked the consul without evidence."

"So, let's get the evidence," I say, inching forward on my chair. "I'm sure the Emperor knows Aurelia is sick. Let's make sure he knows how sick and then we find ways to keep Cornelia out of the palace. If Aurelia improves, we have our proof that it was Cornelia. Even if the Emperor has to wait for the right time and method to expose the consul's treason, *we* will know and can keep Aurelia safe while we investigate this new lead."

Severus rubs his chin, a distracted gaze fixed on the marble floor. "It won't be easy keeping Cornelia away, but it can certainly be done. Discerning if the consul is conspiring with Senator Varro will be more of a challenge."

I shake my head with a growing smile. "Actually, no. It won't be hard at all. We just have to inform Jason and Tacitus."

Chapter XXV

TACITUS

After climbing out of the bath, I reach for a clean tunic on the bench and tense at a presence behind me. Instinct sends my hand to my blade, but my palm hits the linen wrapped around my waist instead.

I turn and inhale sharply when our eyes meet.

"My lady…" I breathe out. I dart an anxious glance around the bathing chamber while Arata scans every inch of me. My body goes cold and then hot beneath her intense stare.

"I was told I could find you in the servant baths," she says, twisting her hand in the ethereal fabric of a gold stola. The color makes her amber eyes glow from another realm as they sink over my half-naked body. Her scalding stare cuts into me before climbing back to my face.

"Captain Atticus sent you to the servant baths to find me? Really?" I mumble in a dry tone.

White teeth sink into her full lip as she returns a coy shrug. "I didn't say *who* said I could find you here."

I shake my head, fighting a smile of my own. When I reach for the clean tunic again, the echo of bare feet on smooth cement claps toward me.

"Don't," she whispers, grabbing my wrist. She laces her fingers with mine and tugs me toward her.

I straighten slowly, my heart pounding.

Still gripping my fingers, she skims her other palm up my chest, guiding me back against the rough plaster-coated wall.

"Arata..." My thin warning is so weak, even I don't believe it.

Dread mixes with impossible desire in the tense stare-down that follows. Water tickles my skin as it drips from my wet hair to the rigid planes of my chest. Chalky plaster scrapes my back, scolding me with reminders of the vast difference between the servant baths and the luxurious marble and tile she's accustomed to.

She doesn't belong here, and I can't bring myself to remind *her* of that fact.

With her imploring gaze locked on mine, she slides her hand up my neck, staking her claim. Humid air fills our lungs as we hover close, her soft lips daring me to ignore the fire ripping through my veins.

"It's been two weeks since we last saw each other. Do you know where I've been?" she whispers, searching my eyes.

I look away, willing my hungry body not to react. "How could I? I've worried about you, though."

"You should worry," she returns with playful chiding. "And not just about me. Lurio hates you, Tacitus. That's why I'm here. To warn *you*. He said he will not rest until he watches jackals rip the flesh from your bones in the arena."

Her words pierce the veil of my consciousness, but the threat feels too far, too blurry to care. All I can comprehend are her bright golden eyes. Her soft skin. Her silky hair.

I don't move, terrified that if I start, I won't stop.

"I face such risks every day," I reply. "It's part of my job. I can't protect without making enemies."

She punishes my defiance with a hard yank on my wet hair. I suck in a breath, my blood pounding heat and hunger through every part of me. Her lips drift along my jaw. Her other hand glides over my chest, down my stomach.

By Pluto's chains, it's destroying anything left of my will.

"I'm not asking for protection," she breathes, torturing me with touch after glorious touch. She presses into me, forcing every inch of my body to acknowledge her. Taunting me with the invitation I can't accept.

"Wait. Arata, please."

I draw on every bit of strength I have to duck away.

We stare in silence, breathing hard. Fighting for control of ourselves, the moment.

"Thank you for the warning," I say in a gentle tone. I distract myself from her pained look by swiping my crimson tunic from the bench. This time, I stay far out of reach as I pull it over my head.

When I dare another look in her direction, glossy, tear-stained eyes shimmer back in the flickering lamplight.

Surprised by the sudden shift, I soften my stance and face her.

"Do you know what it's like to live in constant fear?" she whispers, searching my eyes with a new message. This time, it's pain she's sharing. Fear. "To sense him there, afraid to turn the corner, to constantly feel the marks no one sees."

She takes a deep breath and wipes at the liquid sliding down her cheeks. "And when it's so bad I think I can't take it anymore, I close my eyes for a brief escape. Do you know what I see?"

Heart thumping, I pull in a quick breath. I can't fight these feelings, not with her looking at me like that.

"It's you, Tacitus," she continues in a watery tone. "I see you and what you said that night you took me home from that awful banquet. I was so alone, so lost in my situation, and you gave me hope. Right in the middle of a public street, I was face-to-face with an amazing man, a good man. Strong, compassionate, brave, and I knew there was still something beautiful left in this world. You believed, so I could too."

I look at her then. I have to. My lungs burn, and it's everything I can do not to take her away right then. To rescue her from all of this. What was, what is. What's coming. To finally be able to truly protect her.

To love her the way she deserves to be loved.

It's all there, in my heart, on my face, racing through my veins…

And all I can do is hope she understands I can't do any of it.

Maybe she does. Maybe she just surrenders to her harsh reality, but two hearts break when her shoulders droop in a resigned sigh.

"I should go before someone sees me," she mumbles, turning toward the exit.

"Arata."

She turns back, her expression twisted in conflicting emotions. I'm sure it mirrors mine.

"Keep looking for me when you close your eyes," I say softly. "I'll be looking for you."

A sad smile slips over her beautiful lips before she disappears.

JASON

"Let's go. We have work to do," Tacitus growls as he snatches the bowl of lentil stew from my hands. The other slaves in the kitchen watch in stunned silence at the unexpected confrontation with one of Varro's guards.

"Didn't you just finish bathing after our last training session?" I ask in amusement.

"And I can follow this one with another bath. Let's go!"

"Got it," I say, biting back a smile.

Someone's in a mood.

I offer an apologetic look to the boy currently holding my half-eaten stew and chase after my friend.

Despite his shorter stride, Tacitus remains several paces ahead of me as he marches through the house, across the grounds of the estate, past the barracks where his off-duty companions are lounging, and onto the sand of the training area.

It's late into the evening, and the sun has long set. A few elevated torches cast a small circle of light just large enough for us to spar.

Tacitus grabs a dulled spatha from the stash of weapons and turns on me with fierce determination.

"Choose your weapon, Gladiator! Why are you just standing there?" he barks.

My humor fades into concern as I study him in the quivering light.

"I think I should be asking you that question," I say, crossing my arms.

His gaze narrows on me, but the distracted way he adjusts his grip on the weapon confirms my theory that something else is going on.

"Nothing's wrong," he lies. "I was told to train you, and I will."

I scan his rigid stance with a skeptical look. He's too wound up to be a strong opponent anyway. "Four times a day? In place of meals? In the dark?"

"Your training regimen would be even stricter at the ludus," he fires back.

I furrow a brow as I retrieve a blunt gladius from the pile. "True. But it's not the training regimen I'm worried about. It's the look on your face and the fact that you'd rather be sparring with me in the dark than doing pretty much anything else. I don't mind. I have nothing better to do as a slave whose sole purpose is to fight, but you…"

Tacitus glares at me. A few tense seconds pass before he slams his blade into the ground.

With a slow shake of his head, he runs a hand over his face. "I don't know anymore, Jason. I just don't know."

"What is it? Did something happen?"

Tacitus scans the shadows to make sure we're alone and then steps close.

"It's Arata," he whispers.

"Varro's daughter?"

He nods, dark eyes heavy with rage. "Her husband Lurio—that cursed *luprax* from the pit of Hades—hurts her. She's terrified of him."

Anger swells within me. I feel the burn ignite in my chest and spread through my eager fists. "Ursus's son? The flagrum coward?"

Tacitus nods again. "The same."

"*Caenum*..." I breathe out. "Have you told Senator Varro?"

He runs a hand through his damp hair, a tortured expression on his face. "I can't do that."

"Why not? He may be willing to slaughter districts of poor people he deems undesirable, but I guarantee you, his own daughter is not one of them."

Tacitus darts a surprised look at me. His bleak countenance brightens with a thought in the dancing flames. "Do you really think he'd intervene? It's his main ally's son. His son-in-law. Roman law says—"

"Forget Roman law," I clip out with a firm look. "Trust me on this. For all his faults, Senator Varro would not hesitate to take action against Lurio to protect his daughter. His pride alone guarantees it."

"You think so?" His anxious gaze silently pleads with mine.

"I know it for a fact. He practically said as much after that monster used the flagrum on me. He was so disgusted with Lurio, he reprimanded Ursus right in front of me and said he'd destroy the man if he ever did the same to Arata. You need to tell him what's going on."

Tacitus studies the movement of his palm over the hilt of the spatha. Voices of passing strangers on the street can be heard from the other side of the wall, while the cool evening breeze rustles the trees and plants of the surrounding gardens.

In another life for another person, this would be the perfect night for a relaxing evening with friends. For us, it's another battle plan in our secret war.

"Actually, I have a better idea," Tacitus says.

He yanks the spatha from the ground and tosses it with the others. Then motions for me to follow.

ARGUS

"I made this for you!" a squeaky voice shrieks with excitement as I enter my flat.

I've barely closed the door before a tiny dead animal is being shoved into my hand. I glance down at the mass of fur and sticks, then at the expectant grin of my little houseguest.

"What is it?" I ask, holding up the structured garbage to examine it.

"A lion! The butcher let me have the fur, and I found the sticks by the fig trees near Vesta's Fountain!"

I examine it again, but still fail to see anything except a rotted swatch of goat carcass.

"It took me all afternoon, but I knew you'd love it, so I didn't mind. And look!"

Seia grabs the object from my hand and presses down on its back. The sticks wiggle and shift as she beams with pride.

"It actually walks!"

She thrusts the object toward me again, and I rest it on my palm.

"A lion, huh? And it walks."

She nods vigorously, brunette curls firing in all directions. "I thought you could put it in your satchel if you ever go to war again."

I grunt and deposit the "lion" on the window ledge, which seems like the only safe spot for the impending smell. "I won't be going back to war, but thanks."

I flinch when skinny arms reach around my waist from behind.

"Really? Are you sure?" she asks, her voice muffled against my wool cloak. She squirms around me to look up into my face. "I'm so happy! I'm always afraid you will tell me you have to leave like my parents did. How do you know you won't?"

I bite back a snort at the absurd thought. "I just know. I'm not that kind of soldier anymore. I protect the Emperor now."

Seia gasps and stares up with wide eyes. "The Emperor? The real Emperor?"

"The real Emperor."

"You've seen him?"

"Every day."

"Even today?"

"Every day. So yes, today."

I cross to the kitchen area of the flat and curse at the bare shelf. "Do we have any food left for dinner?"

"I don't think so," Seia says, peeking into the grain sacks and storage jars. "We finished it this morning. You said it was okay because you would buy more on the way home."

"*Frax*..." I mutter and then apologize at Seia's disapproving look.

"You even said sweet cakes," she reminds me.

"Did I?"

She grabs my hand and drags me to the door.

MALLIA

My heart drops to my stomach when our house steward announces the unexpected visit from Tacitus.

I rush from the peristyle to the atrium, my pulse pounding with fear.

"What's wrong? Is it Jason?" I ask urgently, scanning his face for clues.

Tacitus appears startled by my question, and I feel some relief when he shakes his head. "Jason's fine. I'm here on another matter. Can we talk privately?"

Air floods back into my lungs. Thank the gods.

"Of course." I lead him to an empty sitting room off the side of the atrium.

The nerves return at the anxious expression on his handsome face. He adjusts the gladius at his hip and paces for several seconds before stopping abruptly and pivoting on his boot to face me.

"I'm sorry to come unannounced, but I've just left a meeting with Severus." His dark brown eyes scour my face in the filtered sunlight from the atrium. "I have a plan to end all of this, but I need your help."

Stunned, I meet his gaze and breathe through the weight of what he just said. "Of course. Whatever you need."

His chest rises and falls with a deep breath as he studies the floor mosaic with stern concentration. After a long pause, he offers a firm nod.

"You may not be so eager to help when you hear the plan." His pained gaze finds mine again. "It involves betraying someone we care about."

CHAPTER XXVI

MALLIA

I RISE FROM THE BENCH AND GREET ARATA WITH A WARM SMILE WHEN SHE'S LED INTO the peristyle.

Her silky green stola flutters in the gentle breeze as she glides toward me with open arms. "Mallia! I'm so honored by the invitation. It's been too long since we've seen each other."

The spicy floral scent of expensive nard drifts toward me as I return her warm embrace.

"I'm sorry for that. Aurelia has been very ill, so I've been spending a lot of time at her side," I say as I guide her to a bench near my favorite fountain. The large marble basin features a small bronze statue of Venus rising from the sea. Water pours from an urn in her arms, filling the garden with its tranquil, natural song.

"I'm sorry to hear that," Arata says with a frown. She adjusts one of the exquisite pearl fibulae fastening the stola at her shoulders. A simpler version of the decorative clasps secure the drapery at her waist, creating a subtle homage to her elegant taste and high status. The irony that this generous, compassionate woman mourns Aurelia, while the other woman would hate her for owning such beautiful pieces is not lost on me.

"Do they know what ails her?" Arata asks.

Leaning against the fountain, I drag my fingers through the cool water. "No, but she's getting good care now, so we're optimistic the gods will show mercy. Wine?"

"Thank you." Arata accepts a tinted green glass from a slave and takes a dainty sip.

Danae holds out a towel so I can dry my hand and do the same. Her dark brown eyes linger on mine a second too long in the exchange, and I know she's feeling the same mix of dread and anticipation at what's about to come.

I draw in a breath of rose-scented air to calm my racing heart. Deceiving Arata will be harder than I thought.

"I must confess that as much as I enjoy your company, I called you here for another reason," I begin in a gentle tone.

Her smile sags into concern, and I shift on the bench to face her. Amber eyes sift over my face, so trusting, so kind. This manipulation is hard for me, but it must be destroying Tacitus. I saw how much he cared about her while he relayed his plan.

"What is it? Is something wrong?" Arata asks, placing her glass on a table.

I glance around before shifting closer on the bench.

"We have a mutual friend," I say, searching her gaze. "I didn't want to embarrass you in front of Aurelia the day you spoke of Tacitus, but the truth is, he and I are well-acquainted."

Arata shrinks back. Blinking rapidly, she flutters a hand to her hot cheek.

"Of course you are," she mumbles to herself. "He comes from a family of status. I'm sure your paths have crossed."

I manage a tight smile at the unexpected gift. I hate lying more than necessary, but she just offered the perfect cover. "Yes. We're only casual acquaintances, mind you, but you know how it is with him. After one conversation, he is a friend you don't forget."

Arata's blush deepens as a shy smile curves her lips. "That's true. He's not easy to forget."

"Arata…" I take her hands and clasp them lightly. "He asked me to talk to you. He has…feelings…and..." I force in a deep breath as if banishing a thought. "Anyway, he's very worried for you. He hated betraying your trust by talking to me about this, but he didn't know what else to do."

Arata stiffens and jerks her hands away. "What are you talking about? What did he tell you?"

She's clearly upset, and I hate that I'm not sure which of her secrets she thinks is worse.

"He told me about Lurio."

She flinches with a sharp exhale. Her gaze darts to the tiled floor.

"What exactly did he tell you?" she whispers in a pained voice.

"No details. Only that he mistreats you."

"Why would he share that with you?"

"Because he thought I'd be able to help."

Arata glances up, tears in her eyes. "How? Lurio is my husband."

I reach for her hand again, and she lets me hold it. "I know, but I can get you away from him without jeopardizing your reputation."

Hope ignites on her face. Her golden eyes practically glow with it.

Gods, this is brutal. I take some solace in the fact that our plan *does* involve removing that vile man from her life.

"Really? How?"

I squeeze her fingers and muster the warmest smile possible. "We'll explain in a moment. First, there's someone who needs to be part of this discussion." I signal Danae, who moves toward one of the neighboring corridors.

"Tacitus!" Arata cries, jumping to her feet.

The former centurion strides forward several steps as she rushes with equal anticipation. They meet in a swift collision, and he draws her tight against his chest. A weight seems to lift from both of them as they hold on. For a few seconds, nothing else seems to exist for them.

A sudden stab of longing has me forcing away images of Jason.

"I'm sorry for deceiving you," he says softly against her hair. "What we're about to say is too dangerous to discuss at your father's house, and I didn't know how else to meet with you."

She tips her head back, revealing a grave look, but also strength I didn't see a moment ago. She cares about him just as much as he cares about her. Even now, she clings to him like he's already rescued her from every monster.

"Were you serious about getting me away from Lurio or was that just pretense?" Arata asks him before tilting a glance at me.

"We're serious," Tacitus replies. "We want to get you away from him, but we'll need your help."

He pulls her close again, and my chest hurts at the way her fists grasp onto his burgundy cloak. He's holding on just as tightly, which makes the discreet, pained look he sends me above her head that much more excruciating.

Everything in me wants to stop him from doing this, but this moment is exactly what Severus warned us about the day we accepted our commissions. Difficult choices. Betrayal of those we love.

Sacrifice.

We can't afford to be saints, and my heart breaks as I watch Tacitus shatter his own.

MALLIA

"You did the right thing. You had to," I say quietly after Arata leaves to return home.

Tacitus pierces me with an anguished look. "I lied to her, Mallia. I love her, and I knowingly *lied* to her. I'm a monster."

He drops his head to his hands, shoving his fingers through wavy dark hair. I lower to the bench beside him and wrap my arms around him.

"You didn't have a choice," I say softly. "It's the only way you can truly protect her."

"She'll never forgive me," he whispers in a hoarse voice, still not looking at me. "When she finds out the truth of what we're doing…"

He shakes his head in slow movements, a numb expression on his face.

"It doesn't matter if she forgives you. It doesn't matter what she thinks of any of us. You didn't do it for yourself." He aims his tortured gaze toward me, and I squeeze his arm. "What you just did was one of the bravest things I've ever seen."

Tacitus blinks back emotion and fixes his stare on a distant olive tree.

"You'll take care of her?" he asks in a hard tone.

"Like she's family."

"And you're sure no one will find her?"

"Only Danae and I will know where she is. I'll make sure there's a backup plan in case something happens to us."

Tacitus runs his hands over his face. When he straightens, the proud centurion is back in control.

He pushes to his feet and adjusts his cloak. "Then, it's done. Tell me where and when to send her. I'll meet her and face the consequences directly."

I had no doubt about that last part. From what I understand, very few demonstrate a willingness to suffer for their integrity the way this man does.

"I'll prepare the room," I say with a sad smile.

ARGUS

"Argus!"

I turn at the sound of my name to find Eustacius and Decien stalking down the corridor.

"What is it? I'm on duty," I warn.

They glance around the empty colonnade before approaching.

"We know. We checked before we came, and there's no one here," Decien assures me.

Eustacius grips the top of the bronze cuirass over his chest and leans close. "We might have something for you."

I raise my brows. "A job?"

"Pays really well and is the easiest money you will ever make. You just have to agree not to ask questions and tell no one."

"Why not?"

"I said no questions."

I rub my beard while scanning his hard expression. "Fair enough. What's the job?"

He straightens, rustling his deep crimson cloak. "We'll tell you when the time comes. All you'll need to do is guard a corridor."

"One corridor? Where?"

"Here, in the palace. Just make sure no one comes through. That's it."

I survey them slowly, careful to keep my face an acceptable mix of intrigue and skepticism. "No one's getting hurt, right? I'm no criminal."

"What did we say about questions?"

"Fine. How much?"

"Five hundred sesterces."

I fall back a step, breathing a curse. "Five hundred? Are you serious? *Blessed Fortuna…*"

Grins cut through their serious expressions, better reflecting the drunk men I've been manipulating after hours in the tavern.

"Not bad, huh?" Eustacius says.

"That's almost half a year's pay!" I hiss. "You swear I just have to stand watch?"

"That's it."

"And when did you say this would happen?"

"Three weeks," Decien whispers. "Two days after the Aratus Munera."

Eustacius fires a scalding glare at his friend.

"What?" Decien whines. "He has to know if he's going to help us."

"Hey, it's fine," I cut in before this falls apart. "Just work out the details and let me know what you've got when it's time."

Eustacius still wears a scowl when he turns back to me. Guess I wasn't supposed to know about the date. Gods be praised for loose tongues.

"We'll let you know when you need to know. It's important to be exact," Eustacius says.

I hold up my hands. "For five hundred sesterces, I'll skip my mother's funeral. You tell me what you need."

Eustacius nods and drags Decien back down the hall.

TACITUS

The thud of wood on wood echoes through the garden annex as I approach the training ground. Jason is alone, hammering away against the palus with grace, strength, and precision. He really is a remarkable fighter. Despite my sour mood, I can't help but hover several paces away to watch in awe.

Even with a practice weapon, he'd be a deadly threat, which is why I'm not surprised Varro only allows him to use real weapons with direct supervision. Varro also removed the ornamental reminders of Jason's former status from his uniform. The studded belt is gone, along with the military-style tunic. Both were replaced by the simple coarse tunic and plain leather strap of a common house slave. Even more telling, he swapped the subtle bracelet marking him as a slave the Emperor preferred for a more obvious tag around his neck.

Other than those changes, however, I have no complaint with the way my friend has been treated since transferring custody. Varro must be sincere about his intentions for Jason.

I move out of the shadows, drawing his attention. He lowers the wooden gladius and steps back from the man-sized training post. A sheen of sweat glistens over his skin, staining his beige tunic.

Wiping the sweat from his forehead, he squints at me as I approach. Despite the blinding afternoon sun, I feel shrouded in a shadow I can't shake.

"Is it done?" he asks.

My fingers clench in a tight ball at my side. "It will be once Mallia sets things in motion. I just returned from meeting with them."

Jason lets out his breath, his hard expression sagging into concern. "You spoke with Arata then."

I wince through a tightening in my chest. "I don't want to talk about it. There's something else we need to discuss anyway."

He straightens with a nod while I close the gap.

"What is it?" he asks.

I scan the gardens, searching for any unusual silhouettes or movement. It's unlikely since it's too hot for the members of the family to be outside and no other staff would have business here, but we can't be too careful. We live among the enemy. Every word, every breath, comes with risk.

I lean close and lower my voice to almost a whisper. "Severus and Mallia report that they're almost certain Cornelia was poisoning Aurelia. They also think it's related to the main plot because her husband, Consul Matho, would stand to gain a lot once the Emperor is removed." I take a deep breath, casting one more glance around us. "Severus wants us to confirm whether Consul Matho is part of the conspiracy against the Emperor. He's also asked us to investigate Cornelia if she shows up at any events with Senator Varro. Now that they're keeping her away from Aurelia, Mallia no longer has access."

Jason's gaze hardens. "Severus is commanding *us* to investigate her, or me?"

I cringe and drag my fingers along the lining of my cloak. "Well…you."

A muscle moves in his jaw as his focus locks on something in the distance.

"Look, maybe we can think of—"

"It's fine," he mumbles.

"Jason…"

"Let's just train, okay?" He stalks toward the table of weapons and swaps the practice gladius for the real thing. "Now that you're here, we can do this for real."

I sigh and search his stony expression. Nothing about his demeanor says he's fine.

This day—this *world*—is complete *bollax*. I believe in our mission, but sometimes it seems so impossible. What good can five hidden warriors do against an invincible army of evil?

"You choosing a weapon, or what?" Jason snaps, waving toward the pile with irritation.

He shrugs at my wry look, making it clear the discussion is over.

I pull my own gladius from its sheath and settle into a fighting stance.

"You're going to regret pushing so hard to fight," I joke.

"We'll see," he says with a smirk.

We're on our third round of sparring when we spot Varro's approach. We exchange a surprised look before coming to attention. With a hand shading his eyes, the senator advances slowly, as if unsure about this section of his own property. In his fine robes and freshly bathed exterior, he couldn't look more out of place. Based on his hesitant steps and awkward expression, this might be the first time he's visited this part of his estate.

My pulse picks up at the anomaly. "Strange" is rarely a good thing in our world.

"How is the training going?" he asks, passing a look between us.

"Very well, sir," I say, lowering my sword to my side.

Jason does the same, and Varro studies him with open interest.

"He'll be ready to fight?" the senator asks, fidgeting with the sleeve of his tunic.

"He's ready now, sir. True warriors are always ready."

Varro nods in approval and eyes Jason again. "I need both of you to clean up and report to me as soon as possible. I would like to introduce you to some friends."

He casts another long look between us before heading back along the stone path through the garden.

Jason and I watch him disappear around a bend toward the house.

"What was that about?" I mumble. "Since when does the dominus deliver instructions in person?"

My friend squints down the recently vacated path. "When they're delivering instructions they don't want others to know."

I snap a look at him. "And what would that be?"

"If I had to guess, he wants a demonstration."

His hazel gaze brushes mine before he saunters toward the weapons rack.

"But why be so secretive about a demonstration? Isn't that the whole reason he acquired you?"

Jason flickers a look at me and then down at the gladius in his hand. "It's not the demonstration. It's the reason for it. We need to pay attention to the audience. Something big is happening tonight."

Surprised at his insight, I scan him with renewed admiration as he cleans the sword and returns it to its place. He probably read that entire situation the second Varro appeared.

Incredible.

I initially thought Severus recruited Jason for his fighting skills, but every minute we've spent together has shown he's so much more than that. His hard life and unique experiences have given him a perspective on people and circumstances the rest of us will never have. He might be the most important member of our team.

I've always respected him, but I'm starting to rely on him.

"We're probably about to meet more investors," he says in a dark tone. "If we're lucky, we'll have our answer about the consul sooner than we thought."

Chapter XXVII

JASON

Cornelia's devious smile makes my blood run cold when it locks on me.

Although part of me hoped to see her tonight in order to confirm our suspicions, the other part would rather face Ino, Musa, and Basinus again than be alone with the entitled woman.

Thick streaks of charcoal line her eyes, making her brown irises even more piercing in the quivering lamplight throughout the atrium. Embellished hair extensions twist high on her head and cascade down her back in intricate ringlets and braids. Two piercing emeralds glare back from a scorpion fibula attached to one shoulder of her stola. A giant single emerald clasps the flowing gold fabric at the other shoulder.

"I'll catch up with you in a moment," she says to her companion.

I don't recognize the other woman who gives me a quick appraisal before continuing on to the triclinium.

Once we're alone, Cornelia leans against a marble column and studies me with a coy expression.

"Well, this is a pleasant surprise. I heard rumors of Varro's acquisition, but didn't expect to see you tonight. I figured he'd hide his pet away for safekeeping. He had to know the vultures would come out to play."

Dressed like a murmillo statue in a stylized bronze helmet and cuirass, I continue staring straight ahead without acknowledging her. She's a hunter. I have to be the prey if I have any hope of getting something from her.

She slinks several steps closer, stopping just a breath away.

"I see you're still not particularly talkative, are you? I suppose that's a good quality in a slave."

I snap a glare in her direction but remain silent.

"Oh, good. You still have that fire. Varro will appreciate such an attribute in his *champion*." Her gaze slithers over me again, tracing every detail of my body. "I will say, I prefer you without the armor, though."

"I belong to Senator Varro now," I say evenly.

"Yes, but the Senator is very generous with his belongings."

"Varro will be sending for me at any moment."

"I only need a moment," she purrs, tracing my cheek, my jaw. "Our last encounter was too full of distractions."

Her hand moves to my arm where she strokes and squeezes with gluttonous indulgence.

I clench my teeth and force a neutral expression.

"Now is not a good time, my lady. I'm to be presented shortly."

Her thin brows pinch with irritation. "Is that so? Because it seems to me that—"

"Jason! There you are." Tacitus stalks toward us with a stern look on his face.

Cornelia drops her hand and scowls at the intruder. Her expression softens slightly when she scans Tacitus, who looks every bit the dashing Roman hero in his crimson military tunic, studded belt, and matching cloak. The gladius at his hip also separates his free, bodyguard status from my role as enslaved, evening entertainment.

"You don't mind if I borrow him?" he asks Cornelia with a disarming grin.

Her red painted lips tip up in a seductive arc. "Not at all. I'm Cornelia, wife of Consul Matho. And you are?"

Tacitus bows deeply. "Gaius Atius Tacitus, a member of Senator Varro's personal security."

She slides her stare over him in approval. "Noted. Well, I won't keep you from your duties. Jason and I can finish our conversation later."

Tacitus returns a stiff smile, and I'm relieved when she meanders toward the triclinium with the other guests.

"You okay?" Tacitus asks, leaning close.

"Fine. Are they ready for us?"

Tacitus meets my gaze before squinting back at the empty atrium. "Not yet, I just saw her bothering you."

I bite back a smile as he leans past the column to make sure she's gone.

"Bothering me seems to be her favorite activity at these events," I mutter. "Thanks for the interference."

"Of course, but I'm not going to be able to keep her away from you all night. Plus…"

He lowers his gaze to where his fingers fidget with the hilt of his gladius.

Plus, there's the fact that I'm supposed *to let her bother me.*

"I'll figure something out," I grumble. "It will be even easier to keep her interest now that she's been thwarted. She loves the challenge."

Tacitus frowns and looks like he wants to say something, but there's no point in having this conversation.

"I've been watching the preparations for tonight," I continue, changing the subject. "If Consul Matho is part of the conspiracy, we need to pay attention to every detail. I've been to many of these gatherings, and this one is different. This isn't a party, it's a business meeting."

Tacitus nods gravely. "I suspected as much. Everyone we've been watching for the last few weeks is in attendance. Ursus, Pius, Matho. You were right. Something big is happening tonight."

"We may need Cornelia after all." I fire a scowl toward the dining room.

Tacitus sighs and clasps my shoulder. "We'll end this soon. At least we're in it together now, right?"

"True. Plus, I'll have the pleasure of publicly humiliating you in our sparring match tonight," I joke.

"Ha! Not a chance," Tacitus snorts. "Prepare to lose your throne, Champion."

ARGUS

"Can you read?" Seia asks, interrupting my meditation.

Seated with my eyes closed on the edge of my bed, I didn't see her approach. Rain has trapped her in this small room all day, so it's no wonder she's bored, but I can't entertain her at the moment. After my conversation with Eustacius and Decien, I have a lot to consider and need to preserve every detail to memory.

"No," I say without opening my eyes.

"I can't either."

"You don't say."

I try to ignore the rustling as she plops onto the mattress beside me.

"What are you doing?" she asks, swinging her feet. Small vibrations rock the bed with each movement.

"Thinking."

"I like thinking. Can I help?"

I squint at her before returning to the darkness.

"Can you help me think? No."

"But I don't want to just sit and watch you think."

"So, don't. Go play with a toy."

"I don't have any toys."

A twinge runs through me at the casual confession. Is that true? I guess it would be.

Well, frax…

"Okay, then clean or something."

"I already did. While you were guarding the Emperor."

With a low grunt, I push up from the bed.

Seia watches in quiet curiosity as I march to the storage box at the end of the bed and pull out the pouch of coins. After removing a few sesterces, I hold them out to her.

Her brown eyes bulge to alarming levels, and I shake my outstretched hand in encouragement. She slides off the bed and approaches tentatively. When I don't move, she reaches slowly and plucks the coins from my palm.

"What are these for?"

"You." I drop the pouch back in the box. "Go buy yourself a toy."

I push to my feet and return to the edge of the bed to continue my thoughts. Closing my eyes, I try to pick up where I left off, but quickly realize she's still watching me.

I peek in her direction, only to be blasted by big brown eyes stretched wide with emotion.

"What's wrong?" I ask. "That not enough?"

She shakes her head and then nods. Tears obscure her dark irises. "Yes, it's just…"

"It's just what?"

"I never had a toy before," she whispers.

My stomach drops as I take in her sweet little face and rag-covered body. No, I don't suppose she has. In fact…

I glance out the window and sigh. Yes, it's raining. Yes, I'm busy. Yes, I have an entire empire to save, but *by Jupiter's cursed thunder,* I'm not getting anything done until this little mouse is safe and content.

I push up from the bed and retrieve the pouch.

"Where are you going?" she asks. "Are you done thinking?"

"For now," I mutter. "Come on. Let's go to the markets and get you properly settled."

JASON

The sparring demonstration goes well.

Tacitus and I dazzle the audience with our skill and endurance, while the crowd plays its part by showering us with applause and admiration.

Varro and Ursus seem especially pleased that their gamble is paying off so soon.

Ironically, Tacitus and I could say the same. We hid it well, but I know he was paying as much attention to the audience as he was to our fight, just as I was. We noted who was in attendance, who was positioned in the places of honor, and who seemed most engaged with the violence, food, drink, and other indulgences.

Now that the scheduled fight is over, the real battle begins.

"Ladies and Gentlemen, you will be pleased to know that Jason will be representing me in the primus match at the Aratus Munera in three weeks' time!" Varro announces. "Only the best will be put forward as we lavish the people with brilliance they have not yet seen!"

His purple-lined tunic shows off his senatorial status and places him on par with many of the other prestigious guests. Those not dressed with the insignia of the senatorial class make up for the lack of social stature with expensive fabrics and fine jewelry. While not everyone present can claim senatorial status, all can claim vast wealth.

I recognize several of them from previous encounters, although not all.

The guests applaud at the announcement, and I bow my head in acknowledgement before resuming my place among the other slaves against the wall. Tacitus waves to the onlookers as well when Varro credits him for his stellar training.

I bite back a smile at his discreet glance, which is just short of an eye roll.

"Now it's time for the business portion of the gathering," Varro says. "We'll host that here while the rest of you can enjoy some additional food and entertainment in the outside gardens."

Tacitus and I exchange a knowing look from across the room. This is the moment we've been waiting for. Whatever sinister plan has been simmering in the shadows is about to boil to the surface. My heart races as the guests disperse according to their roles.

Tacitus maneuvers to a location behind the central couch which will be the best position to observe without drawing attention to himself. I'm looking for a similar advantage when my search is interrupted by the house steward.

"You're finished here," the man says. "Go join the others in the gardens. I've had several requests for a personal introduction."

Pluto's chains…

I force down a wave of disappointment as Tacitus's gaze cuts to me. *This* is where I need to be—the heart of the conspiracy—not flirting with fans in the gardens.

But I have no choice in the matter as the steward dismisses me with an impatient wave.

I pull in a calming breath and make my way toward the exit.

"I'll make sure they let me stay," Tacitus whispers as I pass.

MALLIA

Voices drift out of my father's study, and I flatten against the wall beside it. Grooves from the relief carved into the marble press against my back and arms, but I barely notice.

The second my father chose to receive this evening's guests in his private office, I knew there'd be a conversation worth hearing.

"Something's wrong. None of it makes sense," my father's deep voice growls.

"It's strange, sure, but maybe worth considering," an older man responds. "What harm could come from strengthening the Emperor's reach? Who's campaigning for the measure again?"

"Olennius," my father responds.

The other man barks a dismissive laugh. "Olennius? The kid with the chip on his shoulder?"

"He's probably pushing the legislation to get in the Emperor's good graces and salute his tail," a third voice reasons. "What better way to earn favor than to give the Imperator more power?"

"You're both forgetting one important detail," my father cuts in. "Varro actually *supports* it."

"Wait. Varro supports the measure?" the older man says.

"I've heard from two separate sources that Varro is encouraging his allies to vote in favor," Father says in a dark tone.

"Vote in favor of giving the Emperor *more* power? Marcus Aratus Varro?"

"Exactly! That's why I called you here. Something isn't right. Varro would never champion a measure like this if there wasn't something in it for him."

"I don't see how there could be," the older man says. "It was pretty straightforward. Matters of city planning will be taken out of the hands of the senate and given to the Emperor. The only person who stands to benefit is the Emperor himself."

Someone clears his throat. "Yes, but why change a law no one was asking to change?" the other stranger points out.

"Are you saying we should fight the measure?" the older one asks.

My father grumbles a curse. "That's the problem. It's an impossible situation for us. We don't trust the motivation behind it, so we can't support it, but we can't fight it either. It would look like we don't have faith and confidence in the Emperor, which we do."

"We have to talk to him," the third voice says.

"Approach the Emperor?" my father retorts. "And say what? That we suspect Senator Varro is up to something because he supports a proposal to grant the Princeps more authority? Do you want to have that conversation? I know I don't."

Several seconds pass in silence, and I hold my breath as I wait for the verdict.

"Continue poking around as best you can," my father says finally. "See if you can find out more details about the proposal, as well as who supports it. Get close to Olennius, too. I'm sure we'll find some link between him and Varro. Varro would never support anything he didn't have his fingers in."

As the men move toward the door, I slip into the gardens of the neighboring peristyle. If my father sees me, he'll find me exactly where he'd expect me to be. As I settle onto my favorite bench by the Venus fountain, I review as much of the conversation as possible and sear it into my memory.

I'm not exactly sure what "the measure" is, but I'm positive Severus will want to know about it.

Chapter XXVIII

TACITUS

"Stay near the senator. This could get ugly," Captain Atticus warns in a low voice as the guests position themselves for the next phase of the gathering. The wealthy visitors seem to settle onto the same couches they occupied during the meal, except for Varro, who remains standing in the center of the room.

I already assumed we'd be in for an eventful evening and appreciate the official command to remain in the perfect vantage point for whatever's coming.

Varro dismisses the musicians to the gardens and crosses a look to Ursus, reclining on one of the central couches. While the main meal table is cleared and cleaned, two secretaries enter the room with armloads of scrolls.

A hushed silence falls over the eleven occupants as the servants deposit the scrolls in neat piles on the emptied table.

Varro raises his hand for silence, and the conversational din fizzles into tense anticipation.

"First of all, thank you for your faith in our vision for a new Rome. A great Rome," he says in a theatrical tone. "The Rome our ancestors dreamed about, but polluted with their soft hearts and lack of foresight."

My blood chills at the way each powerful face beams in approval of their conniving leader.

"So, let's not waste time on pleasantries and commence with the real reason we're here," Varro continues. "You have been chosen to take part in this historic opportunity. I couldn't have asked for better partners as we embark on this mission to clean up our city and transform it into a magnificent display of beauty, wealth, and prosperity. In addition, each one of you also has the privilege of being the first to hear the good news."

He holds out his arms, allowing his luxurious dark blue cloak to cascade behind him. With his impressive stature, distinguished facial features, and close-cropped salt-and-pepper hair, the senator oozes power and influence. If this is how he commands his sway in the senate, we are up against a dangerous enemy.

He steps forward, a triumphant smile on his face. "I am pleased to announce that with the support of you fine patrons, half the senate, and the great Legatus Nepos, in less than three weeks' time, I, Marcus Aratus Varro, will be the new Emperor of Rome!"

Enthusiastic applause erupts from around the room. Varro takes on a grave, stately expression and bows with all the dignity of an emperor. When he straightens, he motions toward the table of scrolls.

"Before us are twenty-seven districts up for auction. These are pockets of filth, poverty, and decay hungry to be transformed by worthy visionaries like yourselves. I will begin by reading the entire list of districts available for purchase. Then we shall commence with the bidding."

JASON

"I first saw you fight over a year ago in the Noster Munera. You were amazing."

"My favorite was the Saturnalia when you defeated all of Cyprias's men!"

"Are all of your scars from the games? Ooh, what's this one?"

"My cousin met you at the feast before the Emperor's accession games. He said you didn't even seem scared! I'd be terrified. How do you not faint with fear before each fight?"

I force a smile at the barrage of attention near the principal fountain in the gardens. A cool evening breeze winds among the patches of vegetation and stone walkways, diffusing fragrant flowers, spices, and burning incense through the air. It's blissful and serene—and I'd do anything to be inside the villa with Tacitus facing whatever atrocity is taking place instead. Better a real horror than pretending this isn't one.

I remain polite but aloof enough to discourage as much interaction as possible. They're engaging a fantasy, not me, and the faster I can relieve them of that illusion, the better.

It takes longer than usual to lose their interest, however, probably because of the recent exhibition. My bored, distracted mind drifts to Mallia and how much she'd love this location in other circumstances. She always seems to find the gardens wherever she goes, and my blood burns with memories of our recent encounter at the palace.

That afternoon was so confusing, so… strangely pleasant. I still don't fully understand what happened or what she wants from me, but I know if she were one of the elite standing here instead of…

I push away the intrusive thought.

"It looks like you've successfully shed your fans," Cornelia says, dragging me back to the present.

My stomach drops at her knowing grin.

Sure enough, the crowd has scattered to enjoy other forms of entertainment once they finally accepted I'm not going to surrender to any of their respective charms.

"And yet, they all seemed to leave without a hint of offense," Cornelia continues, tapping her chin. "Most were even smiling. It's impressive how you've perfected the art of deflecting without offending. If you weren't a slave, you'd make an excellent politician. My husband could learn a thing or two for his own ambitions."

My jaw tightens at her taunt…and perceptive observation. If I'm going to be assigned to battling this powerful woman, I would have preferred an easier opponent.

"I'm doing them a favor," I say in a flat tone. "The person they admire isn't real. He's a fantasy they constructed in their minds."

"Very true." Her stare slices into me, but I don't acknowledge it. "So, you're not stupid after all, are you, Jason?"

"I'm simply a gladiator, my lady."

She scoffs. "A gladiator who's nearly invincible and has gained the attention of the top men of Rome. General Severus…Senator Varro…The Emperor himself…who isn't under your spell?"

I don't respond. Music and laughter float in from the other side of the bronze and marble fountain, but we're alone, except for a few slaves serving honeyed wine.

Cornelia finishes off her glass and motions for another from the slave walking by. The slave fills her glass, and I tense when she holds it out to me.

"Here. Drink," she commands.

I eye the cup, caught between impropriety and disobedience.

"Thank you, my lady, but I'm not supposed to consume food or drink with the guests."

"Oh? Are you supposed to disobey a direct command from the consul's wife?" Her brow arches in an ominous challenge. Even in the dim lamplight, I can see the red sheen of wine on her teeth when she grins.

I swallow hard and glance toward the guards stationed around the gardens.

A hand on my arm draws my attention back to the villain beside me.

"Come. We have a discussion to finish, don't we?"

"My lady, I really can't leave. If they—"

"If they, what? Knew you were entertaining an important guest?"

With a sigh, I drain the cup and follow her toward our showdown.

TACITUS

It's everything I can do to keep an even expression as the horrifying auction drags on. The Fountain District, Hades Hand, the ironically named prostitution district of Little Flower: all are on the list.

When Crassus Pass is called, I nearly choke. Argus and Seia live in Crassus Pass, six blocks of relatively innocuous residential buildings filled with poor day laborers and recently freed slaves. Except for Lepidus's apparent new interest in Crassus Pass, the only "filth" worthy of complaint is the literal animal, food, and human waste in the streets—same as every other street in this gods forsaken city.

Crassus Pass is won by a low-level young senator named Olennius, and I almost break form when the excited man discusses his plan to raze the cheap residential insulae and replace them with private baths surrounded by guest villas for visiting elite.

Less than halfway through the list, I lose count of the total funds raised. It must be in the thousands, if not millions of aurei, the kind of wealth only an emperor would command.

My stomach churns at Ursus and Varro's ever-brightening glow of excitement as the evening wears on. They will see this travesty as nothing short of a massive success. The mirrored exhilaration of the guests is just as alarming.

The idealist in me had hoped the horror of what they were doing would register on them at some point, but if anything, the tone of the event transforms from solemn to merry by the time the last few districts are sold. Bidders joke and laugh, hurling insults and taunts as if they're gambling on bones in a tavern, not sentencing hundreds of innocent people to displacement and death.

"What are you going to do with all your women, Ignatius?" Olennius asks the winner of Little Flower.

The old man snickers and tosses a sly look. "Why? You want some for your urban resort?"

Olennius shrugs. "Maybe. It wouldn't hurt to expand my offerings to the guests. I might be interested in some of your more quality whores."

I aim my disgusted grimace at the floor. My fingers wrap into a fist at my back to keep from grasping the hilt of my gladius. Everything in me wants to draw and start slashing. I'm not sure I'll be able to wait until Severus gives the command to administer justice.

My only solace is that Jason isn't here. If he'd heard half the things that were said, my enraged friend would have ended up with a sword in his throat. *Septem Fideles* can't afford to lose such a dear brother. Nor can we wait much longer to end this monstrosity.

JASON

"I don't understand you," Cornelia says, once we're buried deeper in the gardens. Without lamps, we're left in the shadows of a half-moon and distant flicker of the party closer to the villa.

While we're far from the other guests, the training ground I know so well is just around the corner. A rebellious part of my brain wonders how quickly I'd be able to make it there and retrieve a weapon.

"Most gladiators are honored by the attention of the masses. They consider being desired a perk, not a curse," she says, tilting her head.

I can't read her face well, but her tone is more curious than resentful.

"They also live under the illusion that seeking after the same pleasures as free men somehow makes them free," I counter, surprising myself. The darkness and distance is making me braver. Or maybe it's spending so much time in the company of elites who value my thoughts.

I have to remember that this woman is definitely not one of those.

Proving my point, Cornelia breaks into a grin. "There's that impressive head of yours again. I think I'm starting to understand Aurelia's little friend's admiration of you. What was her name again?"

I school my features, straightening back into a formal stance. She's spent more than enough time with Mallia to know her name. She's just trying to provoke me.

"I don't know to whom you are referring, my lady," I lie. "Lady Aurelia has many visitors, and I was only in her house for a short time."

Cornelia smirks. "So, our encounter in Aurelia's exedra was so common you can't distinguish it from the many others? It appears the Emperor's niece is more opportunistic than I thought. Fortunate girl."

I can't stop an uncomfortable shift, and Cornelia laughs.

After a short stand-off, she waves her hand in dismissal of the topic. "Anyway, I didn't bring you here to talk about Mallia, or Aurelia, or that unfortunate day filled with too many misunderstandings."

She follows her strange speech with a smile that makes my chest go tight. Moonlight glistens off the whites of her eyes, making them glow like a haunting apparition.

"I brought you here because I wanted to give you the good news myself." Her cruel tone indicates there's nothing "good" about what's to come. I brace myself for the next blow.

"As I'm sure you know, my husband is consul. He's inside the villa right now, bidding on the perfect location to build our dream. We are both fascinated by the games. The sights, the sounds, the glory—but especially gladiators like you. He intends to sponsor his own ludus. It will be a thing of brilliance, a spectacle that will dwarf amateur operations like those run by Opius Plinius."

She chuckles with the same sinister delight of her words. Blood drains from my face. An icy chill runs over my entire body.

"It's almost laughable how easily my husband let his loyalties be purchased by Varro, but such are the desires of the heart."

She steps closer and drags her fingers up my arm and across the armor on my chest. "One slave, that's all it took."

I duck away, stunned.

She can't be saying what it sounds like.

Her eyes blaze with indignation at my retreat. "Have I upset you?" she quips sarcastically. "Or am I just being too cryptic?"

Fear trickles through me, cooling the growing flames of anger. I swallow the rush of violent responses and force a stoic expression. "No, my lady. I'm just surprised my master would be willing to sell."

She scans me for a few seconds, considering my defense. I relax when she does. "I can understand that. Varro did just purchase you as his champion."

My fists clench at my side, fresh rage igniting at his betrayal.

Varro *did* just purchase me. With the promise of freedom.

I never trusted the man, and now I have direct evidence that he truly is nothing but a liar. A manipulator. Varro needs his champion to win. He'd tell a slave whatever was necessary to motivate him. What better promise than wealth and freedom?

But once the senator won the people's favor with his magnificent games, he'd no longer have use for a champion gladiator. Why not leverage him for gain, yet again?

None of it matters, of course. *Septem Fideles* plans to stop this coup before it gets that far, but betrayal stings no matter how moot. And nothing burns more than being reminded that I'll never be anything other than a commodity traded among the elite.

"Jason!"

I blink back to the present to find Cornelia inches away, staring up into my face.

My stomach sinks at the familiar look in her ravenous eyes.

I got my information. Now it's time to pay for it.

TACITUS

Although the *Septem Fideles* meeting is being held in my flat, I'm the last to arrive. I shut the door behind me with a hurried apology.

"Sorry. Ever since the auction, things have been hectic around Varro's home," I say. "It was almost impossible to get away without raising suspicions. We're close to reckoning."

Severus nods gravely and kicks back a stool from the table for me to sit. "The details are still muddled, but we need to move on what we have," he says without ceremony. "Argus has learned the assassination is planned for two days after the games, so we can't afford further delay. This may be our last opportunity to strategize together."

"How's Jason?" Mallia interrupts. Her worried gaze locks on me, and I, too, feel his conspicuous absence from the group.

I force a smile. "He's okay. Preparing for his 'fight.' I have an update from him to share as well. He was successful in his assignment," I direct at Severus.

Mallia's eyes narrow as her hard stare passes between us. "His assignment? I thought his *assignment* was to be Varro's champion. Wasn't being sold to a scheming snake enough?"

"It was, until we learned of the consul's involvement and Aurelia's poisoning," Severus explains in a matter-of-fact tone. "You remember."

"Of course I remember, but…" She goes rigid in her seat, eyes burning with anger. "What did you do?"

Severus sighs and seems stuck between compassion and frustration at this familiar line of interrogation.

"Mallia, please, we don't have time to argue the means right now. Not when the end is so close. Jason understands the stakes and his duty, just as you do."

The young woman's glare steels with venom, and I find myself shrinking back in my seat. Who needs a gladius when you can strike with a single look?

"Do I?" she snaps. "Maybe I *don't* understand why it's always Jason who has to pay the highest price for our victories."

She flinches when I take her hand, her gaze cutting to me.

"He's okay, Mallia," I say with a reassuring look. "He understands."

She rips her hand away, and her scowl screams of wanting to hunt down a certain consul's wife and scratch her eyes out—after she's finished with us.

"Mallia, what updates have you brought?" Severus asks, diffusing the tension.

She presses her fingertips into the table, as if physically releasing her anger. "I've learned from my father that there will be a vote to limit the authority of the senate in favor of giving more power to the Emperor. It's being presented as a gesture of support and faith in the Emperor's rule."

"Do you know anything about the measure itself?" I ask, concerned, especially in light of the auction I just witnessed.

"Only that it's related to city planning."

"*Frax*...of course it is," I mumble. "That's convenient."

Severus fires a glance at me before turning back to Mallia. "When is this vote?"

"I'm not sure, but it's imminent. My father was discussing it with Aulus Dexius, one of his good friends and allies. There was another man there, too, but I didn't recognize him."

"Tacitus, this clearly means something to you," Severus aims at me. "You think this is a legitimate threat?"

I nod, gritting my teeth. Images of frolicking monsters, literally laughing as they sentence others to death, haunt the shadows of my head.

"The measure will easily pass," I say in a bleak tone. "Varro's allies will approve it, knowing the true beneficiary of the vote. His enemies will approve it as well, thinking they're supporting a move that gives more power to the Emperor they defend. They'll have no idea they're handing Senator Varro the power to burn half the city to the ground when he's Emperor."

"Tacitus is right about the vote," Mallia confirms. "Even worse, Varro has been careful to keep suspicion off himself. My father said the motion is being campaigned by another senator named Olennius. My father and his allies only mentioned Varro because they were surprised he supported the measure."

"Olennius? You're sure?" I ask, nearly falling from my stool.

Mallia nods, and I pound a fist on the table in frustration.

"What is it?" Severus asks.

"Olennius was at the auction. He's definitely working as Varro's puppet. He bought your Crassus Pass, Argus."

"What?! *Bestia filius!"* Argus roars, jumping to his feet. *"Fraxing sputax wort-ridden son of a she-wolf!"* He kicks his stool—*my* stool—into the wall. Storming back, he shrinks when his gaze collides with Mallia's. "Sorry, my lady. That makes me mad."

Mallia bites her lip, fighting a smile. "Yep. We got that."

"What other districts were on the list?" Severus asks me.

"More than I can name," I growl. "I counted at least twenty-five, although many were smaller factions split from larger ones. Three people bought pieces of Little Flower. Almost all were poorer areas of the city like we suspected."

"We have to move Seia," Argus says urgently. "She can't stay there. What if they start the cleanse before the games? Or decide to test their methods first?"

We exchange concerned looks while several horrible possibilities swirl around us.

Severus nods and shifts forward on his stool. "You're right. Seia needs to be moved somewhere safe until all of this is over. I wish we could evacuate everyone, but that's not possible. Our best hope is to stop it. Mallia, do you have any idea where we can hide the girl?"

Mallia swallows and aims a quick glance at me before nodding. "I do."

My glare cuts into the table. Pain spreads through my chest, sinking into my gut.

"We can keep her with Arata," Mallia says. "She'll be safe and hidden."

Argus sighs and lays a hand on my shoulder. "I guess that means we're moving forward with your plan?"

"It's already in the works," I say through gritted teeth. "I sent Arata a note to meet me tomorrow evening after my shift ends. She thinks we're running away together."

"It's a brilliant plan, Tacitus." Mallia's soft tone only makes it hurt more.

I've spent my entire life being punished by my "brilliance."

"She's right," Severus says, grasping my forearm resting on the table. "Legatus Nepos feared your strategic intellect for a reason. What happened the night you were discharged was no accident, I can assure you."

My shoulders strain as their words grate through my ears. There's no joy in betraying someone you love.

"It could also fail terribly," I mumble.

"No," Severus returns. "Even if it doesn't end the threat, the casualties will be confined to the ranks of our enemies. Your plan is perfect. Pitting Ursus against Varro is a stroke of genius, not to mention, it allows *Septem Fideles* to maintain its anonymity. We eliminate both without the need for a fabricated narrative."

"But what about Nepos?" Argus asks. "Consul Matho? The horde of merchants and senators Varro has in his collection?"

Severus exhales slowly. "Unfortunately, right now we can only attack the head and hope the body withers away. Based on the evidence, I don't believe any of the others will pose a major threat without Ursus and Varro to lead the effort. We can handle them later, if necessary. For now, we have to eliminate the immediate threat, which is Ursus and Varro."

Hands clasped on the table, he leans forward with a probing look at each of us. "It's time to make our move. We can't predict what's to come, but I have faith that you will be strong enough to handle it. You each have your role to play. Gods be with you, and may the next time we meet be in celebration."

Once we're dismissed, Argus and Severus launch into a private conversation about the assassination attempt. I head toward the door to return to my post, but Mallia grabs my arm from behind. I turn and wince at the pleading look on her face.

"Tacitus, when you see Jason, will you…" She draws in a shaky breath, and my heart hurts as I infer the rest of her question.

"I'll tell him how much you care about him."

"Thank you," she whispers, rubbing at her eyes.

"You're going to see him again. I promise," I say gently.

She nods, but we both know I can't promise that. We can't promise anything in light of the violence looming just on the horizon.

As I make my way back to Varro's estate, Mallia's words haunt me in a new way. The fresh revelation tears at my stomach and drags me down the street with heavy steps. At least if Jason and Mallia don't make it through this, they'll die knowing the truth about each other.

If I don't, Arata will remember me as the man who betrayed her and broke her heart.

Chapter XXIX

MALLIA

Tacitus scans the large storeroom for the hundredth time. The empty chamber tucked deep within the servants' quarters at my family's dormant country estate has been converted to a one-room flat, complete with a comfortable pallet for sleeping, a small couch, a wooden table, chairs, and stores of food, water, and wine. Several lampstands sprinkle the room, providing plenty of light for the windowless space. I even included bones and dice for games, a hoop for exercise, and copies of some of my favorite works by Homer and Aesop.

As far as prisons go, this "cell" would be worthy of housing a rebellious goddess, let alone an endangered senator's daughter.

"Are you sure it'll be warm enough?" Tacitus asks, combing his fingers through his hair. "Not too warm, though. What if your father brings this villa back to life?"

"It's plenty warm, and he won't," I say with a gentle smile. "This estate has been vacant for months. Even if he has plans to return, it won't happen in the next few days. Arata will be fine. I'll have Danae here at all times to make sure she has everything she needs."

Tacitus nods, but there's no masking the pain in his dark brown eyes. He scrubs a hand over his face and resumes his anxious pacing.

"What if there's another way, Mallia? What if I'm missing something?"

"You're not," I say patiently. "We went over every angle. This is the only risk-free option. Even Severus thinks your plan is perfect. It has to be done. This isn't about us. It's bigger than any one person. You know that."

He shakes his head, and I'm starting to wonder if it was a mistake having him involved in this part. This must be brutal for him, given how he feels about Arata.

Would I be able to do the same to Jason? Lie to him—*hurt* him—to save his life? A shudder runs through me at the thought.

"But maybe if we just talked to her," he says in a pleading tone, pivoting toward me. "Explained the situation."

"Explained what? How you're using her to orchestrate the murder of her husband, her father, and her father-in-law? If there's even a chance she chooses her father over us, something even more catastrophic could happen. We can't take that risk."

"I know. I just…" He stops cold, his eyes fixing on something behind me. I follow his gaze and inhale sharply at Arata's presence. Danae waits several paces behind after leading her here.

Dressed to travel in a fine wool cloak and sturdy sandals, Arata takes in the scene before launching a tentative step toward Tacitus. Her radiant smile at seeing him fades when her eyes rest on me. She tightens her grip on a small satchel of belongings.

"Mallia, what are you doing here?" She glances between us, before focusing back on Tacitus. "I thought I was meeting you to leave Rome. Your note said…"

"I'm here because this villa belongs to my family," I explain.

Her amber eyes dart from me to her surroundings. Her hands are shaking, and I brace myself for what's about to happen. I can't even look at Tacitus.

"Why is this room so well-furnished? It was intended to be a storage chamber, no?" Her voice quivers as she retreats a step. Tacitus reaches for her, but she ducks away.

My chest hurts when he's forced to maneuver around her to block the exit.

"What's going on?!" she cries. "Tacitus?"

His eyes fill with pain as he shakes his head, unable to speak.

Juno's breath, this is brutal.

"I love you, Arata," he whispers. "This is the only way."

Arata's eyes go wide. Shock becomes fear as she backs away from him.

Tacitus holds up his hands, a pleading look on his face. "We're not going to hurt you. We're not—"

She bolts for the door, leaving him no choice but to grab her and wrestle her further into the room.

"Arata, please! We're not going to hurt you! I swear!" he cries as she struggles against him.

"Let me go!" she shrieks.

She elbows him hard in the side, breaking free. He recoils with a grunt, and I have to block her escape until Tacitus can regain his hold.

"Please, just listen!" he says, wrapping her in his arms. "We'll explain! Just give us a chance!"

Arata goes still, fire blazing in her eyes and singeing every inch of us.

I raise my hands in peace and approach with a calm expression.

"Arata, your father and Ursus are planning to assassinate the Emperor and murder hundreds, if not thousands, of people," I say in a steady tone.

I'm not surprised when her gaze narrows in disbelief followed by anger.

"That's ridiculous! You're a liar!"

"She's not lying," Tacitus echoes quietly, still holding her as gently as possible. "A war is about to break out in your house, and this is the only way to keep you out of harm's way. To protect you."

"By kidnapping me?" she hisses, turning on him. She shoves at his chest with disgust instead of fear, and he releases her when it's clear she's prepared to fight, not run. Steeled in the center of the room, her gaze is fierce with betrayal as she crosses her arms. "Is that what this was all along? You pretended to care about me as part of some sick plan for ransom money?"

Tacitus flinches like she slapped him. His mouth opens and then closes again. He shakes his head, scrubbing at his face. He's fighting so hard to hold it together. Deep worry lines and unshaven stubble make his handsome face look ten years older. Even his eyes are heavy with anxiety and lack of sleep.

"There's no ransom," he says in a strained voice. "It's exactly what I said. I'm sorry it has to be this way, but I will not let you leave here until it's done, so please don't make this harder."

Angry tears collect in her eyes as she glares daggers at him. "I trusted you," she seethes, pointing at him. "You made me fall in love with you! You're worse than Lurio! At least he makes no secret about the monster he is. I hate you. I hate you for using my love against me!"

Tacitus's expression crumbles, along with the rest of his proud bearing. For a man who's faced war and torture, watching him shatter like this is excruciating. After a brief pause, he somehow schools his features back into the hard line of a centurion.

"I'll be outside standing watch," he mumbles to me. "Find me when you're ready."

I nod, fighting to keep myself together as well. As much as I'd love to comfort him, all I can do is gather the pieces after the storm.

Once he closes the door behind him, I take a deep breath and confront Arata's icy scowl.

"So, this whole time, you were just pretending to be my friend in order to get me here?" she accuses.

I shake my head, drawing on every ounce of patience and strength I can muster. "No, the opposite. You're here because you *are* our friend. It's destroying Tacitus to do this, but he knows it's the only way to keep you safe."

"*Keep me safe?*" she fires back. "By holding me prisoner in some storage room on an abandoned estate? Even if I believed any of the lies about my father, what right do you have to make such a decision for me?"

"What's about to happen is going to be treacherous and violent one way or another, Arata. You would've been at the center of the coming war, and almost certainly a casualty. You will be safe here and far from danger. Tacitus was willing to sacrifice your love for your life."

Her forehead creases as her eyes conduct more rapid scans of the space. She's clearly working through a battle in her head, but I can't guess where it's going.

"How long do you intend to keep me locked in here?" she spits finally.

"We don't know. Until it's over and we can guarantee your safety. Maybe a few days, maybe a few weeks."

"A few weeks?! Vah!" Arata throws her hands up in frustration before dropping to the couch against the wall. I don't know what else to say as she buries her head in her palms.

"I'll never forgive him for this," she hisses, looking up again. "Never."

I swallow hard, my heart cracking open at the sincerity of her oath. Gods, what if Jason looked at me like that? I pray I'll never have to do what Tacitus just did.

"Tacitus knows that," I say softly. "He loves you enough to go through with it anyway."

"Enough! I don't want to hear another word about his love. About *his* sacrifice!" Air seems to leave her as she deflates into the cushion. She closes her eyes and shakes her head in slow movements.

I soften my stance and step toward her. "Tacitus didn't have a choice, Arata. He serves something greater than himself, greater than his love for you. He's a servant of Rome, and right now, your father and father-in-law are intent on destroying it. We can't give you any more information, but know that if Tacitus didn't love you more than his own life, you wouldn't be here."

I can't tell if my words are getting through, but at least she seems to be resigning to her fate.

"My own personal maid will stay with you to attend to your needs and make sure you're not alone," I continue. "All you have to do is knock on the door, and she'll pass whatever you need through the opening there." I wave toward the small cut-out in the wall beside the door. "I will also visit as often as I can. You don't have to see me if you'd prefer, but I'll still be coming to make sure you're okay."

I pause and wait for her gaze to lift to mine. When it does, I flinch from her wounded expression.

"Arata, I'm sorry. Truly. I know how terrible this is, and if there were any other way to get you away from Lurio and guarantee your safety through this coming fight, we would have done it. Tacitus is about to go to war to save many lives, and he needed to know you would be one of the survivors. He knows he may not be."

She winces at the last statement. Her scowl falters into a flash of fear. Maybe there's still a chance for them.

MALLIA

Tacitus straightens from the wall when he sees me emerge from the storage room. The hope on his face drains away when he reads mine.

"She still hates me," he says through a dismal sigh.

"She thinks she does, but the betrayal is fresh. I didn't tell her everything, only the parts she needed to hear. We're doing the right thing."

My reassurance doesn't seem to be helping as Tacitus closes his eyes and slumps back against the wall. His chest moves in deep, measured breaths. His fingers clench and unclench in absent fists at his side.

He's breaking apart, and that can't happen. As hard as this was, he still has to face the most dangerous part of the trial. I close the distance between us and slide my arms around him, trying to do what my useless words can't. He eases into my embrace and holds on tightly.

"We're doing the right thing," I repeat, and I will keep repeating it until he's able to accept it. "One day, she'll see that. I know it, but it's too much for her to accept right now. She would have needed time, and we don't have it to give her."

For several long seconds, I do my best to infuse my strength into him while he pieces himself back together. Finally, he steps back with an embarrassed look.

"Is Danae ready to look after her?" he asks, clearing his throat.

I offer a sympathetic smile. "She's waiting just outside. I'll review everything with her again shortly."

"And she's of strong will? She won't be swayed and let Arata out?"

I've never been so sure of anything in my life. "Danae is exceptionally strong, compassionate, and smart. Arata will be in good hands, I promise. Now, go before you're missed. You still have a lot to do if you're going to pull this off."

Tacitus grunts and swats at his eyes.

"It's going to work," I say earnestly, searching his face. "It has to."

With a heavy sigh, he runs a hand through his hair and pushes away from the wall.

"Whose twisted plan was this anyway?" he mumbles as he marches down the corridor.

TACITUS

It's excruciating waiting almost two days to enact the next stage of my plan. I can't eat or sleep thinking of Arata in that room, but we have to be patient. If we act too soon, the scheme won't work either. Her disappearance has to be absolute and long enough to raise concern—one of several reasons why hiding her anywhere she might be seen, even by strangers and slaves, wouldn't work.

When the time is right, I find Captain Atticus bathing in the staff caldarium reserved for high-status employees and servants. Memories of my own recent encounter in this room claw at my head, forcing me to grit my teeth. The last thing I need right now is images of Arata's exploring touch and beseeching gaze.

Atticus glances toward the entrance of the heated room at the sound of my footsteps and waves me in.

"Tacitus, how can I help you?"

Water sloshes around him as he flips to face me and rests his arms on the ledge of the rectangular basin. I salute and take a few nominal steps toward him.

"I'm sorry to bother you, Captain, but I've learned something and I'm not sure what to do about it."

Concerned, he props himself higher out of the steaming pool. "What is it, son?"

I glance around with exaggerated paranoia and crouch to his level. "Sir, I don't know how to say this, so I'll just be out with it. I've recently learned that Arata's husband Lurio is abusing her."

Atticus sinks on his arms, breathing a curse. "How do you know this?"

"She confided in me. Remember the confrontation I had with Lurio after the gathering at Ursus's house? Well, yesterday, she brought it up again and told me the truth about what I witnessed." Very real anger leaks into the fabricated performance as details of that night come screeching back. "She showed me evidence, Captain. I think she trusts me because I saw what he was and defended her against him that night. She's terrified and said he threatened to kill her."

The captain curses again and lowers back into the water, deep in thought.

I settle back on my heels, reading him for any clues we can use. "I'm sorry to burden you with this, but I'm sure Senator Varro would want to know his daughter's life might be in danger."

Atticus waves his hand, splashing water with the abrupt movement. "Yes, yes, of course he would. You did the right thing in coming to me."

His wet brows knit in concentration, and I watch for signs he's reaching the conclusion we planned.

"I suppose we don't have much choice," he says, straightening to attention. He wades toward the single step at the edge of the pool. "We need to go to the senator and share this distressing news. This is a serious accusation that could do a lot of damage. Are you prepared to convey this to him directly? You believe the report enough to stake your life on it?"

I suppress my relief and push to my feet as he climbs from the basin. "Of course, sir. I wouldn't be here if I didn't."

Atticus snatches a linen towel from the bench. "Well, if there's an imminent threat, it does us no good to wait. After finishing here, I'll find the steward and request an audience with Senator Varro as soon as possible. Wait in the barracks. I'll send for you when we're ready."

Chapter XXX

MALLIA

Danae is waiting for me in the dark corridor outside Arata's "prison cell" when I return to the abandoned estate with Seia. My maid eyes the little girl clinging to my hand but says nothing as I lead them further down the hall to talk.

"How's Arata?" I ask once we're a safe distance from the door.

Danae sighs and tucks her cloak tighter around her shoulders. "She cries a lot. I've tried to talk to her, but she mostly refuses. She reads sometimes. I also hear her singing quietly to herself."

I nod and force a sad smile for the sake of our little audience. I don't want Seia to be scared by what's coming, but she also has to be prepared.

Although my heart still aches for Arata, I'm slightly encouraged that she's stopped pleading and doesn't make a run for the door anymore. It gives me hope she's starting to accept the possibility that there's some truth to our claim. At the very least, she's accepting her situation.

Right now, though, we have another challenge. Part of me also hopes this could prove to be a small blessing in a violent, ugly mess.

I gently tug Seia forward to face Danae. "This is Seia, Argus's friend."

The little girl grins and takes Danae's hand like she's seen us do. "Pleased to meet you," she clips out in her version of a formal tone. Danae's surprised amusement flutters to me before settling back on the girl.

"Pleased to meet you, too," Danae says, fighting a smile.

Seia, still clinging to Danae's hand, swings it between them. "Argus says I get to stay in a nice room with a nice lady where I'll be safe from the bad man."

Danae bends lower to address her. "Argus is right. I'm one of those ladies. There's another one in that room who is also very nice. The only thing is, she's sad right now."

Seia's bright smile sags into a frown. "Sad? Why?"

"Because she's in danger and is very afraid," I explain.

"But she's safe here!" she cries. "Argus says so."

"Yes, but she doesn't understand that yet."

Brows pinched, Seia taps her chin. "Oh, okay. I will tell her."

Despite the heavy air, I can't help but smile. If anyone deserves a burst of human sunshine, it's Arata. I motion for Danae to follow us back to the room.

Arata looks up from her place on the couch when we open the door. Her surprise spreads into suspicion when I lead Seia inside.

"What's this?" Arata asks. "You're kidnapping children now, too?"

I sigh and cringe at Seia's look of confusion. I'm about to respond when the little girl steps forward with rigid confidence.

"No, I'm Seia. Mallia is my friend. Argus, too. They're hiding me from the bad man and said I'll be safe here. You must be the other nice lady."

Arata's gaze darts to me. "The bad man?"

"Lepidus, from the Fountain District," I explain.

Her eyes widen in shock and then repulsion. "The brothel owner?"

I nod and take Seia's hand to lead her around the room. "See? I told you it was nice. And look."

From a satchel of supplies, I pull out the toy "lion" Argus turned over to me.

"Argus asked me to make sure you had this so you can keep it safe as well."

Seia gasps and scoops it from my hand. "My lion!" She skips toward a bronze table beside a lampstand. "Can I keep it here?" she asks Arata. "He'll protect you, too."

Arata's hard-fought anger wavers at the girl's eager grin.

"Right there is fine," she says civilly, then directs a hard stare at me. "You won't change my mind with a little friend."

"That's not why she's here," I say, meeting her gaze. "Seia means a lot to us as well, and right now, this is the safest place we know."

Arata's familiar scowl returns, but with less conviction than before. And when her attention rests back on the little girl, I sense a subtle shift in her rage. Seia has that effect on a lot of people.

"We can share my lion. I made it for Argus." Seia rushes to her side and kneels in front of the couch. "Look it walks!"

Her demonstration on the cushion draws the slightest smile from Arata.

"I see that," she says gently.

"Your turn!"

Arata's smile lifts further when Seia shoves the lion toward her.

"Oh, and look! Argus bought me this, too!" She produces a small, carved figurine. "I never had a toy. He got it for me because he likes to think with his eyes closed, but I can't help with that."

Arata bites back another smile, probably to hide it from me. I breathe easier knowing once I'm gone, she'll allow herself to enjoy the energetic company.

"Seia, you remember what Argus also said about this room, right?" I ask her.

The girl bobs an emphatic nod. "Yes. He said I need to stay here and only talk to the nice ladies until he comes back."

"That's right. He will visit you when he can, but he'll be very busy, so it might be a few days."

"He works for the Emperor," Seia explains to Arata. "He sees him every day!"

"Is that so?"

"Argus is a close friend of Tacitus," I clarify. "He's in the Praetorian Guard but also has an apartment in Crassus Pass, which is where he found Seia." I wince when the girl fires a sharp look at me. "Or I should say, where Seia found *him*," I correct.

Seia beams and pops back to her feet. "I hid in his flat when he wasn't there so the bad man wouldn't get me."

Arata's concerned gaze finds mine and something shifts in the silence. It feels positive, like maybe she's starting to understand we're not the enemy, but I'm careful not to hope for too much.

"I'll visit as often as I can," I direct at Seia, even though it's meant for Arata.

"What's happening out there, Mallia?" Arata asks in an urgent tone. "What about my father? Lurio? Aren't they worried? I've been gone for so long. It must be days by now."

I force a tight smile and move toward the door. "It'll all be over soon," I say, ignoring her questions.

She sinks back in frustration, but I can't give her the answers she wants. Not when I've been asking the same questions myself.

TACITUS

Senator Varro does not take the news about his daughter well.

"And you're sure about this?" he asks, pacing his study.

His short hair sticks up in wild spikes from running his hands through it.

"I am. She had a bruise on her arm when she told me," I say in an even tone.

"Then why didn't she come to me?" He spins toward me, eyes blazing.

I remain calm, knowing this reaction is shock and the anger is not meant for me. I just need to direct it at the right target.

"She was scared, my lord. She feared you'd be upset and might…" I let my voice fade into a dramatic pause.

"*Might*…say it! Might—what?"

"Retaliate, my lord."

"*Retaliate?*" he roars. "Strike back against the rotten *bestia filius* who thinks he can lay his hands on my daughter? You can bet every denarius you have that I'm going to retaliate! To the lions with that cursed *bracca!*"

Face hot with rage, he stomps toward Atticus with murder in his eyes. "Find him. Both of them. Arata will stay under my protection at my house while Lurio answers for his abominations. Oh! And send Jason to me."

I go numb.

Jason? That wasn't part of the plan.

Up until now, everything had gone the way we hoped. What would he want with Jason?

"Yes, my lord," Captain Atticus assures him with a salute. He marches toward the door and signals me to follow.

ARGUS

"Seia! Time for food." I drop the loaf of bread on the table and unclasp my cloak.

"Seia! Come on, I'm starving!"

The silence is deafening.

A shadow flickers across the empty room, but it's just a bird flying near the open window.

Then, I remember.

She's not here. I'm alone again. The small pile of blankets where she slept still holds the indent of a tiny body.

"*Frax*…" I mutter, running a hand over my face.

Cursed Vesta, I hate caring about stuff.

I rip off a chunk of bread and toss the rest at the wall.

JASON

"You asked for me, my lord?" I say to Senator Varro.

"Yes, come in."

I enter the tablinum and wait while Varro dismisses the rest of the slaves.

"I have an important job for you," he says once we're alone. "In some ways a reward, really, since I know you must be anxious for revenge."

I remain silent, gaze fixed on the floor. My heart races as terrible possibilities mixed with troubling certainties worm through my head.

"You and I have a mutual enemy," he says in a cold tone, leaning against the desk. "My son-in-law, Lurio."

I glance up in surprise. "I do not consider him an enemy, my lord. He was only—"

"Please," Varro scoffs, waving his hand. "Of course you do. He acted like an animal with his cowardly display at Ursus's banquet. He humiliated you. You have every right to hate him."

Fists clenched, he pivots on his heel and paces in front of a large fresco of Hercules strangling a lion.

"That man has proven to be an even worse kind of coward," he growls. "I've learned he hurts my daughter, and I will not stand for that. I've been mocked and embarrassed by him for the last time."

Varro pauses in front of the desk again and faces me. Our eyes lock, and I resist a surprised flinch when he clasps my arm. "I've sent men to find my daughter and bring her here. I've summoned Lurio as well." His deadly gaze bores into me. "When I give the signal, I want you to kill him, Jason. I will say it was a sparring event gone awry so the house slaves won't be executed, but I want him dead. He will not embarrass my family any longer."

I go cold, my lungs freezing in my chest. My head spins, but no words form. Varro's command is punishable by death if I obey…and if I don't.

"I know what I ask is unusual," he continues in an urgent tone, "but we make difficult decisions to protect our interests. I'd do it myself, but I'm sure you can understand why I can't murder my own son-in-law. Do you understand the instructions?"

I fight through the chaos in my head, the turbulence in my soul. "Yes, my lord. I understand."

"Good. Then return to the training grounds and wait there. You'll be summoned when the time comes."

Chapter XXXI

JASON

Relief flows through me when Tacitus approaches the training grounds. At least we'll have a chance to talk before this terrible twist comes to pass.

"Atticus sent four men to Lurio's home to retrieve him and Arata," he reports. "Once they find her missing, they'll assume the worst, and the next phase of our plan will be set in motion. I heard Varro summon you. What did he want?"

"He wants me to kill Lurio."

Tacitus goes still. Moonlight glistens in his wide eyes as he scans my face. "Just like that, in cold blood?"

I force a grim nod, jaw tight.

"Frax!" he hisses, rubbing at his face. "We should have known he'd be smart about it. He wants you to be responsible for his death so he can protect his alliance with Ursus."

"Exactly. I take the blame and suffer the consequences, while Varro solves his Lurio problem," I confirm in frustration.

Tacitus smashes his foot into the sand. *"Pluto's chains!* What about the other slaves? He would send the entire house to the arena for his greed?"

I stare into the obscure gardens behind him, my chest tight. A swift breeze carrying the musty scent of rain rustles the shadows in the distance.

"He said he'd claim it was an accident to preserve their lives, but that won't absolve me," I say quietly. "I die either way."

"You're not going to be executed," Tacitus snaps. "We won't let that happen."

I shake my head, forcing a hard, protective edge back in place.

They are afraid. They are afraid.

This is the world I know. Violence and death. Fear and revenge. It was those few blissful moments as Severus's valet that were the anomaly in my tortured life.

"I don't see a way out," I say, squinting at the sea of stars above. "It's already been decided. He's going to send for me at any moment."

A cold trickle of panic festers in my stomach. It's the same feeling I get before a match, except this is different. There's no hope of victory in this fight. I lose no matter what happens next.

"You only have one choice," Tacitus declares, drawing my attention back to him. "You can't go through with it. If you do, Varro will have to make a public arrest on the spot and turn you over to Ursus for vengeance. He might even execute you right then. We know he'd do anything to serve his ambitions."

"But if I go against his orders and *don't* kill Lurio, he'll have me executed for disobedience."

"Yes, but he won't be able to punish you for a crime no one knows you're supposed to be committing. He'll have to wait until it's over to execute his sentence. It's not ideal, but it gives us time."

Phantom pain burns through my body from the coming punishment—another reality I know better than anyone. "I'll face the lions."

Tacitus shakes his head and grips my arm in reassurance. "Not if we end this before then."

I slide my gaze back to the leafy shadows, and he drops my arm. Somewhere in those trees, new life is replacing the old. And somewhere, young life is expiring too soon. I've been a rebellious blade of grass since the day I was born. Hero and victim. Champion and casualty.

Tacitus sighs and follows my stare into the dark void opening up ahead of us. "We'll have to see what happens before plotting our next move, but for now, you can't do it, Jason. You have to refuse and give us more time."

TACITUS

I'm on my way back to the villa when Jason is summoned to the atrium, along with the guards.

We enter the cavernous room to find Lurio kneeling on the tile in front of Varro. The swords of Messor, Glabrio, and Helveticus surround him on all sides, while Captain Atticus supervises with a grave expression.

"Where is she?" Varro roars down at Lurio. "What have you done with my daughter?!'

At the senator's command, Glabrio smashes his fist into Lurio's face, sending the man crumbling to the ground.

"I don't know," he whimpers, holding up his hands. Blood trickles from the side of his mouth, and I wonder if this is the first he's ever tasted the substance in his privileged life. "I haven't seen her in two days! I assumed she was here!"

"Liar! Your wife disappears for days, and you don't bother to look for her?"

Varro plants his foot in the man's ribs. Lurio curls onto the floor, sniveling like a child. Varro's volatile stare sears into him, until suddenly, he goes deathly still. His eyes go wide, filling with fear and revulsion.

"You've killed her," he whispers in horror. "You *bracca!* You killed my daughter! *Verrux bestia filius!*"

"I didn't!"

Livid, Varro draws his dagger and whips the handle toward Jason. "Do it. Now!" he growls. "This monster murdered my little girl!"

From the furious tears in his eyes, he actually believes it's true.

"My lord!" Captain Atticus cries behind them, and Varro twists back a glare to silence him.

Jason's blank expression reveals nothing, but his clenched fists make it clear he's still not sure what to do.

Say no. Say no!

"I can't, my lord," he says in an even tone. "I'm sorry."

Thank the gods.

"You *can't*?!" Varro shrieks. "I said, do it! Now!" He shoves the knife flat against Jason's chest, but my friend lets it clatter to the stone. Varro's fist comes next, and Jason reels from a hard blow to the cheek. He straightens again with a blank expression, and Varro's eyes take on otherworldly rage.

"Out!" he barks at his guards. "All of you out except the slave!"

The men hesitate, surveying the scene.

"Leave us!" Varro bellows.

At the captain's orders, they finally move toward the exit, and I have no choice but to follow.

I can't guess what Varro is about to do, but maybe Jason was right. There was no solution to this mess. My stomach aches as I pass him, but if he notices my apologetic look, he doesn't react.

In the neighboring corridor, I wait until the others disappear around the bend to duck into the shadows just out of sight. One of us has to know what happens in there, and if Jason doesn't make it out alive, that person will have to be me.

Lurio pushes to his feet, only to crumple again when Varro smashes the hilt of a sword against his head.

Lurio groans, clutching at the wound, and Varro leans close.

"Last chance, *porca*," he hisses. "Confess! Tell me where she is!"

Lurio lifts terrified eyes to his attacker. A brief look of surprise flashes in his irises before they go blank.

Varro's sword is still in the younger man's neck when his body collapses to the floor.

Jason stares in mute horror at the lifeless body. He must have seen death dozens, if not hundreds, of times, but probably never like this.

Varro straightens slowly, his hatred turning on Jason.

"You refused me," he seethes, closing the gap between them. My heart pounds with fear that the senator intends to kill Jason next. Will I allow it? I have to. There's only one way to stop this coup and killing Varro now will destroy everything.

"You did this," Varro growls, shoving the bloody sword into Jason's hand before the gladiator can react.

Jason drops it and steps back, but it's too late. Varro has already stained him with the evidence.

"Guards!" Varro shouts. "Guards! Come quickly! He's done it!"

Seconds later, boots echo down the corridor behind me as Captain Atticus and his men rush back to the scene. I carefully slip into the group as they pass.

Jason still hasn't moved, a sheen of stunned disbelief covering his face.

By the time the others arrive, Varro's mask has already morphed from vengeance to fake distress.

"I told him I changed my mind! I told him not to do it! He's killed my son-in-law! Now, I've lost both my children!" Varro wails, dropping to his knees.

"My lord?" Captain Atticus asks in confusion. His gaze passes between the small smear of blood on Jason's hand and the growing pools around the body. Any soldier who's spent a second in combat would see the events didn't happen as Varro claims.

"Take him!" Varro orders, gesturing toward Jason. "He will die for this!"

I strain forward, relieved when Atticus hesitates, clearly conflicted by the command.

"What's this? Is my entire house filled with traitors?" Varro roars. "Get this murderer out of my sight! Now!"

"Of course, my lord. Of course." Atticus motions to the other guards, who grip Jason's arms and shove him toward the back of the atrium.

"Secure him at the training ground and begin the interrogation! I will check on your progress shortly. You, Tacitus! Come here."

I'm tempted to disobey as well while they drag Jason away. I can't bear the thought of what's happening, but we're too close to lose it all now.

Jason's only hope is for *Septem Fideles* to put an end to this once and for all.

"Yes, my lord," I force out as I approach the gruesome scene.

Like so many times in my life, I'm careful to step around the specter of death in pursuit of my own.

"Find a messenger and send him to Ursus," Varro commands. "Tell him I need to speak with him, but say nothing about what happened. He's a dear friend, and this is a very delicate matter. We need to make sure it's handled properly. Return to me as soon as you're finished."

"Yes, my lord. I'll do as you say," I lie.

JASON

I gasp when the flagrum rips into my back.

The ropes held by Glabrio and Messor also cut into my wrists as they absorb the weight of my body with each strike.

Atticus straightens and wipes at his forehead with his arm. Helveticus hovers with a grimace several paces away.

The uncomfortable pall over the proceedings settles even heavier in the lengthy pause. None of us knows how to react to a punishment for a crime no one believes I committed.

Atticus must be studying his handiwork when he mumbles a curse.

"You have to, sir," Glabrio urges in a cold tone. "Varro will know you disagree with his command."

"He's right," I manage through clenched teeth. "Varro is vindictive. He's angry and will expect you to react in kind. You have to keep going."

Atticus and his men exchange a long look. Disgust mixed with resignation.

The weapon falls again. And again.

My head hangs low as I struggle back to my knees after each strike. My bare back is on fire from the torn flesh, but this is only the beginning. I've been flogged many times, but for this one, death will be the only way to stop it.

"Frax!" Atticus cries suddenly, swinging the grisly whip into the ground.

He marches around to face me, his expression hot with anger. "This is wrong! We all know you didn't kill Lurio. The cursed rats in the alley know that!"

I don't respond. There's nothing I *can* say. I can't call my master a liar, but it's pointless to pretend otherwise.

All I can do is grit my teeth and glare at the sand beneath my knees. How many times has my blood painted these surfaces? Maybe it's fitting I finally meet my end in such an ironic twist. Spared from the arena only to die anonymously on another patch of sand.

Atticus curses again and runs his hand over his head. "Those *braccas*, Ursus and Lurio! Savages, the lot of them! And what of that cursed auction! What in Pluto's chains was that?! This entire city is going to hades and taking us with it. We stand by with our swords, waiting like dogs. 'Yes, my lord. No, my lord.' 'What injustice do you require of me today, my lord?' 'Let me slaughter the women and children standing in your way, my lord.' *Bestia filius thunder of Jupiter!"*

We flinch when Atticus draws his gladius, only to fling it into the ground.

He stomps on the blade and shakes his head in disgust.

"He's going to give me to Ursus for revenge," I say quietly. "You'd be doing me a favor with a merciful death now."

Atticus meets my gaze, eyes blazing. "No! I'm sick of this! I'm tired of shedding blood in the name of convenience. I took this post to protect, not to become a cold-blooded murderer!"

He retrieves his gladius, and my heart pounds as he approaches with venom in his stare.

I draw in a deep breath, preparing for the death blow.

But the blade comes down on the rope Messor is holding instead. Glabrio drops the other side, freeing my arms.

"Varro will be here soon to finish what we started," Atticus growls. "But I will not be part of it anymore." He turns to his men. "I don't expect you to follow, but if you do, I will have a new commission within a week. It's up to you."

The men stare at their captain, still in shock.

Atticus turns back to me as I stagger to my feet. "Here. You'll need this." He flips the sword and holds the handle out to me. "If you use it to kill Varro, you will still die, but at least you'll die for an actual crime. As for real justice, there is no such thing."

He nods once and then stalks away.

We stare after him until he disappears into the garden.

Glabrio mutters a curse before grabbing the dangling rope again. He uses his dagger to slice through the knot on my wrist. I lift the other, and he cuts that away as well.

"Good luck to you," Messor says to me.

"And you," I reply.

The three men nod in my direction before following their captain into the shadows.

A second later, I'm alone with a bloody back and a clean sword.

Chapter XXXII

TACITUS

Ursus isn't home when I arrive, but he's expected back shortly. I tell the steward my message is extremely urgent and I'll wait in the tablinum.

I refuse refreshments in favor of violent pacing throughout the attached office off the atrium. My thoughts rage in my head, echoing along with the slap of my boots on polished stone. Arata, Varro, Ursus.

Jason.

I wonder how my friend is faring, terrified I'll return to find the mangled corpse of my fearless brother. I can't help but relive images of the brutal exhibition in this very room not so long ago. The pristine marble floors have been cleared of the blood, but nothing can erase the cruelty soaked into these stones.

Captain Atticus is a good man, an intelligent man, and an old friend of Severus. Their bond is what granted me this commission in the first place. There's no way he hadn't seen through the farce of Varro's accusations, but he would also be duty-bound to carry out orders, regardless of how unjust.

It's a situation I understand all too well, and I grow even more impatient waiting for Ursus to return. The sooner this confrontation begins, the sooner we can end this travesty.

It's all or nothing now for me at this point. I blew my cover the second I disobeyed Varro's orders and left his villa to deliver the message to Ursus myself. I won't be able to return as an employee after this, only as an enemy.

"What do you want with Ursus?" a voice growls behind me.

I twist back to find one of the guards from our spat outside the storehouse weeks ago. How silly that little skirmish seems now.

"I have urgent news from Senator Varro," I return in an irritated tone.

"What news?"

"It's for Ursus's ears only."

The man's ice-blue eyes sear into me beneath bushy dark blond brows. "If you think we're leaving you alone with him, you're even less intelligent than we thought."

I adjust the gladius at my hip in a subtle warning. "I will leave that up to him, but I'm not saying a word until he's here."

My adversary grunts and rests his hand on the hilt of his own sword. He leans against a marble column, locking a fixed stare on me. His posture is an attempt at casual, but there's nothing relaxed in his rigid stance. I know a coiled serpent when I see one.

"How's your friend?" he asks with a sneer.

"Which one?"

"You know which I mean. The hairy one with the big mouth."

"Doing a lot better than you and I. He was promoted to The Guard."

The man barks a bitter laugh. "The Praetorian Guard? That animal? Please."

"That *animal* could gut you with one hand and no weapon," I quip. "How's *your* friend?"

"Which one?"

"The dead one."

The man quiets with a fresh scowl, and a smile pokes through my stern resolve.

"You got lucky," he spits out. "You didn't play fair."

"It was two on five!"

"Well, two of our five were drunk."

"Then maybe you should have considered that before picking a fight with a seasoned centurion and legionary."

"Seasoned? Argus, maybe. You're still a child."

I brush off the insult, not about to be goaded into another pointless battle. Besides, I'll have my chance at the bully soon enough. Maybe even tonight if Ursus ever returns to receive his lethal message.

It's a miracle I haven't gutted my unwanted companion by the time the dominus finally enters the atrium, a stream of servants in his wake. His cheeks burn red from drinking or women, maybe both, which concerns me. Drunk men are unpredictable and difficult to control.

"You! You're one of Varro's men. What is it?" he snaps as he stalks toward the tablinum. His tone and mannerisms seem sober enough.

"I've come with a message, my lord. It's of a very urgent and sensitive nature."

His wiry brows furrow as he smooths out his crimson, gold-lined tunic. I note the ceremonial dagger shoved into his belt, but doubt he knows how to use it.

"Leave us!" he barks at the servants. "You, too," he directs at the annoying guard.

The man fires a resentful look at me, but takes his leave as instructed.

Once we're alone, I face Ursus with a grave expression. "Forgive me for what I'm about to say, my lord, but I didn't know what else to do."

Ursus flutters his burgundy cloak in yet another display of pretend power. The man would give the peacocks strutting through the imperial gardens competition for displays of vanity.

"Well, out with it," he demands with an impatient gesture.

I lower my voice and adopt an urgent expression. "I've just disobeyed Varro's order and come to you directly. He told me to send a messenger to lie to you."

Ursus shifts closer, revealing a sheen of sweat at his temples. "I don't follow. Is this a joke?"

"No, my lord. I wish it were." I pause and inhale deeply for dramatic effect. "Varro learned that Lurio was beating Arata. When he also learned Arata has disappeared, he summoned Lurio to confront him."

Ursus shakes his head in disbelief, and I continue in a pained voice. "He murdered him, my lord. Right on the floor of his atrium. He's now trying to blame Jason, the gladiator, but we all know it was Varro. I watched him command Jason to do it, but the slave refused."

Ursus doesn't move. Perspiration trickles from his hairline, while his nostrils flare in rapid, shallow breaths. Several interminable seconds pass until the silence is broken by a piercing laugh.

"Now, I know you're joking!" he cries. "Did Varro put you up to this? Is it because I disagreed about the slave shipment from Gaul?"

Footsteps rush toward us through the atrium, and the house steward approaches the open wall of the tablinum. "Urgent news has just been delivered, my lord!"

All humor drains from Ursus's face. "What news?" His question comes out as a squawk.

"The staff at your son's estate have reported that Varro's men took him by force. That's all we know at this time. They said they were looking for Arata as well, but couldn't find her. No one has seen her in days, apparently."

Ursus's eyes bulge as he shakes his head in numb arcs. "No. *No!*"

I step into his line of sight, every bit the compassionate friend in this time of crisis. "My lord, I'm telling you the truth. I was there."

His gaze sears into me. "You were there?! Then you saw him murder my son? Did you stop him?"

I shake my head. "I didn't see him do it, but I saw him order it. He sent us away first. I presume, so there would be no witnesses to counter his story that it was the slave, but—"

"The slave? The gladiator Lurio beat with the flagrum?"

"Yes, but Jason refused. That part I saw. Varro ordered him to kill Lurio, but he wouldn't do it."

The man seems plagued by questions but is struggling to put them in a coherent order.

"He's dead?" he moans, clutching at his thinning hair. "He's…no. No! Why should I believe you?"

"Because if I'm lying to you, both you and Varro will have me executed," I argue in a calm voice. "I've already betrayed him by coming here, but I want no part in another murder. I thought you should know the truth so you can avenge your son. That's all."

Ursus wipes a hand over his face and then dries it on his tunic. "And if I still don't believe you? If that's not good enough?"

I shift my weight and motion toward the exit. "Then go to Varro yourself. He told me to send a messenger to summon you. He's expecting you."

Ursus launches into absent pacing, his sandals clapping on the marble floor like my boots did an hour ago. He never even changed out of his street attire. If all goes well, he'll be needing it very soon anyway.

"He's expecting me," he mumbles to himself as he stalks back and forth. "He's expecting me…"

He freezes and pivots in my direction, eyes wide. "He intends to kill me, too! He already has my money for his ascension. I'm just a liability now! That's what this is about! He doesn't want to share the spoils!"

I shrug, having no idea if that's true, but there's no downside to letting him believe it. "It's possible, my lord. I didn't know his intentions when he sent me away. If you go to him, however, I would urge you to make sure you go well-armed and protected."

"*If* I go?" he growls. "Of course I'm going! And I'm taking my army with me. Aias!" He stomps into the atrium toward an eastern corridor. "Aias! Summon my guards! Every last one of them! We're going to war!"

I remain in place. And bite back a smile.

JASON

Freed from the ropes, I leave the training grounds in search of a hiding place.

Tacitus will need my help for the final battle, so I have to stay alive until then. If Varro finds me, he'll kill me, especially when he learns about Atticus and the desertion of his top guards.

I roam the perimeter of the gardens, hoping to find another exit from the estate. My best bet is to escape the villa and position myself with a clear view of the main street so I can see when Ursus arrives with his men. I don't know the new plan, but I know Tacitus, and have faith that my quick-thinking friend will find a way to get us back on course.

I scour the stone paths, structures, and vegetation, frustrated when every turn leads to the main house, a wall, or back where I started.

It seems I'll have to hide on the grounds until the final showdown.

"There he is!"

A shout rings out behind me, and I twist back to see several guards striding toward me. They must have been sent to check on the sentencing progress and found the area abandoned.

"I don't want to hurt you," I warn, gripping the sword Atticus gave me. "Captain Atticus and three of his men have deserted their posts. You should, too."

"Deserted?" the man sneers. "Why would they do that?"

I stand tall, calm, and confident like this is just another verbal sparring match before the real fight in the arena. "Because they knew I was innocent and grew tired of being part of a farce."

"Or maybe you killed them also," the guard spits back. "Is that the captain's sword?!"

I follow his gaze to the distinctive weapon and nod. "Yes. Given to me by the captain before he left. He knew I'd need it to defend myself."

"*Rot with maggots!* You killed them!"

"I was restrained and being flogged!" I fire back, my own anger rising. I hold up my left wrist to show the fresh welts from the rope. My back would be stronger evidence, but I'm not about to present that to a hostile opponent.

He snorts a harsh laugh. "You expect us to believe he stopped the beating and walked off? After handing you his sword?"

My fingers tighten on the handle as the tension grows. I don't want to hurt these men, but nothing will keep me from finishing this mission. "Believe it or not, but it's the truth. I understand how it sounds."

"It sounds like a lie."

"I didn't kill the guards and I didn't kill Ursus's son."

"There's a bloody corpse in the atrium proving otherwise," another guard says, lining up beside his companion. "If it wasn't you, then who did it?"

"I can't answer that, and you know it," I growl. "I will say this. Do you think so little of your captain and fellow guards that you believe a bound slave sentenced to death would be able to free himself, defeat all four without a weapon, and dispose of their bodies in the time it took for you to find us missing?"

The guards flinch and exchange a concerned glance. One steps back from the line and then another. The remaining two harden their stances as they scowl at me.

"I don't want to fight," I say in an even tone. "Not here, not like this, but I will because I refuse to die a criminal's death for a crime I didn't commit."

The main guard's skeptical expression sinks into warning. "Even if we believe you, you are still a slave disobeying orders, and we serve Varro."

"I'm disobeying orders to let Varro kill me for no reason," I fire back.

"It's his right."

I adjust my sword and steel myself for the coming battle. "Fine. Then let's settle this."

"He's a champion gladiator," one of the retreating guards mutters from behind.

"What if he's telling the truth?" another says.

"What choice do we have?" the first guard snaps back. "Desert like the others? Then what? Atticus has General Severus to protect him from Varro's wrath. What do we have?"

He focuses back on me, and I shift into a defensive stance.

"You don't have to die today," I say, scanning their faces. "I'm a killer by law, not by choice."

A tense silence settles over us. The soothing trickle of a nearby fountain lies about the violence of the moment. While they consider their situation, I consider how I will dispatch all four of them.

After several long seconds, the head guard releases a hard breath and lowers his weapon.

"If you run, they will find you and execute you," he cautions. "If not for murder, then for theft of yourself."

I swallow a smirk and relax my stance. "I'll take my chances."

Chapter XXXIII

SEVERUS

"General Severus! What a pleasant surprise. How can I help you?"

Senator Justus clasps my hand in greeting and waves toward a chair in the tablinum.

"Thank you for seeing me," I say, straightening my cloak behind me. "Is Mallia home?"

Justus's brows pinch at the mention of his daughter, and he shakes his head. "No, she's with Aurelia. She hardly leaves her side these days. Would you care for refreshment?"

"No, thank you. My visit will be brief."

Justus nods and takes a chair near mine. Servants waiting at the opening to the neighboring atrium will be able to hear our conversation, so I'll have to be careful.

"You asked about Mallia. Is there a problem?" he asks in a concerned tone. His light brown eyes and straight, slightly rounded nose remind me so much of Mallia. Even more, his compassionate strength and fierce loyalty.

I return a tight smile. "Not at all. Mallia has been instrumental in Aurelia's recovery and a celebrated guest at the palace. The Emperor is grateful for her service."

Justus glows at the praise and motions to one of the slaves. The boy pads over with a glass of wine. "Yes, she is my pride. A gift from the gods."

"She is. And more."

Justus's smile wavers slightly, and I lean forward with a grave expression.

"There's something we need to discuss, Senator. Something I'm sure will come as a shock to you, but may not be so surprising once you have time to digest it."

I cast a pointed look at the line of slaves. Tension mounts when he catches my meaning and places his glass on a small marble table.

After he dismisses the staff, I lower my voice to keep it from echoing through the high walls and ceiling of the attached atrium.

"You have always been a loyal supporter of the Emperor and a trusted ally," I begin. "We, in turn, think very highly of you. What I'm about to tell you is a dangerous secret only a few select friends of the Emperor know. You have been chosen not only to be privy to this secret, but you will also be asked to aid his cause."

Justus adjusts his robes with a solemn expression. "Anything in service of the Emperor is a privilege, my lord. Rome has been waiting decades for a leader of his character."

"Indeed." I shift in my chair and lean toward him with conspiratorial zeal. "Your opposition to Senator Varro is well-known. You don't trust him, just as we don't. You were right to question his motives. We've learned that Varro has orchestrated a coup against the Emperor to take control of Rome for himself. His plan is far-reaching and well-funded."

I pause to allow my words to sink in.

As hoped, Justus's expression crinkles with concern, but not shock. A truly intelligent, perceptive person would not be surprised by what I just said. He must have already suspected Varro was plotting something.

"I've heard rumblings," he says, confirming my suspicion. "The measure put forth by Olennius—is that related?"

"Yes. Olennius is a close ally of Varro. They're granting the emperor more authority in preparation for Varro's ascension to the throne."

"Pluto's chains..." Justus hisses as he sinks back into deep concentration. After a heavy silence, he shifts forward on his chair again.

"I assume if you're sharing news of this threat with me, there's more to tell."

I nod, encouraged he's proving to be every bit the intuitive and strategic ally we hoped. "Quite a bit more. I won't burden you with every detail, but you should know we have a unit of agents working to contain the threat as we speak. They've sacrificed greatly over these past weeks to gather intelligence and sabotage Varro's efforts. The final phase is underway, and by tomorrow, we will have successfully brought an end to this conspiracy, or be lost to a dark force intent on destroying Rome."

Justus falls into silence again, his gaze fixating on something through the open wall to the atrium.

"What is it you want from me?" he asks finally. "How can I help?"

I scan the open space to make sure we're still alone. "We need you to construct the narrative for the public," I say in a somber tone. "You are a trusted leader in the Senate and a respected name among the people. We need your voice and influence to explain what happened in order to bring the truth to light and mitigate any lingering threats."

Justus sits back, lips pressed together in thought.

It's a heavy request, but I'm confident the senator will not shy away from his duty.

"Yes, of course, I'll do it," he says with firm resolve. "If it's in service to the Emperor, I consider it an honor."

I relax into the chair, enjoying a brief oasis of relief. "Thank you, Senator. We will share more details when we can. In the meantime, there's something else you should know."

His brows knit again, and I brace for the most volatile revelation of all.

"Senator…it's time you knew that Mallia is one of our spies. Your daughter has been instrumental in saving this Empire."

TACITUS

Ursus gathers his men with all the rage and vigor of a bloodthirsty provincial bandit. I remain on the periphery of the action, observing as much as possible before joining the small cohort's short march from Ursus's villa in Amethyst Hill to Varro's lavish estate in The Laurels.

A sudden storm of punishing rain clears the streets of activity and forces us through filthy streams of water, waste, and debris. Rain pelts my skin and reddish-brown cloak with each step. I'm glad I wore the more rugged paenula today as I tug the hood over my head.

The villa belonging to Senator Justus looms ahead, only two blocks from Varro's estate. Many members of the senatorial class have villas in this neighborhood, making the stakes of this final showdown even more treacherous. The risk of it spreading and claiming additional victims torments the back of my mind. I'm relieved Mallia and Arata are a safe distance from the coming battle.

"Varro will kill you when he learns you've betrayed him, and we will kill you if you're lying about this," the captain of Ursus's small army of ten shouts as we near our destination.

"I'm not lying," I call back, squinting through cold drops of water leaking from my soaked hood and lashes.

"No, I don't believe you are." He eyes me with a wary expression. "Although I still don't understand why you'd help us."

I yank my cloak firmer around my shoulders. "I have my reasons, and for now, our interests are aligned."

The other guard can accept selfish ambitions, and he nods before addressing his men.

"You know how this goes," he shouts through the thunder of pouring rain. "Varro will be well-armed. You're familiar with his men, so remember they're top quality and will be similarly motivated. Avoid any civilian casualties unless they pose a direct threat to Ursus. Do you understand?"

The guards return a jumble of salutes and confirmations, while the captain signals the valet standing beside Ursus's litter.

Slaves hold up a waterproof cloak to protect Ursus as he descends to the flooded street. The rain makes it impossible to hear the words he exchanges with his captain, but the emphatic command to proceed requires no audible sound.

JASON

Varro's estate is in chaos.

Ursus's approaching army has been spotted.

Reports of missing guards are spreading.

Varro's son-in-law lies dead in the atrium, while the violent gladiator who murdered him has escaped and is probably on the hunt.

Worst of all, Varro himself is in a fit of rage and on a rampage for blood.

Rain clatters the terracotta tiles of the roof, while more sheets of liquid pour through the open ceiling of the peristyle. I duck behind a column in the corridor lining the private courtyard as a slave scurries past and then another. I creep to the next column when it's clear.

After reaching another corridor, I slip into an alcove shared with a bust of one of Varro's ancestors.

"I've never seen him like this!" a servant hollers to another as they dart past. "He's lost his mind!"

"A slave murdered a member of the family! Varro will kill all of us! He's possessed by the Furies!"

Once they move out of sight, I continue my journey toward the front of the house. Any action will most likely be taking place there.

"Ursus is here! May the gods have mercy on us! They're here to slaughter us!" a slave cries, his bare feet smacking the tile floor with each frantic step.

If that's true, the action has begun. It's time to fight.

To die.

Tacitus and I will leave here as sole survivors, or not at all, and I'm glad Atticus and some of his men chose to desert rather than suffer the fate of the rest. I have no desire to kill more than necessary.

The shouts grow louder as I move closer to the front of the house. Fleeing slaves serve as markers that I'm on the right path. Concerned for their own lives, they barely notice me, let alone try to stop me.

I grip my sword and continue forward against the flow, bracing myself like I do every time I prepare to step onto the arena sand.

"Murderer!"

Ursus's accusation blares off the towering stone walls ahead, and I peek into the atrium to see a crowd of his men lined up between the entrance to the villa and the shallow pool in the center of the room. Varro and the remainder of his contingent occupy the other side of the pool, protecting the rest of the house. The guards I confronted in the garden are among them, and I feel a twinge of regret that I might have to kill them anyway.

I can't see Tacitus from my weak vantage point, but there's no way to position for a better view. Events are unfolding exactly as planned, and I can't risk distracting the powerful adversaries from confronting each other.

Rain continues clanking off the roof tiles and pouring through the cut-out in the ceiling. Thick drops ping the sheen of water collecting in the rectangular basin below.

"Only because he killed my daughter! My beautiful little girl!" Varro roars.

"That's not possible! My son would never! Where's your proof?"

"Your disgusting son was all the proof I needed!" Varro shrieks, spittle flying from his mouth. "He was an animal! He was beating her!"

"Even if that were true, it's his right as her husband!"

"How dare you!" Varro snarls, charging toward Ursus with his gladius drawn.

One of Ursus's guards steps in to block the thrust, igniting Varro's men in response.

Both sides erupt into action. The clank of metal on metal mixes with shouts and screams of pain. Blood spatter stains men and marble alike, painting new grotesque mosaics over the floors and walls.

With the battle raging, I step out of my hiding place and inch closer. For now, I'm an observer, watching elite men brutalize each other like they'd done to me so many times. The more they annihilate each other, the easier it will be for Tacitus and me to clean up the rest.

Varro swings his sword wildly as he backs toward the corridor where I'm hiding which leads to the servant wing of the home. His blows neither defend nor land, and his terrified gaze keeps glancing behind him instead of the battleground, as if preparing to flee.

That can't happen.

He doesn't see me as he launches into a run and storms past me down the corridor. I pick up my pace to follow as he heads toward the servants quarters, probably planning to hide or escape through the service exit. He cuts left toward a storeroom near the kitchen, clapping his sandals on the floor at a furious pace. It would have been an excellent plan for a coward.

I close the distance and grip my gladius.

"Turn and fight," I growl from behind him.

The shocked man spins back, his confusion turning to terror as his expression fills with recognition. "You're supposed to be dead!"

I release the smirk I've been holding for weeks. "Without giving you the chance for a rematch? Let's have a fair fight this time."

Varro's eyes widen as he backs toward the wall. He lifts his blade with little conviction.

"You will die if you kill me. I'm your master," he stutters out.

I bark a laugh at the absurd threat. "You were going to kill me anyway. I'll die if I don't."

"I was going to free you!"

My gaze turns cold as it sifts over the despicable man. "Were you? Or were you going to sell me to the consul? What was the price of his allegiance?"

He flinches, confirming my accusation. Not that it makes a difference at this point. Varro's list of crimes is too long to be concerned with this one.

He lets his sword clatter to the floor and holds up his hands in surrender. "You wouldn't murder an unarmed man. It goes against your code as a gladiator!"

"That's not in the code," I snarl, stepping forward with my gladius pointed at his chest. The tip indents the fabric of his white, purple-lined tunic.

"You think I won't kill an unarmed man?" I seethe in a low tone. "What about an unarmed man conspiring to commit treason and orchestrating the murder of his emperor? What about an unarmed man who was prepared to slaughter hundreds of other unarmed men, women, and children by auctioning off their lives like herds of cattle? You are not armed with a sword, my lord, but you are armed with something far more vile."

With a bitter curse, I sink my blade deep into his heart.

A look of shock remains frozen on Varro's face as blood gurgles up his throat, past his lips, and down his chin. It's the look of unexpected death, a look I've seen more times than I can count. And for once, the man deserves it.

I stand in solemn silence for several long seconds, watching for any sign of life. I learned long ago to leave nothing to chance. There should be no mercy for one so merciless.

With a swift blow to the neck, I deliver a stroke of insurance.

Chapter XXXIV

TACITUS

I remain in the vestibulum just inside the gates of Varro's estate while Ursus and his men continue to invade the atrium.

Seconds pass like hours as I listen for evidence of the chaos inside. A fierce exchange of words between Ursus and Varro quickly explodes into the familiar cacophony of violence and death.

After several minutes, when I'm sure both sides are depleted and distracted, I finish the journey into the home and monitor the remainder of the civil war unfolding in the atrium. If I join too early, I risk my own death, which means a failed mission. Too late, and I risk survivors who can counter our narrative.

I mumble a curse when I spot Varro running from the action on the opposite side of the massive hall like the *bracca* he is, but there's no way for me to give chase without exposing my presence. I can't cross the room openly, so I commit Varro's path to memory, deciding to hunt him down once the fight is over.

For now, I watch the former allies' small armies rout each other, and wait for the perfect moment to strike.

Ursus's men outnumber Varro's, and I notice Atticus, Helveticus, Messor, and Glabrio are missing. A sick feeling runs through me that they're still punishing Jason, or even worse, disposing of his body. Then again, they wouldn't concern themselves with such a trivial matter if there was a war raging on the property.

There must be another explanation for their absence.

Despite being outnumbered, Varro's men are far superior fighters and hold their own against Ursus's larger contingent. With Varro in hiding, perhaps they're not as distracted by the challenge of protecting their master and can focus on a more offensive strategy.

A scream pierces the air, and I follow the sound to see Ursus dropping to his knees, clutching his stomach. Blood seeps through his fingers and saturates his expensive robes.

His closest guard runs to his defense and fatally wounds the attacker, but not before taking a blow of his own. Another of Varro's men fills the gap and finishes off Ursus's guard.

Ursus collapses, his expression lifeless as he hits the floor.

By the gods, it's happened. One down. Two, if we count Lurio.

I take a deep breath, relieved that Ursus is gone, but the battle is far from over. At this point, all these men must be considered enemies.

Ursus's death seems to fuel the fire of his remaining army. Vengeance is a powerful motivator, and his men charge with a furious cry.

It's four-on-two now, and despite their gallant stand, Varro's entire guard is soon defeated.

Only two fighters remain standing in the sea of bodies when I emerge from the shadows, gladius drawn.

"You missed one," I say in a nonchalant tone.

They turn at the unexpected voice, narrowing their eyes in disdain when they recognize me.

"You! You've betrayed both sides," one man hisses. "The worst kind of traitor."

I toss a smirk and casually twirl my sword at my side. "I can't betray a side to which I never swore allegiance. I am loyal to neither of these monsters."

"How dare—"

Yeah, I'm not here to chat.

I charge forward, spurring my adversaries to do the same.

I recognize one from the clash at the warehouse. If I remember correctly, the heavy-set man has a powerful strike but is slow to deliver it. I quickly re-position myself so that Slow Man is on my weaker side.

The other man is taller and faster, but not as focused, so I'm careful to vary my attack patterns on that opponent.

The strategy pays off, and I'm able to confuse Unfocused until he's not sure when to strike, which exposes him when he tries. It doesn't take long for me to draw first blood by lodging my gladius in the soft tissue of his abdomen.

I yank my sword free, but not in time to block a lunge from Slow Man.

Pain radiates from my left thigh, and I adjust to block a second attempt from

Slow Man. I follow it up with an immediate strike to the ribs that leaves him shaken, giving me time to deliver a fatal blow to Unfocused.

The man grazes my arm with a desperate slash as he goes down, but he won't be causing any more problems for me. I barely notice the fresh pain and dedicate my full attention to Slow Man.

My opponent has regained his footing and charges again, but I easily block the thrust and follow with a counterstrike before he recovers his stance. One more hit to the side, and Slow Man is down as well.

I finish him off with a plunge through the neck.

With a deep breath, I survey my wounds and mutter a quick prayer when none seem fatal.

Any sense of triumph fades as I scan the red-streaked marble floor, littered with mangled bodies and pools of blood. More drips from my gladius, leaving a grim testimony to the cost of justice. The war may be won, but I feel no sense of accomplishment.

I've seen too much death and violence in my life to ever call such carnage a victory.

Instead, I take a deep breath and brace myself for the gruesome task of ensuring there are no survivors.

JASON

The echo of boots on tile crash behind me as I straighten from my confrontation with Varro.

I spin around to face the next opponent…and sigh with relief.

"Jason, thank the gods. I…" Tacitus slows to a halt as he surveys the bloody scene. "…was afraid I'd find a corpse," he finishes with a wry smile.

I glance down at Varro's blank face. "I suppose you did."

Tacitus nods, fighting a smirk. "So it appears." He grimaces when his focus returns to me. "*Caenum,* brother. Your back. Are you alright?"

"Fine," I mumble, wiping the sword on Varro's cloak. "Nothing I'm not used to. You don't look so great yourself."

"Took a few hits, but I'll live."

I straighten again and peer past him toward the corridor. The silence is blaring after the shriek of battle. "How is the main conflict?"

"Over," Tacitus says, following my gaze toward the empty hallway. "Varro's men killed Ursus, and then the rest of the guards took each other out. Well, all but two of Ursus's men, whom I finished. I also made sure there were no survivors."

He motions toward the service exit, leading to the street. "We need to go, though. We can't be seen here. I'm sure the slaves have already run for help, and no one can know we had anything to do with this."

I take a step to follow and then stop, overcome by the enormity of what we've done.

"Is that it, Tacitus? Did we actually stop this?"

Tacitus turns back and sighs with a solemn expression. "It doesn't feel like much of a win, does it?"

I grit my teeth and pass a slow scan over Varro's body. "Death isn't always an end," I say in a distant tone. "Often, it gives birth to a greater enemy."

Tacitus moves beside me and places a hand on my shoulder. "True. But for today, this will have to be enough."

Chapter XXXV

TACITUS

Mallia runs to greet Jason and me as we turn the corner toward the storeroom.

She barely acknowledges me before clinging to Jason with everything she has.

A tiny smile tugs at my lips, and I can't help but wonder when those two will finally admit their feelings for each other. I understand why they hesitate, and truth be told, there's probably no happy ending for a love as impossible as theirs. Then again, I'm not exactly the one to lecture about doomed romance.

I leave them to their reunion and brace myself for my own heartache.

Danae waits just outside the door to the safe room.

"You're okay, my lord!" she says with a relieved smile.

It feels good to know at least one person cares that I'm alive.

"Yes. Jason, too," I say with a quick twist of the lips. "He's with Mallia in the corridor. How is Arata?"

Her smile fades as she hands me the key. "It's probably better you see for yourself. I shouldn't be involved."

My stomach sinks as my heart launches into a furious pace. With a deep breath, I open the door and duck inside.

I freeze when Arata's amber stare locks on me from across the room.

"Tacitus," she whispers, rising from a couch and interrupting a game with Seia.

Her expression is a mask of conflicting emotions as she takes a tentative step forward.

"Argus's friend!" Seia shrieks, running past her to give me a hug. I return the exuberant embrace, but she quickly pulls away to resume her game, forcing me back to Arata.

"I want to hate you," Arata says in a shaky tone. Her gaze slices into me as it runs over my face. "I know what you've done. Mallia told me everything. She didn't want me to find unexplained blood. If I were going to hate you, she wanted it to be for the right reasons."

I lower my gaze to the stone floor, my heart cracking at her expression.

"You killed my father, Tacitus!" she cries in a shattered voice. "You used me to *kill* him!"

She charges toward me, eyes blazing. "Say something!"

I shake my head in numb arcs as she pounds a fist into my chest.

"Say something, Tacitus!"

I flinch but remain silent, letting her take out her anger on me. What is there to say?

"You're a murderer!" she sobs. "How could you sit there by the fountain that night and pour out that story about those children you refused to kill as a centurion, while you were scheming to murder my father?!"

Tears stream down her face. Angry, hostile drops that would probably burn my flesh if they touched it.

"You lied to me! Used my love for you against me!" She winces and goes silent when a tiny hand takes hers. Dragging in a ragged breath, Arata glances down to find Seia staring up with wide, confused eyes.

"He saved my life," the little girl says in an earnest voice. "There are a lot of bad men, but he is a good one. I know he is a good one."

The older woman covers her face and breaks down in open sobs.

"Arata…" I say, moving toward her.

"Stay away from me!" she hisses through angry tears. "I'm not ready for you! Not now, maybe not ever!"

But I don't want to stay away. Every piece of me wants to comfort her, to take her pain.

She shoves me back when I approach. "Leave! I don't want to see you!"

I swallow a surge of emotion as well.

"I love you, Arata," I say quietly. "I'm sorry it had to be this way, but I'd do it again. I'd do whatever was necessary to keep you safe."

She won't look at me. My chest aches as I wait in silence. For her wrath. Her forgiveness. Gods, for any cursed thing.

But I get nothing.

It takes all I have left to turn and leave her, but there's no other choice.

I manage a step.

Then another.

And another.

"Tacitus!"

I turn back, heart pounding as my gaze meets her tear-stained eyes. A flicker of hope ignites in my chest at the change in her expression. There's something different there now, something I can't begin to understand. It's haunting, pushing and pulling at the same time.

"I want to hate you. I *should* hate you." Her broken heart is all over her face. "But I don't. Which is why I hate *myself*."

I swallow hard against the sudden pressure in my throat.

"I know," I whisper. "I will be patient. *'I am, and always will be, your servant, my lady.'*" I echo the promise I made that fateful night and then leave her alone with her grief.

MALLIA

At the sound of approaching footsteps, I crouch in my hiding place, dagger in hand.

I've been standing watch for hours, waiting for news. If we lost, I'll be ready to fight for as long as I can. If we won…I'm not ready to hope for that yet.

But when I recognize the tall figures striding toward me, I drop the knife and jump to my feet.

"Jason! Tacitus!"

Both men are bloody and exhausted, but very much alive.

I ignore everything else as I rush toward Jason and slip my arms around his waist. He stiffens at the surprise contact and then draws me close.

The sweat, the blood, the violence, none of it matters as I nestle into his chest and enjoy the rapid beat of his heart. There were so many moments over these last few weeks when I had to live in fear of never hearing it again.

Never touching him like this.

"I was so worried about you," I whisper. "I didn't…"

The tears I've been fighting for days come racing in now. I quiet so they won't be revealed in my voice.

As we stand in silence, I realize we're alone. Tacitus must have gone in search of Arata.

"Is it done?" I ask, still holding on. I'm not sure I'll ever be able to let go.

"It's done." His deep voice rumbles through me. "Varro, Ursus, and Lurio are dead."

"And the narrative of what happened?"

"Their bodies tell the story of a civil war. Tacitus's plan worked."

I exhale a heavy breath, my arms still wrapped around his waist. "What about you? You're okay?" I lean back just enough to see his face.

A weak smile skims his lips. "Of course. The battle was easy compared to what I'm used to."

"That's not what I was worried about. I know you can fight." I reach up and trace a bruise on his cheek.

He frowns, averting his gaze to something behind me. "You worry about things outside of our control."

"And you think such a truth will stop me?"

Hazel eyes dart back to mine, and his sweet smile settles deep in my chest. The quick kiss he brushes on my cheek nearly wrecks me.

I'm still in shock when he pulls away.

"I was worried about you, too," he explains softly.

"Jason…"

My pulse races as the confession I've been holding onto for so long climbs up my throat.

Eyes locked on mine, he shakes his head in a silent plea. "You shouldn't speak right now, my lady." There's a waver in his tone I've never heard before.

A flood of unspoken words passes between us in the heavy silence. It's all right there, blazing hot and violent in his eyes—that cursed confusion about me that makes my heart pound and break at the same time. Somewhere deep, somewhere trapped, there's a longing in him as well. It's burning through his defenses, even if he can't—or won't—recognize it for what it is.

He's so beautiful in this rare moment of vulnerability, so tempting. I can't stop my hands from sliding up his chest and curving around his neck to draw him close. I press into him, held captive by an infinite hazel gaze that would take a lifetime to explore.

The tension in his body makes my blood rush, radiating a torturous heat that burns through every part of me. Igniting a deep craving I'm not allowed to satisfy. Jason is forbidden, in so many ways, but he has to know how I feel. I *need* him to know.

The ache overwhelms me. The words are taking on a life of their own.

"Don't speak, my lady. Please."

I close my eyes at his plea, my body on fire. He doesn't want me to make the confession that will change everything. Words I'm not allowed to say, and he's not allowed to hear. They're scorching my mouth, attacking my lips.

I want to tell him that I don't care about the rules. I don't care that he's a slave and can never be mine no matter how much I'm willing to sacrifice. I want him to understand the beauty of who he is, how different that truth is from what he's been taught his whole life.

I want him to know how my heart is slamming against my ribs in a desperate attempt to get to him.

But I can't. He's not ready to face the consequences of those treasonous words, and the gods know, I'm not either.

After what feels like an eternity, I finally release my hold on him.

It physically hurts to separate our bodies and break the connection that stopped time. As I catch my breath, the battle to reconstruct his walls flashes across his chiseled face.

"We should see if Tacitus needs any help with Arata," I say softly.

Emotion closes my throat, presses against my eyes.

I have to go before it crushes me.

I turn to leave, but a strong grip grabs my hand. It pulls me around, and I suck in a breath at the sight.

His eyes. His smile.

Gods, I can hardly breathe.

Jason squeezes my palm, and I blink back tears when his fingers lace with mine.

Stunned, I stand frozen as his shy smile cuts into me.

My heart bursts while I squeeze back with everything I have.

Because in all the unlikely battles we've fought since our secret war began, this might be the greatest victory. A miracle that will change two souls forever and rewrite what's possible.

The statue took a breath.

Love *can* melt stone.

EPILOGUE

MALLIA

IT'S A GRAVE DAY FOR ROME AND THE SENATE WHEN NEWS OF THE MASSACRE SPREADS throughout the city.

Two weeks have passed since the events at Senator Varro's estate, and although many of the details still seem caked in blood and controversy, the bulk of the mess is settling into a clearer story.

My father, Senator Lucius Mallius Justus, has risen up as a pillar of strength in the aftermath of the bloodshed, maintaining his poise and courage while he broadcasts the treachery that led to such horror at the urban villa.

What happened was clear: Senator Marcus Aratus Varro and Vibius Acilius Ursus had a dispute over their insidious plot of murder and treason. They intended to raze Rome and rebuild their own empire, killing and destroying the lives of thousands in the process. A plan like that is rife with potential for internal quarrels, and ultimately, the men betrayed each other in a gruesome clash of greed and spite.

In the wake of such terrible events, several senators, including Olennius, chose to resign from public life, suddenly preferring provincial living or the promise of distant opportunities. As a result of Varro's supporters removing themselves from the public eye, the balance of power in the Senate has shifted in favor of those who support Senator Justus and the Emperor.

"Your father certainly has a way with words," Tacitus says to me when we finally meet again in his flat.

I huff a short laugh. "He's a politician. Words are what he lives and breathes."

"Yes, and his influence is proving to be tremendously valuable," Severus says, gazing out the window. He turns back to face us. "Varro's allies are on their heels."

"We arrested Decien and Eustacius as well," Argus says, standing with his boot braced against the opposite wall. "I'm sure they'll be executed for their role."

Severus nods and moves toward us. "It's good you were able to weed them out. The Emperor did not take the news well that he had traitors under his roof."

"You mean, in addition to all the visiting ones," Argus mutters.

"They will be dealt with in time," Severus says in a firm voice. "For now, we can be comforted by the fact that they've been forced into hiding."

"What about Prefect Falco?" Tacitus asks from where he leans against the writing desk. "He's retained his post as Prefect of the Praetorian Guard."

Severus releases a sigh and scratches at his cheek. "We have no evidence to suspect the prefect had any knowledge of the scheme. He played his role in the arrest of his men without reproach. But I've made it my personal mission to confirm his loyalties. Until then, we will watch him closely. The last thing we want to do is give a kingmaker a reason to betray us."

Argus grunts a dry laugh. "Falco would make Nepos's threat seem like a minor nuisance."

"Emperors can trust no one, least of all their own Guard," Severus says in a somber tone. "Tomorrow's enemies are most likely today's friends."

"At least Cornelia won't be around anymore," I say, picking at a scratch in the table. "There's one known traitor ejected from the palace."

"I'd be shocked if you see her again," Severus confirms. "The consul has been stripped of his title and exiled. They're lucky they weren't executed."

"Does the Emperor know about the poisoning?" Argus asks.

Severus nods. "He knows, but he must proceed with caution. Like it or not, Matho and Cornelia are well-connected and powerful. Executing them for unproven allegations would only start a new war we're not ready to fight."

"And we can't exactly prove the allegations without revealing the existence of *Septem Fideles* and all that we've done," I reason. "At least Telemon and I got the credit for Aurelia's recovery."

"Oh, so you'll be leaving us to be a physician now?" Argus jokes.

I snort a laugh. "It was an easy remedy when all I had to do was remove the poison."

"And yet, Aurelia is alive because of you, Mallia," Severus cuts in. "Don't underestimate your role." He passes a stare over each of us. "That goes for all of you. We recognize your individual sacrifices and the magnitude of what we just accomplished. The Emperor, Aurelia, Arata, and hundreds, if not thousands, are alive because of the four of you."

Tacitus flinches at the mention of Arata, and we toss a sympathetic look in his direction.

"She's been through hades," Severus directs at him in a gentle tone.

The younger man scrubs a hand over his face as he wrestles with his demons.

"My father has spoken to her many times," I add softly. "She knows what her own father tried to do. She knows why we had to act."

Severus places a comforting hand on Tacitus's shoulder. "She just needs time to come to terms with the reality. She's a reasonable and intelligent young woman."

"I'm sure the money and property will help," Argus quips, drawing a sharp look from the rest of us. He shrugs with a sheepish expression. "What? It's true. She just became one of the wealthiest people in Rome. Taking control of the Varro and Ursus estates? I'd forgive anything."

Tacitus fires a searing glare at his friend. "Maybe *you* would, but she's not the type to be soothed by wealth."

"Arata was highly praised by the Emperor and Senate for her role in exposing her family's plot," Severus says. "With no surviving male heirs of age on either side, the Emperor thought it best to grant the estates to the only person in their respective households he can trust. At least, until Ursus's young son is of age. For now, he resides with his mother in Capua."

"In light of her husband's disgrace, I doubt Ursus's wife and son will want to travel back to Rome any time soon," Argus snickers.

"Managing those estates will be a heavy burden in itself," I observe with a sigh. "My father has been helping her get them in order. He is very impressed with her intuition and administrative abilities."

I study Tacitus's grim expression in the afternoon sun streaking through the open window. He looks years older than he did when we met just a few weeks ago. It's hard to tell if this conversation is helping or hurting him.

"None of that surprises me," Tacitus says after another long pause. "She's a remarkable woman."

"And Seia is thrilled to live with her in a real home," Argus adds.

Tacitus's chest rises and falls in a deep breath. "She couldn't have a better guardian. You okay with losing your bunkmate, Argus?"

The other man grunts and kicks away from the wall. "Why wouldn't I be? One less mouth to feed and squeaky voice to keep me awake."

We fight back smiles as his expression sinks into a scowl.

"I'm sure Arata will let you visit whenever you'd like," I offer. "She doesn't resent all of us equally."

I can't look at Tacitus as the words come out, but it's an obvious truth. Arata even transferred ownership of Jason back to Severus and the Emperor. She had no need of a gladiator at her villa.

Jason…

The young man has been noticeably quiet, and I'm surprised to find his striking features looking as troubled as ever. After our victory, I hoped he'd have at least a short reprieve from his mental torment, but clearly that won't be the case.

"What is it, son?" Severus asks, noting his grim expression as well.

A muscle moves in Jason's cheek as he gathers his thoughts. "I'm concerned, my lord. The worst thing we can do right now is be overconfident and revel in a victory. We won a battle, not a war. I'm worried about the losers."

"Legatus Nepos," Tacitus says in a dark tone, and Jason nods.

"The legate will be our biggest and most immediate concern," Jason continues. "Nepos will soon learn what happened to his allies. He'll be out for blood, and we should not assume he's not a threat just because he's far away in Britannia. If anything, that makes him even more dangerous. And what of Matho and Cornelia? The Emperor stripped them of their rank, but they're still alive to return as a threat. If anything, they have even more incentive to remove the Emperor since they'll be desperate to regain their status."

"Yes, but as I said, they have many connections," Severus counters. "The Emperor had to spare their lives to prevent the creation of more enemies."

Jason leans forward with an animated look. "Exactly, my lord! Nepos, Matho, Cornelia, maybe Falco, are all powerful losers who will not disappear. If my time as a gladiator has taught me anything, it's that you don't assume an opponent is defeated until he is dead."

"Not to mention Lepidus and whatever that demon spawn has cooking in my neighborhood," Argus mumbles. "I'm glad we prevented the destruction of Rome, but that's one snake and his lair I wouldn't have shed a tear to see burn."

"We saved the slaves inside," Jason reminds us quietly. A chill spreads over the room at the pain in his voice.

He sets his jaw against whatever memories are haunting him and continues. "But Argus is right. For every Senator Varro who's capable of pulling off massive conspiracies, there are dozens of Lepiduses poisoning the Empire on a smaller scale. What about all the elite cowards who were happy to attend Varro's auction and then went into hiding when it was exposed? We can't assume none of them will have further ambitions."

"Olennius is well-connected. I believe he even has links to Matho," Tacitus says darkly.

A deathly pall settles over us as we consider the new threats blooming in the shadows.

"Jason's correct and has illustrated a timely reminder for all of us," Severus says with a solemn look. "Varro and Ursus were just the beginning of your commission. When you accepted the seal of *Septem Fideles,* you turned your lives over to the pursuit of the one opponent that will never die. There is no claim to victory, because as long as there is Evil we will have to challenge it. We saved the world today, but that means nothing for tomorrow's threats."

His gaze bores into each of us. "You are *Septem Fideles,* ghost warriors, chosen for an eternal purpose that will follow you until your last breath. There is no rest, no reprieve, no celebration. You can go now with a smile because today is over, but prepare yourselves, because tomorrow we start again."

We exchange a somber look as his meaning sinks in.

"Well, *frax,*" Argus mutters.

***

Thank you for reading! Did you enjoy? Please add your review because nothing helps an author more and encourages readers to take a chance on a book than a review.

And don't miss more in the SEAL OF ROME series from Eden Maddox coming soon!

Until then read THE LAIRD OF DUNCAIRN, by City Owl Author, Craig Comer. Turn the page for a sneak peek!

Also be sure to sign up for the City Owl Press newsletter to receive notice of all book releases!

Sneak Peek of The Laird of Duncairn
By Craig Comer

Effie exposed her hand to the growling bear. Her fingers found Rorie's head and gave him a few soothing strokes behind the ears. A rumble came from deep in his gullet, as fierce as his wee body could muster. Frigid wind blasted them as they hid behind a large boulder atop the crown of Ben Nevis, the highest peak in the Highlands. A stranger had come to speak with her employer, Thomas Stevenson. Not an odd occurrence, but for a fortnight Rorie had groaned and whined, pawing for her attention as if disturbed by dark thoughts, trying to plead with her that something was amiss. And now that the stranger had come, Rorie's discomfort had turned into malice.

"If only I could peer into that head of yours and see what the fuss is about," she said, planting her hands firmly on her hips.

Rorie squatted on his haunches with a big huff, turning his head away. Though preferring the wild of the forest, he behaved himself around others when she asked. And only because it was she who asked. The bond had something to do with her Sithling blood, but Effie couldn't explain how it worked. It was as much a mystery to her as any of the uncanny bonds she'd made with woodland creatures, lazy housecats, and goofy hounds over the years. As much a mystery as why the queen and all the lords of London abhorred her kind, though she'd done nothing to warrant their wrath.

Rorie had been loyal to her ever since she'd convinced Stuart Graham to rescue him from a carnival the prior year, saving him from a brutal—and probably short—life of baiting. But he'd never acted so ill-tempered. Had the stranger come to take him away? Or was it she who should be fearful? By sight alone, the stranger wouldn't know her for a Sithling. Short of stature, with a young woman's curves and chestnut locks clipped about the shoulders, she lived her life amongst the Scots all but unnoticed, the truth of her mixed fey blood hidden.

Yet such reliance on appearance was a false safety.

Her hair whipped about her face, blinding her until she swept it back. The lodge of the Scottish Meteorological Society perched only a short distance away, a cozy, timbered house well-weathered from years of driving gales. Its chimney puffed white smoke, teasing her with thoughts of hot tea and honeyed biscuits. But that was where Mr. Stevenson had taken the stranger, and he'd instructed her not to return until he bade her. She blew into her hands for warmth, vexed by the riddle of the strange visitor, unable to contain her curiosity any longer.

"I'm going for a closer look," she said to Rorie. "Wait here." Hoarfrost crunched as she shifted her weight and slunk forward. The frozen dew crusted the fern and bracken around the lodge, radiating a cold that sank into her bones. Her olive-colored dress and drab woolen coat were serviceable enough, but they did little against the cutting winds atop the mountain, winds that drove in the damp air as if she wore nothing as all.

She understood why Mr. Stevenson wished her to hide. He was a man who believed in prudence. He would not jeopardize one of his great works, nor his reputation nor her safety, on the off chance a stranger would find her out. There were some who could recognize her fey nature if they stood close enough. The scientists of the day, many of whom had their pockets lined by London's coin, said fey blood corrupted the flesh, giving off an odor that some could smell. Catholics and Protestants alike said it was the sins of the fey that radiated a cloud of evil around them, allowing those pure of heart to perceive them. Other tales held that a fey's eyes glowed in the dark or that they would burst into flame if they touched iron. All of it seemed foolish to Effie. She drank her tea and let it pass the same way as anyone she'd ever met, regardless of their blood. How some knew her for a Sithling while most did not was as random as why some seeds took root and others wilted.

A whistle shrieked, drawing her attention. Next to the lodge, Mr. Stevenson's plans for a great observatory were coming to fruition. Steel beams braced half-raised walls as masons slathered on stone and concrete by the ton. The pipes of a steam crane shuddered, and a burst of gas exhaled as another beam was lifted into place, soaring thrice the height of a man to the workers waiting above. The construction was what had brought them to Ben Nevis, and Effie guessed the stranger would not have come if he weren't involved with the great project in some manner.

She stalked forward, half-crouched so the wind wouldn't stagger her, and reached the sill of one of the lodge's thick windows. Grabbing the smooth, lacquered wood for support, she peered through the glass into the lodge's main room. It held several tables of a dark and sturdy teak, and a stone hearth large enough for a royal estate.

The stranger stood with his back toward her. His coat and polished shoes bespoke a city, but not the odd leather cap with its flaps that clung tight around his ears. She didn't recognize the tartan on his trousers: blues, greens, and purples all jumbled together as if shouting at her. She recalled he'd driven his own steam carriage up the winding road, working the levers and knobs as if he were used to the task, an odd thing for a wealthy man.

"I will take your concerns into account, Mr. Crofter," said Stevenson. The window's frame had warped over the years, allowing her to hear him clearly. He stood by the hearth. A dark coat fit snugly around his stout frame, its wool threadbare from years of rugged service. His balding head held tufts of hair around the ears, yet they served to dignify his face rather than embarrass it.

"They are not just my concerns, Mr. Stevenson. They carry the weight of the Society. It is time to distance ourselves from such relations. Lord Granville will have his way, and you must choose where your loyalties lie—with the Society or with your fey friends."

Stevenson's face darkened. "We have pushed back these threats before and should not wilt so easily to tactics of hatemongering. Parliament has no grounds, and Lord Granville not enough allies."

A shadow moved from the corner of the room, and Stuart Graham's stocky frame came into view from where she crouched outside. The man's knee-length boots were coated in mud, a workman's badge he wore proudly, and his white locks curled in ringlets atop a face as cheery as it was round. "Bah, let us speak plain, Mr. Crofter. You knew of Mr. Stevenson's associations before you funded the observatory. It was his name alone which brought in enough benefactors to ensure the completion of construction."

Mr. Crofter grunted. "Do you think any of these benefactors will stand against the threat of an Inquiry? No, Mr. Graham, they will scatter like rats." The stranger turned to Stevenson. "You will do as we ask, or we will sever ties and throw you to the wolves. One noted engineer is easily replaced by another. Now I bid you good day." He slapped his gloves together and strode for the door.

Effie recoiled. The news from London must be dire for Mr. Crofter to speak to Stevenson as he had. She crept to the front corner of the lodge and watched the small yard of trampled grass where the stranger's carriage sat. Graham emerged from the lodge's main door. He pulled a worn and battered watch from his pocket and studied it before casting his gaze to the skies. Mr. Crofter came out on Graham's heels, walking cane thumping the dirt as he ambled. The pair exchanged a cordial nod, similar to one shared by passing gentlemen in a city street. Effie didn't understand such manners. It was clear Graham was in a foul mood and Mr. Crofter the cause of it, but they pretended like nothing cross had occurred between them.

Rorie wasn't as polite. A low growl came from behind the boulder where she'd left him, and the bruin's head popped into view, teeth bared. She waved at him to stay back, but the noise had already drawn Mr. Crofter's attention. He peered at the boulder, his eyes growing wide. He muttered something, a scowl on his face, before clambering into the waiting steam carriage. Graham stood stiffly while the other man brought the boiler into action. The carriage's engine was a monster of steel and wood, with copper tubes lashed in a lattice across its flank and a charred snout thrusting upward from its roof. With a parting nod, Mr. Crofter threw open the valve, and the carriage sputtered forth with a burst of burnt coal perfuming the air. Only when the squeaking of the carriage's axles had faded down the mountain road did Graham turn to stare right at Effie.

As he beckoned her, brooding clouds rolled over the surrounding hills, darkening the sky. The wind gusted, flapping his leather coat about his legs. Neither were good omens. She stood and crossed to him, her cheeks flushed in embarrassment. He greeted her with a grin forced from pursed lips, and he spoke in a rushed manner, barely taking a breath.

"Och, lass," he said. "You took a risk. If my waistcoat weren't as round as an ox, ye'd surely been seen. It's like to piss down any moment. Let's get into the warmth before it does. Mr. Stevenson wants a word."

Effie nodded sheepishly as the steam crane's whistle shrilled again. Black smoke belched from its boiler, the engine fighting the strain of the wind. But she needn't watch the work progress to know the shape of the observatory. Its structure had long been affixed in her head from the drawings she'd rendered of the project. That was her place in the endeavor. Stevenson had discovered her talent for depicting his designs years before when she was just a lost girl sheltering under his protection. She'd sought him out after the death of her mother, the famous lighthouse engineer who designed edifices powered by stardust—the glowing azure silt, forged by Fey Craft, that burned hotter than oil and slower than coal. Her eyes grew glassy. The time was a blurred memory that still haunted her dreams. She'd come close to starvation and almost succumbed to exposure. Worse, she'd been captured and beaten by the queen's Sniffers, those who hunted fey, and only managed to escape by sheer luck. Yet none of those trials compared to the sorrow of isolation, the sense that all her warmth and cheer had fled. That she was alone, the last of her family, nearly the last of the Sithlings.

Alone and yet not alone. She glanced at the dark shadows of forest sprouting from the hills ranging beneath the peak of Ben Nevis. How many of the other fey races hid there watching them? Pixies and brownies, gnomes and hogboons all still dwelt within the Highlands. The remnants of a Seily Court existed, yet her mother had taught her to be as wary of it as of the Scots. She could count on a single hand the number of fey she'd ever met, and none were likely to take her in if the need arose. Such was the way for many Sithlings. Despite their appearance, they lived between races, not quite human and not quite fey. Their blood derived from a sect of the Daoine Sith interbred with the Votadini, an ancient human clan whose might had receded under an onslaught of Scoti tribesmen. What remained centuries later could claim neither as kinsfolk.

Effie followed the man she considered an uncle into the lodge. Heat from the hearth enveloped her the moment she stepped inside, soothing away the bite the cold wind had left. Laid out on one of the tables were Thomas Stevenson's plans of the observatory, his lines and notes as formal and stiff as he was. On another perched the casing for one of his famous screens, a protective box for meteorological instruments. Its sides were angled slats designed to keep moisture from the instruments contained within, allowing them to collect data for weeks on end unattended. Her own worktable rested in a corner. A collection of colored charcoals, neatly arranged within a tin, sat atop a rendering of the observatory. Her drawings always held more flora than the bleak locations Stevenson chose to build on, and the observatory was no exception. Ben Nevis' crown boasted none of the hearty pines and spring flowers her depiction held, but that never seemed to bother her employer.

Stevenson greeted her with a curt nod and gestured to a chair by the hearth. He didn't make her wait long, once settled. "Our caller was Mr. James Crofter, a noted engineer whose father worked with Thomas Telford on the Great Canal." Effie's lips tugged at a smile. To Stevenson, names were always linked to matters of accomplishment. His own noted a long family line of engineers. "He came to us in haste with news from the coast. Murder has been done in the village of Duncairn."

Effie started. If given a dozen guesses, it was not the news she'd expected to hear. She read Stevenson's face, but it remained a stone mask. "Was it someone you knew?"

"A fisherman," answered Graham, bringing her a cup of tea, "An Ewan Ross. His boat capsized in the Bay of Lunan."

She took the cup, piping hot and full of sugar the way she liked, and breathed in its sweetness.

"The importance is not whom but the how," said Stevenson. "Fishermen in the area swear a host of rabid seals tipped Mr. Ross' boat, accosting it in unison. Not normal behavior to say the least."

She stifled a laugh. The poor fisherman deserved better, but the image of a group of seals harassing his vessel, barking and slapping the water with their flippers, was comical to her. "Surely these fishermen are mistaken in what they saw, or perhaps Mr. Ross agitated the seals in some manner. Perhaps they were trying to help the man." She glanced between the two men, wondering if they were jesting with her. "Yet I fail to see how one could call it murder."

"That's what I did say," said Graham. "The Scottish folk are long known for tales of fancy. Any dark bed of kelp becomes the Kraken in their minds."

Stevenson cleared his throat. "Putting Mr. Ross aside, there is a second account Mr. Crofter related. A week ago, a young lass was accosted on the road to Montrose, just outside of Duncairn. She suffered woefully and is much delirious, but describes her attackers as hairy imps slight of stature, with sharp ears and wicked fangs. They battered her as she fled. She recovers now from a fractured skull and other wounds." Stepping to the table, Stevenson rested his fingertips on it. "Short, devilish imps with pointed ears. These creatures have a name. The Shetland folk call them trows."

"Bah, bollocks," spat Graham.

Effie blinked, taken aback by the certainty in Stevenson's gaze. "I had not believed trows real." Her cheeks flushed at the admission. Her knowledge of the fey races, and of Fey Craft, were scarce at best. Much that she knew had come from Stevenson.

"Real enough," said Stevenson, "though not seen in the Highlands for centuries. They are fell creatures not of the Seily Court."

She frowned. "I thought all fey were bound to the Seily Court, before the Leaving at least. The binding is what gave Fey Craft power in this world." That power had dwindled ever since the Daoine Sith abandoned Sidh Chailleann, their ancestral home.

"There are some fey the Seily Court cannot control. They form their own covenants, Unseily Courts they are called, though decades have gone since the last rumors of one's appearance."

"Oh," she said. She stared into her cup, feeling a bit lost. It seemed, every time matters of fey lore arose, she understood the least.

Graham read her expression. "Don't fret, lass. You still ken more of your blood than all of us together. Mr. Stevenson's just got more years of hearing tales than you." He winked. "Many more, by the top of his head."

She forced a smile. Graham often reminded her how young she still was. For all her curves, she was still recent to adulthood by human standards, let alone fey. Thinking on the accounts of Duncairn, she drew the simple connection. "You believe the two attacks are linked, and if these trow creatures did the one, then the seals were really—"

"Selkies," affirmed Stevenson.

"But that doesn't make any sense. Selkies are not wicked creatures. They shed their sealskins in favor of human form to lure men and women into loving them. They don't work in packs, nor accost fishermen at sea."

"I have never heard tale of such a thing either," said Stevenson. "Just the same, fey sightings have grown in past weeks across the Highlands, enough to reach the ears of Her Majesty's Fey Finders, and now with these attacks it is almost certain there will be an Inquiry."

Effie blanched. There hadn't been an Inquiry by the Sniffers in almost fifty years. Most in London called the fey hunters relics, the funds used to support them better used elsewhere. Yet as dire as the news was, it did not follow why Mr. Crofter had spoken of such immediate threats. There was more to the stranger's visit Stevenson wasn't telling her, something she hadn't overheard. She studied his face. Her foot tapped impatiently. Cheeks growing red, she forced herself to still and sip her tea. She could be more stubborn than a stone when it fancied her, but secrets foiled her patience. As much as anything else, curiosity had driven her into the world of man after the passing of her mother, the need to explore the enigma of their society. Yet even as a girl she had always quested after knowledge. Her mother had often scolded her, reminding her life wasn't a puzzle to be solved but a great riddle to be savored.

The lesson had rarely stuck.

She would need to pull the truth out of the man. "Rorie is in a foul temper," she said. "He wants to warn me of something, but I can't understand what. I thought it might be Mr. Crofter."

Graham traded a glance with Stevenson. "She's a woman more than twenty years grown. There's no sense as treating her like the girl she was."

Running a hand over his chin, Stevenson worked at the muscles of his jaw. "Parliament pushes for legislation to formally outlaw any association with the fey. That would include the use of Fey Craft—stardust, precisely—and the harboring of those with fey blood."

"Bah!" Graham cursed. "That kind of nonsense comes up every odd year. They'll make no ground with it. We've still friends enough in London."

Pain flashed in Stevenson's eyes. "That is not the worst of it, you well know, Mr. Graham." He turned to Effie. "The Society feels a sacrifice is in order, something to appease the crown and end talk of an Inquiry. They instructed I draw up a document listing the fey I am in contact with and hand it over to the crown."

Stevenson drew up his weight into a rigid posture, clasping his hands behind his back before speaking. "That is why Mr. Crofter came to us—to demand I betray dear friends."

Effie's blood ran cold, and she had to swallow hard to keep the tea in her stomach from surging upward. So that was it—the missing piece. To protect their investments, the Society wished to send her and Stevenson's other fey allies to the gallows. It was not strictly illegal to harbor pro-fey sympathies, but neither was it fashionable, and those who did often found themselves in prison or their fortunes waning. She sensed Rorie's seething hatred for Mr. Crofter and felt a fury of her own spring to life.

"Do they all know of me, then?" she asked.

"Not directly," answered Stevenson. "But they know I have enough involvement with the fey that I could perhaps influence the crown's good graces."

"You wouldn't!" Effie exclaimed.

"Of course not," Stevenson snapped. He turned from her to cool his temper, yet she thought nothing of his outburst. His benefactors had placed him in a horrible position. They would not let their investments fail; they had too much money at stake. Either he sacrificed the fey known to him, or they would find an engineer to run their projects who would. She had heard Mr. Crofter threaten as much, she now understood.

"It's a fool plan," spat Graham. "I should've skinned the man alive for suggesting such a cowardly thing. The Fey Finders would hang the fey and still seek an Inquiry in Duncairn. Better if this observatory falls to ruin."

Stevenson shook his head. "The Society will not allow that. But they do underestimate the devastation of an Inquiry; they see only what it would mean in London. Her Majesty's Fey Finders care naught whether a fey is good or fell, peaceful or sinister of purpose. Their aim is to demonstrate their own worth. Without check, they'll scour the coast and put to the question all they find, as they did during the Potato Famines a few decades ago. They'll use the Inquiry as a grand stage and propel these legislations through. From there, their wrath would spiral out of control." He pressed his palms against the table, though it appeared he would rather knock it over. "We cannot let that happen. We must strive to show the world that fey and human can coexist."

"What will you do?" Effie asked, eager to hear his thoughts. Part of what drew her to Stevenson was his work, always seeking to blend science with nature. He was a pure naturalist who used stardust to power his famous lighthouses, promoted harmony with the fey, and sought to canonize their lore.

"We must sap the hatemongers of their advantage," said Stevenson. "I will stall them as best I can, but we must find the true motive and intent of these attacks before their Inquiry can come to bear. If the truth is known, there's a chance the Fey Finders will find no allies north of Edinburgh. The Scots have no fondness for London's authority."

Effie considered his words. She had no stomach for politics. Large crowds and public debate went against every fiber of her nature. But that did not mean she would wither away like some English violet. She could not let innocent fey fall victim to such a scheme as the Society planned. If Stevenson meant to unravel the truth of the attacks rather than appease his benefactors, it would take all his resources to hinder their enemies in Parliament, leaving nothing for Duncairn.

So to there she must go.

She rose, her mind settled. "If an Unseily Court exists in Duncairn, we must know of it before the Inquiry. It may be our best chance of gaining leverage, and our only chance to forestall Mr. Crofter's designs." Her words were heavy, but she stiffened her back against them. "I will go there and uncover the truth of the matter."

"What!" Graham barked. "You can't mean to go near that village. The queen's bastards will be crawling over it before the fortnight is through."

Effie swallowed to keep her voice from trembling. "There is danger, but to do nothing is to guarantee more fey will suffer." She faced Graham. "I can do nothing here to help; my presence might even bring greater danger if Mr. Crofter returns."

"You can do less against an Unseily Court!"

"If one exists," she reminded him. She tried to keep herself steady despite the knot forming in her gut. Graham and Stevenson had risked their lives and the fortunes of their families to let her in and give her a sheltered life. She would not balk at doing the same for them. "You are both needed here. At the least you cannot be seen in Duncairn. The scandal would link your names to whatever judgment the Inquiry handed down."

"There are others," huffed Graham. "I ken a man near Montrose who often trades with the fishermen of Duncairn." His tone was more tired than she had ever heard. "He knows much of the fey and has befriended a few in the area. I would have him handle this."

"If you could reach him," said Stevenson. "The man is a drunkard and hasn't responded to your missives in weeks."

"I'll speak with the fishermen and the girl's family," said Effie, "and if an Unseily Court exists, we will throw them to your benefactors and limit the crown's hand. It is the least either party deserves. Please, Mr. Graham, I must do something to protect the lives of the fey. I will not run and hide when I can offer aid instead."

"Bah!" Graham stammered, but his shoulders sagged in defeat. He spun on a heel and stormed out, slamming the door behind him.

The cold gust that rushed in made Effie shiver. She smoothed her coat and stepped closer to the hearth. Stevenson's face fell as blank as unmarked parchment, and he bent to scour over the observatory's designs. Effie knew Stevenson well enough to leave him be. Silent brooding was his nature, and she didn't take offense. To others it might seem he didn't care, but she knew he cared perhaps too much.

"Mr. Graham left his coat," she said. "I'll go after him."

She found Graham watching as the workmen set the observatory's giant lens in place. It was a moment they had planned for weeks. She knew a few of Graham's crew by name, but they all recognized her, giving her a cheery nod or word of greeting. Mr. Stevenson thought it a risk, yet she took that sentiment with a grain of salt. Where Stevenson placed prudence above mirth, Graham naturally exuded an honest warmth. He treated the crew like family and didn't employ a man he didn't trust.

"He should be seeing this." Graham had his arms folded across his chest. His cheeks and nose were rose-colored, as if he'd been nipping a few drams, but it was only from the wind.

"He has more pressing matters on his mind," said Effie, handing Graham his coat. She was not in a mood to speak in circles. "How dangerous are these creatures?"

Graham raised his eyebrow and stared at her askance. "If they're real? Dangerous enough you shouldn't go messing with them. It's a thick lad who pokes at a badger and doesn't expect to get bit."

"But you doubt trows exist?"

Graham stomped his boots for warmth. "I think Stevenson's nose has sniffed after funding for so long that it doesn't know a fart from a flower." Her eyes narrowed, and he held up a hand for her pardon. "This observatory is funded by landowners hoping its weather data will lead to better crop growing. They don't give a cuss about Acts of Parliament or the stars or the fey or any other bit of science that doesn't put more money in their pockets."

He pointed down the road. "That man, Crofter, is from Newcastle where the Hostmen lord over the coal trade for the entire empire. They aren't the type of men one should meddle with, and I wouldn't doubt the bugger is afoul of them."

"And Mr. Stevenson has been led down this path before." Effie finished Graham's thought. The affair with the lighthouse engineer, John Wigham, had left Stevenson accused of reckless slander, his name tarnished forever in the eyes of many in the scientific world.

"He's blinded by his own interests," said Graham.

"It is the fey's interest too," said Effie. "We are also his benefactors and have no other voice. The constabularies will not defend us. The magistrates of Edinburgh are bought and paid for by men who proclaim us the offspring of Black Donald." She stopped short of mentioning Graham's own interests, those of the French merchants who stocked his warehouses full of goods.

Graham gave her a cheery smile, but she saw the doubt and fear behind it. "We have enemies, lass. Too right. Some we know of, some we don't. I can't say as I understand what's going on myself, and that's what frightens me most.

There's a strange feeling to this whole ordeal." The smile dropped from his face. "Robert Ramsey is a good man and no drunkard."

She rested a hand on his arm. "I will inquire after him."

He squirmed in frustration. "The tale of this Mr. Ross being killed by selkies is foolishness, and no doubt the other attack was carried out by some drunken rogue. The lass is just mistaken in what she saw or embellishing the tale for some reason." His skepticism made her love him more. It was the concern of a father not believing night had fallen, if only so his child could play in the sun a little longer.

"I've lived a happy life these past years, sheltered from those who would do me harm. That was your doing, yours and Mr. Stevenson's. It's time I repaid you the favor."

Graham's eyes grew moist. "Be careful, lass. The queen's appointed a new Fey Finder General, the man called Edmund Glover. I fear you know him, and he knows you."

Effie's stomach dropped to her toes. The name made her skin crawl. The last time she had heard it, she'd almost died.

Don't miss the next book of the SEAL OF ROME series coming soon and find more from Eden Maddox at edenmaddox.com

Until then, discover THE LAIRD OF DUNCAIRN by City Owl Author, Craig Comer.

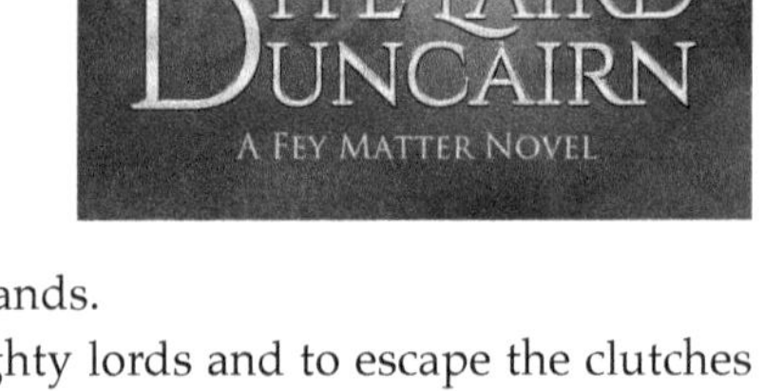

A war is brewing between the worlds of fey and man . . . but only one can prevail. Find out which in this fantasy featuring nefarious plots, dashing knaves, and militant gnomes.

When Sir Walter Conrad discovers a new energy source, one that could topple nations and revolutionize society, the race to dominate its ownership begins.

But the excavation of this energy will have dire consequences for both humans and fey. For an ancient enemy stirs, awakened by Sir Walter's discovery.

Outcast half-fey Effie of Glen Coe is the empire's only hope at averting the oncoming disaster. But she finds herself embroiled in the conflict, investigating the eldritch evil spreading throughout the Highlands.

As she struggles against the greed of mighty lords and to escape the clutches of the queen's minions, her comfortable world is shattered.

Racing to thwart the growing menace, she realizes the only thing that can save them all is a truce no one wants.

Please sign up for the City Owl Press newsletter for chances to win special subscriber-only contests and giveaways as well as receiving information on upcoming releases and special excerpts.

All reviews are **welcome** and **appreciated**. Please consider leaving one on your favorite social media and book buying sites.

Acknowledgments

To all of you reading these pages, thank you for taking a chance on my words. I can't possibly see this as my accomplishment, but an incredible blessing thanks, in large part, to all of you. There are so many people in my heart, and I wish I could personally thank every one of you. Please know that I treasure you all and take nothing for granted.

To my amazing husband who has been there to support me since the beginning. Without you I would not have written these words.

To Hazel James for walking by my side through life and prose. Thanks for being the other half of my brain.

To Danielle DeVor, thank you for believing in this project and helping to make it the best it can be.

To Katie Monson, thank you for your tireless work to make other people's dreams come true.

To Rhon House, thank you for assisting me on this new and exciting adventure.

To Daniele Derenzi and Nicole Kellman, thank you for your insight, encouragement, and support.

About the Author

EDEN MADDOX resides in eastern PA and has been fascinated by Ancient Rome since childhood, but her passion goes beyond the facts. She's always had a keen psychological attraction to the extremes of human nature present in that period. How could a society so advanced and cultured also be so cruel and violent? And even more haunting, what if that volatile time was examined through the lens of modern values?

Rendered by her love of history, suspense, romance, and fantasy, these questions evolved into an epic genre mashup that reinvents Ancient Rome in a gripping, surreal exploration of the best and worst of us.

What if the greatest stories of the Roman Empire are the ones that couldn't be told? Until now.

edenmaddox.com

facebook.com/edenmaddoxwrites
instagram.com/edenmaddoxwrites
tiktok.com/@edenmaddoxwrites

About the Publisher

City Owl Press is a cutting edge indie publishing company, bringing the world of romance and speculative fiction to discerning readers.

Escape Your World. Get Lost in Ours!

www.cityowlpress.com

facebook.com/CityOwlPress
x.com/cityowlpress
instagram.com/cityowlbooks
pinterest.com/cityowlpress
tiktok.com/@cityowlpress

www.ingramcontent.com/pod-product-compliance
Lightning Source LLC
LaVergne TN
LVHW010558100826
845148LV00014B/2764